BLUE BEAR

OR THE IMPOSSIBILITY OF ANONYMITY

Joseph M. Grady

Palazzo Mortimer Press

Fort Collins, Colorado

Cover design by Josh Applegate.

Vespa provided by Matthew Peters of *Moto Italia of Northern Colorado*

PRAISE FOR *BLUE BEAR*

I just finished *Blue Bear* – I think it's amazing, downright brilliant at points.

Marianne Medlin, Editor in Chief, *Catholic News Agency*

Seriously, though, dude, this thing is well written. I've read plenty of people's attempts at fiction and this is, by far, the best self-published thing I've read.

Fr. Scott Valentyn, Diocese of Green Bay

I really wanted *Blue Bear* to be terrible, that way I could make fun of Grady. But as I kept reading it, I kept getting more and more mad at him, because it was so good, and because I lost so much sleep staying up and reading.

Fr. Michael Niemczak, Archdiocese of Santa Fe

It was a really fun read, and I enjoyed it a lot.

Samantha Cohoe, Author

I've probably read over three hundred books in the last five years. *Blue Bear* is the only novel.

Fr. Matthew Rensch, Diocese of Burlington

TABLE OF CONTENTS

You stare ahead of you, and behind your back stands your Life! It calls to you, you turn and cannot recognize it. Your eyes, unused to light, can grasp nothing. And then an abrupt word: your name! Your own dear name ... your being, your very essence – yourself – bounding from the mouth thought dead ... O word, O name, my own name! Spoken to me, breathed forth with a smile and a promise. O stream of light.

Hans Urs von Balthasar

CHAPTER ONE

'STE CHIAVI

Running is a pretty universal activity. You throw one leg out in front of the other, then repeat the process with the other leg. Around the world, and from person to person, you have variations in time, distance, speed, terrain, etc. But the essentials are always the same: two legs and rapid succession of one after the other. It is also a pretty much universally understood rule of etiquette that when a person is out for a run, it can be rather rude to interrupt. It's okay to stop a walker, no problem, but there is a rhythm and focus that sets the runner apart from the rest of the pedestrian world. This fundamental axiom is valid the world over, with only one notable exception: Italy.

If a lost Italian needs directions in downtown Rome, he surmises that the stranger going by at a walker's pace could very well turn out to be a tourist, so it might be a waste of time to stop and ask. But a runner — it is, of course, unimaginable that a sane person would spend precious vacation time exercising — a runner is most certainly a local, eager to dispense intimate knowledge of neighborhood shortcuts. Anywhere on the peninsula, that respect for the runner's rhythm is not at all sacred. Rather, it is eminently interruptible. But speaking of sacred, this also is the same place where people manage to stay updated on village gossip and fulfill their Sunday obligation in one fell swoop, the same place where any given *nonna* will spend more than half of her time kneeling in the box confessing not her own, but her husband's sins. Even though, on the whole, Lucy Fox found certain aspects of Rome to be a runner's paradise — a good number of large parks, a long path by the river, ancient monuments and aqueducts anywhere you look — there was always that one drawback of the fact that any long run would almost always be interrupted, at least once, by a boorish Italian seeking directions.

So while I was wasting time puttering around St. Peter's Square, seeing the sights and smelling the smells, at 3:30pm, Lucy exited Via del Gianicolo number thirteen, like she did most every afternoon. She took a knee to tighten her left Brooks and, because Gambetti wasn't in the porter's office, she spent a moment stretching before leaving. The horizon threatened her with a rainstorm, but a little water won't stop a true addict from getting her fix. At a warm-up ten minute per mile pace, she headed towards Villa Doria Pamphili, a spacious park just outside central Rome.

I used to do a lot of my normal afternoon puttering around in that park too, and, believe it or not, even sometimes accompanied Lucy on very short stretches of her runs. It's a common misconception. People think I should have poor vision. I don't. My eyes are just normal. I'd sit there on the hill by the gate, and if I was awake, I'd see her coming from a long ways off. Even with good vision, it didn't matter. I knew her athletic running gait well. Efficient. Precise. Not like most Italian women, who bounce around aimlessly in their stride. Now, okay, I realize my habits already sound kind of strange. And it's true. I didn't have much else to do in those days. But I am certain that there has never been a more platonic relationship than that which existed between me and Lucy. So then what was it? It's hard to say. I would simply maintain that our interactions were on such a level of particularity that anyone would be hard pressed to find an analogue in any other friendship. At least I've never found one.

A mile from home, she cruised through the park gates at eight and a half minutes per mile, her tied back wavy black hair barely moving from side to side. At this point, she would be warm enough to cross that threshold into a perfect flow and cadence, where the morning's stress would melt away, ceding ground to the simplicity of breathe and numbing exertion. Her eyes squinted up to the grassy knoll where I like to lie and soak up the sun. (I was still in the piazza, evaluating the salesmanship of a team of immigrants hawking lightweight scarves and rosaries to passersby.) Lucy's fixed gaze on my usual patch of grass prevented her from noticing a disgruntled Italian man in a red tracksuit and red Nike sneakers running down the path in her direction. His form was terrible, but he was really hauling, and his form was not helped by the way he kept looking back over his shoulder.

Nobody would have thought too much of this, except that when the two of them finally did converge at a point on the path, the upset tracksuit man looked straight at Lucy with faint recognition in his eyes. He stopped, threw out his arms and shouted at her, "*Oi, Ragazza! Puoi fermarti un attimino? Mi fai un grande favore?*"

Before she could pretend to ignore him, Lucy failed to avoid eye contact and stopped in her tracks. *Come on,* she thought, *This is a park! Who the hell needs directions in a park?* So she put on a thick foreign accent and called upon her backup tactic for avoiding conversation.

"*Non parlo italiano.*"

"Yes you do," the man didn't skip a beat. His own accent was thick, but his English was quick and efficient.

"I'm sorry?"

"You speak Italian! You are the American girl from the Palazzo Mortimer. Yesterday you were speaking the Italian. I was there. I heard."

Lucy turned beet red. The odds of running into an Italian who spoke English well, and who also somehow knew that she spoke Italian, were extremely low. She'd made a good bet, but even good wagers sometimes lose.

"At any rate, it is of no importance," he went on, and had already thrust a pair of keys into her hand, which Lucy, because she was too embarrassed by her failed attempt at language ignorance, did nothing to resist receiving. "I have need of a very big favor from you."

"Um... wait... but who are you? Do I know you?"

"I am nobody. You make a great favor for me, okay? And you listen to me clearly, okay? These keys, you are to render them only to me, or to Ginevra."

"Um… sure… but why? Do we know each other?"

"Only to me or to Ginevra! Nobody other. Understood?"

"Yeah. Only to you or Ginevra, but… I mean…" Lucy even added local emphasis by placing both palms together, with fingers pointed in the air, thrusting forward with each syllable. "Yeah, but who are you?"

"Already I have told to you that I am nobody. You give them just to me only, or to Ginevra only!"

An old digital ringtone started playing, and a small cell phone emerged from his pocket. He rattled off something into it using a funny sounding language that Lucy couldn't recognize at all (a bilingual Italian is a rarity; trilingual is off the charts), "*Hallo? Wat maak jy hier? Is jy in Italië? Nee, jy moet nie hier nog wees! Bly net daar, ek kom om jou te kry. Bly daar!*"

He hung up and looked back at Lucy, "Now I must go. Thank you! Thank you!"

The man took off running again in the direction of the park entrance. A black Subaru Impreza pulled up right in front of the Park's gate. Lucy could just barely see the outlines of two large men in black leather jackets getting out of the car. The tracksuit man got a view of them too and suddenly changed direction, heading off towards the other end of the park. The leather jacket people, meanwhile, got back in the car and sped off.

Lucy slipped off the path up to the hill, hoping I might be in the vicinity. Finding nothing, she zipped the keys in the small back pocket of her running shorts, told herself that nothing weird had just happened, and did the one thing she did compulsively whenever she really felt the need to clear her mind (which was also the one thing she did compulsively even if she didn't really feel the need to clear her mind). She ran.

The lap around the lake and the rolling hills of the Villa grounds did something to alleviate the queasy intuition the tracksuit man had left in her gut, but not much. She steadily quickened her pace, but the slight increase in lactic acid ebbing into her thighs and calves was not enough to eliminate that gut reaction. In the more populated areas of the park she had to zigzag around, giving a wide berth to anyone wearing a tracksuit. But the deeper she plunged into the old estate property, the thicker the tracksuits got, so earlier than normal, she changed her bearings and headed back towards the Palazzo, avoiding the walking paths altogether.

The park gate spilled out onto Via Aurelia Antica. Ahead of her, a very familiar massive figure — lighter than me, though — was steadily traipsing forward in the same direction. He was hard to miss in a yellow onesie with red polka dots and blue frills on the collars, cuffs, and ankles. His head was covered in white make up, a white bald cap, and fake curly blue hair around the ears. Two clown shoes dangled from his right hand, and a plastic Carrefour bag with a payload full of chips and Pepsi from his left. The truly remarkable thing, though, was that his appearance no longer struck her as remarkable.

Instinctually, without even realizing what she was doing, and without skipping a beat, Lucy quieted her steps. She bit her lip to keep herself from grinning. She had to stay focused on her mission. Making her approach, she matched his footsteps and pace until she was directly behind him. As the clown shifted his weight to his left leg, and started moving his right knee forward, Lucy held her breath and lifted her own right foot off the ground. She waited, poised in the air for just a quarter of a second until the critical moment. Then she unleashed her foot, tapping the precise point on the backside of the clown's leg, just below the knee, at the exact moment of vulnerability in his stride that would cause a loss of balance. His whole right side faltered and gave way. He almost collapsed, but was able to stumble forward a few steps, catching himself and recovering, even lunging forward to cradle the grocery bag like an infant in danger of being dropped.

"Fricking-A, Lucy!" he yelled, even before he could see who his attacker was.

When his balance was back, he turned and swung his clown shoes at her huge smile, just barely grazing her dry fit t-shirt. Lucy backpedalled. The clown launched one of his shoes at her, striking her hip, but causing no real damage. Lucy laughed all the more. Whenever running failed to calm her nerves, the only surefire backup was picking on Brian.

"Lucy, this is not the time to be messing with me! If you had any idea what kind of day I've had."

Now at a safe distance, Lucy pretended sympathy, "Oh no, is somebody having a bad day? Oh, you poor thing. Come on. Let's go get you a coffee. You want some coffee?"

"Lucy, you are a disease."

"Come on. Let's go. Sounds like you need a little pick me up after a bad day."

"You've been out running. I don't want to be in a public place with someone gross like you."

"Brian, I barely even went four miles, and it's chilly out. I'm hardly sweating."

"Four miles? Do you want to know what *I* would look like after running four miles?"

"Actually, I would like to see that."

"Whatever. Let's go." They started walking. "I swear, though, Lucy. Some day, you're going try to pull some crap like this, and you're going to get what's coming to you, and you're going to deserve it, and I am going to laugh at you for it."

"Hurry up. It looks like it's going to rain."

They headed towards their local coffee bar, at the base of the Janiculum hill in Piazza della Rovere. Across from the piazza and the traffic they could just make out the banks of the Tiber River, if they sat up straight. But most of the time, when seeking refuge in coffee, they preferred to forget they were in Rome. Brian and Lucy's antagonism of one another had grown over a number of years of being the only Americans living together in student housing in a foreign country. Lucy had been the first English speaker at the Palazzo, arriving one year before Brian. Their mutual teasing had nothing to do with flirtation. That's not to say it was without affection. It was just closer to sibling rivalry than anything else.

The afternoon clouds had been spitting rain when they started walking together, but it really started to pour once they reached Piazza della Rovere. Lucy sprinted ahead and got out of the rain before it had a chance to soak her. She gloated from underneath the awning at Brian, who was waddling as fast as he could.

Inside, Lucy ordered for both of them, as Brian was too out of breath to speak, "*Ciao Giorgio. Due caffè, un'americano e uno macchiato.*"

The strong coffees came served in small ceramics, perched on mini saucers. Brian turned towards Lucy, resting his elbow on the bar and stirring sugar into his coffee with his free hand. Regaining his breath he said, "Alright, so do you want to know how I spent my day today?"

Lucy nodded and stirred.

"Okay, so it takes me an hour and a half to get way the hell out there to Via Boccea. The metro, then two busses. So I finally get to this nursing home, where this hundred year old lady is supposed to have her birthday party, and nobody knows who the hell this lady is, and nobody knows what I'm talking about. All they see is a foreign clown trying to explain why he's there. Fricking Italy. I even called and confirmed with the guy just last night. And of course, he has his cell phone off all day. Wonderful. So I walk around the whole neighborhood trying to find these people. Nothing. Then I sit in the lobby reading *Io, Donna* for two hours and leave. And then it gets even better. I go to my next appointment at the car dealership, and guess what."

"You bought a car?"

"Another hour on the bus to get there, and the car dealership doesn't exist. It's been closed for two years! Or at least that's what the guy across the street tells me."

"That's weird."

"Yeah, I know. Like… what the hell? Italy could be a paradise for clowns. People get us here. They love us. Clowns in America were done fifteen years ago. If only they could learn to make appointments in this country I'd actually have a job."

"I don't know if you can blame this one on Italy," said Lucy. "I know they're not great at appointments here, but I've never had something that bad happen to me. Who are these people?"

"I don't know. They said they found me on Craigslist."

"That sucks."

"Yeah, I know."

"Hey," Lucy changed the subject, "so something really weird just happened to me in the park."

"Oh, I guess it's time to talk about you now."

"No, really, this was weird."

"That's fine. That's fine. Let's talk about you. Let's talk about all the things you want to talk about."

Lucy plowed ahead. "So I was just running through the park and this random guy I don't know flags me down and gives me a pair of keys. He tells me to hold on to them for him and then he runs away. And now I've got his keys."

Brian thought for a second and could only say, "Yeah, that is weird."

"Coming from you," she pointed out what he was wearing, "that means something. Do you think he was trying to steal something?"

"If he was, it was stupid. Runners don't carry wallets."

"Yeah, I know."

"Did he look like a gypsy?"

"Not really."

Brian arched his eyebrows. "Did he get your number?"

"No!"

"Maybe he's some kind of operator. He thinks you're some innocent study-abroad girl. Giving you some keys is his way of getting his foot in the door. He can make sure that he gets to see you again some other time and take your purse."

"I guess," she said. "But that kind of freaks me out, because he said he recognized me as that American girl from Palazzo Mortimer."

Brian shrugged his shoulder. "Maybe he's new on staff and he just really needed to get his keys back to the Palazzo for some reason. It's probably nothing. And even if he is an operator, you've got a head on your shoulders. He probably tries the same trick on tons of girls who are much dumber than you. We'll see what happens. I wouldn't worry about it."

Lucy sipped her coffee and tried not to worry. It didn't work. "Wait, what do you mean girls dumber than me? I can't tell if that's supposed to be a compliment or not."

"Well, if you don't get what that means, then you probably know how you're supposed to take it."

"And aren't I just some innocent study-abroad girl?"

"No, you've been here too long for me to call you a 'study-abroad-girl'... I was talking about the *innocent* part."

It took a good twenty-five minutes for the rain to let up. As it did, Lucy and Brian headed up the Janiculum hill to Palazzo Mortimer.

Coming around the curve, they found an ambulance and a huge variety of police vehicles parked in front of the building with lights blazing. About twenty yards off, she finally saw me, standing there in the middle of the scene. I'm hard to miss, at least for Lucy.

She quickened her pace up the sidewalk towards me, leaving Brian to chug up the hill by himself, but a police officer jumped out and blocked her way, "*Lei non può entrare, c'è stato un omicidio. Ha capito? Un omicidio!*"[1]

"*Sì?*" she gasped. "*Qua? Ma io abito qua. Chi è stato?*"[2]

"*Eh, a 'sto punto, non lo possiamo dire. Ma adesso Lei deve stare qui,*" said the officer pointing at the ground, "*E Le facciamo un paio di domande.*"[3]

The officer brushed past her to intercept other pedestrians. From where Lucy stood, she could just catch glimpses of the main entrance to Palazzo Mortimer. The door was propped open, and a twisted shape lay beneath a plastic tarp in the doorway with two feet sticking out. The legs had red Nike sneakers and red track pants.

---

[1] "You can't come in. There's been a murder. You understand? A murder!"

[2] "Yes," *she gasped*, "But I live here. Who's been killed?"

[3] "Uh, at this point we can't say. But now, miss, you have to stay here," *said the officer pointing at the ground*, "And we'll need to ask you some questions."

CHAPTER TWO

LE RAGAZZE NON FANNO VISION QUEST

I still clearly remember, twelve years, two months and five days earlier, when I first met Lucy. After quite a few years of inactivity, they finally told me I might be given a new assignment, if everything lined up as it should, and if the guide request was both valid and licit. Now, I had been told the same thing a number of times already, but nothing had ever come of it, so I logged that information in the back of my mind, and endeavored to keep it there. There's little sense in getting all stirred up, you old bear. You know it will all probably come to nothing, so why start making plans before you're damn sure?

And so I waited. In moments of weakness I would let my guard down and envision what it would be like to be back in the field: the hunting, the practical advice, the wilderness. But then I would snap out of it, and remind myself that I already had a comfortable life without solid work. Sure, it would be nice if it were still like the old days, when there was no lag time whatsoever between assignments. But things change, and even I appreciate some of the advances of modernity: Volkswagens, martial arts classes, white noise machines.

Despite my doubts, one day I actually did get the call. The higher ups — that is, men in starched linens, ancient enough to bear esoteric names like Emile Durkheim or Henry James or Rudolph Otto — delivered a name and an address, and ordered my deployment. I was unable to hide my delight at the fact that the address they gave me was not some anonymous urban jungle, but was deep in the hinterlands of Montana. Wide open space. Backcountry. Woodlands. Freedom. Too many these days are commissioned to the cities. I had really dodged a bullet. It is difficult to describe that thrill I experienced when I turned off the paved road, and felt that gravel beneath me for miles and miles, and that even greater thrill when I came around a bend, the hill crested, and the camp came into view: a lake full of kids in canoes, and twenty large teepees beyond that. Perfect. This is it. This is the wilderness. I had stopped believing assignments like this could still exist.

But with that thrill, I also received the first sign that something was wrong: the sound of a perfectly tuned engine roaring around the bend, and the startling sight of a brand new Rolls Royce careening past me along the dirt road towards camp. The second indication that something was wrong came before I arrived at the teepees: a big wooden sign reading *CAMP IWIFABLOF: the Initech Wilderness Institute for American Business Leaders of the Future.* Well, at least it says 'wilderness,' I told myself.

I got to work right away canvassing the area, looking for anyone on a quest. Nothing. So I bid my time. The address given was right here. I knew the assignment was here. Patience. Everyone really sucked at archery, and they were using velcro arrows. Okay. Calm down. That's alright. We'll have something to work on. It looked like they were decent swimmers, but there was a man in a suit and tie with an "Office of Risk Management" badge. Whenever anyone approached a water level that was above the neck, he nodded to the life guard, who would whistle and bring the kids back in. Then the man in the suit would write everything down on a clipboard. Strange.

At the end of the day, hundreds of forms from various adults wound their way back to the "Legal Teepee." I thought these might be the people in charge, but after a while it became obvious that they were only advisors. They documented everything twice, and would grow twitchy if anyone mentioned the word lawsuit. Finally, I found myself listening to the proceedings in the meeting teepee with the adult who seemed to be running the show.

A frightened twelve year old boy poked his head in the flap, "Miss, do you have a moment?"

"We'll be moving forward with a guided reading on paradigm shifts in ten minutes. Can you be quick?"

"Absolutely."

"Come on in."

"I wanted to dialogue briefly about the implementation of our new project based learning procedures in the Cheyenne Arapahoe Teepee," said the twelve year old.

"Our wheelhouse learning goal for that was yesterday," responded Miss. "You know that."

"And my guys have been very proactive at meeting that goal set."

"Then what's the delay? This is an early stage: archery, canoeing, that kind of stuff. Core competencies."

"There's been a few roadblocks towards synergy in the group — well, just one really."

"Yes?"

"We've had one asset with serious HR objections about adaptive learning and seamless cooperation. First amendment objections."

"Did you touch base with legal?"

"Oh, absolutely. They've been wonderful."

"What did they say?"

"Well, we've got our hands tied. We're one hundred percent committed to openness and mind-sharing, which means we can either accommodate or lose our 501(c)3 tax-exempt status."

The woman in charge sighed. "If that's what we've got to do, at the end of the day, that's what we've got to do."

"Then we have your go ahead for a reevaluation of my teepee's Talent Relationship Management procedures?"

"You can tee off, but we'll circle back on this tomorrow morning, alright?"

"Perfect. Thank you, Miss. Thank you for your time."

"Always a pleasure."

Individually, I understood each word used in the conversation, but when put together in those combinations, the whole dialogue sounded completely foreign to me. So I stayed away from the adults, and focused in on the campers. None of them seemed to be doing anything remotely resembling a vision quest. There were three kids in the medical teepee. One of them was actually sick, and the other two just wanted some attention from the nurses. Nobody was fasting or meditating. There was one boy with autism who could see me just fine, but he didn't pay me any attention. There was a girl on a juice diet. She spent her days in a teepee by herself reading Harry Potter, clearly not wanting to be at camp. There was one counselor who, on the sly, every once in a while, ingested some kind of hallucinogen. He saw me too, but was usually too incoherent for conversation. Nobody was the boy I was looking for.

By the time Thursday evening rolled around, I was getting pretty impatient, and was beginning to wonder whether or not this was all going to fall through. I started rehearsing all the old rationalizations. It'll be fine. You'll have so much free time. People aren't interested in this kind of stuff these days. I was wandering away from camp, by the lake, when I finally heard someone say something.

"Oh, shoot, I guess I've been on a vision quest, or something, for a few days now." The voice sounded high. It went on, "Um... so I think it's getting close to the end of camp. So... my dear spirit animal, or whatever I'm supposed to see on this quest thing, if you're going to show up, I suppose you don't have a lot of time left."

I stood up high on my back paws. The voice was coming loud and clear from the isolation teepee on the other side of the lake. I barreled over there as fast as I could, and burst inside. But I was immediately confused. The only person in there was a thirteen year old girl who was staring right at me while clutching the arms of a lawn chair, with a pale face and a slack jaw. It looked as though she wanted to scream, but just couldn't get it out. Though she did have black hair, she looked white. Very white. Even her clothes were white: a hoodie with *Skyview Academy Middle School* written on it, blue jeans, and — the worst — a cheap pair of those moccasin slippers made of fake polyester. I waved my paws in the air to try to calm her down and whispered, with the most soothing voice I could muster, "Shhh, shhh, it's okay. I'm a friendly bear."

Unfortunately a talking animal was just enough to push her over the edge. She let loose and finally did scream.

One of the hard parts of being a bear is that it's really hard for us to cover our ears. I can barely reach mine. We have excellent hearing. When a terrible noise happens, you've just got to shrug your shoulders, close your eyes and grimace until it stops. And eventually she did stop. Maybe she realized after a while that I wasn't interested in mauling her.

When I opened my eyes I was balled up in a corner of the teepee — or at least as balled up as a four hundred pound blue bear can be and insofar as teepees have corners. The girl was still motionless on the other side, still clutching the arms of the lawn chair. *Harry Potter and the Order of the Phoenix* had spilled out of her lap onto the ground, next to the small lantern, the only faint illumination available. She was staring at me, hardly blinking, and taking short quick breaths.

I picked myself up. Hey eyes followed me. I made no sudden movements. She didn't react. Looking around the teepee, there was no one but the two of us.

"Well, I guess you can see me?" I said.

She nodded, then narrowed her eyes to listen.

"And hear me?"

Another nod.

"That's very strange."

A third nod.

"No I mean... strange that *you* can see me. You didn't see, by chance, if there's somebody around here doing a vision quest?"

No response.

"You know... is there a boy or young man who's spending his time fasting and waiting for a vision?"

She paused to think. I let her. But I was desperate to find him. Bit by bit, a look of wonder and understanding crept its way onto her face. She sat up straight and ran her fingers back and forth through her wavy black hair and said, "Holy shit, it worked."

"What do you mean?" I asked. "What worked?"

She pointed at me and said, "I mean... you're here. It worked."

"You mean there *is* a boy doing a vision quest somewhere around here?"

"No, no, no," she pointed back at herself. "*I'm* on a vision quest."

"Are you sure?" I gave another look around the teepee, and was about to start searching outside.

"Well," her eyes followed mine around the teepee to see what I was looking for, "Yeah. I think I'm the only one. All the other kids are busy with camp stuff. I would have to do camp stuff too, but I started talking about my rights and all that, and now I don't have to hang out with Cheyenne Arapahoe teepee anymore."

"What?"

"I imagined that you would be a fox, though."

"Okay, sure," I said, trying not to take offense at the fox comment. "That's fine. But girls don't do vision quests."

"What is that supposed to mean?" Now she looked offended. I didn't respond right away, so she kept talking. "Fine, I guess it was more of a 'vision quest' than a real serious one." At the words "vision quest" she made quotation marks in the air with her fingers. "But it looks like it's working. I can't say I was expecting a talking bear. I've just been on this juice diet... that's never made me see things before. But who knows what they're putting in juice these days. I think it was just juice. Are you real, though, or is this just a hallucination?"

"This is a real *experience*."

"But are *you* real?"

"You're really not going to understand this right now. Did you see if anyone else is on a vision quest?"

"It's pretty important to me. Are you real?"

"Metaphysically... that's not the point. It's about the narrative reality, not the material reality. But speaking of narrative, let's go back to my other question."

"Okay, so then *what* are you?"

"Please. I don't have time for this. Maybe I'm just some tasteless cultural stereotype, something that doesn't really correspond to any real tradition, but is still hanging on somehow in a misguided ethos. Fair enough? I don't even qualify as a misappropriation, because there was never anything there to misappropriate in the first place. Is that alright?"

She shook her head no.

"Don't they teach Emile Durkheim and totem theory in middle school anymore?"

"No."

"This is the last thing I'm going to say about it and then no more questions. Look, it's 2003. I really shouldn't be allowed anymore in popular society, but hopefully you'll let this slide. I'm part of your personal experience of the *mysterium tremendum et fascians*. I'm a projection of Rudolph Otto and late 19th century stereotypes. That's it. I'm more real than you, but not. Just let it be. Think Clarence Odbody or James Cricket. I understand. It's not kosher anymore, but just let it be. It's okay."

But I didn't have the patience for this kind of circling philosophical discussion. Neither did the girl. Her face was beyond confused, and I had successfully used big words to convince her that seeking an answer was not within her ability. I came across the teepee and sat in front of her lawn chair. Even with my butt on the ground and hers up in the chair, I was still looking down on her. I didn't want to waste any more time. I looked her square in the eyes and put on a disappointed principal face. She crossed her arms and sat back farther in her lawn chair.

"Alright, sweetheart, I need you to be as clear and honest as possible. What's going on here?"

I kept my eyes right on her, and she kept her eyes anywhere but me, as if the answers were written somewhere on the teepee walls.

"Hey!" I snapped at her. "I'm over here. Focus in, child. This is very important. You need to be very honest with me for a second. What's going on here?"

She looked down at her belly button and muttered quickly and quietly. I could make out some words, but not many. "Liberal chaplain lady… special project… be yourself… find your meaning… but they were like… but I said okay… then I talked to this lawyer, and he said… so they got all scared and said yes —"

"Whoa, whoa, whoa," I interrupted. I reached out and raised her chin with my paw so that she'd look me in the eyes. I intensified my expression from disappointed principle to police interrogator — a four hundred pound police interrogator with fangs. "You need to slow down, look me in the eyes and use full sentences. Can you do that? Can you talk like a big girl? If not, you don't want to know how serious the consequences will be. I need the truth and I need it now."

This tactic was a mistake. The girl burst into tears and became twice as incoherent as before. Between sobbing and gasping for air, I could just catch small bits and pieces of phrases: "... it wasn't even, like, my idea... just trying to fit in... other kids... stupid, like, juice diet... sorry! The camp food just sucks... get away from this place for just a while... I'm sorry... and she was all like, sure, you're a quarter Cree... but I'm not even a quarter, I'm just an eighth!... but whatever... so she was like... why don't you just go find your spirit animal or something... whatever the hell that means... like you said, it's just 19th century projections from shoddy anthropologists... but the teepee committee was like, no, we need to streamline our new learning goals... and I was like screw you... and they were like, let's talk team cohesion... which is their bass ackwards code for 'hey, so it turns out you're actually a terrible person'... so then I went to legal and they were all like, hey everybody, back off, we don't want litigation, do we?...but I'm only in eighth grade, what the F do I know about litigation?... anyways... sorry... this wasn't supposed to happen. I'm sorry... it's not my fault I'm even here... five weeks in the middle of nowhere with no friends... mom and dad were like, tough cookies, you're going... but I was like, just 'cause friggen' Kelly loved Camp Iwifablof doesn't mean I have to... sorry... I'm sorry."

This was a whole new world to me. Now I started looking around the teepee. The answers were not written on the walls. She looked pathetic, like I'd just caught her doing something terribly wrong. I couldn't decide whether or not to just leave her there and start looking for whoever was really on a vision quest. But she was the only clue I'd gotten thus far, so it only made sense to stick around and see if there was any more relevant information, and perhaps the only thing that kept me there was her shocking indication that she actually had understood my big words. Who is this girl? Playing bad cop had only made things go from bad to worse. I'd have to try good cop.

I leaned forward and extended one paw onto her shoulder, making a first attempt at sympathy by giving two firm pats and saying, "There, there."

I sat back and observed the effects of my sympathy. Nothing. The hysterics and mumbling just went on. I ventured another "there, there." It turned out to be equally ineffective.

And so I swallowed my pride. I grabbed her by the shoulders and lifted her straight up out of the lawn chair and transferred her into my lap and did what everyone assumes bears are good at. And I guess we are actually pretty good at it. The girl intuited what was going on, and pulled me in tight. I wrapped my arms around her — each of which was bigger than her. She kept on sobbing, but stopped mumbling. By now it was clear that she was hugging out all kinds of baggage that had nothing to do with me. I patted her on the back as I imagined a bear was supposed to do when comforting a young girl. Like I said, completely new territory. She held on tight, filling my blue fur with snot and tears. I rocked back and forth, and, though I didn't admit it to myself then, I did feel some genuine sympathy for her. The terrifying realization also started to dawn on me: what if this is my new assignment?

I asked the obvious question that I should have started with. "What's your name, child?"

The crying stopped. From somewhere below my chin I heard her say, "Lucy Fox."

"Really? That's a girl's name?"

"Yep."

"Hmm."

This was truly puzzling. Completely unprecedented. What are the odds? Well. Whatever. At least I would have something to do now. It beats doing nothing. About like anything else.

"Well, little girl, it looks like I'm your spirit animal. You can call me Blue Bear."

"Okay, Blue Bear."

CHAPTER THREE

IL PALAZZO

"Oh my God, oh my God, oh my God, oh my God," Lucy repeated again and again. She put her hands over her eyes, looked down and did her best to keep control of herself.

"Okay, okay, how about we go and wait over there," said Brian, taking Lucy by the arm and pulling her down the block.

"No, wait, no," Lucy gave slight resistance, but still let Brian drag her down the block. "No, you don't understand, Brian. You don't understand."

She finally rooted her feet on the sidewalk, stopped him, and shook his hand off her shoulder. Like everyone who knew her, Brian had long since learned that sometimes Lucy was to be listened to, but not understood. This was one of those moments. He just stood there and let her have her moment of panic, wishing it didn't have to happen this time at a crime scene. He shifted his weight from foot to foot and looked around at everything but Lucy. Lucy's main focus became controlling her breathing and looking normal.

In a solid show of support, I stayed away from her, and took the liberty of ducking underneath the police line to check things out. I'd never actually been in a real crime scene before — odd considering all the opportunities I would have had. All kinds of people in classy uniforms ran about from place to place, each one trying to look more important than the next. And of course, in proper Italian style, tasks that should have been carried out professionally, were done, yes, professionally, but also dramatically. Beyond an analysis of their behavior, though, I wasn't really able to grasp much more about *what* they were being dramatic about. The guy dead under the tarp exactly matched Lucy's description of him to me. One of his feet stuck out of the entrance door of Palazzo Mortimer, and the rest of him remained crumpled up by the counter of the porter's office. The more I watched official people come and go, the less I understood.

I couldn't say I was surprised that Daniele Gambetti was the one who found the body. He was Palazzo Mortimer's porter. Or at least that was his job title. On any given work day, he'd spend most of his time in other parts of the building doing anything and everything that had nothing to do with the porter's office — or just doing nothing at all. Come to think of it, that's not too far from what I was doing with my life. Unlike me, though, Gambetti was pushing forty, had an emerging gut, was single, and was always willing to stop and chat with anyone as a pretense for work. Like many Italian men, whenever Lucy was forced to stop and chat with him, or whenever she was anywhere near him, he always seemed to have trouble keeping his eyes anywhere above her neckline.

At the moment, he was talking to the police explaining how he'd found the body. He included far more detail and passion than necessary, but I sat nearby and patiently discerned the relevant details: after lunch he smoked a cigarette out on the sidewalk. There was no dead body on the floor. Half an hour later, after wandering around upstairs, trying to look busy, he came back to the porter's office. There was a dead body on the floor.

That's all I needed to understand. Whenever they show crime scenes on T.V., they've got people who follow the camera around and subtly fill in the audience on all the relevant information. It was a bit of a let down to discover that crime scenes are not nearly as exciting without a narrator. No storyline, no script, and lots of strangers in motion, yelling at each other in rapid fire Italian. I headed back over to the sidewalk.

The police had herded Brian and Lucy into a small group of people standing around. Two men in uniform stood there supervising, while a third and fourth called people over individually, asking them questions, and taking down information on notepads. Everyone was on edge. And when Italians are on edge, they smoke. Lucy's shoulders tensed every time she heard the sound of a lighter and every time she caught a scent of that soothing smell of smoke. Her sense of smell is terrible, but she knew that one well. Only once, though, did she permit herself to gaze longingly at a cigarette, and she was even able to convince herself that she didn't want one.

I shuffled back through the group, up to Lucy and Brian and told her, "Yeah, that's definitely the tracksuit guy from the park that you were telling me about."

She didn't look at me. She fixed her eyes on a point across the street and moved her lips as little as possible, "I don't need to know that. You never told me that."

"But don't you think the police will want to know about the keys?" I asked.

"Blue Bear, look, this is not my problem. Stop talking to me, okay? I need to look normal."

Brian went fidgety again. "So I guess you think this is a good time to start talking to yourself?"

Lucy's eyes remained on their spot across the street, she ran her fingers through her hair, taking deep breaths.

"I'm not saying... I'm just saying," said Brian, "now is probably not the best time to be the twenty-five year old with an invisible friend, okay?"

"I don't have an invisible friend."

"How many times have I caught you carrying on a conversation with nobody?"

"Is this really the time for this?"

Brian seemed to agree. "Just try to look normal."

"Said the guy dressed as a clown," responded Lucy.

"You can't always use that one. At least people see me dressed like this and they know I have a job."

Lucy went silent again.

"Why don't we try and get closer to the scene?" said Brian. "Let's see if someone from the Palazzo can tell us what's going on."

"No!" She almost yelled. "Don't you get it? I don't know anything. You don't know anything. And it's better that way. It's not my problem and it's not your problem. End of story."

"But why would this be your problem?" asked Brian. "*Do you know something?*"

A guy on a motorino pulled up next to the group and parked on the sidewalk. Before dismounting, he stood there observing everything with confusion, running his fingers through his fluffy koala-like hair. He finally said to Brian and Lucy. "Hi there, mates. What's going on here?"

Brian raised his shoulder. "Oh hey, Andrew. Nobody knows. I guess there's been some kind of murder or something in our building."

"Really... struth!" said Andrew, looking concerned, and employing his usual array of unintelligible Australian slang.

"Yeah, just get in line," said Brian. "The cops are going to want to talk to everyone."

"That's crazy, mate." Andrew shook his head. He finally dismounted and joined the group, chatting with Brian. He was the exact same height as Lucy, had an average build, fuzzy hair, and a large nose. "So a weird thing happened to me today, yeah? The University phoned me and said I had to come see them immediately to verify that I've got an Italian visa. Otherwise, they said, they would have to discontinue my registration."

"But I thought you were an Italian citizen," said Brian.

"Right, and that's just what I told them!" Andrew was born in Australia, but both of his parents were Italian immigrants from somewhere in the south of Italy. "They told me they had records of me being born in Sydney, but no immigration documents. But the thing is, I didn't need immigration documents, because I've already got citizenship and a passport, you know? Anyways, I had to drive over there this afternoon to show them my documents, before they report me to the immigration police."

Lucy had long since checked out of the conversation. Her body was still present among the other two, but her mind had wandered elsewhere. She got that same look on her face that people get when at the free throw line or about to make a critical throw in beer pong or drunk ball. And whatever interior psyching up she was doing paid off. By the time it was her turn to talk to the cops, she was perfectly in character.

"*Scusi, signorina, potrei vedere i suoi documenti?*"[4]

"*Eh, sono in camera là sopra, che sono andata a correre.*"[5]

"*Poi nel caso li andrà a prendere. Nome, prego?*"[6]

"*Lucy.*"[7]

"*Cognome?*"[8]

"Fox.*"[9]

"*Non è di qui, giusto?*"[10]

"*Sì, sono americana.*"[11]

"*Immaginavo. Lei sa che cosa è successo qua?*"[12]

"*M'han detto che c'è stato un omicidio.*"[13]

"*Ha visto o sentito qualcosa?*"[14]

"*No. Sono andata a correre e sono tornata adesso. Non ho sentito né visto niente.*"[15]

"*C'era qualcuno con Lei?*"[16]

"*Cioè, nel parco, no, ma andando a casa mi sono fermata nel bar col mio amico qua, Brian.*"[17]

"*Neanche Brian ha visto niente? Giusto? Me lo potresti indicare?*"[18]

"*Eh, sì, è quello vestito di pagliaccio.*"[19]

---

[4] "Excuse me, miss, can I see some identification?"

[5] "Um, it's in my room upstairs, because I was out running."

[6] "Alright, we can go get them in just a second. Name, please."

[7] "Lucy"

[8] "Last name?"

[9] "Fox"

[10] "You're not from here, I take it?"

[11] "Yeah, I'm American."

[12] "Of course you are. Do you know what's happened here?"

[13] "They told me there's been a murder."

[14] "Did you hear or see anything?"

[15] "No, I was out running and I just got back. I didn't hear or see anything."

[16] "Was there anybody with you?"

[17] "Well, in the park, no, but on the way home I stopped at the coffee bar with my friend Brian, here."

[18] "And I'm sure Brian didn't hear anything either, right? Can you point him out for me?"

"Ah, 'namo bene. Siamo a posto. Lo farò schedare al collega.[20]

Lucy thought she was about to get let off the hook, until the officer added, *Intanto se vuole venirci incontro potrebbe mostrare i suoi documenti."*[21]

"Va bene, saliamo."[22]

It's more than unnerving when you need permission from a stranger to enter your own front door, especially if you have to pass under crime scene tape to do so. The main entrance — the only way in and out of Palazzo Mortimer — was just ten yards from the property gate on the sidewalk. The officer escorted her past the spot where, just moments earlier, the body had been found. For her sake, it was probably good that it was gone, but she couldn't help but be a little disappointed that nobody had drawn a chalk outline.

Palazzo Mortimer was a five-story U-shaped structure with three wings. The main entrance faced the street and was in the wing that composed the bottom of the U. The officer and Lucy hurried across the main lobby towards a massive marble staircase. At the same time, a man in a slick suit came barreling down the stairs at them. He held up his arms at them and stopped to look down on them from his spot on the stairs above.

"Ferma, ferma!" He asked if Lucy was a student resident.

"Sì, lo sono."

"È inglese?"

"Americana."

"My name is detective Luca Speziale, special homicides unit, province of Rome." He held out his hand.

"I'm Lucy Fox."

---

[19] "Um, yeah, he's the one dressed as a clown."
[20] "Oh, great, that's just what we needed. I'll have my colleague here ask him some questions."
[21] *Lucy thought she was about to get let off the hook, until the officer said,* "In the meantime, we can go upstairs and have a look at your identification."
[22] "Alright, let's go upstairs."

"A pleasure." His English was not great, but workable. "I would like to understand some things about the student residents here. Will you show me where you live?"

"Um… sure."

"You students are retirement home employees?"

"No."

"No matter. Please show to me your residence rooms."

"Okay. This way."

A narrow hallway behind the fancy staircase led to an ancient elevator. Since the renovation, more modern elevators had been installed at the tips of the U, to carry beds and wheelchairs, but the staff and students were required to take the 1924 elevator. Besides Lucy and the two police officers, two other large men in suits were waiting for the elevator. In typical Italian fashion, they bent the laws of physics and shoved all five of them into the phone booth sized carriage.

Getting in, Lucy thought she had been lucky to get a spot in the corner, but ended up with Detective Luca Speziale crammed right in next to her. She crossed her arms in front of her chest, and unsuccessfully tried to touch and be touched as little as possible. When he had been glaring down at her in athletic position from the staircase, Speziale had somehow seemed impressive to Lucy. For five floors, though, this first impression fell apart as she contemplated his profile in the awkward elevator silence and tried not to breathe too heavily on the top of his balding head, which was right beneath the path of any air coming out of her nose. His lips were extremely long and thin and his closely trimmed beard ran rampant over his face: down from the tops of his cheeks, all the way to somewhere below his tie. What was left of his retreating hair was trimmed the same length as the beard, giving the impression that the beard had orchestrated a coups d'état against his hair and expanded its own sphere of influence to the top and back of his head. The elevator stopped abruptly on the fifth floor. Someone with a range of motion still available to his arm swung open the old gate, and everyone unfolded themselves from the tiny box.

"Now, explain to me, perhaps from the start," Speziale turned to Lucy. "What is this building? What was it for in the beginning?"

"In the beginning?"

"Yes."

"Well, they built this place at the turn of the century as the Roman residence of the Fasani family," said Lucy. "You know who the Fasani's are, right? The rich and famous Italian noble family?"

"I know. I know who they are. Of course. Everybody in Rome knows them. So it no longer belongs to them?"

"No, it does."

"It does? Then why is it a retirement home?"

"They lost all their money in the wars and the fascist period. But the old prince, Giovanni, made friends with an Englishman – something Mortimer – who had a lot of money."

The group turned a corner from the elevator. The only eyes that watched them as they escorted each other down a long white marble floored hallway with high corniced ceilings and crystal chandeliers were the eyes painted on the numerous portraits of now defunct Italian nobility. Lucy stopped in front of a canvas with two men seated in frock coats smoking cigars.

"Okay, so this is Prince Giovanni and Mortimer," explained Lucy. "Giovanni had a title, but no money, and Mortimer had money, but no title, so they were great friends. At some point in the eighties, the Fasani's *really* had no more money, so they renovated the whole palace into a swanky series of retirement apartments for upper crust Romans. It got named after the main investor in the project."

"So it's a *retirement* home, not a nursing home?"

"The second floor is a nursing home. Everything else is apartments for people over sixty."

"And the Fasani's still own it?"

"More or less. The old prince moved in in the '80's and died not long after that."

"And the current prince?"

"The current *princess*," Lucy turned around and pointed to a painting of a little girl on the opposite wall, wearing cowboy boots and sitting on a rocking horse, "lives in France. She keeps an empty penthouse for when she'll need to move in. She makes visits on holidays, but that's about it."

"But then why do you students live here?"

"Um… come upstairs."

They approached the turn in the hallway, which should have sent them up another wing of the U-shaped building. But hidden in one of the massive marble framed doorways, was another slender door. Lucy stopped in front of it, fumbling with the zipper in the back of her track shorts as she tried to pull out the correct key. Petrifying visions of the cops recognizing the wrong set of keys raced through her mind. She braced herself, half expecting them to yell at her, slam her to the wall and throw her in handcuffs. It was at least comforting that the officers, like all Italian police, didn't seem to be in a hurry, nor did they seem to notice that the difficulty in getting the keys was caused by the trembling in her hands.

Instead, she pulled out the correct key, and the doorway opened as normal. Behind it there was a poorly lit and narrow steel corrugated staircase with no decoration at all. It had once served as a way for butlers and maids to move between floors without being seen. Lucy went first, leading the officers back and forth along the short flights of stairs ending in a steel door that, when unlatched, led to a rooftop terrace. They exited one of those triangle structures that you see on the tops of buildings, that make it look like streams of people emerging from a clown car — even more so when Brian comes out.

A ten-yard long outdoor covered area led from the triangular roof access door, through a gamut of lounge chairs, patio furniture, and potted plants, towards what appeared to be a completely undecorated one story structure, built right on top of Palazzo Mortimer. In the previous two weeks, Brian, Lucy, and Andrew – Andrew was an architecture student – had volunteered to build the wooden roof over the patio furniture so that they could walk from their front door to the roof access point without getting wet in the rain.

"This is the old servants' quarters," said Lucy, "where we live."

"And you pay rent to the princess for this space?"

"No."

"It's free?"

"Kind of."

"So you work for her, then?"

"We *volunteer* for two hours a day."

"I see."

And that was the end of his line of questioning about their irregular housing situation. With just a few words, Lucy had implicitly become a tax evasion informant, and Speziale tacitly acknowledged to her that such matters were outside of the scope of his investigation.

For those unfamiliar with the rule of law in Italy, here is a brief explanation of the meaning behind this exchange: sometime in the mid 2000's, someone forgot to bribe the property tax inspector, who thereupon noted, for the first time, that there was a ten bedroom building that had never been included before in his assessment. Given the awkward location on the roof, the space was unusable as a retirement home residency, but changing the zoning to normal residential would have been a tax nightmare. So they decided to make it available as free housing to poor grad students, which, with enough bureaucratic red tape involved, could eventually provide a backhanded tax loophole, the legitimacy of which was entirely questionable, depending on whether or not any possible auditor was well compensated.

Having the students work as employees would have been a payroll nightmare. What's more, if the students had an income, they would no longer be poor, thus rendering their tax loophole null. So the students were asked to volunteer for two hours each day, chatting with the residents. This, in turn, became a huge unexpected benefit for the retirement and nursing home community, as resident morale went way up. Italians – and I guess all people, really, but especially Italians – need someone to talk to in order to feel normal. Some residents, who would usually only get monthly visits, at best, now had constant company. It turned out to be a huge benefit for the students too. There was always more than enough food at all the meals, and as long as you sat next to a resident at lunch or dinner, it counted as part of your volunteer hours. Free food.

Out on the terrace, Luca's phone buzzed, and he looked at a text message. "Thank you, Lucy, for your explanation. I have need to return downstairs."

They shook hands, and Luca departed.

Once the ranking officer disappeared from sight down the roof access door, the other cop became a tourist, pulling out his phone and snapping pictures. He stepped to the railing to admire the view – one of the best from the whole Janiculum hill. You had St. Peter's Square and basilica to your left, and all of the center of Rome directly below your feet in front of you. As of 2015, standard Italian police were not yet equipped with selfie sticks, so Lucy was required to snap photos of him smiling in front of the Roman skyline.

"*Ma che figata 'sto posto dove abitate, no?*" he said with a big grin on his face.[23]

"*Sì, sì, è proprio bello.*"[24]

He pointed out and identified all of the monuments and hills of Rome from their bird's eye angle: the pantheon, the coliseum, the *Altare della patria*, the Vatican, Santa Sabina, and in the distance you could just make out the roofs of St. John Lateran and St. Mary Major.

Eventually the officer got back to work, "*Allora, i documenti.*"[25]

She used the same key that was still in her hands to open the door to the old servants' quarters: one long hallway, white tiles, white walls, bright white fluorescent lighting, and ten white doors. Nonetheless, it was home. From the end of the hallway a portrait of the old prince from the seventies – and in his seventies – smiled down at them with a flock of seagulls haircut and a baby blue leisure suit.

Lucy's door was the third on the left and was closed, the door across from it, though, for the first time in a year, stood open. All the furniture from that room was scattered in the hallway. As they came inside, a strong stench of bleach became more and more overwhelming, culminating at a point in the room across from Lucy's.

Inside her own room, she opened the curtains, which had been drawn shut, casting orange light on the whole interior of the room. His polished shoes and ironed pants strolled in uninvited, and Lucy could feel the officer's condescending gaze on the back of her neck. How old are you? Didn't you ever learn to clean up after yourself? The room was arranged with inordinate piles of things and furniture surrounding a red Moroccan rug.

And of course, just when she needed it, Lucy could not find her wallet. She dug through everything she owned, and the officer

---

[23] "Damn, this has to be an awesome place to live, huh?" *he said with a big grin on his face.*

[24] Yeah, yeah, it's really nice.

[25] Alright, let's go look at that I.D.

eventually gave her some space by looking only at the walls and what was on them: Botticelli's *The Birth of Venus*, Caravaggio's *Judith beheading Holofernes*, Vermeer's *Girl with Pearl Earring*. One wall was covered in photos of famous Italians eating spaghetti, and another with a massive print of the Denver skyline. A small portrait of the prince reigned from above the sink and mirror.

Her wallet was not in her jacket, which was crumpled up on her unmade orange bed sheets. Nor was it in her school bag, left on the antique leather footstool. It was not on the desk, which had always served more as a place to pile things than as a desk, nor was it near the 19th century stained glass lamp, nor was it anywhere in the antique wardrobe with inlaid Chinese soldiers. It was not in the small Christmas tree — left out since the previous December — nor was it anywhere in her laundry basket

The officer heard movement in the room across the hallway, and abandoned Lucy to examine all her dirty clothes without an audience. In frustration, she gave up, stood in the middle of the room, and covered her eyes. Come on, Lucy, think! Think! What was I doing before I went running? Bits and pieces of conversation distracted her from the hallway, so she covered her ears as well. You were wanting to take a nap, but couldn't fall asleep, so then you started reading and then... that's right! She went straight over to one of the large piles of books surrounding her orange Ikea easy chair, picked up García Márquez's *Cent'anni di solitudine*, and removed the objects she had been using as a bookmark – a U.S. Passport and an Italian visa card.

Her triumphant exit from her bedroom interrupted an exchange between the cop and a gorgeous blond haired blue-eyed girl that had been going nowhere. Rome is not particularly cold in October, but the girl was wearing a turtleneck, jeans, leather boots, and a down vest. She held herself in such a way that said: I have spectacular posture, I'm a much better person than you, and I'm very cold right now.

Lucy didn't like her.

"*Ciao*... um... I'm sorry, I don't speak Italian yet. Are you the person who lives across the hall from my room here?" the blonde girl asked Lucy. She had an English accent, or rather, her accent sounded mostly like an English accent, but some of the vowels came out slightly different, and a few of the r's were almost rolled.

Lucy nodded.

"Oh, thank God. They said you might be American, but you speak Italian. Do you speak Italian too?"

"Yeah."

"Great. I definitely haven't understood anything that this officer is trying to explain. God, my Italian is downright dreadful. It sounded like he said there's been a murder just downstairs. But that can't be right."

"No, that's right. Somebody was just killed an hour ago in the lobby."

"Holy shit," she whispered. Her eyebrows went up, and she shuffled back aimlessly, knocking into a mop and bucket that she had left on the threshold of her bedroom.

"*Signorine,*" said the cop, "*Vi dà fastidio se vi interrompo un attimo?*"[26]

"*Oh, sì, sì, ci scusi, signore,*" responded Lucy.[27]

"Oh, thank God, you really do speak Italian," said the new girl.[28]

The officer turned to Lucy and said, "*La dica, per favore, che voglio suo nome, cognome e documenti?*"[29]

"He wants your first name, last name and I.D.," translated Lucy.

"First name, Natálya Nikoláevna," said the girl, "last name, Abramova." She produced a Russian passport and an Italian visa card.

Lucy translated the same line of questions that she had received outside on the sidewalk. Natálya hadn't heard or seen anything. The officer thumbed through the Russian passport and halfheartedly attempted to copy some of the Cyrillic script to his notes, but gave up halfway through the word *Natálya* and scratched it out.

---

[26] "Young ladies," *said the cop,* "do you mind if I interrupt you for a second?"

[27] "Oh, yes, sorry, sir," *responded Lucy.*

[28] *"Oh thank God you really do speak Italian," said the new girl.*

[29] *The officer turned to Lucy and said,* "Can you please tell her that I want her first name, last name and some I.D.?"

He then turned and took the U.S. Passport from Lucy – who was feeling indignant at the pretty girl for having cut her in line.

"*Ah, bello,*" said the officer, "*tu sei di* Colorado*? Mio fratello una volta è andato lì a vedere il* Grand Canyon*! Bello, no?*"[30]

"*Non lo so. Io non son mai andata.*"[31]

"*Caspita. Io c'ho una zia che abita a* San Francisco. *Una volta mi piacerebbe un sacco andare a trovarla. Forse andrei anche a* Denver*, non lo so. È Bello? Denver è attacata a California, no? Cosa? Cento chilomentri da* San Francisco*, no?*"[32]

"*Più o meno.*"[33]

"*Va be',*" said the cop with a note of finality in his voice, seeing that Lucy was not interested in chitchat, "*Vi Saluto. Se sentite qualcosa, vi mettete subito in comunicazione con la polizia.*"[34]

"*Certo.*"[35]

"*E vi raccomando. Rimanete qui sopra e non scendete per almeno un paio di ore.*"[36]

"*Ok.*"[37]

He turned on his heels and walked straight down the hallway. Lucy stood rooted on the spot, digging her fingernails into her palms, until the cop left the servants' quarters. She stared at the closed door, sensing her whole body slowly deflate. But as the rest of her relaxed, her shorts felt heavy. The weight of the dead man's keys in her running shorts hung heavy on her waist. Without saying a word to the new girl, she returned to her room, locked the door, hid the keys, and melted into her easy chair.

---

[30] "Oh, nice," *said the officer*, "you're from Colorado? My brother went there once to see the Grand Canyon. Beautiful isn't it?"

[31] "I don't know. I've never been."

[32] "Wow, I've got an aunt who lives in San Francisco. Sometime I'd love to go see her. Maybe I'd hit Denver too. Is it beautiful? It's right next California, right? About sixty miles?"

[33] "More or less."

[34] "Well," *said the cop with a note of finality in his voice, seeing that Lucy was not interested in chitchat,* "I'll take my leave of you. If you hear of anything get in touch with the police immediately."

[35] "Of course."

[36] "And please, stay up here and don't come down for at least a couple more hours."

[37] "Okay."

CHAPTER FOUR

L'INCULTURAZIONE FALLITA DEL CAFFÈ

Lucy finally crawled out of her room the next day at eleven in a bathrobe and sandals and crept down the hall towards the dorm room style bathroom, the first door on the left when entering the servants' quarters. She stopped at the door and closed her eyes, greeted again by the strong stench of bleach. The floor and shower tiles were sparkling clean — smug and happy, having recently been granted parole after a twenty year sentence of soap scum. After dressing, she went to the kitchenette – the last room on the right, next to the smiling prince – and wondered why the light had been left on. She hit the switch, and the lights turned *on*. Wait. No. The lights had not been on at all. The kitchen tiles were just a shade brighter than she'd ever seen them before.

Her daily allotted two stale cups stared back at her, lurking at the bottom of the American coffee machine. The green warning light had already switched itself off three hours ago. It was cold, and tasted like burning. She swallowed, cringed, set her cup down on the counter and frowned at it. To make a new pot or suffer though this cup? Yesterday's events came to mind. Well – shit – I deserve it.

"Oh! Caught red handed!"

Lucy jumped and almost dropped the coffee pot as the last of the old batch circled the drain. Brian, of all people, was there to see her wasting precious community coffee.

"Hey," he said, throwing his backpack on the table and maneuvering his large mid section into the space between the wall bench and the kitchen table, "just so we can keep an accurate budget, could you let me know whether or not you're going to waste half a pot of coffee every time you sleep in and skip class, or is this just a one time thing?"

"Brian, I'm having a bad day. Now is not the time."

"Well, I mean, just for budget purposes, could you give me a ballpark figure of how often you're going to have a bad day this year?"

Lucy didn't answer. Brian's watchful foreman eyes supervised her every movement: one filter, the water filled to the very top of the pot, five level scoops – not an ounce more – of the absolute cheapest coffee available in Italy.

"Well," Lucy hit the 'brew' button, turned around, and leaned against the counter, "did you have a good day at school, dear? Were the other kids nice to you?" In Italy, university doesn't start until the first week of October.

"Yeah, it was alright, I guess. It's good to be back at Mamma Greg. We had two hours of this new Polish professor who teaches Johannine literature. The poor guy can barely speak Italian. I kid you not, he just read to us for two straight hours from his book. It was brutal. But it'll be nice having two hours free on Tuesday mornings. But then, at least, we had a great hour of anthropology with this feisty little Italian woman, *Professoressa Verace* or *Tenaccia* or something like that. Oh, and Scott says hi."

Lucy blushed and turned around to watch the coffee drip. "So you saw him at class? They're all back now?"

"Oh yeah, the NAC guys have been back for a few weeks now."

"A few weeks! And that ass hasn't come to see me, yet?"

"Those guys have been pretty busy with conferences or something. I'm sure he'll come visit now that real classes have started and he doesn't have to work." Brian put his elbows on the table and rubbed his eyes. "Maybe I will want some of that coffee you're making. Oh, and yes, the other kids were nice to me."

"I don't know, Brian. It looks like you already drank two cups this morning. I don't think it's in the budget."

"Hey!" Brian sat up and yelled – half pointing at himself, half thumping his chest – "I'm the coffee Tsar here! I will make the decisions."

"Well, I've got some bad news for you about the coffee Tsar thing," said Lucy.

"What's that?"

"We've got a real Russian in the servants' quarters now. No more Tsar jokes."

"Russian? The new girl? She told me she's South African."

"Really?" said Lucy. "That would explain why she spoke English. But I saw her Russian passport when the police came up here."

"We'll find out soon enough, I guess," said Brian. He changed his tone of voice, leaned in towards the center of the table and asked, "So, do you want to talk about why you were freaking out yesterday?"

Lucy looked at the door, back at Brian, and back at the door. She pulled out the chair straight across from Brian and sat down, leaning in towards him, "Do you remember the guy I was telling you about? The guy in the park?"

"Yeah, the creeper who gave you the keys?"

"Yeah, him," she gulped and continued, leaning further into the table with an even quieter voice, "He's the guy who got killed here yesterday."

Brian rubbed his forehead and remained quiet. Lucy's breath had quickened, and Brian tried to put it all together at once. "But how on earth would you know that? They haven't released a name yet, have they? And you told me you don't know who that guy was, right? And he was in the park, what would he be doing at the Palazzo?"

"The track pants and the shoes sticking out from under the tarp, they were the same. Why do you think I was freaking out?"

"I don't know. You saw a dead body. Some people freak out at that kind of stuff. But come on. Shoes and track pants are pretty common. We can't know it's the same guy."

"The *exact* same shoes, and the *exact* same pants on the guy who said he was from Palazzo Mortimer? It's the same guy."

"But what about the keys?"

"I put 'em in the storage room."

"Really? The cops didn't want 'em?"

Lucy leaned back in her chair and didn't answer.

"Are you kidding me? You didn't tell the cops?"

"What do you think I was talking about when I kept saying, 'This is not my problem'? This is not my problem!"

"Oh yeah?"

"Look, if some totally random person gives you keys and then shows up dead on your front porch, that is not your fault. What do you do? You let the cops cart off the body, and get on with your life. Or… like… I don't know… If you open your front door, and there's a flaming bag of shit there, what do you do? Put it out with your boots? Hell no! You close the door, go to bed, and let that sucker burn."

Brian paused to contemplate that final image. "Yeah, but no matter what, you've still got shit on your doorstep. Sooner or later you're going to have to deal with it."

Lucy shrugged her shoulders. Brian shook his head. Both of them straightened up, hearing footsteps approaching towards them from down the hallway. The new blonde girl stood in the door frame.

Lucy was comfortable in jeans, a polo – collar popped, of course – moccasins, and her leather headband. Brian was in khakis and a button up, and looked less than comfortable, still sweating from having walked up the Janiculum. (That is, he's not always dressed as a clown. Whenever he would be getting ready for a job, Lucy would make fun of him because, despite his short hair and receding hairline, he still put on a rubber bald cap.) The new girl, though – wearing tight jeans, leather boots, a jacket, a light scarf and a headband – looked cold and pale, but with rosy cheeks. She kept her hands tucked into her jacket sleeves.

The gurgling sound that the coffee machine makes when finishing a pot finally interrupted the short tense pause created by the new girls' interruption of a serious conversation. The blonde sensed something was odd, but plowed ahead anyways, with the nicest tone possible. "Oh, you're making coffee? I'd absolutely love a cup if you're making a full pot."

"Oh yeah, definitely," said Brian. "It's Natasha, right?"

"Indeed. And you're Brian, correct?"

"Correct."

"And I don't remember if I caught your name yesterday afternoon," said Natasha, turning towards Lucy. "I'm awfully sorry about all the drama with the police and the translations. You really did save my life, there."

"My name's Lucy," she said, extending her hand, but not getting up. "It's no problem."

Natasha came into the kitchen, hesitated for a split second looking at Lucy's hand, but eventually shook it. She pulled a chair out from the table, looked down at it, removed a Clorox wipe from a packet in her pocket, gave the chair and her right hand a once over with the wipe, and finally took a seat. Her posture was impeccable.

During the ritual, Lucy's eyes met Brian's. They both had an oh-crap-who-the-hell-just-moved-into-our-builing look written on their faces. Lucy stood up and filled three mugs with coffee. She placed Brian's sixteen-ounce Starbucks Singapore mug in front of him, her own favorite mug with the entire calendar year of 2010 printed on the side (with all the months in German) at the head of the table, and – as a tacit assertion of her own power and authority – she unilaterally decided that the ownerless dark blue Knights of Columbus mug would now be assigned to Natasha.

"You don't mind American drip coffee do you?" asked Brian. "Or what do they drink in South Africa anyways?"

"Oh, the tea is wonderful everywhere, but Cape Town is one of the only places with a real coffee culture. In a lot of the country they've just got instant coffee. Terrible. I had been trying to drink stronger espresso to see if I could get used to it before coming to Italy." She took a sip out of her mug. "But I suppose inculturation only goes so far. Anyways, can I ask you both a question? Do either of you have a mobile in Italy?"

"You mean a cell phone?" asked Lucy?

"Don't answer that question," said Brian. "She knows what you mean. She's just got this habit of making everyone in Europe use American vocabulary when speaking English."

"Well, when I first got here, I had a *cell phone*," said Lucy. "But I never really had anyone to call over here. It was just a waste of cash, so I got rid of it."

Lucy slouched down into the seat at the head of the table – an exaggerated slouch in the face of Natasha's incisive angles – and put her feet up on the empty seat next to Natasha to see if she couldn't provoke a germaphobe reaction.

"I've got a *mobile*," said Brian. "Some of us have real jobs and need to be in touch with people.

"Well, my boyfriend gave this to me in South Africa and he told me it would work in Italy." Natasha gingerly placed one of those miniature brick cell phones with a manual keypad on the table. "I can't seem to get any calls to go through. Yesterday afternoon, everything was working just fine, but now I can't get ahold of him."

"Your account's probably just out of credit," said Brian. "Everything here is pay as you go. No contracts. What company do you have? You'll just have to go to a *tabaccheria* and fill it up with credit."

"Oh my God!" Natasha turned to look at the feet on the chair next to her. Lucy tried not to smirk and Brian rolled his eyes. Natasha looked even closer at her feet and said, "Where on earth did you buy these shoes? I absolutely adore them!"

Brian now tried not to smirk himself. He knew exactly what Lucy was trying to do, and he knew that Lucy had failed to provoke the desired reaction. She wasn't going to give up that easy, though.

"I slaughtered a bison, tanned the skin, and sowed them myself," Lucy answered with a straight face.

"Really? They do that sort of thing in America?"

"What? You've never been on a bison hunt?"

"Not at all."

"Oh, come on. I'm just messing with you," Lucy finally laughed. "Have you ever heard of Hobby Lobby?"

Natasha shook her head. Her cheeks turned even redder and she tried to laugh along. Except when running, Lucy almost always wore handmade moccasins. I had tried to convince her to go and hunt an animal by herself, but she insisted that leather and other materials could be found at this place called *Hobby Lobby*.

"G'Day, mates!" all three turned their heads to watch Andrew stride through the door, throwing his school bag on the floor. A huge cheesy grin spread across his face as he patted Natasha on the back, "Who's the most excited here for her first day on the job? Oh, you're gonna love it! Two hours of chatting with old ladies. Get ready!"

"But don't get too big of a head on your shoulders," said Brian. "They always love the new student for the first month or two. You're going to be the most popular girl at lunch today, and everyone will want you to be at their table."

"It's true," said Lucy. "There's these three old ladies. We call 'em the 'mean girls'. They sit by themselves, or sometimes they let me sit with them, but nobody else. You'll probably have to sit with them today as a test, which is a very special thing."

"Yeah, it's a big day for you," said Andrew. "When I started, I was as nervous as a gypsy with a mortgage. I only got just one day with the mean girls before they decided they didn't like me. Brian got four before they didn't like him anymore. Today could make or break your whole career at the Palazzo. You might be spending the next few years with me and Brian in the nerds section. No worries, though. Brian and I will keep you company."

"But I hardly speak Italian," said Natasha. "They're going to hate me."

"But it's not about speaking Italian," Lucy shook her head and caressed her popped collar. "It's about being a bad ass, and that's it. You either are or you aren't."

Very soft footsteps came down the hallway in their direction. A young Asian man in black pants, a grey clerical shirt, and a black blazer made a bee line through the kitchen to the fridge. Before opening the door, he stopped and performed a slight head bow towards the table, solemnly pronouncing, "*Buon giorno*," and left the kitchen with a Mountain Dew and a Tupperware of fried rice.

"That's Master Miyagi," explained Lucy. "If you're interested in learning Karate or Feng Shui, he's the guy to talk to. Or actually... he doesn't really talk much at all, but you can give it a shot."

"But then why was he dressed as a priest?" asked Natasha.

"In Asian cultures, they use western clothing differently," said Lucy. "It just means he's a black belt in Zen. If you're awake at the right hours, you'll even see him levitate sometime."

"Okay, just to be clear," interrupted Brian, "that's Fr. Damien. He's not a Karate master or Zen or anything like that. He's just a normal Catholic priest from Korea, and he's another one of the grad student residents on the hallway."

"But he doesn't have to volunteer like the rest of us," Lucy rolled her eyes at the grave injustice.

"He *does* have to volunteer like the rest of us," said Brian. "He's the chaplain. He has to say Mass every day in the chapel, hear their confessions, and be there to anoint anyone who's about to die."

"It's a pretty good deal, actually," continued Lucy. "The residents all love having a priest around who doesn't ever talk with them. They know he barely understands Italian in the confessional. And even better, they know they'll have someone to wipe some magic oils on their heads to get rid of their sins before they die, so they don't have to worry about behaving or going to church or anything like that. It's great. If I were Catholic I'd definitely want to live here, because then I could sin as much as I wanted, and still get a free ticket to heaven just before checking out. They've really got everything figured out in this country."

You could almost see the gears working in Brian's head, quickly flitting through different theological arguments that had already been hashed out a number of times without success. Reason can almost always prove useless against the impenetrable fortress of Lucy's sarcasm. She sat back, waiting to see what ridiculous thing Brian was about to say, hoping she would get to make fun of him more. Probably because of the new girl's presence, though, he skipped a serious response, and matched fire with fire, "Well, even without being Catholic, Lucy, you seem to sin as much as you want anyways, so what's the point?"

She opened her mouth to respond, but the surprise of his comment took her off guard. What the hell was that supposed to mean? After she'd done the math, it was clear that what Brian had said was more biting and personal than any of the old abstract theological things he'd said before. In the heat of the moment, she forced out a courtesy chuckle, shrugged her shoulders and pretended she thought he was funny. But in her eyes it was clearly a fake laugh. Her eyes also said that the comment had cut much deeper than Brian would have intended. A keen observer would know that she would try to ignore it for a few days, then she'd spend a week ruminating on it, and finally, in a moment of weakness, she'd explode at me or at Brian for something completely unrelated. Hopefully nothing expensive would have to be broken in the process this time.

"But what does Fr. Damien do the rest of the day?" asked Natasha.

"Smoking, sleeping, and studying," said Andrew. "I've got the room right next to his. He does the *exact* same thing every day. His alarm goes off at 11:40am. He smokes his first cigarette on the terrace at 11:45, showers at 11:53, returns to his room by 12:06, has a Mountain Dew, a cigarette and fried rice for breakfast at 12:17, goes to the chapel at 12:30 for twenty minutes and stares at some book, leaves for the Greg at 12:43, and sits at the exact same spot in the library until Mass in the chapel here at 7:30. He eats dinner at the table by himself in the dining room until 8:20. Then he comes back upstairs and works on his doctoral thesis, taking a smoke-o every forty-two minutes out on the terrace before going to bed at exactly 3:40 every morning. The man is a machine."

"So he's already a priest, but he's still studying at the seminary?" asked Natasha.

"No, he's not a seminarian. He's getting his doctorate at the Gregorian University, where I go," explained Brian. "So he can go back home to Seoul and teach in their seminary there."

"But what do they do if they die in the afternoon?" asked Natasha. "If Fr. Damien's at the library, how do the residents get the anointing, or confession, or whatever it is they call it?"

"Oh, that's the thing," said Lucy, having quickly suppressed her rage and now back to her normal salty personality. "They don't die in the afternoon, they always hold on and wait for Fr. Damien to come in the evening. It's really bizarre. They all like to die in style here with the distressed family members standing around and all the religious rituals. Yeah, and now that you mention it, it was really weird to have someone die in Palazzo Mortimer in the afternoon yesterday. That's never happened in the three years since I got here. I guess that guy must not have been Catholic."

Lucy started to chuckle, but fell silent, fidgeting with her mug, when nobody else laughed. Natasha looked down, and Brian looked across at Lucy with a mocking grin. The rage in Lucy's eyes flickered back on and off for just a moment.

"So where are you going to study?" Andrew asked Natasha.

"Right now I'm just hitting the Italian pretty hard," said Natasha. "But I'm looking into a few viticulture marketing programs."

"Viticulture?"

"Yeah, wine production," said Natasha. "It's an agriculture specialization. That's what I've got my undergrad in. But now I've got to figure out how to sell the stuff."

"You need to sell wine?" asked Brian. "I'll buy some."

"That's exactly the point," said Natasha. "How do South Africans get Americans to pay more for our wine? You'll pay top dollar for swill with 'Italy' written on the bottle, but you won't pay half as much for highly rated stuff with 'Africa' written on the side. You heard it here first. The New World — Africa, Australia, the Americas — we've got to stick together, and we've got to figure out why the Old World can sell sub-par wine for twice as much as it's worth!"

"I thought you were, Russian, though," said Lucy.

"I'm not sure if Russia counts as 'Old World,' but yeah, I've got dual citizenship," she answered. "Daddy's Russian and Mum's South African. I only spend a few weeks or so every year with Daddy in Moscow, so I'm really not much of a Russian at all. Mum and I have been on our own in Cape Town since whenever the wall came down, and Daddy was allowed back into Russia."

Nobody quite knew what to do with that last statement, either, and it was followed by a pause, until Andrew, again, saved the day, "Alright, well I'm interested in hearing all about South Africa and Russia. Right now, though, we'd better head down to lunch."

CHAPTER FIVE

LEI È LA SIGNORINA LUCY FOX?

That day at *pranzo*, morale was absolutely through the roof. Two new things. First, the new girl. The residents would spend the next two weeks analyzing and dissecting her appearance, her dress, her words, and her gestures. So who's that new girl? How long has it been since last time we had a blonde? Maybe '07 or '08 when there was that funny looking German one, remember her? *Ma questa qua invece, che belle chiappe che c'ha, no? Hai ragione, è proprio carina.* Where'd they say she's from? Must be Milan. No, no, she don't speak no Italian. Maybe German? Polish? No, no, I heard say she's from Africa. What are you crazy? A blonde from Africa? Yeah! You mean *Africa Africa* or just *Sicily*? No, Africa Africa. They got blondes in Africa? Sure do. You gotta go down far enough, though. What? Yeah, keep going down south. They've got winter when we've got summer, just like we've got Norway and Sweden up here in Europe. You don't say. Yep. So you're telling me they've got blondes on the other side of Africa? Course they do. I got a cousin who spent the whole war in Mozambique. Told me all about it. So why's she all bundled up? What do I know? Think about it. She was just coming out of winter down there, but we're headed into it up here. Should take a few weeks to adjust. You think it's real blond hair or just dyed? No, I think it's real. No, that's bleached for sure. Look it only goes down past her ears. Real blondes from Sweden have long hair. This one's a fake.

Second, and more importantly, a murder. Finally they had something to talk about that wasn't the weather or what their children might be doing with their money. The residents were in such a good mood that the staff was wondering if they could have a dead body delivered to their door every Monday afternoon. Did you see the body? I've seen plenty of Saudis. No, I said did you see the body yesterday? What? The body? The dead body? Did you see it? Carolina saw the body, I thought. She said it was under a tarp, though. What? A tarp! I bet it was the mafia. I'll bet it was the staff, I know exactly who it was, but I'm not telling. They were after money, I'm sure, it's all about money. No, it was sex and drugs. All the killings these days are about sex and drugs, not money. I know a guy in the police department, he told me he's gonna bring me all the files to look through tomorrow. I once knew a guy from Brescia who got killed. I knew a guy from Perugia who got killed. Oh yeah, I knew three guys who got killed *in* Perugia! Mafia? Gambling? I bet it was the wife who couldn't take it no more. Did you hear the gun fire? Was it a gun? No, it was a knifing. I heard the gunfire, loud and clear, and I said, Antonio, somebody oughta call the cops 'cause that ain't no firecracker, that's a gun. Oh, you're full a crap, it was a knifing. You haven't heard anything more than ten feet away from you since '97. What? Like I said. You didn't hear nothing. What? Forget it. What's for lunch? Again? We just had that yesterday. That was two weeks ago. Yesterday we had the lasagna. All right. Let's eat. let's eat. Can we eat now in peace or are you just gonna stare at that food? What? Let's eat! Yeah, pasta's made of wheat. Forget it.

Lucy was the first student to come downstairs to the dining room, strolling through, indifferent to the Tiffany stained glass windows and the enormous high ceilings with intricately painted panelling and trusses. The mean girls flagged her down. She stood by the one empty seat at their table, but waited to sit down, knowing exactly what was going to happen. Natasha finally came through the door and stopped. Her eyes flew up, and her jaw fell down, awestruck at the windows and ceiling.

The ringleader of the mean girls, Signora Pironi, held up her hand to Lucy, telling her not to sit down. *"Oh, ma aspetti un attimo. La ragazza là è la nuova che è appena arrivata?"*[38]

"Sì.[39]*"*

"Grande, la dica di venire qui. Vogliamo conoscerla."[40]

"Certo."[41]

Lucy walked over to Natasha, and took her by the arm, interrupting her wonder moment and dragging her over to the mean girls' table. *"Ciao, ecco, ti voglio far conoscere alcune delle più illustri residenti qua al palazzo. Signora Pironi, questa è Natasha Abramova, la nuova arrivata fra noi studenti."*[42]

"Piacere."[43]

"Piacere mio."[44]

"E poi, la Signora Sbarra."[45]

"Piacere, signorina."[46]

"Piacere mio."[47]

"E poi, la Signora Torretta."[48]

"Piacere."[49]

"Piacere mio."[50]

---

[38] "Oh, could you wait just a second. That young lady over there, is she our new arrival?"

[39] "Yeah."

[40] "Splendid. Could you tell her to come over to us. We'd be delighted to make her acquaintance."

[41] "Certainly"

[42] *Lucy walked over to Natasha and took her by the arm, interrupting her wonder moment and dragging her over to the mean girls' table.* "Hi, I'd like to introduce you to some of the more illustrious residents here at the *palazzo.* Mrs. Pironi, this is Natasha Abramova, the newly arrived student in our group."

[43] "It's a pleasure."

[44] "The pleasure's all mine."

[45] "And then, here we have Mrs. Sbarra."

[46] " It's a pleasure, miss."

[47] "The pleasure's all mine."

[48] "And then Mrs. Torretta."

[49] "It's a pleasure."

"Prego," said Signora Pironi, pointing to the chair in front of her. *"Si accomodi."*[51]

"Grazie, molto gentile."[52]

"Lei, da dove viene?"[53]

"Sono sudafricana."[54]

"Bello."[55]

Lucy walked away to sit at the vulgar old men's table that was always closest to the mean girls. So it wasn't true that Natasha was *completely* inept at Italian.

The vulgar old men were the definition of exhausting personalities. They demanded constant attention, and they kept Lucy from eavesdropping on the mean girls' conversation with Natasha at the next table over. When the daily four courses were finally through – *primo, secondo, insalata, frutta* – Lucy looked up from her fruit salad to find the adjacent table already empty. She was burning to know how bad things had gone. What magnificent Roman insults had Natasha been served? Afternoon programming in the lounge, immediately after lunch, involved a game of Tombola – a kind of Italian Bingo – led by Brian, and virgin daiquiris served by the paid staff. Natasha and the mean girls were AWOL. Lucy made a tactical mistake and for the full duration of the social hour was locked into a seat on a couch next to a clingy lady who grew more and more tipsy after each non-alcoholic cocktail. The chatty resident finally passed out five drinks in, right in the middle of a slurred anecdote about the time she went out dancing during World War II with American presidents and sailors. Lucy, not giving the woman a chance to wake up and rally for another round, gently lifted herself out of her spot. She abandoned Brian to hand out the Bingo prizes by himself, and snuck off to find Natasha or the mean girls and hear about lunch.

---

[50] "The pleasure's all mine."

[51] "Please," *said Mrs. Pironi pointing to the chair in front of her,* "have a seat."

[52] "Thank you, that's very kind."

[53] "Where are you from?"

[54] "I'm South African."

[55] "Splendid."

Following a thorough search of all the likely places, unable to locate anyone, she returned to her room, changed into her athletic clothes, and walked out onto the terrace to head out for a run. And there she was, seated at the patio table next to Andrew and in front of a Mokka stovetop espresso maker, two thimble sized espresso cups, and a newspaper. Andrew – being a second generation Italian/Australian in Sydney – had always refused inculturation with the roommates and their American coffee.

Lucy lowered her aviators over her eyes, and sauntered over to the table. But before she could drum up a demoralizing conversation about lunch, Natasha started talking about something else. "Hi Lucy, looks like you're keen for a run with your trainers on there. Are you a big runner?"

"With my *what* on? And did you just call me *big*?"

"*Ach*, sorry, no. Gosh, I'm so sorry. I mean, are you an *avid* runner? And by 'trainers,' I mean your shoes. That's the way that we say it – "

"Wait, wait, wait," interrupted Andrew. "Don't answer that question. Lucy knows damn well what you mean. She and I had it out a few months ago on the whole trainers/sneakers argument. You'll do well to not humour her too much. She's just giving you a hard time. Don't worry. She's a little edgy to all the new people. She'll warm up to you."

Lucy didn't respond, but looked off in the distance and started stretching.

Natasha smiled. "I sure bet I'll need to start exercising too. What, with living and eating in Italy and all. I simply don't understand how everyone here can eat so much pasta and stay so skinny."

"I think it's all the stress and cigarettes," said Lucy. Natasha started to chuckle, but stopped, when she realized Lucy wasn't laughing along.

"Here," said Andrew, tipping the espresso pot in Natasha's direction. "We've got to finish this."

"Oh, no, no, I really shouldn't," said Natasha. "Virginia made me take a cup of espresso with her straight after lunch in her rooms."

"Virginia?" asked Lucy. She stopped stretching and finally looked Natasha in the eyes. "Did you just say *Virginia*?"

"Yes, I think that was her name."

"You mean *Signora Pironi*?"

"Right. Her. The mean girl in charge."

"Did I ever tell you that her first name was Virginia?"

"No, I don't think you did," said Natasha. "Because, I remember that I called her *Signora Pironi* a few times at lunch, and then she stopped me and told me to call her 'Virginia' instead. The other two did the same as well. Martina and Elena."

"Are you kidding me!" Lucy put her hands on her head. "You got *oh-just-call-me-Virginia* on your very first day? And you got invited to coffee in her rooms?"

"Yeah, I think so," said Natasha, with a worried expression. "Is that a bad thing?"

"Is that a bad thing? It's incredible! Do you realize it took *me* six months to get on a first name basis with Virginia?"

"Yeah, and I've been here for almost a year," added Andrew, "and I don't think I'll ever achieve first name status. Good on you, mate!"

"Good night! They must really be losing it," said Lucy. "That's too bad, though. Those girls can be mean as hell, but they're the only three normal residents here."

"Or maybe they just like Natasha," suggested Andrew.

Lucy looked off in the distance again. What she had just said could easily have been taken as an insult. Natasha's expression, at least, remained unoffended. But what was more startling for Lucy was how much the mean girls had rubbed off on her. Come on. It's just the mean girls. A silly group of old ladies. Does it even matter which student resident gets to be the fourth wheel? Really, who cares?

Andrew was quick with a subject change, "Did you see the newspaper today? They've identified the murder victim."

"Oh yeah? Did they say why he got killed?" asked Lucy, coming around to lean on the table beside Andrew. He turned to the local news section of *La Repubblica* and shuffled through to find the article. Natasha started examining her fingernails.

"Yeah, the police haven't made any statements about motive," said Andrew. "At least I don't think. Okay, yeah, here's the article. Something about a body... blah, blah, blah... some guy named Eugenio Galli... no motive... no information... no known connections to anyone at Palazzo Mortimer. It doesn't really give us a lot of information."

Andrew looked up from the paper and found both girls now squeezed in around him, standing to his sides, leaning over the table and reading the article. Lucy took it slow, reading each paragraph from top to bottom, but Natasha – whose cheeks had gone from rosy to pale – hurriedly ran her fingers over paragraphs in no particular order, as though touching them might make the Italian any more intelligible. She finally let her fingers rest, trembling just slightly, under the name of the victim, before straightening up, turning around as gracefully as possible, and disappearing down the roof access door that led downstairs.

"Well," said Andrew, "we'll just have to keep our eyes on the papers and see what else they can tell us."

"Yeah, I guess so," said Lucy, who was now lost in her own thoughts and hardly paying attention to Andrew. She walked to the railing and looked out over the city below them. Andrew flipped through the paper trying to find the soccer article he had been reading before Lucy came along. It took him a while, though, as he had to stop and examine every advertisement along the way that featured beautiful women.

Lucy eventually wandered off towards the door, and when it slammed shut, Andrew looked up and said out loud, "Oh, okay, goodbye, then," to no one, except the Banana Republic models beaming back at him from below his coffee cup.

Lunch with the new girl had been distracting enough, but Andrew's newspaper had yanked her mind straight back into the previous day's events. She left the building as quickly as possible, with an implicit certainty that clarity of thought would somehow be achieved somewhere outside the Palazzo.

"*Oh, Ciao, Bella. Dimmi, come stai, Lucy?*" said Gambetti in the lobby.[56]

"*Sto bene. Grazie, Gambetti. Ciao!*"[57]

---

[56] "Oh, hey there, beautiful. What's up? How are you?" *said Gambetti in the lobby.*

[57] "I'm fine thanks, Gambetti. See you!"

And as soon as she crossed the threshold, her legs began pumping automatically, with the same urgency as a junkie who can find a vein even blindfolded. But Lucy, at least, wasn't interested in the kind of escape offered by drugs. She sought that nirvana made possible only by prolonged physical movement, that beautiful and paradoxical state wherein she simultaneously found a jarring impact with reality in the present, and at the same time, an intense distance and detachment from it all. This was also the state in which Gambetti loved to see her the most. He got up from his chair and stood by the door, to narrow his eyes at her aft side as it ran up the street. It's the little things in life.

Before she could round the next switchback up the Janiculum hill, though, five police vehicles raced by her. She would have kept going, without looking back, had she not heard the tires of the first vehicle screeching in front of the Palazzo. They all parked quickly and a swarm of officers descended on Gambetti and the lobby.

"Not my problem," she mouthed to herself. She faced away from the Palazzo and let her legs carry her up the hill towards the park, convincing herself that it was just like any other afternoon. She had only planned on running six miles, but ended up doing thirteen – not because she felt a lot of energy, but to avoid thinking about yesterday's events and to avoid going back to the Palazzo and the police. She even stopped a mile from home, and slowly lolly gagged her way back.

In the meantime, I had been upstairs, dozing in my storage room – the room across from the bathroom, which was now used exclusively for two purposes: getting rid of piles of unwanted things and providing a place for a bear to sleep. Five officers with surgical gloves woke me up and systematically sorted through *everything* – boxes of clothes, golf clubs, skis, luggage, power tools, mops, brooms, cleaning supplies, empty cases of Folger's, Christmas decorations, piles and piles of textbooks – all the things that had been abandoned or forgotten by people who had once been student residents in the servants' quarters.

They sorted it all out in the hallway, swabbing and dusting with all kinds of expensive machines. Other teams searched through each individual room. Andrew had been the only one home when the police arrived. He was told to remain seated on the terrace, so he read the newspaper again, or rather, read all the articles about soccer and studied all the ads.

By the time she walked around the switchback in front of the Palazzo, there were no police cars parked out front. Lucy stopped in the lobby and looked around. Nobody was there. Completely empty. No Gambetti. No police. Good. She began her ascent, relieved. The extra seven miles had been worth it. She clambered sloppily up the final stairs to the roof access, threw open the steel door, and her heart sank. In unison, ten officers turned their heads towards Lucy, now frozen in the door frame. I had been too interested in watching the police work to think about warning Lucy downstairs. Ever so slightly, she scowled in my direction.

"*Lei è la signorina Lucy Fox?*" one of the officers asked her.[58]

"*Sì, sono io.*"[59]

"*Va bene. Venga con me.*"[60]

She was told to sit in a patio chair on the terrace. Detective Luca Speziale and his expensive shiny suit appeared in front of her. She made to stand up, but he gestured for her to remain seated. He scowled down, and took an athletic position in front of her. She crossed her legs and arms and stared back, not having to raise her eyes much to look into his.

"Please remain seated," he said. "And do not look at your friend over there."

He pointed at Andrew, and of course, the first thing Lucy did was look at him. Andrew looked up from the Dolce and Gabbana models that he'd been studying to smile and wave at Lucy.

She jerked her head down and said, "Sorry."

"It's okay. It's okay. Just do not permit yourself to let it happen again. We have to hold all of the persons here in a separated way so as to verify that all stories are in accord. I am certain that you are understanding. Here I give to you your passport and and your permission of Italian visa card." He handed them off, and scratched the short bristle behind his receding hairline.

---

[58] "Are you Ms. Lucy Fox?" *one of the officers asked her.*

[59] "That's me."

[60] "Okay, come with me."

"But… wait… why do you have these? Have you been in my room?"

"For sure," said Luca. His way of speaking in itself was distracting, his wide mouth wiggling inside his shortly trimmed beard. A stack of papers full of Italian legal language, stamps and seals landed in her lap. "I can now offer to you a series of documentations permitting for us to search all of said property. Okay? You are to stay here. I am coming back."

As soon as Luca walked off, I took a seat on the ground in front of Lucy's chair, at eye level with her. "Is there something that you know that I don't know?"

She just barely shook her head from side to side, indicating no.

"Are you sure?"

She nodded yes.

"The keys are in the golf bag. Are you going to tell the police about them?"

Negative.

"Alright, well, you've got to decide right now what you're going to do," I said. "You can either explain yourself – fully – right now, or, in the next few months, you can get caught lying to the cops about critical evidence in a murder case. They *will* find out. I for one, however, do not want to spend significant portions of your life puttering around an Italian prison cell. I get the feeling you don't want that either. This assignment's already been strange enough for both of us already. Just be upfront and tell them what's going on."

Giving advice to Lucy was usually like trying to convince a full grown cat to suckle sour milk from my own male breast. Her jaw dropped open and her scowl intensified, with her bottom lip twitching, full of desire to upbraid me. But she glanced behind her. Two officers stood guard over her patio chair, so instead she tried to give as much meaning as possible to her nasty glare.

When Lucy and I had first met, I used to give her all kinds of advice about everything – as spirit animals are wont to do. Middle school girls are not usually in a good place to mount a sufficient argument against the bad advice of a giant bear with centuries of experience, so she would often go along with my somewhat antiquated ideas. Over time, though, she grew to resent this more and more, but not without good reason. It took me a while to figure out that the things I used to say to young men hundreds of years ago, did not always qualify as sound guidance for a twenty-first century adolescent girl in south suburban Denver. You live and you learn. In time, we had reached a tacit agreement about how our relationship would work, an agreement that I had just violated. That afternoon I didn't really need to tell her that she was at a crossroads. She knew. Her eyes grew determined, no longer focusing on anything in particular. By the time Detective Luca stood in front of her again, it was clear that she had made up her mind. She wasn't going to listen to me.

"Ms. Fox, I have some notes that one officer took concerning your conversation with him yesterday," said Luca. "You say that you were absent from this building at the time of the homicide, that is, you were absent from approximately 15:30 until 16:45, and that you did not see nor heard nothing at such times. You say that you were at the Doria Pamphili park and at the coffee bar in Piazza della Rovere. Is this all true?"

"Yes."

"There is nothing else you would like to add to this statement?"

She turned away from the detective, looked me straight in the eyes and said slowly, "No."

"Okay, please come with me for a moment."

She followed him to the side of the servants' quarters. An officer held a tape measure against the exterior wall. Andrew was gone.

"Your visa document says that you are 1.68 meters in height," said Luca. "Is this true?"

"Maybe."

"What do you mean 'maybe'?" Luca was not happy. "You are telling to me that you do not know how tall you are?"

"I'm five six… five feet, six inches."

Luca sighed. "Just stand there by the tape. Take off your shoes."

She was 1.68 meters tall.

"Please return and be seated and replace your shoes." The officers placed her in the spot at the patio table where Andrew had been. The newspaper was gone. Luca left for another half an hour. I sat by the terrace railing and glared at Lucy. She crossed her arms and pouted back at me, the same way she used to pout when she was thirteen.

Sick of me, she made an attempt at conversation with the officers watching over her. "*È una bella giornata, oggi, no?*"[61]

"*Signorina,*" responded the tougher looking one, "*è meglio se noi non parliamo. Grazie.*"[62]

When Luca came back he had an armful of electronic equipment. He took her fingerprints, which should have already been on her police files from her entry visa. She finally started to look worried – a small place in her stomach opening up. I got worried too. It was hard to tell what Luca was up to, but whatever it was, it didn't seem to be for Lucy's good. Why would he need to take her fingerprints again? It made no sense unless he was convinced she was involved somehow, and needed to make some sort of extra verification. Lucy realized the same.

Luca placed an iPad in front of her. Lucy and three of her friends from her time as an undergraduate smiled up from the iPad, drenched in rain at the top of a mountain in Colorado. The other three were having a great time. Lucy's smile was forced.

"Is this you, Ms. Fox?" Luca pointed at her.

"Yes." Lucy looked back, puzzled.

"We have found this picture of you on the Facebook. You are wearing a green North Face brand rain jacket and black rain pants. Do these items belong to you?"

"Yeah."

"Where are they?"

"They're on a hook on the wall beside the wardrobe in my room."

"Both the rain jacket and the rain pants?"

"Yeah. In fact I'm certain the pants are there, because I've never even worn them or touched them since I got to Rome. They've just been hanging on that hook for three years.

Luca nodded at two cops, who went inside the servants' quarters.

---

[61] "It sure is nice out today, isn't it?"
[62] "Miss," *responded the tougher looking one,* "it's better if we don't talk. Thanks.

"No, they are not there. We have thoroughly searched every room in this facility. They are not here."

The two cops came out of the building and shook their heads.

"But you can for certain verify that these are your rain jacket and your rain pants?" asked Luca, pointing again at the photo. "And it is true that you have had them with you in this building quite recently?"

"Yeah. Of course. It rained just, like, last week, and I wore the jacket. But not the pants. I've never worn the pants in Rome."

I was shaking my head at her saying, "Stop talking! Stop talking! Ask for a lawyer! Ask for a lawyer!"

It was already too late. The small hole in Lucy's stomach got bigger. She started playing with her shorts, and looked down, saying everything at once and as quickly as possible. "No. Wait. No. No. No! What are all these questions even all about? I want to see a lawyer! I didn't even consent to any of these questions. What is this, like... what is this... like... even all about? I need a lawyer. You didn't give me a lawyer. You can talk to my lawyer, not me. I'm not talking to anyone!"

It didn't matter. Luca had already gotten all the information he thought he needed. He had understood only two words of Lucy's quick English: *no* and *lawyer*.

"We are a long ways from the United States," said Luca. "That will be all, Ms. Fox."

Luca turned away and made a phone call to someone more important than him. Lucy sat, watched, and worried. Luca returned with handcuffs. He planted his pricy leather shoes at shoulder length, and gave her an evil smirk. The two officers behind her gripped her upper arms and lifted her straight out of her chair. Cold bands stretched tight around her slender wrists. Her pulse struggled to get by the metal – a pulse now beating hard and fast.

Talking up at her 1.68 meters, from his 1.48 meters in height — enjoying every syllable — Luca solemnly pronounced, "*Lucy Fox, La dichiaro sotto arresto per l'omicidio di Eugenio Galli il quinto giorno di Ottobre di 2015. Lei ha il diritto di rimanere in silenzio. Qualsiasi cosa dirà potrà e sarà usata contro di Lei in tribunale.*"[63]

It had been a while since Lucy had been arrested. I thought that part of her life was behind us. Neither of us were used to it any more. And she'd never been arrested for anything this serious. Murder. Her face contorted. Tears flowed. Her breathing became quick and irregular. But she did exercise her right to maintain some sort of silence – mostly because of the shock. All sorts of cops started moving around the terrace, performing all sorts of jobs associated with a murder arrest. I stood there in the middle. Helpless. Unable to do anything.

---

[63] "Lucy Fox, you are under arrest for the murder of Eugenio Galli on the fifth of October 2015. You have the right to remain silent. Anything you say can and will be used against you in a court of law."

CHAPTER SIX

I MOBILI SPEZIALI

Probably the most enjoyable part of working for the Roman homicide unit was making arrests. Luca always fixed in his mind the images of the looks that murderers got on their faces when caught, so he could spend the next months relishing in that memory. Men usually became stoic. Women, dramatic. Clearly, Lucy was guilty. That much was obvious from the evidence against her. Her tears made the experience all the sweeter, especially knowing that her tears were all fake. Or rather, they weren't fake. For sure, she was going through some intense emotions: shock, anger, surprise, guilt, regret, etc. But she was certainly not crying because of a *false* accusation. She was crying because she'd been caught. And why are murderers always so surprised when they do get caught? The poor souls don't realize how clever detectives like Luca Speziale are.

In any case, Detective Speziale in some way even admired her for putting on such a good show. She was at least smart enough to redirect her real emotions of guilt and surprise in order to give the appearance of innocence. Working in the international homicide unit, Luca hardly ever got the chance to arrest Americans. And he'd never gotten to arrest a beautiful young American woman. People from other places could learn something from this one. He was looking forward to the interrogation. She's putting on the right face now — but does she have the energy to keep up that show in the interrogation room? Definitely not. I'm going to break you.

"*Portala via, la piccola assassina schifosa!*"[64]

Luca turned on his heal and headed over to the other side of the terrace. Were it not for the two cops gripping her arms, she wouldn't have been able to stand at all. Luca's thoughts were clear and decisive. Lucy's were not. The shock of an arrest — a murder arrest — was too much. Too many details. Too many distractions. She would try to think, but the massive hole in her stomach cried out for attention. Why the hell did they care about her North Face rain jacket? She would try to ask herself, but the derision on Luca's face was too much. That big mouthed sneer kept jumping up in her mind, and she'd have to start crying all the more. What did they care about 1.68 meters? Hearing the words *arresto* and *omicidio* was too much. Those words lurched in the pit of her stomach and tied her insides to knots. *Arresto. Omicidio.* Murderer. *Piccola assassina schifosa.* The cops held her arms too tightly to allow her to wipe off her tears. She tried rubbing her cheeks on her shoulders, but only ended up wiping snot all over her already sweaty dry-fit t-shirt.

Luca looked out over the city, stroking his beard. He jotted down notes, pondering how to proceed. This would be an important moment for his career, to say the least. Was it worth dropping hints — "dropping hints" i.e. "selling hints" — to friends in the media? His sneer became a smirk as the officers dragged her towards the stairs. She could hardly walk straight. Perfect. She'll break. In the end she'll break.

The lobby was empty when they walked her through. They had backed up a squad car just a few feet from the main door, that is, just a few feet from where Eugenio lay dead the day before. Two strong men gripped her limp arms while a third moved the cuffs from behind her back to the front. Through her tears she could see that the group of smokers that always congregates at the side entrance to the hospital across the street had stopped to look at her.

---

[64] "Take her away, the disgusting little murderer."

They all stared shamelessly. The poor girl getting arrested in handcuffs and everything. Wonder what she did? Among them stood a large clown in a yellow suit with red polka dots. He dropped his grocery bags and put his hands on his head in shock.

And the sight of Brian made her weep all the more.

"Brian!" she yelled, gasping and then choking on her own saliva. And then even louder, "Do something! Help!"

The last thing Lucy saw before being shoved into the back seat was the clown with two empty helpless hands aloft in the air, full of confusion and hesitation.

The ride to the police station, or wherever it is they take you in Italy after getting arrested for murder, was quicker than she expected. She had managed to calm herself down just slightly. The two officers up front, talking about their weekend plans, and the sharp turns in the middle seat without a seatbelt helped to bring her back to reality. They parked in a garage and and waited for the door to close before pulling her out. They brought her to a concrete room with no windows, a heavy steel door, drains on the floor, a few hoses with shower heads on them, and five very large female police officers wearing blue plastic gloves that extended past their elbows.

The biggest and ugliest of them came forward holding the shower head in a threatening way and told Lucy, "*Allora, ragazza, tutto ciò che hai addosso ormai appartiene alla Repubblica di Italia. O lo togli tu, o lo togliamo noi. Scegli tu.*"[65]

Lucy's dry fit t-shirt was full of thirteen miles of sweat. Another officer held it at a distance from her nose and said, "*Oh, ma che puzzo! Dovrebbe essere difficile la vita di una piccola assassina americana.*"[66]

The rest of the officers laughed, and even Lucy smiled.

Lucy exited that room half an hour later feeling more invaded than she'd felt in a long time, but also — at least physically — much

---

[65] "Alright, young lady. Everything you're wearing now belongs to the Republic of Italy. You can take it all off yourself or we can take it off for you. You decide."

[66] "Oh, what a stench! Life must be difficult as a little American assassin girl."

cleaner than she'd felt in a long time. The Republic of Italy had taken all her clothes from her, but in return, it had generously allowed her to borrow a pair of thick white socks, a white t-shirt, white underwear, and a khaki prison jumpsuit that was five sizes too big. The officers had first tried to force her into a jumpsuit that was far too small for her, but then gave up, and folded her up in a large. There must have been too many prisoners the same size as Lucy. She had to hold onto the elastic strap on her pants whenever she walked anywhere. The ladies told her she would have to throw some elbows to get to the front of the group on the next laundry day. At least the rubber slip-on sandals fit surprisingly well. Despite their best efforts, the officers were unable to find anything on Lucy's person. They even let her keep her leather headband. Somewhere between the shampooing and the rinsing, and four hair dryers going at once, Lucy stopped crying. Despite their threatening appearance, and their invasive work, the ladies were normal people. They didn't talk to Lucy except to give her instructions, and they made quite a few jokes among themselves that Lucy either didn't understand or didn't think were funny. Their light hearted mood at such a moment caught her off guard. For them, shampooing murder suspects was just another day at the office — the same job as a hair stylist, but with the tact of a pet groomer. The rest of the world went on as normal, even if Lucy was in crisis.

I tracked her down, just as they were pulling her out of the washroom. They left her in a room with three walls of solid concrete, and one wall of thick metal bars. Her cuffs came off, and we again heard that iconic clink of prison bars as they rolled shut. They made the same sound in Italy as they did back in America. She sat on the small bed attached to the wall, and I sat on the floor across from her, next to the all in one prison toilet/sink. She was exhausted. Too tired for any more emotions. But at least she was back in control of herself.

"Lucy," I said, "you used to be good at being here."

"I used to deserve to be here." She spoke with complete indifference, looking at the blank wall above my head.

"That's true."

"I used to *want* to be here."

"That's not true."

She rolled her eyes.

"Either way," I continued, "it's time for you to get back into that frame of mind. You used to love these little chats with police and social workers. Or, well, you didn't love it, but you clearly used to get something out of playing the game, and playing it well."

"I stopped playing that game a long time ago."

"In your life, and in this bear's life that wasn't that long ago. You've still got it in you."

"I don't want to play games any more. What do you think we're doing in Italy in the first place?"

"It doesn't matter. Look where you are. Look at what you're wearing," I said. She kept on staring at the wall. "It doesn't matter if you *want* to play or not. You're in the game. You can play it well, or you can lose. You decide."

"Alright." She stood up and walked the length of the cell, back and forth for a good five minutes. Her pacing looked much less confident than she might have preferred, having to hold up the elastic strap on her extra large prison pants. In the end though, she was not trying to look confident to me or anyone else, but only herself. She finally stopped by the bars, turned around, looked at me, and said, "I'll play."

I got up and put on my best rapper voice and recited by heart the first two lines of Eminem's *Lose Yourself.*

She didn't skip a beat, and still remembered all the words by heart. She put one hand in the air — leaving the other on her pants — and used her best white-girl-rapper voice, shuffling around the room with a gangster walk and perfectly delivering every line of a song she hadn't thought of since middle school. I knew that if I laughed, or even smiled, I would have broken her concentration, so I had to get out of there. This was supposed to be serious. Very serious. It's amazing the power that music can exert on some people. She looked ridiculous. She'll never make a convincing rapper.

But one hour before that moment, she had been right in the middle of an acute emotional breakdown, barely able to put two words together through all the sobbing. Ten minutes beforehand, her zombie gaze had been completely incapable of even the simplest emotions. But after just the introductory verses of a rather innocuous suburban rap song, if you looked in her eyes, you would have believed her capable of murder.

I snuffled around the facility until I ran across an unmistakable stench of Armani cologne. I followed it into a room with all sorts of electronic equipment in front of a thick window with a view into another room, which was furnished with just a table, two chairs, and a lamp. Luca stood above the equipment, staring through the window, systematically cracking one knuckle at a time.

Luca and I watched two officers drag Lucy into the room and plop her down into a plastic seat. At the same time, a grey haired man, wearing an even more expensive suit than Luca's, entered the room on our side of the glass and stood next to Luca. Among the various electronic devices on the panel in front of us, one was an old fashioned tape recorder. When the grey haired man began to speak, my claw accidentally slipped onto a red record button, and a tape began rolling.

"Luca, ti rendi conto quanto potrebbe essere importante questa interrogazione per tutti noi e per te?"[67]

"Sì, capo."[68]

"Ripassiamo i fatti. Uno, lei ha commesso un omicidio. Due, è una americana giovane, addirittura più bella di quell'altra che hanno beccato a Perugia qualche anno fa. Sul serio. Guardala lì. Bella, no? Tre, se puoi provare, come sospetto io, che c'è anche in gioco l'adulterio o qualcosa del genere, sarà il caso più importante della tua vita. Le media amano 'ste cose. Capito?[69]

"Sì, capito."[70]

"Scriveremo dei libri su quest'interrogazione e faremo un sacco di soldi con gli intervisti. Tu verrai promosso ed io andrò in pensione in una villa in campagna."[71]

---

[67] "Luca, do you realize how important this interrogation could be for all of us and for you?"

[68] "Yes, boss."

[69] "Let's go over the facts again. One, she's committed murder. Two, she's a young American girl, even prettier than that one they caught in Perugia a few years back. Three, if you can demonstrate, as I suspect, that there's also some sort of adultery or something like that involved, this will be the most important case in your life. The media love this stuff. Understood?"

[70] "Yes, understood."

[71] "We'll get book deals; we'll earn a ton of money on the interviews; you'll get promoted, and I'll retire at a villa in the countryside."

"Ti ho mai deluso, capo? Sono proprio all'altezza del lavoro."[72]

"Sicuro che non vuoi un traduttore?"[73]

"Capo, non c'è nessuno nel dipartimento che può parlare l'inglese così bene come me."[74]

"No, ma non dico nel dipartimento. Ci sono dei professionali traduttori di madre lingua che potrebbero venire a dare 'na mano proprio stasera. Dimmi tu."[75]

"Proprio non ce n'è bisogno.[76]

"Va bene."[77]

The older man took a seat in front of the window and a microphone, leaned back, and lit a cigarette. Luca struggled to fix a wire to his ear. I went into the interrogation room to explain an idea to Lucy.

Even if she agreed, on principle, she usually would find some way to contradict me. So I was a little nervous when Lucy accepted my suggestion, nodding her head with enthusiasm. Maybe even too much enthusiasm. Luca strutted into the room, slammed his pad of paper on the table, sat down, and looked her straight in the eyes. Lucy stared back. Hard. Unflinching. She sat up, leaned forward, put her elbows on the table, and folded her hands in front of her chin. In a completely calm voice, she quietly and clearly said, "I've got something to say before we begin."

Her new behavior caught him off guard. He touched his earpiece and looked at the mirror. "Sure. That would be fine."

Luca glanced at his notes, and started to rehearse to himself all the responses he had already prepared to her requests for a lawyer. You're not in America. This is an interrogation, not a courtroom. Etc. Etc.

---

[72] "Have I ever let you down, boss? I'm entirely up to the job."

[73] "Are you sure you don't want a translator?"

[74] "Boss, there's no one in the department who speaks English as well as I do."

[75] "But I'm not talking about in the department. We can bring in professional native speaking translators from outside by tonight, if you want."

[76] "There's really no need."

[77] "Alright."

But she didn't demand a lawyer or a phone call or anything.

"I just wanted to try and be nice to you," said Lucy, staring him down, as his eyes flickered up and down between his notes and the mirror. "And I'd like to at least give you a warning."

Luca dropped his pen and looked up.

"You can either let me go right now, or you can lose your job." She crossed her arms and leaned back. "That's all I have to say. If you'd like, you have my permission to ask questions."

Luca fumbled through his notes, completely unsure where to begin. Her introduction was not in any of the scenarios he had prepared. The ideal plan was to walk in, raise his voice, shine a light in her eyes, get her to cry at the right moment and spill the beans, and be home by dinner. In any case, the first punch had been thrown, and Luca wasn't the one who had thrown it.

Police interrogations are not as interesting in real life as they are on TV. In fact, they are actually designed to be lengthy, boring and repetitive, precisely to wear out the suspect and catch her in a contradiction. Luca asked hundreds and hundreds of straightforward one-word answer questions, scrupulously analyzing every detail of her responses. He went directly for what he thought was her weak point, the alibi. Luckily enough for Lucy, she had a true alibi. She told him everything, exactly as it had happened, leaving out only the thirty second encounter with Eugenio in the park. Luca pressed her on every detail, and every detail of every detail. Again and again and again and again.

Hours later, he abruptly switched to the jacket. Where was it? When had she last seen it? When had she bought it? Where was the receipt? Had she ever lent it to anyone? What size was it? Where did she hide it after the murder? Why did she throw it away after the murder? Did her accomplice hide it for her? She had never before spent so much time talking about one article of clothing.

Finally he asked, "Alright, we have been talking now for some time. It would be beneficial for both of us if you would stop playing at being a stupid innocent girl. Why did you dress yourself in the jacket and the pants when you killed Eugenio?"

"You're saying the girl who killed Eugenio was wearing the green jacket and the rain pants?"

"Yes. Why did *you* wear them when *you* were killing Eugenio?"

"Why don't you just tell me what's going on?"

"No, Lucy. Why don't *you* just tell me what you did yesterday afternoon?"

"Are you saying you want to talk about the park and the coffee bar again? I think we've both heard that story enough already. We can talk about it again, though, if you really want to waste more time."

"No, why don't you tell me why you killed Eugenio Galli, not at the park, not at the coffee bar, but in the lobby of Palazzo Mortimer?"

"Why don't you just tell me why you think I killed him and then maybe I could help you understand why you've mistaken me for the murderer?"

Luca didn't take her up on the offer. They switched to talking about "the weapon." At no point did he ever tell Lucy what it was, though. He did, however, ask her hundreds of questions about where she got it, how long she had owned it, whether or not she knew how to use it. Did she know how to load it? Did she know how to shoot?

Lucy racked her memory. Had she ever touched a gun in Italy? Her clearest memories of such things were all from America, where it is not outside the ordinary. Luca, of course, wanted to know all about her history of firearm usage. For her, it involved the usual weekends growing up in the the great American West, that is, going off to isolated ranches with friends in Colorado or Wyoming, getting tipsy and picking off beer cans and chipmunks from four wheelers. For Luca, such lethal behavior sounded tantamount to proof that she was a trained killer. For Lucy, such lethal behavior sounded like the natural consequence of two margaritas.

"So you're telling me the murder weapon was a gun?" she asked.

"I did not say that."

"So it wasn't a gun?"

"I am the question maker, not you!" he shouted.

He then plied her with seemingly endless questions about the victim. This part was harder for Lucy, but just slightly.

"When did you first meet Eugenio Galli."

"I've never met him."

She didn't flinch at all. I was impressed. In the end, if we want to take things extremely literally, she wasn't exactly lying. She had run into him and she did have a brief conversation with him. But could she say that they had really *met*? In any case, Luca plied her with endless questions about a non-existing relationship. She was a fantastic liar. At the end, I was almost convinced it was true.

Around one in the morning, he finally left the room. Lucy set her head on the table and pretended to sleep, forcing herself to relax every muscle in her body one at a time. Just minutes later, Luca returned, slamming the door as loudly as possible. Lucy didn't budge. He grabbed onto her hair — in that sensitive spot where the hair meets the neck — and pulled her up, removing a small clump of curls as he yanked back. Following that sharp sting, a few seconds later, every muscle from the top of her head to the bottom of her toes snapped into tension, as he threw a scalding hot splash of tea on that same spot on her neck.

Lucy cringed. It burned. Badly. Luca lit a cigarette and walked in slow circles around the room, stopping on every lap behind Lucy to flick the ashes on the back of her neck. She wiped the salt water from the side of her face as soon as it leaked out, but kept a blank expression. When he finished, he extinguished the cherry on her leather headband, and dropped the filter down the back of her shirt.

He took his seat across from Lucy. She breathed deep and told herself her neck didn't burn at all. She leaned back, tried to look comfortable, crossed her arms and legs and forced a large smile across her lips, looking straight back at him. Luca hid his clenched fists under the table. But he could not hide his red face, or the vein, which was now popping out of his forehead. She had correctly read his pithy violence for what it was: a clear sign of how desperate he had become. He had been working her for hours with no results whatsoever. Now both of them knew he was desperate, and she told him as much with her smile. His little display of power had completely backfired.

The interrogation took yet another unexpected turn when Luca wanted to know every imaginable detail about every single piece of furniture in Lucy's room, most of which had been recovered from defunct residents of Palazzo Mortimer whose heirs had failed to recover their belongings. Here too, she gave a very broad interpretation to honesty.

As the night went on, Luca's diction, grammar and pronunciation had all begun to suffer. His English skills started the evening at about the same level as Marlon Brando's Vito Corleone in the 1950's, but as the hours dragged on, he was rapidly approaching the level of Roberto De Niro's interpretation of the same character, fresh off the boat in the 1920's. On her side of the table, Lucy began to mumble and speak more quickly. At certain points, it became clear to her that Luca did not understand her for entire sentences at a time. However, he never once admitted to this, and never asked her to repeat anything. So she took a risk, following my suggestion, but taking it much farther than what I had imagined.

"The old lamp on your desk, from where had you gotten it?"

"Oh, that's just a reflupper dox that I froopled from Brian."

Luca nodded, looked at the mirror, and took notes on his pad of paper.

"Okay, and when did you froople said dox from Brian?"

"Recently, I think. Maybe even just twelve or fourteen parsecs ago."

He wrote that down too, and wiped off the perspiration that was now forming on his forehead. "Okay. And is it normal for all of you to go frooping furniture amongst yourselves?"

"Well, I prefer to glozzom, but Brian likes to jellop. You understand, don't you?"

"Okay. Yes. Yes. That makes sense," said Luca. "So the furniture is just borrowed and shared?"

"No. None of it is borrowed. Like I just said, it's glozzomed or jellopped. You understand, right?"

Luca looked at the mirror. "Right. Of course."

The interrogation went on this way for at least another hour, both of them talking complete nonsense about all of the furniture in Lucy's room. At no point did she ever give a response that did not include at least one completely non-existent english sounding word. And she did it all with a completely straight face. Luca never let on that he did not understand. Her gamble was absolutely crazy and reckless, but I don't know if I've ever been more proud of her.

At one point, Luca looked down at his notes and pointed at her in triumph, having finally caught her in a contradiction. "That sounds great, but explain to me why you said the wardrobe which you gruntled from a dead scrittle was flabulous, but now you affirm that it's a puffalope. This is clearly contradictory. Which one is it?"

"Well, do you mean flabulous in the British or American usage? I guess you're right. In Europe you'd probably say that it's more of a grob than anything else, wouldn't you?"

Luca stared blankly at her, finally showing signs of miscomprehension. Lucy glanced at the mirror, and so did Luca. "Yes, I guess that's right," he agreed, jotting down her answer.

CHAPTER SEVEN

IL GIORNALISTA

At a quarter to three in the morning, Luca finally gave up and left, promising to return early in the morning. I slept soundly on the floor next to Lucy. She tossed and turned for a few hours, until, as promised, Luca came back to the cell, accompanied by two officers. The fluorescent lights struggled to flicker on so early in the morning. Luca looked down, exhausted and defeated.

"Take this." He slipped a sheet of paper full of seals, stamps and loads of Italian legal jargon into the gap in the bars, where her tray of cold dinner still sat untouched. "You are free to leave prison for now. However, it is absolutely forbidden for you to leave the province of Rome. You are on — how do you say in America? — the probation? Understood?"

Lucy propped herself up on one elbow, and pulled the ratty prison blanket higher up on herself. She squinted back at him.

"Understood?"

"I can go?"

"Get the... just get out of here."

Luca swiveled on his heal, and stormed off. Only a few minutes later, she was alone on the sidewalk outside the police facility, without a clue where she was. The streets were empty, her running shorts and t-shirt did little to protect against the chill, and she had no money for a bus ticket. The eastern sky was just beginning to grow lighter. She turned around a few times, getting her bearings about her. She tucked her passport firmly in the front pocket, checked to make sure the keys were still zipped into the back pocket, and gave her sore legs a few stretches. Wherever she went, she'd have to run to stay warm.

She jogged to the end of the block and would have crossed, if there were not a pair of headlights careening down the street in her direction. A black limo slammed on its brakes right in front of her and a short, stout, blond man came out of the back door, with hand outstretched to introduce himself.

"Good morning, Ms. Fox. My name is Dr. Mârek Mikulaštik. My firm represents your father's legal interests in the Europe. Please board vehicle." His voice was loud, and never once changed in volume or tone through all his speech.

She shook his hand, got into the back middle seat of the limo beside him, closed the door and looked up to find six tired middle aged Italian men in suits staring back at her.

"May I introduce you to legal team," said Marek, holding out a brand new, perfectly fitting, black fleece jacket, followed by a pastry and a cappuccino. "Dr. Pietro Paiusco, Dr. Nicola Robotti, Dr. Andrea Sidotti, Dr. Simone Valentini, Dr. Marco Vignolo, and Dr. Matteo Torresetti."

"*È un piacere, grazie*," said Lucy, snuggling herself into the warm jacket.

They all smiled back, "*Piacere nostro*."

"And this is nurse Chiara Carbone from hospital," said Dr. Mikulaštik. "She will document injury."

A woman in scrubs, who was sitting next to her, pushed back Lucy's head, and started applying all kinds of stinging ointments to her neck, while one of the lawyers snapped pictures of the burns.

"These men are finest legal minds in Rome," said Dr. Mikulaštik. "I flew to Rome from Prague last evening for to assemble team, and we spend all night working hard in order to provide for your release. Roman police department perpetrated several errors of clerical and procedural nature in process of arrest, and we have possible accusation ready of police brutality. We have just filed sixteen injunctions, which shall delay your case in legal process for at least one year."

The Czech lawyer's words were not easy to follow, especially with the stinging on her neck. The nurse finished and sat back, and Lucy tried to look out the windows and bite her lips. The limo raced through Piazza Venezia, just down the street from the Roman forums and the coliseum in front of the giant white marble Italian unification monument, the *Altare della Patria*. She had only ever seen these things from the comfort of a privately owned vehicle a handful of times. Every morning, coming to and from class, she was sardined into a city bus, where it was hard to fight for a place near the window.

Dr. Mikulaštik handed her three large packets full of documents, but her hands were already full, so he just set them on her lap. "These are relevant case materials. You will find all of injunction documentation, sworn statement from barista at coffee bar, memory stick containing surveillance footage of you from coffee bar on Monday afternoon, sworn statement from your friend Brian, and memory stick with audio recording of entire interrogation last night, as well as our own transcript of said interrogation. There are three copies of everything. One is for you to keep on your person at all times. One for Brian. A third is to be placed in a safe."

The car stopped outside of a building along Via del Corso. All of the lawyers and the nurse climbed out one by one, each shaking her hand before exiting the vehicle.

The car set off again, and so did Dr. Mikulaštik, "Of course, you will not be staying in the Italy. If media decide speak about your case, it will be too difficult to maintain injunctions." He placed three more things on top of the envelopes. "These are keys to grey Fiat Panda rental car with Swiss license plates. She is parked on Via del Gianicolo near your residency. Here is fake American passport with your picture — your new name is Emily Green. Please memorize information regarding your new identity in passport. And finally, here is one-way ticket for a flight departing tomorrow night from Zürich to Denver. Drive from Rome to Zürich will last about nine hours, so you must depart quite early tomorrow in morning. There should not be difficulty at Swiss border, but just in case, here is my card."

"But the police told me I can't leave the province of Rome. How could I go back to America?"

"Sure. Strictly speaking, it is not exactly legal for you to leave. Once you are in the America, though, there is almost nothing that they can do to you. It is much safer for you outside the country. You are indeed clearly innocent, but the circumstances are volatile enough that your exit from Europe is necessitated."

"But with a violation of the terms of my probation, how do I get back into Europe?"

"Coming back to Europe is out of the question. Tomorrow is the last day for you in Schengen zone. But do not tell anyone of your intentions for departure. You must leave quietly without the noticement of others."

The limo stopped in front of Palazzo Mortimer.

"Remember," said Dr. Mikulaštik, "call me if anything whatsoever is to happen. I wish you the best, Ms. Fox."

He took the still full cappuccino cup and the untouched pastry from her with his left hand and shook her with his right. She put everything she could into the pockets of her new jacket and her track shorts. She barely got her feet on the ground before the car drove off.

To her right, dozens of rapid-fire explosions, clicking, and flashing set off. A man was slowly jogging towards her on the sidewalk.

"Ms. Fox, Ms. Fox!" he yelled. What appeared to be three Italian supermodels with cameras firing were following at a short distance behind the man. "Ms. Fox, could I speak with you for a moment?"

He was probably in his mid to late forties. He had a few days' worth of beard stubble, dark black scruffy unkept hair with grey patches on the side, and very square glasses. He looked skinny even in a large black coat, black pants, and a grey scarf, but somehow he still had a double chin. While his height was average — slightly taller than Lucy — the women following him with their cameras, on the other hand, were exceptionally tall and skinny, and they were dressed to kill in the latest fall fashions. The man couldn't believe his luck when Lucy didn't run away. When he got close, the cameras stopped firing and he held out his right hand towards Lucy.

"Hi, my name is Cristiano Ludovici."

She looked at the hand, but did not shake it.

"I work for *La Repubblica*. I was wondering if I could talk to you for a minute."

She considered the hand for another second and shook her head, running up to the front door of Palazzo Mortimer. Gambetti had yet to arrive, so the door was still locked. Lucy fumbled with one hand to open the zipper in the small back pocket of her track shorts to get the key. The cameras relaunched their attack from their position on the sidewalk outside the front gate. She was about to insert the key, when a thought occurred to her. She paused, turned around and looked back at them. Cristiano held up his hand, and the photographers lowered their weapons.

Lucy returned the key to her track shorts and zipped the back pocket shut. She sauntered down the little driveway, stopped in front of Cristiano, and looked up and down the road. It looked empty.

"Are you the only journalist here?"

"As far as I know, yes."

"Can we talk first off the record?"

"Of course."

She led him in silence up Via del Gianicolo, around the other side of the hospital to an overlook from the Janiculum hill. There was an outdoor coffee bar and snack shop that wasn't going to open for another twenty minutes. The only people around were the occasional hospital staff passing by to get to work early. The photographers went to the other side of the overlook and took turns snapping and comparing photos of the Roman skyline at dawn.

Lucy and Cristiano sat down opposite one another just as the tip of the sun peaked over the Apennines on the opposite end of the city. Her running shorts were not long enough to protect her bare legs from contact with the frigid metal chair. At first she pretended not to care, but as she sat back and hit a damp spot on the seat, she involuntarily shivered and scooted up as far forward as possible in the chair, crossing her legs and arms. Across from her, Cristiano leaned back, warm and comfortable in his puffy black coat and grey scarf. He lit a Lucky Strike and offered one to Lucy, who used every ounce of moral strength left in her to smile and politely decline.

Cristiano waited for her to begin the conversation, so she forced her way through a few minutes of small talk. He was from Milan, but had gone to journalism school in New York. He rooted for AC Milan and the Yankees. She did not care much for Italian soccer. The Yankees response, though, did not inspire trust. But if he could be trusted, perhaps he could be valuable. Small talk ended up going nowhere resulting in establishing said trust, so Lucy took an Italian approach. Direct.

"How can I trust you?"

"I work for *La Repubblica*. We are a professional sophisticated news source, not a tabloid. If we make promises, we keep them."

Lucy turned around and looked at the photographers — who were now playing with each others' hair and checking their make up in small mirrors — and back at Cristiano. "Professional?"

"Absolutely. Professional. I've been able to get much better shots ever since I started recruiting photographers from modeling agencies instead of photography schools. In homicide news stories, readers aren't interested in clean artistic shots. They want grungy shots with murder suspects looking at the camera. They want to look the killers in the eye. A professional photographer can guarantee a beautiful shot, but they cannot guarantee that the target will be looking at the camera. A beautiful model can, because her job is not to look at the subject, but to get the subject to look at her. They may not be as skilled, but in the end, they produce a much better final product. And if that's not professional, I don't know what is."

"Do you know who else is covering this story?"

"There's one guy from *Corriere*, but I get the feeling he's busy with other projects."

"Does he know about me?"

"As far as I know, I'm the only journalist who knows about your arrest so far."

"How can you be sure?"

"I can't be one hundred percent sure. But in my experience, I'd say it's a foregone conclusion that no one else knows about your arrest. Think about it. It's a murder case, so that's interesting for the Roman tabloids, to a certain point. A standard murder might appear on page five or six, and the story about Eugenio's murder already did appear yesterday in most newspapers. But it's obvious that neither the tabloids nor the international outlets know that *you* are the main suspect. At least they don't know *yet*. Maybe they know your name, but they certainly don't know that you're a beautiful young American girl. If they did, there would be fifty or sixty photographers stationed outside that door, and I wouldn't be talking to you."

"Come on? You think this case is really that interesting?"

"Absolutely. Don't you watch the news?"

"Not that much."

"If it can be suggested that there's sex involved somehow," he raised his eyebrows, "this will be a total media frenzy. There will not be an Italian or American who doesn't know your name. Think of recent Americans getting accused in Perugia. People love this stuff."

Lucy rested her elbows on the table, no longer noticing the cold. Some last bit of tension in her finally broke, and her right hand, without permission from any other part of her, automatically reached for the pack of Lucky Strikes on the table. Unable to think — completely disconnected from the well rehearsed motions that had once been habitual — she was a mere observer of her own hand as Cristiano placed a flame in front of her face, as her chest filled up deeply, and as sweet smoothing smoke hastened in and out of her throat.

"But nothing is certain yet," said Cristiano. "Maybe nothing else will happen. Maybe the case will be forgotten by next week. Maybe we'll forget that we ever had this conversation."

"Really? Do you think that's likely?"

"I don't think it will happen. But anything's possible. What's important, for you, Ms. Fox, is to make sure that when your story does get out, it gets out on your terms."

"Just call me Lucy." She pulled another hard drag on her cigarette, a cigarette that she was still not smoking actively, but passively. It was happening to her.

"Okay, Lucy."

"And you want to be the one who breaks the story on my terms?"

"Absolutely."

"Do you think I'm innocent?"

"I don't care."

"I care what you think."

"Listen, I don't know."

"Come on, be honest. You said we're off the record."

"Alright. Just based on the evidence, it looks pretty bad for you. There's probably not enough to convict you, but since we're being honest, I would say it looks like you did it. But, like I said, I don't care if you did. From the stories I cover, it seems like a good amount of murder victims probably had it coming, anyways. Having met you, I'm willing to believe that the person you killed probably wasn't entirely innocent, either. Look, Lucy, I don't know who Eugenio was or what he did to you, but that's not what I'm interested in talking about."

"So you want to get to know me, even though you think I'm probably a murderer?"

He shrugged his shoulders. "You've been in this country long enough to understand how things work. Hell, things work the same in America. I'm not here to help you because I think you're a charity case, or because I'm just a nice guy. And you can tell that I'm not some uptight puritan — like most of you Americans — and judging from my first impression of you, you don't seem to be one either. You've got a past. I've got a past. *Va bene*. Everybody's done things that they regret. For the present time, though, I've got to carry on and do my work, and you've got to get along with your life. Unfortunately for you, my present work involves talking about other peoples' past. And in order for me to do that work in the present, I've got to make friends with people who have a much more colorful past. People in your situation. And I make friends with them by helping them, by allowing them to talk about their past with someone who will give them a fair hearing. Let's not pretend that journalism isn't a business."

"And what do I get out of it if we do work together?"

"A professional newspaper that's going to treat you with respect. Go talk to the tabloids. See what happens."

"That's not enough. I want time."

"Honey, you don't have time. The best thing that you've got going for you at this point is the fact that you're having this conversation with me, instead of some cheap tabloid writer."

"I could offer you more."

"You don't have what I want. I don't take money. In my line of work I can see where bribery ends." He looked over at his photographers, and back at Lucy. "And don't get me wrong, you're quite pretty, but I'm already a very satisfied man."

"God, that's not what I meant." She took a final long pull on the end of her cigarette, reached for another, and lit it off the cherry of the first. "I'd agree to an interview — a long extended interview. A book deal, even, if this story is really as fascinating as you claim it is. And right now I could give you some documents." She threw one of the packets of paper from Dr. Mikulaštik on the table. Cristiano reached over to pick it up, but Lucy put her hands on top of it. "You'll find a few interesting things in this envelope. I'm sorry to let you down, but you'll find proof of my innocence and a watertight alibi. But you'll also find a great story about police incompetence and brutality, if you're interested. There's a recording and a two-hundred page transcript of my interrogation with the police last night.

"I'm interested."

"You say the best thing going for me right now is the fact that I'm talking to you. If you're serious about my story being such great material, it sounds like just the opposite: the best thing going for you right now is the fact that you're talking to me."

Cristiano smiled in admiration, and leaned back to consider. He lit another cigarette. "You say you just want time?"

"As much time as you can get me, yes. And one more thing."

"Yes?"

"Do you know Detective Luca Speziale?"

"I cover homicides in Rome. Do I know Luca Speziale? We see each other on a weekly basis."

"There's more than enough information in that recording to prove his incompetence and brutality. Get him fired."

"If that's true, this is Christmas come early. I would love to see that man fired."

"Can you do it without breaking the story?"

"The department owes me a long list of favors already. It would be my pleasure to call one in. It would be a very simple call to the station chief, letting him know that I have the transcript, but that I would prefer not to release it on the condition of Luca's quiet disappearance from the force. If you want, we can have him boxing up his office by this afternoon. Of course, you have to promise not to release the transcript to anyone else but *La Repubblica*, nor speak with any other journalist before me."

"It's a deal then."

"Oh, and one more thing." Cristiano waved his hand at her outfit. "We are going to need to get some decent photos of you for when the story eventually breaks."

"Fine."

They stood up and shook hands. Cristiano got in his black Fiat500 and drove off. The photographers, meanwhile, took Lucy up to her room. As they walked through the front gate, Gambetti was unlocking the main door. For the first time ever, he was completely speechless. Once upstairs, the models dressed her, washed and brushed her hair, covered her in makeup, and told her she didn't know how to walk. She was forced to spend the next hour strutting around the neighborhood in high heels, pretending to do ordinary things — drinking espresso, buying a newspaper, trying on shoes — while the three sirens took candid paparazzi photos of her from afar.

When they were finished, she bought a pack of cigarettes and slugged her way back up to her room, exhausted. Opening the door to the servants' quarters, the portrait of the old prince greeted her with his ever-present smile. A different pain hit her stomach. This would be her last full day living at the Palazzo. She tried to smile back at him, but her eyes just watered up.

She removed piles and piles of things from on top of her luggage, which had sat untouched in my storage room for three years. Back in her room, she surveyed the mess in a whole new light. Having departed America in haste, she had arrived in Rome with just a carry-on and a half full suitcase. It's amazing the amount of stuff one person can acquire in just a few years, without even purchasing most of it. She didn't feel like departing Italy carrying any more baggage than what she had brought from America, so thus began the long and agonizing process of choosing what to bring to America and what to leave behind. A post-it note went up on the outside of her door: "Sick with the plague. Go away!"

So of course, a little after twelve, Brian knocked on the door three times. After the third, Lucy yelled, "Go away!" and Brian came on in.

She was seated cross legged on the floor in front of the open suitcase, deciding between a nice cashmere sweater, abandoned by some long gone aristocrat, or her favorite 2010 Austrian calendar mug. Brian closed the door behind him and sat down at her desk chair, surveying the chaos.

"That bad, huh?" he asked.

"Yeah, it's that bad."

"When do you head out?"

"Tomorrow morning."

"For what it's worth, I think I'm the only one who knows."

"Don't tell them I'm going. I want to go unnoticed."

"No, I mean I'm the only who knows you were arrested."

"Really?"

"Yeah, surprisingly enough," said Brian. "I think I was the only one who saw you getting arrested and put into the cop car, even though you were making all that noise."

"Not even the staff?"

"It's possible. I don't know. But if you think about it, the distance from the elevator to the entrance is almost nothing, and if Gambetti wasn't in the porter's office — as he usually isn't — it's actually pretty easy to get in and out of here unnoticed. People don't go to the lobby unless they're leaving, and there wasn't a shift change when you got hauled away. Sure, I guess there'll be security footage, but nobody ever watches that stuff unless they're actually looking for something. After they drove off with you, I went upstairs and tried to ask all the cops what was going on, and they acted like you didn't exist. Nobody would say anything to me."

"There's security cameras here?"

"We're in Italy. There's security cameras everywhere."

"How 'bout that."

"Yeah, you lucked out running into me."

"Why did you call my dad?"

"I don't know. I guess it just seemed like the thing to do. I've never had a friend get arrested."

"But how did you get ahold of him?"

"I never actually got ahold of him directly. I remember you mentioned his name and where he works, so I called corporate headquarters to see if I could get his contact information. It took forever to get in touch with a real person, though. None of the phone tree options were 'press seven if an employee's daughter has just been arrested while abroad.'"

"So you never talked to him?"

"Once I got to a real person who believed my story, I just got sent from secretary to secretary until they finally connected me to your Dad's staff. Those guys sure as hell move quick. The crazy thing, though, was that it almost seemed like they already had some sort of policy in place for what to do when the CFO's daughter gets arrested. They already had a list of questions prepared for me. And then, maybe, like just two hours after, I went out for a walk, and I got kidnapped by a black limo stuffed full of Italian lawyers."

"Two hours. That's a long time. If I'd been arrested in America, I bet it would have been just half an hour. Maybe fifteen minutes."

"You never told me your Dad was CFO of Initech."

"Does it matter?"

"That's a Fortune500 company."

"So what?"

"You live in housing for poor grad students."

"Just 'cause my dad's rich doesn't mean I am."

"Well... no... I'm not saying... whatever... it's fine. I'm happy you're here. Just. Nevermind. But why did you tell me last year that he's just a 'middle management grunt' at Initech?"

"Because he's right in the middle between the stockholders and the rest of the company."

"Lucy, that's not what middle management means."

"I know. Whatever. Brian, I just don't want to talk about it, okay?"

"Do you want to talk about why the cops think it was you?"

"You know it wasn't me, Brian."

"I know."

"Here. You've got some reading." She passed him his packet of information from the lawyers. "I'll just call you sometime next week from America and explain everything else, okay?"

"So you're definitely going back to America, then?"

"Yep."

"Damn, that sucks."

"I know. Well, no, I mean. It should be great to get out of friggen' Italy for a while, and back into a normal country. It just really sucks to…" she stopped, unable to put her finger on it. She looked at Brian, and back at her bags, and fought to speak over the lump that had just showed up uninvited in the back of her throat. "It just really sucks to… I don't know… you know… it sucks to — "

Brian stood up chuckling. "Good God, you better not start getting all sentimental on me your last day here. I'd think a lot less of you for it." He moved to the door. "Anyways, I'll leave you to it. Let me know what you want to do your last night in Rome."

She kept her door locked that night, and didn't respond when Brian knocked. At a little past two in the morning, she came to the storage room and woke me up.

I looked up from the floor. "Can't sleep?"

She shook her head.

"Lucy, you haven't slept in two days, have you?"

Another head shake.

I followed her back to her room, and lay on the red rug on the floor. She curled up next to me, using my arm as a pillow. Half an hour later her breathing deepened, and she finally got some rest.

CHAPTER EIGHT

PICCHIATO IN FACCIA

She rolled over in bed. Sunlight was already peaking through the orange curtains. Sunlight? What the... what time was it? She reached over for the alarm clock and swore at the two hours that had already gone by from when she had planned on leaving the Palazzo. With her heart pounding, she jumped out of bed, and got ready as quickly as possible. She'd be cutting it close at the airport in Switzerland. She wheeled her suitcase into the hallway, careful to keep her back towards the smiling portrait of the old prince — there would be no tears on the way out.

But the sound of frying, the greasy smell of Mexican breakfast, and one familiar booming voice all hit her from behind, coming from the kitchen. She hadn't heard that voice since it had left Rome for summer break at the end of June, and she'd spent the better part of July and even August imagining and idealizing the person attached to that voice, again and again and again, until she'd grown bored of it. Stupid fantasies. She was already late, but she found that her legs were carrying her one last time down the hallway to the kitchen.

He threw his hands in the air and yelled in his thick Wisconsin accent, "Scott's here!"

He left his hands in the air — one gripping a spatula, the other a pepper shaker — until Lucy came into the kitchen and gave him the Italian/Mexican greeting of two kisses, one on each cheek. She'd spent hours over the summer wondering what this moment would be like, knowing she'd be flustered and coy upon seeing him back in Italy. The odd thing was, though, that she wasn't. Her imagination, running free, had grown disconnected from reality, such that reality was so different from what she'd imagined that she couldn't swoon freely — reality was different, but much more pleasant and satisfying.

"So you *did* miss me?" he joked.

Lucy just smiled.

"You want some eggs?"

"I'm good thanks." Ever since she knew she'd have to leave the Palazzo she could hardly eat.

"Good 'cause I'm not making enough for three," said Scott, nodding at Natasha, who was seated in front of an empty plate.

Three? Lucy only then realized that Natasha was even there. Finally she felt something. She had not expected it to be a pang of jealous rage, but it was something.

"Good morning, Lucy," said Natasha.

"Oh, hey," she responded, without removing her eyes from Scott.

"Wait a second, Lucy," said Scott. "Did the guy who founded *L.L. Bean* die at the Palazzo recently? Or is this really happening? Are you finally going to leave Rome for a day?"

"You mean Leon Leonwood Bean?" she asked.

"What?"

"The guy who founded *L.L. Bean* — Leon Leonwood Bean? He died in Florida in '67."

Lucy looked down at herself, embarrassed. She was wearing a carry-on back pack, something you'd want on a mountain expedition more than an airplane. Growing up, she was always required to use a rolling carry-on suitcase and to wear business formal whenever they went to the airport, which always left her uncomfortable and ill prepared. Anything can happen on an airplane and you have to be ready at all times. Now, as an adult, free to make her own decisions about proper attire for international flights, she sported hiking boots, jeans, and a white thermal long sleeve shirt beneath a plaid chamois button up. Tight french braids were held back by her leather headband, a handkerchief and aviators. On every flight there's always one or two people dressed like this. Very few of them are actually going camping. The rest, like Lucy, just get really intense about flying. Of course, the essential thing about Scott's comment was not the fact that he made fun of her clothes, but the fact that he commented on her appearance at all. He noticed! He looked at what I was wearing! He was looking at *me*! She finally started to get flustered.

"No... Scott... I'm just gonna... just gonna... y'know, I have to go across town to get some things from some people."

"So it's true what Brian said? You spent the whole summer without leaving Rome?"

She looked down at her boots and turned redder, "yeah."

"Good God!" he yelled. "You must be the most boring person I know! That sounds miserable."

"The plants out on the terrace don't water themselves. And somebody's got to talk to all the old people here."

Scott Valentino was Brian's best friend and classmate at the Gregorian University. He lived just down the block from Palazzo Mortimer at the North American College, a massive seminary — where young men train to become priests — that sat adjacent to the hospital. On Mondays, Wednesdays and Thursdays he would usually come up to the servants' quarters in Palazzo Mortimer to eat breakfast on his way to class, because those were the days the college cafeteria didn't serve eggs. "I gotta get ripped. How'm I gonna get ripped without protein in the morning?" His parents were migrant workers from Mexico, but he was born — literally — and grew up on a dairy farm outside Green Bay. He had olive skin, spoke a very sophisticated form of Spanish, but in English he had a loud booming voice and a thick Wisconsin accent. He wore a black clerical shirt, black pants, a black jacket, and black Air Force Ones.

"Oh, Lucy," said Natasha. "Where were you the other night? I saw your room door was open all night."

Lucy looked at Natasha from the corner of her eyes, but didn't turn her head or body away from Scott. Why, thought Lucy, does this cretin need to interrupt my last Scott-moment ever? "I was just out," she said.

"Out?" asked Natasha, looking kind of excited at the prospect of having a roommate who sometimes stayed out all night partying.

"Y'know… just out at some friends' house. It was kind of a weird night, actually. I just fell asleep early on their couch and stayed there." She said this with a tone of finality, and was glad that Natasha didn't insist.

"Well, anyways," said Natasha. "Scott and I were just having an argument. He thinks I would belong in Gryffindor, and I agree, but just based on my first impression, I told him he's probably a Slytherin. What do you think?"

"Yeah, I mean, I'm a Ravenclaw myself, so it's hard to say," she squinted and kept her eyes on Scott. "But I see what you're saying. Scott's definitely got a Slytherin ego."

"What are you talking about?" he yelled, while turning towards the stove and pushing eggs around in a pan. "I'm definitely in Gryffindor!"

"This is good. In one room, we've got Slytherin, Gryffindor, and Ravenclaw. We're just missing Hufflepuff. Speaking of which, where's Brian?" Lucy asked, suddenly noticing his absence. Brian was always there whenever Scott was around.

"I haven't seen him today, but he texted and said he wanted to go to class early," said Scott.

"So then how did you get in?"

"Oh, do you remember how Brian lost his keys last year? We found 'em in my couch last week, and I'm definitely not going to give them back. Finders keepers. He's got a new set anyways. It's great, too. Now I don't have to wait for Brian to come down and open the door for me. I've finally got the keys that I deserved two years ago."

"You're right, Lucy," said Natasha. "That's exactly the sort of egotistical thing a Slytherin would say about himself."

Scott emptied a frying pan of chilaquiles and eggs onto the empty plates on the table, and sat down. Across from him, Natasha had a cup of coffee in front of her. And in defiance of Lucy's authority, she was not using her assigned Knights of Columbus mug, but a green and white mug with the word "Wimpy" written across it in bubbly letters.

"You don't understand," Scott raised his voice. "I'm Harry! I have to be in Gryffindor. I'm clearly the most important character in the story. Harry. Me. Ergo, Gryffindor. I am Harry." He considered that last sentence and added, "I mean I'm H-A-R-R-Y, Harry, not H-A-I-R-Y, hairy... or... I guess I'm both."

"Scott," said Lucy. "You can't even grow a beard."

"Neither could Che Guevara, but that didn't stop him. In fact, he had one of the most important beards in Latin America."

Lucy opened her mouth to respond, but paused and decided to take things in a different direction. "All beards aside for a second, there was this one time in middle school when I had to spend the whole summer at this stupid outdoor leadership camp between seventh and eighth grade. The only good part about that summer was that I bought... or... well... I guess there were a few good things about that summer... but the best thing that I *bought* that summer was this awesome souvenir t-shirt that had a picture of the Montana Rockies in the background, and a cute little otter in the foreground, sitting in a lake and dressed like Harry Potter. The top of the shirt had 'Hairy Otter, and the Adventures of Montana' written on the top. I remember the first day of eighth grade, I was so excited 'cause I knew I was going to have *the* coolest t-shirt that day." Lucy went silent.

"So what happened?" asked Scott.

"All the boys just laughed at 'Hairy Otter' and made jokes about their... well... anyways, the point is, I never got to wear that shirt again." Lucy sighed. "But wait a second. Why are we talking about Harry Potter?"

"I just met Natasha," said Scott, "and she claims she's not English, even though she clearly sounds English. And I know that all English people love Harry Potter."

"Now if you could really recognize English accents," said Natasha, "you would know that I'm not English! Absolutely, the schools I attended while growing up in South Africa forced the Queen's English onto my lips, but if you would listen carefully, you might hear something else."

"The funny thing about meeting Natasha, though," said Scott, "was that it was completely normal. We introduced ourselves and made conversation."

"Oh please," said Lucy, knowing where he was going.

"No really, Natasha, would you like to hear the story of how I met Lucy?"

"I would."

"Me and my friend Brian — you know Brian — we went out to the Ikea this one day, and Brian tells me that this crazy girl from his building was going to meet us for lunch. So we're sitting there, minding our own business, eating our Swedish meatballs in the Ikea cafeteria, and who should show up, but this girl, here. Brian introduces us, and do you know what the *first* thing she says to me after we shook hands was?"

"What?" said Natasha.

"You tell her, Lucy," said Scott.

"Nothing," said Lucy. "I just asked a completely normal question, given the circumstances."

"Which was?" said Scott.

"I'm not saying," said Lucy.

"So Lucy sits down," Scott turned to talk to Natasha. "She sees that I'm Mexican, and the first thing she does is ask me if I own a poncho and a sombrero."

"A completely normal question," said Lucy. "It was totally fair game, given my specific needs at that time in my life."

"No!" yelled Scott. "That's not something you just ask a stranger. Oh, hey, you're a white girl, can I borrow a French press and a yoga mat? Can I see your copy of *The Notebook*?"

"But what was the answer?" asked Lucy. "Natasha, ask him what the answer was. Did he own a sombrero and a poncho?"

"The answer is irrelevant!" said Scott.

"Do you own a poncho and a sombrero?" yelled Lucy.

"You're white. Does that mean this is fair trade coffee? Can I borrow your frisbee later today?"

Lucy smirked and leaned back, "And anyways... I'm an eighth Cree — "

"Guys!" Andrew came running into the room in pajamas holding a piece of paper. "Did you see this? I just found an anonymous letter tucked under the door to the servants' quarters."

"Who's it from?" asked Natasha.

Everyone went silent for a second, looking at Natasha.

Lucy gladly took the opportunity to be a jerk, "*Anonymous…* you know… without a name."

"Well… right… of course," Natasha attempted a recovery. "I mean… how is it signed?"

"Here, just read it," Andrew threw it down on the table and everyone gathered around.

It was a normal piece of office paper, with a letter written on it. The first half was written in letters cut out from newspaper headlines and glued onto the page:

Dear Residents of the Servants' Quarters,

We are well aware of the situation that all of us find ourselves in, and we are writing you to make sure that you, as well, are aware of what is going on. We all need to be on the same page, so that nobody has to get hurt. In fact, there are others in our family who are in favor of kidnapping and hurting some of you. We have managed to convince them otherwise, confident that you will be willing to cooperate with us. Unfortunately not everyone has cooperated with us, and poor Eugenio had to be killed, but...

The letter then continued in black marker and block letters:

(IT TAKES WAY TOO MUCH TIME TO CUT OUT AND GLUE THOSE LETTERS. WE ARE SURE YOU WILL UNDERSTAND IF WE CONTINUE THIS THREAT LETTER IN MARKERS AND BLOCK LETTERS, INSTEAD. PLEASE DO NOT INTERPRET THIS CHANGE IN FONT AS A DIMINISHMENT OF THE DANGER YOU FIND YOURSELF IN.) ...WE ARE CERTAIN THAT YOU WILL BE VERY COOPERATIVE AND NO SERIOUS ACTIONS WILL NEED TO BE TAKEN. AS YOU MAY OR MAY NOT BE AWARE OF, EUGENIO WAS IN THE PROCESS OF STEALING A LARGE BIT OF INHERITANCE THAT BELONGS TO US. WE ARE ALSO AWARE OF THE FACT THAT

EUGENIO SHARED THE ACCESS CODES TO SAID BANK ACCOUNTS WITH ONE OF YOU JUST BEFORE HE WAS SO UNNECESSARILY ELIMINATED. SAID PERSON MUST PRESENT HIM/HERSELF TO US WITHIN A REASONABLE AMOUNT OF TIME, AND NO ACTIONS WILL BE TAKEN, AND SAID PERSON WILL EVEN BE HANDSOMELY REWARDED. YOU CAN REACH US AT (+39)7202265517.

IF SAID PERSON DOES NOT COME FORWARD, PUNITIVE ACTIONS WILL BE TAKEN AGAINST ALL OF THE MEMBERS OF THE SERVANTS' QUARTERS. TO BE CLEAR: YOUR LIVES ARE IN DANGER. DO NOT THINK THAT LEAVING ROME CAN BE A SOLUTION. WE ARE A VERY SOPHISTICATED ORGANIZATION. YOU WILL BE FOUND. BUT WE ARE ALSO CONFIDENT THAT THIS WON'T NEED TO HAPPEN.

YOURS TRULY,

THE TRUE HEIRS

Lucy was the first to finish reading. Scott, for the first time in a long time, was quiet. And Natasha kept a puzzled look on her face.

"What on earth does that mean?" asked Andrew.

"I think it's pretty clear," said Lucy, casting aside her intentions of leaving without telling anyone. "It means we all have to get the hell out of here."

"What if this is just some kind of sick joke?" said Scott. "I get it. Somebody here got murdered. But that doesn't mean you guys have to take this thing seriously, does it?"

"If it is a joke, it's not very funny," said Natasha.

"You guys aren't interested in trying to find out who wrote the letter?" asked Andrew. "You don't want to figure out what the whole bank account thing is?"

"I could care less," said Lucy.

"Why? Because you don't think you could find out?" he pressed. "Afraid of — how do they say it in America? — being a grade '7' investigator?"

"It's letters not number, you know that. And anyways, I'd make an A+ investigator if I cared," said Lucy. "I'm not interested in finding out who wrote this. But I am interested in *not* ending up cold beneath a tarp like that other guy."

"So you really think leaving is the best thing?" asked Natasha. "Where would you go?"

"Hell yeah, leaving is the best thing! Probably today. And you guys are idiots if you don't do the same. If anything, we probably shouldn't tell each other where we're headed. Did you guys just read the same letter that I just read?"

"Wait a second," said Scott. "You bum around this town for how many years — scared shitless to move an inch out of Rome — then all of a sudden you read a stupid letter, and you think you can just up and leave?"

This was exactly how her final moments with Scott were *not* supposed to go. She opened her mouth to respond, but couldn't find the words, and instead, bit onto her lower lip to keep it still. She almost felt she needed to tell Scott everything, and maybe he could figure it all out. She probably would have, but the others were there. Speaking of which, why did that stupid blonde have to be here to ruin the moment anyways? And who invited the Australian, who was still talking about that stupid letter?

"Really, though," said Andrew. "The security here is not bad. We just need to keep an eye out for each other. That's all. But who am I to judge? Go on. Get the F out of here, if you want to let yourself be intimidated by some thugs pretending to be real mafia. Sounds to me like you'd make much more of a B- investigator than an A+."

Lucy's face went blank. She stood to face Andrew squarely, their eyes level with each other. "What did you just say about me?"

"Isn't that how the marks in your schooling system work in America? 'B' would be the second best mark, right?" and then — noting her aggressive posture and not wanting to cede ground — he upped the ante. "There's a few other words in the English language that start with the letter 'B', aren't there?"

"I dare you to say that again." Her voice became cold and threatening.

Andrew slowly pronounced each syllable, staring Lucy back in the eye, "Bee... minus..."

The last thing Andrew remembered was Lucy's right shoulder dropping backwards and her fist approaching rapidly at him. For the next week and a half he couldn't see out of his left eye. When he regained consciousness thirty seconds later on the kitchenette tiles, Natasha was kneeling on the floor beside him, wearing surgical gloves and filling his bleeding nose with Kleenex.

Andrew reached for his face, and Natasha swatted his hands away. With a plugged nose, and a pounding pain on the left side of his head he asked, "What the bloody hell happened?"

Meanwhile Scott stood in the doorframe laughing and hollering down the hallway, "That's my girl, Lucy! That's my girl! Yes! Damn, you threw that punch like a bear!"

CHAPTER NINE

LA "B"

The first time Lucy ever got arrested was a Friday in October. Her class had just received their first quarter grade reports, following the first two months as freshmen in high school. Eighth grade, for Lucy, had ended with all B's and C's. Freshman year, though, I got on her case, and forced her to do her homework. And when necessary, I guess I might have also sometimes stood next to her during exams and I may have happened to check her work once or twice. That first quarter, all of our grades... I mean all of *her* grades were much better, except for one math grade. There had been a surprise pop quiz when I was busy taking my usual afternoon nap in the janitor's closet.

Like most Friday nights during that first year of high school, she was not hanging out with friends, but was in the family's ten car garage, putting together a Volkswagen Beetle. After she met me, I convinced her to give up playing Legos with her little brother and get into the real thing: automobile mechanics. Her father was happy enough to allow her to use his tools — which he himself never touched — but only if she always put them back where they belonged, keeping them organized in neat rows and even numbers. He did start to get nervous as the Volkswagen neared completion, though, as this would make for an odd number of cars. There were already four parked in the garage. He looked around for a car for Lucy's older sister, Kelly, who had already turned sixteen. Of course, he was really more worried about keeping an even number of vehicles in the garage, than getting a car for Kelly — who felt she really needed a car and now saw Lucy as the main obstacle to that end. But it was just too hard to decide at what exact point Lucy's project would no longer be a pile of car parts and start being a fifth car in the garage, thus necessitating a sixth vehicle.

Lucy was beneath the car on one of those rolling boards with a plastic puffy headrest, working on installing a very large and shiny exhaust pipe — that I insisted did not belong on a classy Volkswagen beetle — and talking to me, when Kelly stormed into the garage. She was two years older and taller than Lucy, but was almost the spitting image, just with a slightly lighter hair color and less light in her eyes.

"Blue Bear, can you pass me the number nine? I think the ten is too big," said Lucy. "Yeah, the ten is too big. Blue Bear? Are you there?"

I didn't respond.

"Hey!" Lucy yelled as Kelly grabbed her ankle and pulled her out from under the VW.

She stood over Lucy with her hands on her hips. "What the hell are you still doing out here with your imaginary friend?"

"Working on the Volkswagen."

"God. Why do I have to be the only sane person in this family?"

Lucy shrugged her shoulders.

"We have our performance evaluations in five minutes!"

"That's not 'til tomorrow. I checked the schedule this morning."

"Did you read your e-mail today?"

"No."

"You're such an idiot, Lucy! There was even a memo posted on the main bulletin board this afternoon. I am gonna kill you! Dad's board meeting in Dubai got bumped forward. The performance evals are right now, 'cause he's going to the airport tonight."

"What? I can't be there in five minutes!" Lucy face turned to horror. "There's no time to change. Tell him I'm sick or something."

"Come on, get your ass upstairs, right now!"

Lucy dropped the number ten wrench, got up, and sprinted out of the garage and up to her rooms, trying to unbutton her overalls and run up the stairs at the same time. Kelly followed, yelling, "*Juanita! Juanita! Ven aca, ahorita! Necesitamos ayudo!*"[78]

A stocky Hispanic woman in a smock ran up the stairs after them. Juanita held down Lucy's arms over the sink and scrubbed off all the auto grease, swearing below her breath at Lucy's father in Spanish, while Kelly picked out business formal clothes from Lucy's closet.

"Just so you know," said Kelly, as she buttoned up Lucy's blouse, and as Juanita circled around tucking the blouse into her skirt, "I'm not doing this 'cause I want to help you. I just don't want to deal with another meltdown."

Juanita and Kelly each grabbed hold of one of Lucy's arms and stuffed them down the sleeves of her suit jacket. They managed to have Lucy more or less presentable forty seconds ahead of time. They ran down the stairs and lined up beside their younger brother, John, holding grade reports in leather folders and trying not to breathe too hard. Their father opened the door to his study two seconds early at 4:59 and 58 seconds and called in Kelly. John and Lucy waited in silence on the bench outside, for exactly ten minutes. The door opened at 5:09 and 54 seconds, Kelly came outside, took the seat beside John, and Lucy came into the study.

"Lucy, please, come in. Good to see you. Have a seat. Make yourself comfortable." He shook her hand at the door, and invited her to sit in the chair in front of his desk. He straightened his tie and asked, "Can I get you something to drink? Water? Ice tea?"

"No thanks."

"Alright, well, let's get straight to it, I guess," he said, taking a seat in his captain's chair behind a long desk. "I've just had a look at your chore reports from Juanita and your mother. It looks very positive, as always. Your mother's report also tells me that your

---

[78] Juanita! Juanita! Come here now! We need help!

attendance at extra-curricular activities is up to 96%. Those are encouraging figures. That's a four percent increase over last quarter. I see that you've joined the cross-country team. That'll look great on your college applications. After two years you'll be eligible to letter in that sport. This looks like a great performance overall. Keep up the good work."

Lucy remained silent. Her father shuffled through some more pages, "And I see you've already drawn up a first draft of your goals and objectives for personal growth for freshman year printed out on official family letterhead. I do apologize. With the meetings getting bumped forward in Dubai, I didn't get a chance to review these before our sit down meeting tonight. We'll table that discussion to our next appointment in November, alright? Well, let's have a look at those grades."

She sat forward, set the leather bound folder on the desk, and leaned over to slide it across to him, getting excited, but keeping a straight face.

"Okay, let's see what we've got," he said, scanning down the page. "Spanish, A+, Freshman P.E., A-, Geography, A, English Literature, A-, Advanced Algebra, B-, Chemistry, A-, Photography, A+."

Lucy looked down, and forced herself not to smile too much.

"Well, that certainly is different," he studied the page again and again. "One B minus." He started rubbing his forehead, and then his cleanly shaven chin. "Indeed, that is an improvement. Of course, last year, you had an even number of classes, and an equal number of B's and C's... This year, on the other hand, is really quite different. Definitely very different."

Lucy stopped smiling.

His gaze turned slightly agitated, and he started to shake his head back and forth making *hmmm* noises as he thought to himself. "Yep. A nice even number of B's and C's. Here we've got just one B, and an odd number of classes. Alright. Alright. That's alright, I guess. That'll do."

"But it's an advanced algebra course," she finally said something. "It's weighted the same as an A. Look at the top. It's still a 4.0. That's, like, a whole 1.6 points higher than last quarter."

He continued to scratch his chin. She bit her lip and dug her fingernails into her palms to stop her eyes from moistening. Her father now had his elbows on his desk, and his forehead in his hands. He raised his voice, more so trying to convince himself than Lucy. "It's fine. It's fine. No, it's not just fine, it's great. It's just great." He started breathing hard and, ever so slightly, rocking back and forth. "It's just that... it's just that... you know I like symmetry. You know I just like to see clean and clear results that I can expect. But this is fine. No, this is great. It's just great. You did good."

Lucy crossed her arms and looked down.

He stayed in his trance for a few more seconds, then stopped rocking back and forth and said very quietly, his hands still folded in front of his face, "Why don't you go tell your brother John that it's his turn?"

"Five minutes early?" she sniffed.

"No. Wait a minute, and have him come in four minutes early."

Later that evening, their mother, Amy, and all three kids were lined up outside the house in front of the black airport limo. He came out of the house at precisely 6:14pm, shook all of the kids' hands, pecked his wife on the cheek, got in the car and sped off. That was also the first night their mother ever dared to change the schedule. She sent Juanita home early, got in the car, and returned twenty minutes later with a case of white wine.

Amy changed the dress code for dinner from business formal to business casual and ordered Chinese food. She set the table with the Flora Danica porcelain set, which was usually only ever seen on Christmas and Thanksgiving. If you're gonna have Chinese, there's no sense in not using the china set, right? Everyone was poured a large glass of wine.

At the beginning of the meal, their mother hoisted up her Waterford crystal wine glass and proposed a toast, "And our shrink says I'm the enabler. Here's to co-dependency all around, kids. Cheers."

"I'm not hungry," said Lucy.

"We're going to have a nice meal."

"May I be excused?"

"Lucy, I would like just *one* relaxed meal in this house."

"Mom."

"Honey, your Dad's been going through a lot."

"What else is new?"

"Don't you dare start with that tone of yours."

It took all of Lucy's strength not to roll her eyes.

"As we all know," continued her mom, "they stopped using Led Zeppelin in Cadillac commercials and he finally realized how old he is... well we've all been under a lot more stress, that's all. So let's just have a laid back evening. Would it really be that hard?"

"Mom, I just —"

"Absolutely not. You will stay and we will socialize."

"Can you please pass the soy sauce?" asked Kelly.

Young Lucy stumbled upstairs to her rooms after her third generous glass of white wine and not enough sesame chicken. I was on the couch in her sitting room, reading Kelly's latest issue of *Seventeen*. She slammed the door behind her, pointed at me, and yelled, "What the hell were you thinking?"

I turned my paws up and shrugged my shoulders.

"This is all your fault, you know! If you weren't always sleeping, you would've been there on Tuesday for that stupid pop quiz!"

I tried to change the direction of the conversation. "You know, in the past when young men found themselves frustrated, I used to always try to find the source of the frustration, and see if we could channel that energy towards something positive, like hunting, or some kind of mission — stuff like that, y'know? You can only lick your wounds for so long. Channel that energy. Find the source and channel it. It'll make you feel much better."

She paused and considered my advice.

"Hunting," she repeated to herself. "Mission."

"Or whatever the equivalent of that is for twenty-first century teenage girls."

"I'll channel that energy," she said. "I'll let her know what she is. I'll give her what she deserves."

"Who?"

"That asshole who made today possible. I'll channel some energy and tell her what I think of her."

She left her sitting room and went into her bedroom. I continued reading that month's featured article: "Ten Times the Disney Princesses Totally Explained Your Life." Lucy came out of the bedroom five minutes later in jeans, a *Regis Jesuit* hoodie, sneakers, a backpack on one shoulder, a bandana tied around her neck, and a mission consciousness. She left without saying anything to me.

I followed her down the stairs. "Where are you going? Hey, I'm talking to you! What are you up to?"

In the garage she got on her bicycle — there were an even number of very expensive bikes in the garage — and headed down the half mile tree lined driveway that led off the family property. It's hard for me to keep up with her on foot for long distances, so imagine a bicycle. And she was hauling. I followed at a distance as fast as possible, sniffing the air and ground as I went. Three miles from home, her scent turned off the main road into a large housing subdivision full of hundreds of identical houses and lawns. When I finally caught up to her, she was standing on a sidewalk next to her bike, with the handkerchief covering her face, holding a bottle of spray paint, and admiring a large red letter B that now decorated the front of someone's garage. The mailbox bore the same last name as her math teacher, Mrs. Fleschner.

She turned to me and said calmly, "It's not working."

"What's not working?"

"You said I'd feel better if I channelled my energy."

"Well…" I was at a loss for words. "I'm not sure this kind of thing counts as channelling energy."

She took off her backpack and removed a small crowbar.

"Hey, what are you doing?"

"You're right. I need to channel my energy in other ways."

"Give me that crowbar, right now."

She tried to make a break for it and run away from me, but luckily I reacted quickly enough to catch up with her in the front yard, just in time to snag the crowbar and hold onto it. She pulled back, and started screaming, "Give it back! It's mine! Give it back!"

The handkerchief fell from her face. She put one foot up on my gut and pushed me away, while pulling back on the crowbar with both of her arms as hard as possible. Unfortunately for her, I was three hundred pounds heavier, and she didn't have any chance of ever prying it from my grip. But she still kept on screaming, "Give it back! Give it back, right now, or else!"

When Mr. and Mrs. Fleschner looked out the window with the police on the phone, all they saw was one of Mrs. Fleschner's more talented students with one leg held aloft in the air, holding a crowbar out in front of her with straight arms, and yelling at a point in space just beyond the crowbar, "Give it back!"

"I'm going to let go," I tried to tell her. "Lucy, listen to me. I'm going to let go."

But she wouldn't listen, and kept screaming and tugging. So I just let go, and she tumbled back hard. She took the fall like a champ, though, because she sprang up right away, ran over to the Fleschner mailbox and treated it like a piñata. By the time the two cop cars pulled up, she had dropped the crow bar by her feet and was breathing hard, standing on the sidewalk and looking down through wet cheeks at the pile of wood and metal that had once been a mailbox.

On a Thursday in October eleven years later, Brian came home from class and opened the door to Lucy's room.

"Oh, sorry," he said. At first he was startled to have woken her up, but then he was startled that she was there at all, lying in her orange Ikea chair — the mabbled palioderm that was more trib than bibble — with her feet up on her antique leather ottoman — the one they had flunged during their Appalachian werbgurbling expedition last June. An ice pack was perched on top of her right fist.

"What's going on?" she asked, shielding her eyes from the light now streaming in from the hallway. "Did you want first dibs on all of my stuff?"

"No, I just wanted to make sure... nothing... just wanted to see if... if... nevermind. Sorry, I thought you'd already left this morning."

"Look in there." She pointed at her trashcan.

It was empty, except for two scraps of paper at the bottom. Brian pulled them out, and put them together at the place where they had been ripped apart. It was a one-way ticket for a Swissair flight from Zürich to Denver.

CHAPTER TEN

ROMA, SEI BELLA.

On Saturday morning, Lucy's eyes pealed open in bed at the sound of yelling and gunfire coming from Brian's room next door. She closed her eyes and let out a noise that was somewhere between a sigh and a groan. She rolled onto her left side, and stacked a pillow on top of her right ear, with her right arm on top of it. No results. The noise was too loud, and the pillow didn't help. She rolled onto her back, and hit the wall next to her bed once with her right fist, but she immediately had to use a choice word and choke back tears. The impact with the wall gave her a sharp reminder of the bruised and purple state of her right fist. Andrew's skull had not been a soft target. So she reached across with her left fist and banged on the wall yelling, "Brian!"

The shooting sounds let up, but Scott's voice fired back, "Don't speak unless spoken to!"

"Guys! It's Saturday morning!"

"Ms. Fox, don't think we didn't hear that word that you used a second ago. You had better think about cleaning out your mouth, young Lady," Scott yelled back from the other room. "And give us a break. It's ten thirty. I slept in more than normal too, but I've been awake for three hours."

The explosions and bedlam set off again. Lucy made another attempt at banging on the wall and yelling, "Shut up!"

So Scott took a different approach, "The rest of the world is awake and taking the bull by the horns, Lucy. We're getting stuff done. You can spend your life zoned out and detached or you can wake up and focus. You had better take some time and think long and hard about what you're doing with your life."

They gave her twenty seconds to stare at her ceiling and contemplate the direction of her life, before Brian lobbed another plasma grenade and Scott went to town with the sniper rifle. Lucy closed her eyes and pressed both of her palms to her ears. This is how I found her when I came into her room, after having spent the entire morning out searching around Rome.

I took hold of the edge of her mattress and gave it a shake.

"Are you serious?" she yelled. "What the hell do you think you're doing in here? Get the fu — " she opened her eyes and saw that it was me. "Oh… sorry… I thought you were…"

"You thought I was…"

"Nobody… um… " she sat up in bed, clearing the sleep out of her eyes. "Can nobody ever let me just sleep in this place?"

I threw a green North Face rain jacket onto her lap.

She yawned and fiddled with the zipper, "Oh, hey, you found my rain jacket." She stopped moving her hands and squinted at it, as a vague and distant memory slowly passed through her mind. Her head shot up at me and with her eyes wide open she yelled, "You found my rain jacket!"

The shooting in the room next door came to a stop again.

"What was that?" yelled Brian.

"Nothing," she hollered back.

"Lucy," said Scott. "What did we tell you about not speaking unless being spoken to?"

She didn't respond.

"That's right!" yelled Scott. The shooting picked up again.

"Yeah, and you're never going to believe the best part about that jacket," I told her. "There's blood on the sleeves."

Her hands flew off the jacket into the air, and she crawled out from under it, to ball herself up on the other side of the bed, looking suspiciously back at the jacket.

"That's disgusting!" she said to me, now keeping her voice down so that they wouldn't hear her in the other room. "I'm not a germaphobe, or something — like some people here — but come on! You don't touch blood. It could have AIDS all over it or something."

"That blood's been on that jacket since Monday. Viruses don't survive that long outside the body."

"Yeah, but still," she responded, employing that universal comeback, valid in any situation, regardless of the weakness of your argument. She leapt out of bed, and went to sit at her desk chair. She pulled her feet up onto the seat, and wrapped her arms around her legs, still looking at the bed with suspicion. Having put a safe distance between herself and the jacket, she then got curious. "Where did you find that?"

"Well, this morning, I was having this really awesome dream about that great pile of trash that I'd found in Boulder that day after Thanksgiving a few years ago. Remember that one? I think I told you about that, right? It had all that salmon and raw turkey legs, and something with a hint of fermented fruits. Oh my gosh. That was a day."

I closed my eyes for a second in ecstasy, and Lucy scrunched her nose at me.

"Well, anyways," I went on, "I was dreaming about that pile of trash this morning, and this group of Roman trash collectors came running at me with those giant witch brooms yelling, 'It's trash day, it's trash day, it's trash day!' and I was like, 'No way, it's Saturday. It can't be trash day!' But they were like, 'We work on Saturdays too, Blue Bear. It's trash day!' and then I realized. Oh crap. Those guys are right. They do collect trash on Saturdays."

"Okay..." said Lucy, not seeing the point.

"Then I woke up, and I thought, wow, they're right. They do collect trash on Saturdays. If there is still any evidence from last Monday, it's probably going to get collected by today at the latest."

Lucy nodded her head in understanding.

"So while you were getting your beauty sleep, I got my ass out of bed, and spent the whole morning canvassing every garbage dumpster within a mile radius of Palazzo Mortimer and Doria Pamphili."

"Don't you do that most days anyways?"

"Well, yeah, but not this early in the morning. And this time I was looking out for any smells that I could recognize from the Palazzo."

"Where did you find it."

"There's a lot of great dumpsters in Rome, but there's a few that always smell pretty bad. Do you remember that one on Via dei Corridori, just off Via della Conciliazione?"

She shrugged her shoulders.

"You know the neighborhood, right?"

"Yeah."

"Okay, so there's that one set of dumpsters on that street, those ones that always smell pretty bad over there."

"Blue Bear, they all smell bad."

I sighed. Poor creatures with a completely unsophisticated sense of smell should not be the judges of these things. "Just trust me. That one smells *bad.* Anyways, there was a trash truck pulling up, ready to empty them all, but I got there just in time, because the two guys driving the truck all of the sudden stopped, and decided to take a smoke break. So I shimmy up to it, and what do I smell?"

"What?"

"Well, I smelled a lot of things, actually. But among others, I caught a *very* faint whiff of," I pointed at her with my paw, "you."

"Of me? I haven't been over there in months."

"Yep. Of you. So I dug around for a little while, and towards the bottom, I managed to pull out that green jacket, and," I threw the black rain pants onto her bed next to the jacket, "these too."

"Blue Bear!" she said, curling herself up even tighter into her chair, "those pants have been worn by a murderer. They've got blood all over them. They've spent a week in a Roman dumpster — a dumpster that even you think smells bad. What the hell makes you think that I would want them on my bed?"

I've definitely made some progress over the years, but I don't think I'll ever fully adjust to civilization. Why are there so many completely incoherent rules about what sorts of things can be placed next to other sorts of things? Okay. I get it. It's true. In her defense, the dumpster did not smell great. I understand her confusion. But in my defense, the absolute best smelling thing in that dumpster was her rain jacket and pants. Any other normal creature would have taken it as a huge compliment if I had thrown those things on her bed. But modern humans, who have no sense of smell, have all these pretentious ideas about these things, so much so that they get all bent out of shape when more sophisticated souls behave rationally and try to express our admiration. I had been giving up my precious sleep to work my butt off all morning, and all she could do was scold me for not being human. Great. I'll admit that I was a little bit offended. However, not offended enough to really make a scene. But despite that, I also knew I needed to gain some leverage in the conversation. So I rolled my eyes and sighed again. She realized that she had just broken one of those tacit rules of how our relationship would work.

"Blue Bear, come here," she reached out from her chair, grabbed onto me, and wheeled herself over to the middle of the room, where I was sitting, throwing her arms around my shoulder.

I nudged her with my nose, in acceptance of the apology, and then shook her off of me. She kept her feet off the ground, and wheeled herself away from me by shaking her hips until the chair had jerked itself back to the spot in front of the desk.

I had gained the moral high ground, so I pressed it to my advantage. "I mean, I guess the point is this. The last two days, you guys haven't done anything. Okay, yeah, you've read the newspaper, you've re-read the interrogation transcript, you went to class, you've sat around thinking. That's all something. Sure. But if we're gonna figure out who did this, we've got to get active. We've got to start looking for stuff."

"Sure. But where do we start?"

"We start with what we've got."

"A bloody jacket? Some random keys? What do you want me to do? Should I just walk around and try the keys on random locks?"

"Somehow you're still not in the papers," I suggested. "If you are planning on walking around doing shady stuff like that, it's probably better to do so sooner than later. If they ever do decide to publish something, people are going to recognize you."

Three different people in Rome were listed in the yellow pages under the name "Eugenio Galli." Nobody with a Facebook account under that name lived anywhere near Rome. Sunday morning, a train carried Lucy to Gemelli hospital, where one of the Eugenio Galli's was listed as a hematologist.

At the front desk, assuming hematologists don't work on Sundays, she asked the lady, "*Buon giorno. Io sono una vecchia amica di un dottore ematologo che lavora qua. Stavo qua in giro e pensavo, magari ci sarebbe anche lui oggi. Sarebbe bello poter salutarlo.*"[79]

"*Come si chiama?*"[80]

"Eugenio Galli."[81]

"*Oggi, sì, c'è.*"[82]

The receptionist's response at once verified that Dr. Galli was still alive — thus eliminating him as a candidate for the Eugenio Galli that Lucy was looking for — but also caught her unaware. She hadn't been prepared to actually meet him.

"*Grazie,*" she said with wide eyes, then turned and walked away.

But the front desk lady yelled back after her, "*Aspetta! Eccolo arrivare adesso.*"[83]

A young man in a white jacket turned the corner before she had a chance to escape. Lucy turned bright red, and backpedalled out of the lobby, explaining that she must have confused him for another friend of hers who was also an Italian hematologist named Eugenio Galli. It was always in moments like these that speaking Italian became difficult again. The doctor and receptionist both squinted at her, as she tried to find the right words, before she gave up, turned around and high tailed it out of the hospital.

Another series of busses took her out to the residence of the second Eugenio Galli, on Via Nomentana. Both of the mystery keys found no success in opening the front door of the apartment building, so she puttered around outside until she got the chance to follow

---

[79] *At the front desk, assuming hematologists don't work on Sundays, she asked the lady,* "Good morning. I'm an old friend of a hematologist who works here. I was in the area, and thought I might drop in and and see if he was around. It'd be great to say hi."

[80] "What's his name?"

[81] "Eugenio Galli."

[82] "Yeah, he's here today."

[83] "Wait! Look, he's arriving right now."

someone inside. The keys were equally useless on the door of the apartment itself. Not ready to give up, she put on her sunglasses and sat down on a bench outside the apartment entrance, contemplating her next move. Dr. Eugenio walked right past her and up to the apartment building. Lucy stared and Dr. Galli smiled politely back. Once he reached the door, though, he did a double take. He opened the door quickly, slipped through it, and slammed it shut behind himself. Lucy's stomach doubled over and she turned even redder than before, speed walking away from the building.

So there were not three people with the name Eugenio Galli listed in Rome, but only two. At least one of them was still alive, but was listed twice in the phonebook: work and home.

"Well, he didn't have to slam the door so quickly, did he?" she asked herself, walking away. "A lot of people would be flattered to have me as their stalker."

Monday morning she left Palazzo Mortimer like normal. Now close to mid-October in the Mediterranean, it was getting a little chilly every morning, and like most Italians around her, Lucy had, over the years, without realizing what she was doing, started dressing in heavier clothing than she ever would have imagined wearing in similar weather in Colorado: a thick white fisherman's sweater, jeans with the cuffs rolled, one of those light scarves that Europeans wear at the first sign of a breeze, aviators, thick walking moccasins, and a leather school bag with frills — also of her own making.

She hurried past Gambetti at the porter's station without looking at him — "*Ciao, bella, come stai?*" "*Ciao Gambetti. Sto bene, grazie.*" — and descended the Janiculum hill. Across Piazza della Rovere she took Ponte Savoia to get to the other side of the Tiber, where, most mornings, she would catch the number forty or the number sixty four.

At the high point on the bridge, a motorino slowed down and stopped next to the sidewalk where Lucy was walking. It was Andrew.

Most Italians thrive in the midst of conflict. They can't live without it. Most Americans prefer to avoid conflict. They avoid even awkward situations for as long as humanly possible. Even though she was sporting a heavy sweater in relatively mild weather, Lucy remained American. Conflict aside, though, the absolute worst thing imaginable, in Lucy's book, was having to apologize, especially in a situation in which the other person was mostly at fault. Lucy, of course, was convinced that Andrew was one hundred percent at fault for last Thursday's incident. Even living in close quarters, she had done an exceptional job of not crossing paths with Andrew, ever since her right fist had made contact with his left eye. Luckily enough for Lucy, Andrew had not been the type to insist promptly on a formal apology, or the type to initiate a group discussion on roommates and boundaries, or even worse, the type to propose helpful tips to improve interpersonal conflict resolution management skills. Thank God there were no RA's at the Palazzo.

But out in the open, on the bridge, with him staring her down, there was no avoiding him. So she halted and shot him a blank stare, putting all of her effort into communicating a nonverbal *Don't you dare even think about bringing up last Thursday, because you don't understand the half of it.*

And he didn't. "You off to class, then?"

"Yeah."

He nodded at the space behind him on the scooter. "Well, hop on, love."

She stood there for a moment questioning his motives, hoping that once she was on the bike he wouldn't turn it into an opportunity to bring up an unwanted conversation. In other circumstances she would have refused, but the offer of eliminating up to twenty minutes of travel time off of her normal morning commute was too good to pass up. He had already opened up the compartment beneath the seat and was passing her the extra passenger helmet.

"Do I have to wear that?"

"If you care about your head, yes. I always wear my helmet. You know that. And nobody rides on my scooter without one."

She snapped on the helmet, tightened her school bag, and swung her leg over the back of the scooter.

Organized is not the first word anyone has ever used to describe Roman traffic. It's not that there are no traffic rules — there are — it's just that those rules, like with all things Italian, are less about the rules themselves, and more about the relationships between persons. (In this case, vehicles are seen as extensions of personhood.) For example, the lanes are not Kantian categorical prescriptions of where a vehicle absolutely must be, in and of itself, rather, they are indications and suggestions about how one ought to behave towards others. That is, any area that is not already occupied by a car, becomes *de facto* scooter territory. Using a motorino is not for the faint of heart. Riding as a passenger, even more so, means placing your life entirely in the hands of another person. And depending on the size of the scooter — Andrew's was on the small side — there's also really no way of being the passenger without getting very close to the person in front of you. It has little to do with your affection, or lack thereof, for the driver. Instead, out of affection for your own bodily integrity, you grab onto whatever is available and hold on tight, even if that means grabbing onto the person in front of you.

Despite the high level of physical proximity, given the noise of traffic, there's little way to communicate with one another, except when parked at stoplights. Lucy was thrilled when the first three intersections were green, thus eliminating the possibility of conversation. But between three and four, a question presented itself to her with urgency, so much so that on Corso Emmanuele in front of the Chiesa del Gesù at stoplight number four, which was red, she felt the need to break the silence herself.

"Andrew."

"Yeah."

"Can you drive with just one eye?"

"Everything's legal on the road in Italy."

"No, not *are you allowed* to drive with one eye, but *can* you drive with just one eye?"

"I can drive a lot better with three eyes on the motorino."

"What?"

"Nevermind."

"Oh, I get it."

The light turned green, Andrew hit the accelerator, the scooter gave a little bang and a shimmy, puffed out a good deal of smoke, and they sped off again down Via del Plesbitico towards Piazza Venezia. That was as much as they needed to say about Thursday's incident, or at least, that was as much as Lucy needed to have said about Thursday's incident.

Driving from the Janiculum to Sapienza University, they passed directly through the heart of 2,600 years of history layered in circles around itself. Lucy sometimes felt like Rome is just one giant museum disguised as a city, or a museum surrounded by a city. The most ancient parts that are still visible above ground are the ruins of the Roman forum, in the kilometer between the capitoline hill and the Coliseum. Most everything after that, from the middle ages, has been thoroughly destroyed twice over by invading barbarians, so the forums are surrounded by the next layer of history: heaps and heaps of over-the-top opulent renaissance era buildings, stretching between St. Peter's basilica and St. John Lateran. Around these areas, there are nineteenth and early twentieth century neighborhoods with grid street patterns from the time of Italian unification, when Rome decided it needed to imitate every other European capitol. It is precisely this contrast between ancient ruins, renaissance exuberance, and nineteenth century elegance that makes Rome one of the most beautiful cities on the planet. Lucy enjoyed the great privilege of taking it all for granted, and looking down on those who didn't.

Andrew, for his part, was more interested in another of Rome's beauties. Flying through the giant roundabout in Piazza della Repubblica, his head turned to observe three supermodels with cameras around their necks. Once his eyes returned to the road, though, he suddenly swerved to avoid a near collision with a slow old man on a bicycle. Lucy instinctively leaned in and grabbed even harder onto Andrew's abs, as he clenched them in fear. Once he regained control of the motorino his midsection started to shake, and she could tell he was laughing. It took her a moment to release the tension in her limbs, and take stock of how close she had just come to certain death. It's strange how adrenaline can produce affection in humans. Her tight grip on Andrew became less mechanical and almost endearing, natural.

Beyond Piazza della Repubblica they entered the areas where most of the population lives, the blocky 1930's fascist neighborhoods and the mid-century modern apartment complexes that surround the old city. Uneven cobblestones gave way to potholed pavement. After WWII, Italy had an unexpected decade of economic boom, (cfr. Fellini's *La dolce vita*) when everyone decided, for a short decade, that they were going to work like capitalists. Unfortunately the building boom was contemporaneous with the 1950's, a decade when they still hadn't gotten over the idea of fascist block architecture. As a result, most of the buildings in the most populated areas of Rome, despite what you'll see on TV, were built in that style, and not in the more beautiful aforementioned areas. Palazzo Mortimer was old enough to have been spared this fate, but the main campus of Lucy's school, Università Sapienza, was directly from this era.

Moving from the Janiculum to Sapienza every day meant hurtling herself through every epoch in the history of Western civilization, from the most jaw-droppingly gorgeous to the most cringe-worthy ugly, all while trying to avoid becoming a part of that history by way of an automobile accident. Every commute, whether she was aware of it or not, was a thoroughly human experience.

Andrew parked the motorino at a lot just outside the main entrance to the campus — a massive series of imposing block gates. If you didn't already know it was a university, you would think you were entering an evil villain's fortress or some kind of socialist prison block.

Lucy handed off her helmet to Andrew, adjusted the strap on her bag and stood next to the bike as Andrew locked up the helmets and wound a medieval chain through the front wheel.

"Thanks, Andrew. Have a good one."

"No problem. Yeah, I've got class every Monday at this time. Just let me know whenever you'd like a lift."

"Alright. Thanks. I will." She made a mental note to run into Andrew again next Monday morning, then turned and walked against the flow of students in the direction of Eugenio Galli number two's apartment building, which was near Sapienza.

"Or wait... no," he called out after her. "Next Monday I'll be at my cousins' house down south, but every Monday after that, yeah."

"Okay. Thanks!"

She turned and took another two steps away before Andrew called out again. "Lucy, isn't the Lit. building over there?" He pointed towards the gate.

"Oh yeah... you're right. I guess I've just never been to this side of campus before," she lied.

She turned around and joined the stream of 130,000 people who filtered in and out of the Sapienza University system. Of course, not all the faculties were housed on one campus, but the sheer volume of people at the main campus made it impossible to tell. Her white fisherman sweater stuck out among the cynical European students, walking with their heads down, sporting little to no color in their apparel. They all marched on through the imposing gates into a small city of buildings, a walled-in ghetto of European intellectuals, detached from the rest of reality. The most acerbic characters joined Lucy at her faculty building: literature. Most of Lucy's classmates were the type to be seen reading Nietzsche and Dostoevsky on the morning subway commute, complain to their girlfriends about their profoundly complex existential angst at dinner, and take the train home to the countryside every weekend to make sure that mamma could cook them a good meal and do their laundry. Welcome to Europe.

Inside the literature building, she killed time perusing the bookstore, and even considered attending her morning lectures. After standing among the shelves and reading the last paragraphs of part I of Wendell Berry's *Storia della vita di Jayber Crow*, adventure called, and she came skipping out the front steps of the building.

Eugenio Galli number two lived in a mid-century modern apartment building on a block full of mid-century moderns, maybe a half mile from Sapienza. The keys did not work on the main entrance to the complex, so she took a seat outside, hoping that Eugenio number one did not own two apartments. After just ten minutes, sitting paid off. A grumpy old man flew out of the building in haste, allowing Lucy to get up and lodge her foot between the door and the doorframe just in time.

Upstairs, the keys did not work. This was almost a relief. What was she going to do if they did work? Break in? Dust the place for fingerprints? Exiting the building, she held the door open for a woman in a yellow *Poste Italiane* uniform, carrying a letter bag. Lucy stood rooted on the spot in the doorway staring at the mail lady and holding the door open as a thought crossed through her mind. The woman turned and glared at Lucy, who rummaged through her bag, pretending to have forgotten something. She came back inside the building and disappeared up the apartment stairwell. Once she heard the mail woman leave, she scampered down to the lobby and searched for the mailbox to Eugenio number two's apartment number. The first key did not fit. But the second —

"Holy shit," she said to herself, as the key slid smoothly into the keyhole.

Opening the little metal door, she removed four items, closed the box, and left, walking quickly and keeping her gaze pointed towards the ground. She intended to go home immediately, but curiosity was too strong.

She sat down at the table farthest from anyone else at the first coffee bar she passed, and ordered breakfast, waiting with her bag shaking up and down on her knee. The waiter dropped off a pastry and cappuccino, Lucy shoved them to the far side of the table, and took out the letters. The first was an advertisement for local painters. Great. Lots of information there. The second was a weekly news magazine, *L'espresso*. She thumbed through it and was glad not to find herself anywhere. The third was a hand addressed birthday card for someone named Irene Spiga.

"Hmm. Does this mean he was married?"

Inside was a long note covered in loopy cursive from a distant relative down south. A certain part mentioned "Eugenio and the kids."

Finally, she opened a white envelope with one of those plastic windows so that you can see the address is printed on the letter itself. It was one of those checks with a detachable receipt.

"Oh crap," she whispered, as her conscience allowed itself to be felt for just a split second. It's true, she had fully intended to steal someone's mail. But she hadn't planned on stealing money — especially not a check she wouldn't even be able to cash. She distracted her conscience by taking a closer look, hoping that it would prove to be a useful clue. But her conscience roared back on the scene when she saw the little box with the quantity written on it: 352,673.61.

"Oh shit, oh shit, oh shit. I'm an idiot," she stared down at the huge number and ran her fingers through her hair. "Oh, shit I'm an idiot. Oh my God, I'm an idiot."

She stuffed all of the papers back into her bag, getting up with the intention of returning everything to the mailbox. But — she stopped, standing up halfway — what good would that do? If the family got an open check in the mail, they'd get suspicious and look at the security footage. But then again, if a €350,000.00 check went missing, they'd get suspicious and check anyways, right? Well, maybe not. The check could have been lost anywhere, not just from their box. And come on, stealing a check isn't stealing money. They'll just have to cancel it and write another one, right?

She took out the slip of paper and looked at it more closely. It was written in English. Strange. It was from a company called *Furniture Exports, Inc.*

"So that's why Luca wanted to know about all my nice furniture," she nodded her head.

Her jaw dropped open, though, when she saw the address of the company: Cape Town, South Africa.

"That bitch."

In one blinding moment, her conscience was clear. How on earth were the police so incompetent? How did they not catch such an obvious connection? Italy. Fricken' Italy.

There was also another relief, "Okay, so I didn't just steal 350,000 euros. That's probably just, like, what? Twenty bucks in South African money?"

She chugged her cappuccino, wolfed down her pastry and almost ran out of the bar, needing to talk to me or Brian or anyone. Passing by a Wind cell phone store, she stopped and said out loud, "I've really got to stop talking to myself," and went in.

The number forty from termini took her to Piazza Dodici Apostoli, a two minute walk to Piazza della Pilotta, the Jesuit owned square surrounded on four sides by the campus of the Pontifical Gregorian University. The Gregorian, in contrast to Sapienza, was in the heart of old Rome, spitting distance to the Coliseum, the forums, and the capitoline hill. Ignatius Loyola founded it himself five hundred years ago, but the campus was rebuilt in the 1930's, because the Masons had stolen the original structure during the Italian nationalist craze in 1871 and turned it into a public high school.

She ignored the beggars stationed at the entrance — seminarians are such suckers — and headed into the massive atrium in the center of the main building. The campus was extra-territorial Vatican property, ceded by Italy to the Holy See in the 1929 Lateran Treaty between Mussolini and Pius XI (or, depending on how you look at it, part of the property *not* ceded to Italy by the Vatican), when the Italian state and the Vatican finally recognized each other's existence. This is just a long way of explaining that the Gregorian campus, even though it was built in the heyday of fascist architecture, had been spared the popular style of the time, because it was technically not in Italy. Instead, it fit in well with the beautiful renaissance façades of the surrounding neighborhood. The students were not swallowed up by the building. Even though it was sizable, it still respected and affirmed your humanity.

Mamma Greg, as her English speaking students affectionately referred to her, had only about three thousand students, most of them priests, seminarians, religious sisters and a small smattering of lay people, like Brian. Everyone was decked out in the most bizarre mixes of prescribed religious uniforms. Lucy, who was neither a priest, nor a seminarian, nor a religious sister — far from it — in some strange way, stood out less at the Greg than at her own school. At Sapienza, nobody followed any official dress codes, but everyone ended up wearing the exact same depressing shades of European fashions. At the Greg, most everyone followed some kind of a religious dress code, but they were all wearing diverse and unique outfits. Lucy — someone with light colored fabrics and hope in her eyes — was not out of the norm. That's not saying much, but it's something.

An enormous stained glass ceiling covered her head, fifty yards above, held up by a two story colonnade that surrounded the main atrium's walls. The handful of seminarians and sisters who were ditching class occupied tables set up on the marble floor underneath. In one corner, an automatic sliding glass door led to the student coffee bar, *il Greg Bar*.

At exactly a quarter after ten, Lucy positioned herself outside the door to one of the larger lecture halls, with its entrance right off the main atrium. The bell rang and hundreds of international students began to trickle and then stampede out of the various lecture halls. The whole stone building echoed with voices now having to yell at each other in almost every modern language known to man. Some ran to the bathrooms, and others — Scott Valentino among them — jockeyed for position to be first in line at the Greg Bar. Scott smiled at Lucy and then did a double take.

"What are you doing here? They let people like you in here?" he stopped to ask.

"Have you seen Brian?"

"Watch out Lucy. This is a Jesuit school, but they still have a chapel. You'll want to avoid it. I wouldn't want you to burst into flames or something."

"Thank you. That's very thoughtful of you. So Brian's not here today?"

"I thought I saw him earlier. He's here somewhere. But come on, Lucy!" Scott made an angry gesture towards the rush of people now forming all the way out the door of *il Greg Bar*. "Look what you did! Now I'm going to have to wait in line for coffee."

Scott stormed off towards the entrance of *il Greg Bar* and Lucy entered the lecture hall with stadium seating. The last time she had been to the Greg, over a year ago, Brian had explained to her the dynamics of the class. The Americans, English, Australians and Irish sat by the windows to control the temperature. The Scots never came to class. The Spaniards, South Americans, and the scrupulous sat up front in the middle. The French sat dead center and kept to themselves. The Italians didn't attend lectures often enough to have an established location. The Indians, Asians and Africans sat on the left, as far away from the windows as possible.

Sapienza was so big that Lucy hardly ever saw the same people twice at different courses. At the Greg, on the other hand, the first three years of theology were spent together in one giant lecture hall with one hundred and fifty classmates who all had an identical class schedule. Of course, on any given day, maybe sixty percent of them would attend lectures. Most people had developed cooperative note taking systems, so that it wasn't necessary to physically come to class every day.

At the beginning of the first year, Brian said, everyone made giddy smalltalk with one another in a new language. Over the second year, people grew tired of repetitive and superficial conversation in an Italian that never improved. By the beginning of the third year, Brian's year, the national and linguistic groups had given up on integration and had all closed in on themselves. During breaks between classes, people stood around chatting in their own circles, staring at laptops, or with their heads on their desks, trying to sleep or imagine they were back in their own countries.

Once she came through the door, she stopped and stood in the front of the lecture hall to observe the flock. Behind her, a Powerpoint slide filled a large screen with a massive hairball of color coded information about a passage from the Gospel of John. A skinny Eastern European Jesuit in a suit and grey clerics struggled to field questions from the more nerdy looking students in a very mechanical Italian. Morale among the troops was at an all time low. A good number of them were slyly packing up their bags and sneaking out the side.

Lucy had already met the majority of the American seminarians in Brian and Scott's class on various odd occasions. A good number of them were great. But still others were either overwhelmingly awkward around beautiful young women, or else they used her as an opportunity to "evangelize." Lucy had once considered herself to be a consistent churchgoer when growing up — consistent on Christmas and Easter, like most reasonably religious people — and had even, on occasions, devoutly thumbed through the Gospels while suffering through long Christmas sermons. From the little that she had read, and she certainly didn't consider herself an expert, she somehow never got the impression that Jesus wanted his followers to use the Gospel as an excuse to talk to the only attractive English speaking woman available within the wide circle of your friends' friends, whenever you happen to find yourself abroad for a few years and are deprived of a consistent feminine presence in your life. Maybe, she thought, that was an innovation in Paul's letters, which she had yet to peruse.

The more interesting and human seminarians — Scott and his cronies — had already cleared out of the lecture hall. She knew she only had a very small window of time to find Brian before one of the evangelizers would mount an attack, so she kept her survey of the field brief. Looking to her left, outside the door, Brian stood in the atrium, with his backpack on his shoulders, motioning for her to come join him, while trying to stay out of the professor's field of vision. One of the evangelizers had already spotted her, and had risen from his seat. Lucy avoided eye contact, scurried out of the lecture hall, and accompanied Brian out of the building into the piazza.

"Lucy, do you realize what today is?" asked Brian, taking her on one of the narrow cobblestoned lanes towards the Trevi fountain. The crowds of tourists grew thicker, and they had to turn down armies of street vendors offering selfie sticks and light up gooey balls that made a squealing sound when splattered on the ground.

Whenever she walked alone, the street vendors never bothered her. Whenever she was with Brian, they never left them alone. The trick is eye contact and confidence.

"October 12th?"

"And…"

"Monday?"

"And…"

"I don't know. The feast of St. Brian?"

"Wait, is today the feast of St. Brian?"

"Brian, how would I know that? You're talking to *me* remember?"

"Oh yeah, that's right."

"So what is it?"

"Well, there's some debate," said Brian. "There isn't really a St. Brian on the calendar, and there isn't really a St. Brian at all. There was this one guy named Edward, whose middle name was Brian. He got martyred in England in the 1590's, and his feast day is sometime in October, but I don't remember exactly when. So, if you really wanted to, you could argue that the feast of St. Brian is coming up. I just forget exactly which day it is."

"No! Today, Brian! What's today?"

"Oh, yeah, today is one of the most important days in Italian history."

"Really? I guess it wasn't important enough to cancel class."

"No, not a *historical* day. *Today*, on this day," he pointed at the ground, "history will be made in Italy. Today, centuries after the fall of the Roman empire, civilization returns to the peninsula."

"What's going on?"

"Come with me."

They took a left turn one block before the Trevi fountain and walked down the street towards the McDonalds.

"You had better not be taking me to McDonalds."

"No, no, no. I told you. I'm taking you to civilization."

A block past McDonalds, he stopped her before they came around the corner. "Alright, stand here for a second, and take a deep breath, and get yourself ready for a surprise. Close your eyes. Okay, now walk towards my voice. Left. Right. Left. Right. Okay. Good. Now stop. Now turn to your right. A little bit more. A little more. Okay, stop. Good. Okay, now open your eyes."

They posed before the glass storefront of a trendy looking coffee shop full of people. Above the door, a naked mermaid relaxed inside a green circle, looking down with condescension as Italy passed by on the streets below her.

"Can you believe this?" Brian shouted and smiled.

"Oh hey," Lucy was completely *under*whelmed. "There's a Starbucks here. Did this just open today?"

"Yes! Do you realize that Italy was the *last* first-world country ever to *not* have a Starbucks? Civilization has returned to the peninsula. We're living it, Lucy. This is history and we're living it."

He opened the door for her and followed her inside. The place was packed with tourists, who were too scared to try something new, and local Italians who were interested in the novelty of American coffee. In front of the register there was a phenomenon not seen at a coffee bar in central Italy since the German occupation: a line. Lucy felt that one of the baristas — all of whom spoke English (already a huge departure from any other Italian coffee bar) — looked familiar, but she could not quite put her finger on which one of them it was until she was at the register and the man behind it asked her a question.

"What can I get for you?" He glared at her with disgust.

The sound of that voice at first provoked in her an inexplicable moment of dread and fear, as though she had done something wrong and had just been caught. But then a light went off, and she recognized who the barista was. But what on earth was he doing here? Oh, that's right. The poor guy was recently let go from his other job. She felt a great surprise, followed by an intense and sweet feeling of victory. It had been clear to her, in an abstract way, that it was going to happen, but she had not expected an actual concrete moment when she would get to gloat over him in her victory. The barista glared over the counter at her and Lucy could not stop herself from smiling. It was a wicked smile, she knew, but she didn't care. It was so full of *sweet sweet* triumph. The barista was Detective Luca Speziale, or by now, just Luca Speziale — no prefix.

"I'll have," began Brian, "a grande, whole milk, one pump hazelnut, two pumps vanilla caramel macchiato."

"Can I get a name for that?"

"Brian."

Luca wrote Brian's name and drink order on the cup, without making a single mistake. He looked at the man next to him in a black apron — the manager — and back at Lucy. He scrunched his nose and asked, "And for you, Miss?"

"I'll have a *caffè americano* — "

"No, she's not going to order that," interrupted Brian.

"But that's what I want."

"This is Starbucks, Lucy. You can get anything you want."

"Yeah, and that's what *I want*. That's what I'd get even if we were in America."

"If you order that, I am going to take it off the counter and take a piss straight into the cup, right here. Right in front of everybody."

Luca stood scowling at the register.

Lucy turned to Luca and smiled again, "I'll have a tall chai latte."

"She'll have that with whole milk, three extra pumps of chai and no water," Brian added. He paid, saw that a table had just opened, and moved towards it.

Lucy waited for the drinks and basked in her moment of victory, closing her eyes and trying to fix this moment in her memory forever. It felt so good and so delightfully bad. When she opened her eyes, the manager was looking away from Luca, who had turned to face Lucy and was scratching his beard using only his middle finger.

One of the baristas called out their orders. "I've got a grande caramel macchiato for 'Brian' and a tall chai latte for 'You bi...' or... wait... No. Maybe it says... I don't know... 'You Brick' or 'You Bick'? I don't know. This one is kind of hard to read."

Lucy picked up the drinks. The name written in Luca's handwriting on the side of Lucy's cup was very clear. She stood by the side of the table where Brian was sitting and said, "We have to leave. I have to tell you something, and I can't tell you here."

"This is Starbucks. You don't have to pay extra to sit down."

She gave him one of her I'm-Lucy-and-I-said-so-so-end-of-discussion looks. Brian knew debate was pointless, so they got up and left. At the Trevi fountain, they held on to their wallets and found a spot to sit by the edge. She told him that their barista was also her interrogator — still with a proud expression on her face.

They tested out the camera on her new smartphone, taking a picture of the profanity scrawled out on her Starbucks cup with the Trevi fountain in the background. Brian also heard all about the apartment, the stolen mail, the birthday card, and the South African address of the furniture company.

It took a few minutes for Brian to absorb the significance of it all.

"Well, we know what that means," he said eventually.

"Yep."

"Our new roommate is definitely involved."

"Would you say she's dangerous?" asked Lucy.

"I don't know. She doesn't look too dangerous. It's been more than a week, and nobody else is dead yet." He took a swig from his caramel macchiato. "We know she was involved, but does that mean she's the dangerous one?"

"Well —"

"And why?" Interrupted Brian. "Is it normal for South African furniture companies to hire young blonde girls as international hitmen?"

"The police obviously thought it was a woman. That's got to mean something. Maybe we shouldn't ask if she's dangerous. She definitely is. But is she dangerous *to us*. She wouldn't get rid of anyone else, yet, would she? She needs to find out about the bank account, or the keys."

"But wait," said Brian. "Why didn't the cops immediately suspect her instead of you? They knew Eugenio was importing furniture from South Africa, right?"

"Well, I know why they thought it was me. There were all the fingerprints and the jacket," said Lucy. "But Natasha's got a Russian passport. The cops don't even realize yet that she's South African. Her real name's even, like, Natálya Nikoláevna, or something sinister like that. I'm surprised she told us that she's South African. She tries hard to come across as cute and naïve, but you're right, she's definitely dangerous."

"This is weird."

"Very weird."

"What do we do next?" he asked. "How are we going to keep an eye on Natasha? Or should we just try to stay out of it?"

"Oh, we'll definitely keep an eye on her," said Lucy. "I have an idea, though. Do you have any idea where we could get some fake I.D.s and lots of fake government documents?"

"Lucy, we were just at the Greg."

CHAPTER ELEVEN

IL BAGNO TURCHESE E IL RIPOSO

They headed back to Piazza della Pilotta — Brian proudly carrying his grande caramel macchiato with the logo turned outwards — and went up the steps to the Greg. They waited for the bell to ring, and Scott was one of the first to come charging out of the lecture hall.

"Why did they have to schedule three straight hours of this guy?" he moaned at them. "Three straight hours of Johannine Lit. It's like dragging dead horses through the mud. This class is literally the same thing as dragging dead horses through the mud."

"Scott," Lucy raised her eyebrows, "do you know what the word 'literally' means?"

"Yes. *Literally*. There are dead horses and mud in that room."

"Why do you guys even go to that class?" asked Lucy. "I thought you guys had that whole note taking system that you were telling me about."

"Yeah, there is the notes system, so I don't actually have to pay attention." Whenever Scott was tired his Wisconsin accent got even thicker. "But two things have happened to me this year. One: the American seminary faculty is going to vote on whether or not to ordain me, and two: we've got snitches."

"Snitches?"

"Yeah, there's these other uptight seminarians who rat us out to the College formators or the faculty if we skip class."

"Wait. Wasn't Judas a snitch?"

"Exactly."

"Hey, Scott," Brian interrupted their exchange, "did you see if Yvette's here today?"

"Yeah, I think I saw her in there." He pointed back at the lecture hall.

Lucy kept flirting with Scott while Brian hid behind one of the pillars of the colonnade surrounding the atrium, until the Johannine literature professor departed the lecture hall. The number of students had significantly dwindled over three hours of the professor's voice droning on at the same pitch, but there remained a small faithful remnant from each national group.

While it is true that the different national and linguistic groups tended not to interact much with each other, like with all rules, there are exceptions. Yvette was one of them. She was a short, slightly chubby, radiant young African laywoman from Burundi. She moved with ease from group to group, smiling and striking up conversation in a delightful mix of French and Italian with anyone who wouldn't run away from her smile. Brian waved at her, and she came down, beaming.

"*Brian! Perché non mi hai salutato oggi?*" Yvette's speech patterns were as close to laughing and singing as you could get while still speaking.[84]

"*Perché sono cattivo. E perché dovevo fuggire da quest'ultima lezione. Tu ci sei rimasta?*"[85]

"*Oh, mon Dieu, son rimasta, e mi sento stanca morta! Quando verrà le Signeur? Dimmi, quando?*"[86]

---

[84] "Brian, how come you haven't said hi to me today?" *Yvette's speech patterns were as close to laughing and singing as you could get while still speaking.*

[85] "Because I'm not well behaved. And because I had to escape that last lecture. Did you stick around?"

"Senti, Yvette, ti volevo chiedere una cosa. Possiamo parlare un attimo?"[87]

"Certo, dimmi!"[88]

Brian took Yvette out into the atrium where they spoke to each other in hushed voices. Lucy observed from a distance, while safely tucked into Scott's circle of friends to stay sheltered from unwanted threats of phony agenda driven conversations. After a few minutes, Brian waved her over and introduced Lucy to Yvette. She placed Lucy in front of a whitewashed wall and took her picture with a cellphone, then repeated the same process with Brian, laughing the whole time to herself, but instructing them not to smile.

Brian stayed for the fourth hour of class, and Lucy walked back up to the Janiculum hill. Gambetti was in the porter's office, but surprisingly, he did not look up at Lucy. He was wearing a brand new expensive looking suit, and was busy scratching away at a pile of lottery tickets. The resident TV lounge was just around the corner from the lobby. Signora Virginia Pironi, the ringleader of the mean girls, was standing at the doorway, eyeing Gambetti. She gave Lucy a head nod, signaling for her to come over.

Virginia handed her a large glass of lemonade with a straw and asked her, *"Hai visto quello là?"*[89]

"Sì. È strano. Non mi ha salutato. Lo fa sempre."[90]

"Oggi, sì, mi sembra un po' diverso. Anzi, molto. Secondo me, in qualche modo è riuscito a pigliare qualche soldo da qualcuno."[91]

"Perché lo dici?" asked Lucy.[92]

---

[86] "Oh my God, I stayed, and I feel dead tired! When will the Lord come? Tell me when?"

[87] "Listen, Yvette, I wanted to ask you something. Can we talk for a second?"

[88] "Of course! Tell me!"

[89] *Virginia handed her a glass of lemonade with a straw and asked her,* "Have you seen him over there?"

[90] "Yeah, he didn't say hi to me. He always says hi."

[91] "Today, yeah, he seems different. Very different. If you ask me, somehow, he's come across some money."

[92] "Why do you say that?" *asked Lucy.*

"Non lo so per sicuro, ma secondo me, guarda, è un tipo molto impulsivo, no?"[93]

"D'accordo."[94]

"Oggi è arrivato al lavoro con un abito nuovo, e non fa nient'altro che andare al bar ogni venti minuti e tornare qui con un mazzo di gratta e vinci. Un tipo così impulsivo non agisce in quel modo se non ha appena acchiappato per fortuna un paio di soldi inaspettati."[95]

"Strano."[96]

"Certo. Dobbiamo tenerlo sott'occhio[97]."

Martina, who was on the couch with two other ladies watching the T.V., turned around and yelled, *"Oh! Zitte! Cerchiamo di guardare Don Matteo!"*[98]

Over the summer, the mean girls had set out to watch the entire first nine seasons of *Don Matteo* — an Italian TV show on Rai1 about a crime-fighting priest in Spoleto — before the release of the tenth season coming up in January. By October they had only reached the beginning of season three, and had recently gotten much more serious about catching up. Virginia made a rude gesture at Martina, and returned to the couch, squeezing in between Martina and... Lucy only then realized that one of the people on the couch was not a mean girl, but Natasha, in a grey peacoat and a pink scarf, playing with mittens in her lap. Lucy's fist clenched, and then she remembered she was a detective. Time to play it cool. Natasha is my friend. But how on earth was she already so tight with the mean girls? And it looked like she was even getting resident volunteer hours by just sitting there watching TV. That's absolutely brilliant.

---

[93] "I can't say for sure, but if you ask me, look, he's a very impulsive guy, right?"

[94] "Definitely."

[95] "Today he came to work in a new suit, and he's not doing anything but running off every twenty minutes and coming back with a stack of lotto tickets. Somebody who's that impulsive doesn't act like that unless he's just unexpectedly come across some money."

[96] "Weird."

[97] "Definitely. We've got to keep an eye on him."

[98] *Martina, who was on the couch with two other ladies watching the T.V., turned around and yelled,* "Oh, shut up! We're trying to watch Don Matteo!"

Natasha looked up and saw Lucy. She got up, and walked up close, "Hey, can we talk?"

"Sure. You want to head upstairs?"

"No!" Natasha responded suddenly and forcefully, grabbing onto Lucy's arm. She looked around to see if anyone had seen her yell.

All three mean girls had turned around to stare at them.

"*Niente, scusate,*" said Lucy to the old ladies, then turned to Natasha, "Come here." They went to a love seat in the back, Lucy sat down, and Natasha squeezed in right next to her. Lucy pretended it didn't bother her.

Natasha still looked jumpy.

"Look, the mean girls have Don Matteo cranked as loud as it can go. Nobody can hear us back here, alright?"

"Alright." Natasha kept scanning the room. "Lucy, have you been upstairs this morning?"

"Not since I left for class. What's up? Is there another note?"

"No, nothing like that. I mean, yes, something has happened."

"Yeah?"

"I just came in — like — half an hour ago and went upstairs to my room and…" she gulped, struggling to say the next words "…and it looks like… it looks like somebody's just broken into my room and has rummaged through all of my things." She paused and breathed easier, like a weight had just been lifted from her.

"You mean somebody searched all your stuff? When was this? Did you see anybody?"

"I don't know what happened. I just opened the door to my room, and there were all of my things all over the place. So I screamed and slammed the door and ran downstairs. I've just been here camping out with the mean ladies watching *Don Matteo.*"

"The mean *girls.*" Lucy thought out loud. "So… somebody searched your room. But why? How is that possible?"

This was unexpected. Why would somebody involved in a murder fake a search of her own room?

"I don't know. Maybe it has to do with that bizarre letter."

"You said you didn't go into your room?"

"No, I've been down here."

"And you're sure the door was locked when you left this morning?"

"Dead certain."

"Has anyone else come down since you've been here?"

"Well, I don't know. I've just been curled up on the couch between Elena and Martina, staring at the telly."

"Let's go have a look upstairs."

"What if he's still up there?"

"How loud did you scream?"

"Very."

"He's not up there."

They left the TV lounge, went behind the staircase and called the antique elevator. The carriage, though, was already in descent with a passenger, Fr. Damien. He stopped, bowed and said to them with inquisitive eyes, "Much screaming this morning and banging of door. Everything is okay?"

Lucy and Natasha looked at each other. No, everything was not okay, but how do you explain?

"It's fine," Lucy answered. "Thank you, Father."

They traded places with him and got on the elevator. He walked down to the Greg and the girls went up to the servants' quarters.

While Lucy's room was usually a constant flux of items heaped on top of each other in uninterrupted movement, Natasha's was normally a static display of rigid and immaculate simplicity. Beige veneer rocking chair, white desk, white sheets tucked mercilessly tight on top of an iron bed frame, white carbon fiber desk with a white plastic chair, logical bookshelf — only four books — and not a speck of dust on the exposed tiles or the perpetually bare surfaces. From day to day, it seemed that nothing ever moved from one spot to the next. Was it a bedroom or an experiment in avant garde minimalism? Hard to say.

Natasha put her back to her closed door, her hand on the nob, and turned to Lucy. "I was thinking we mightn't tell the whole world about what's taken place here today."

"I won't."

"Are you quite certain it's safe to be up here?"

Lucy shrugged her shoulders, "Is it safe to be anywhere in this building?"

Natasha opened the door, and Lucy couldn't believe it was Natasha's room. She glanced up and down the hall to make sure they were at the correct room. It was the right door. All the drawers had been removed, and all their contents dumped on the floor. All of her clothes — mostly cold weather gear — were strewn about on the ground with the pockets turned outwards. The mattress was propped against the wall, the sheets in the sink. Her books were on the floor with the spines rent open. Natasha went up to the pile, picked out one with a blank leather cover, and held it close to her.

"Well," Lucy pretended to be generous, "Do we want to start cleaning up now or do you want to call the police?"

"Oh, I shouldn't think there's need to involve the authorities. I'll just have a glance through these things to make sure nothing's been stolen. I don't imagine I own much worth taking."

"It doesn't look like they took much, if anything," said Lucy. "Is all your underwear here? Maybe somebody's got a weird fetish."

"Or is it linked to what's been going on lately?" asked Natasha.

Lucy's mouth hung open. Natasha looked back with anxiety.

"I don't know," said Lucy finally.

"Me neither."

"Well, where do we start?"

"No, no, no, don't worry about cleaning. I've got it."

"It's really no problem. I can help."

"No, really, I've got it."

Lucy changed her approach. "I've been out all day, so I'm going to go shower, and make sure I'm real clean. Then we'll both sort through everything and bleach this place like none other."

She didn't wait for a response, but backed out of the room before Natasha could say anything else, returning fifteen minutes later with a clean white handkerchief over her hair pulled into a bun, and with the whitest socks she could find. There was a box of surgical gloves on the desk. Lucy helped herself to a pair.

When everything had been spread out on the floor, it seemed like a lot, but in the end, Natasha didn't own much, having just arrived a week before. The leather book had disappeared and Lucy noticed a keyhole on the nightstand drawer. Within an hour they had thoroughly scrubbed everything. Nothing appeared to be broken, and — Natasha claimed — nothing had been stolen. Natasha thanked

Lucy profusely and seemed reluctant to let her go, but Lucy finally escaped back to her own room, having convinced Natasha that she would be right across the hallway. Lucy reeked of bleach, was bewildered at Natasha's behavior, and felt disappointed at not having discovered anything in the room. She regretted her decision to feign generosity.

She leaned back in her Ikea chair and closed her eyes, looking forward to spending the rest of the afternoon doing nothing. But her eyes flew open:

"Security cameras. Gambetti."

Anybody else would have thought that this was obvious. She covered her face with her hands. Why hadn't she thought of this earlier? Well. She had thought of it, but those thoughts were so unpleasant that she had never fully permitted them to surface to the light. But now it had surfaced, and there it was. And it was definitely very unpleasant.

She curled herself up in her chair, already feeling gross about it all, but then she stood straight up, right on one edge of the Moroccan rug, and thought at herself, *No, I'll think this through. I'm a cautious and mature adult. I know my limits. I know I wouldn't do anything beyond a certain point. I certainly don't want to do anything beyond a certain point.*

She considered this, wandering over to the other side of the rug, debating with another part of her that was not happy with that reasoning. Reaching the opposite edge, she turned around and thought back at herself, *Yeah, you're a mature adult, which is why you're not going down that road. That's just gross.* This was true, and she nodded her head in agreement, staying on that side of the rug.

But something in her had to walk back to the other side of the rug. She thought, *What are you talking about? I never said I was going down that road, did I? Come on. Get your head out of the gutter. I just said I want to get close and see how he reacts. You don't have to be such a prude. You said yourself you're going to investigate, and that involves some dirty work, right?*

This was mostly true, but something still felt weird. So she walked back to the moralist side of the carpet and thought, *Yeah, but still.* And this was a hard argument to refute. For some gut reason, that *yeah, but still* was completely right. But the longer she stood on the moralist side of the rug, the longer she still didn't have access to the security footage, and this presented itself as a stiff problem as well.

She decided to give another hearing to the live-and-let-live side of the rug and thought, *Hey, so it's obvious to both me and you that we're not going to do anything too gross. Agreed? So why not just go down there and see what happens? Where's the harm in that? You've got nothing to lose.*

Before the moralist side of the rug got a chance to respond, she tore through her clothes and squeezed herself into a short skirt, a tight sleeveless top, and stood by her moccasins, wondering which ones were the most provocative. But another warning came from the moralist side of the rug, which wanted one last word. *Come, on Lucy. Don't exaggerate. If you go downstairs dressed like that, it'll be too obvious. Just be normal.*

The live-and-let-live side of the rug conceded. She put some normal clothes back on and headed downstairs.

As a method actor, she had to spend a few minutes in the empty elevator with her eyes closed, breathing deeply and convincing herself that bad things were good things. She forced a cool smirk onto her lips, allowed her live-and-let-live side to undo another button of her blouse, and hit the descend button. Crossing the lobby, her heart sank seeing that Gambetti was still there, sitting behind the counter of the porter's office. She took a deep breath, put her elbows on the counter and leaned over.

"*Oh, ciao, bella,*" he said. His eyes were flicking back and forth between Lucy and his lottery tickets, "*Come va?*"[99]

"*Bene. Senti, non c'hai un attimo per chiacchierare?*"[100]

"*Certo, sempre.*"[101]

She came around the counter through the door to the porter's office, and perched herself on the desk in front of him, slightly to his

---

[99] "Oh, hey there, beautiful," *he said. His eyes were flickering back and forth between Lucy and his lottery tickets,* "How's it going?"
[100] "Good. Listen. Do you have a moment to chat?"
[101] "Of course. Always."

right side, on top of his lotto tickets. She put her right foot up on the seat of his office chair, and leaned in close to him.[102]

"*Tutto a posto, ragazza?*"[103]

"*Ah, sì, più o meno.*"[104]

"*Che c'hai?*"[105]

"*Niente. No, alla fine, sto bene. Non lo so. Solo che ... solo che ... tutta questa faccenda dell'omicidio, eccetera, mi lascia un po' sconvolta, no? Capisci?*"[106]

"*Certo, Lucy, siamo tutti un po' sconvolti.*" He placed his hand on her knee, and leaned in. "*Se c'è qualcosa che posso fare per farti compagnia in questi momenti, mi fai sapere subito, eh.*"[107]

"*Sì, certo. Ma ...*"[108]

"*Ma cosa?*"[109]

"*Cioè ... solo che quest'omicidio mi lascia in tanti dubbi, tante incertezze sulla vita qua al palazzo, sai? C'ho tanto desiderio di sapere tutto, ma non so proprio niente su cos'è successo.*"[110]

"*T'ho già detto la storia dell'incontro del cadavere, vuoi che te la racconto ancora?*"[111]

---

[102] *She came around the counter through the door to the porter's office, and perched herself on the desk in front of him, slightly to his right side, on top of his lotto tickets. She put her right foot up on the seat of his office chair, and leaned in close to him.*

[103] "Is everything alright, girl?"

[104] "Well, yeah, more or less."

[105] "What's wrong?"

[106] "Nothing. No. Really, I'm fine. I don't know. It's just that… it's just that… all this stuff about the murder, and all that, it's just left me shaken up, y'know?"

[107] "Oh, definitely, Lucy. We're all a little shaken up." *He placed his hand on her knee and leaned in.* "If there's anything I can do to keep you company in these difficult moments, you'll let me know, right?"

[108] "Of course, but…"

[109] "But what?"

[110] "I mean… it's just that this murder has left me with so many doubts, so many uncertainties about the life here at the Palazzo, y'know? I really want to know everything, but I really don't know anything about what's happened."

[111] "I already told the story about how I found the body. You want me to tell it to you again?"

"No. Solo che ... non so ... voglio vedere. Capisci? Voglio vedere ..." she leaned in closer to his eyes and wet her lips with her tongue. *"...voglio vedere proprio tutto quanto che è successo, così com'è successo."*[112]

"Ho capito."[113]

"Allora, mi aiuti?" She put her hand on her knee and let her thumb lie casually on his hand.[114]

"Ho capito." He took his hand off her knee and leaned back. *"Mi hanno detto che le donne americane sempre parlano in modo meno diretto rispetto a quelle italiane. Ma dai, tu non sei per niente sottile. Comunque, vedo che devo essere molto diretto con te. Guarda. La video registrazione non te la posso far avere. Alla fine, a questo punto ... cioè ... sono passati già parecchi giornalisti e avvocati che hanno lasciato delle offerte enormi alla fondazione Palazzo Mortimer per aver quella roba nei mani – in contanti, se mi capisci. Tu sei una studentessa, neh?"*[115]

"Quanto vuoi?"[116]

"Il più possibile."[117]

"Dai, Gambetti, almeno mi racconti che cosa è successo nelle registrazioni!"[118]

---

[112] "No. I don't know… I want to see. Understand? I want to see…" *She leaned in close to his eyes and wet her lips with her tongue.* "I want to see what happened, just as it happened."

[113] "I get it."

[114] "So you'll help me?" *She put her hand on her knee and let her thumb lie casually on his hand.*

[115] "I get it." *He took his hand off her knee and leaned back.* "They told me that American women always speak in a less direct way compared with Italians. But come on, you're not at all subtle. Anyways, I see that I've got to talk direct to you. Look. I can't let you have the recordings. At this point… I mean… already a good number of journalists and lawyers have offered generous donations to the Palazzo Mortimer fund in order to get their hands on those things — in cash, if you understand. You're a student, right?"

[116] "How much do you want?"

[117] "As much as possible."

[118] "Come on, Gambetti. At least tell me again what happens in the recordings."

"Va be'. Ma non c'è molto da dire. La videosorveglianza ha ripreso questo tipo qua, Eugenio, che arriva alle 14:40, e poi esce alle 15:10. Poi, ritorna un po' di tempo dopo al Lobby. Lo incontra là quest'altro tipo coperto totalmente da 'na giacca e pantaloni di pioggia. Parlano per tre minuti. Uno spara all'altro in testa cinque volte. Si mette nel suo veicolo parcheggiato appena fuori la porta e se ne va."[119]

"Che tipo di veicolo?[120]

"No si sa. L'angolo della ripresa non ci lascia vederlo bene. E basta, dai, Lucy. Non c'è più niente da dire."[121]

"E questo tipo, Eugenio, chi era? Perché era qui? È parente di qualcuno?"[122]

"Ho detto basta. Di lui non si sa niente nessuno e non si trova niente nei nostri file."[123]

"E Ginevra? Chi è Ginevra? Non c'è una Ginevra qua in giro? Oppure uno che ha una parente che si chiama Ginevra?"[124]

"Ma cosa?"[125]

"Ginevra! Chi è?"[126]

"Non lo so, sei fuori. Ho detto basta!"[127]

And that was the end of the discussion. He scooted his office chair away from Lucy, and started collecting his lottery tickets from

---

[119] "Fine. But there's not much to say. The recordings show this one guy, Eugenio who shows up in the lobby at 14:40, and then leaves at 15:10. Then he comes back later to the lobby. There's this other guy who comes in after him completely covered in a rain jacket and rain pants. They talk for about three minutes. The one guy shoots the other in the head five times. He gets on his vehicle which was parked just outside and leaves."

[120] "What kind of vehicle?"

[121] "We don't know. The camera angle doesn't capture it. But that's enough, Lucy. There's nothing more to say."

[122] "But this guy, Eugenio, who was he? Why was he here? Is he somebody's relative?"

[123] "I said that's enough. Nobody knows anything about him, and there's nothing in our files."

[124] "And Ginevra? Who is Ginevra? There's not a Ginevra around here? Or somebody with a relative named Ginevra?"

[125] "What?"

[126] "Ginevra. Who is she?"

[127] "I don't know. What are you crazy? I said enough!"

all over the desk, even the ones sticking out from under her. Gambetti was indeed a man of passions, but unfortunately for Lucy, he was also a man with a strict Epicurean hierarchy of passions. He was only interested in her relative to other passions — money — and she had made the mistake of offering him a lesser satisfaction at the risk of losing what was more important. She wandered back upstairs, wondering if a short skirt would have helped.

At 11:00pm that night, Lucy left her room and walked towards the servants' quarters bathroom wearing just sandals and a bathrobe. She passed by the bathroom door, though, and peeked through the cracked exit door, to make sure nobody was sitting outside on the terrace. She looked back over her shoulder to double check that nobody saw her leave. She slipped out, hurried her way over to the triangle roof access door, and wound her way down, back and forth, on the steep and narrow servants' staircase, all the way to the negative one level, avoiding the elevator so as not to be seen.

Tip toeing around the basement hallways, she crossed through the giant laundry room, and walked up to the door behind the dryer machines that was covered in lightning bolts and several harsh warnings in Italian. Anyone who dared to open the door, it said, would be immediately electrocuted upon entrance, no questions asked. With her hand on the doorknob, she gave one final look over her shoulder, and disappeared through the door. On the other side, there was no sign of anything electrical or mechanical. It was the old basement servants' quarters: a hallway with ten bedrooms, exactly like the one upstairs, but with no windows. Back in the Palazzo's glory days, the female staff lived down here, and the men on the roof. Now these rooms were full of old things, all carefully catalogued, marked, and appraised with post-its written in Gambetti's handwriting. This is where — Lucy suspected — he ran an under the table antique business.

At one point, however, sometime after the end of the resident female staff, and before the remodel into a retirement home, someone had decided that the building missed one essential: a Victorian style Turkish bath. Lucy was the only grad student who knew about it, and she preferred to keep it that way. One half of the old remodeled bedroom had benches to lounge on and soak up the steam room functions, while the other half was occupied by a huge basin, that could be considered a small hot tub or a large bathtub. The stone and tile work had been done so well, that once you shut the door behind you, it was easy to believe you were really in the basement of an ancient Ottoman palace.

Lucy kept a crate next to the tub with just the essentials: a bulk order supply of bubble bath, a loofah, bath salts, soap and shampoo, candles, matches, a shower CD player, a waterlogged copy of *The Poetry of Rumi*, and a rubber ducky.

When I came in, I found Lucy's head surrounded by a massive field of bubbles, listening to Norah Jones, and smoking a *Marlboro Gold*. I grabbed the steam nob, just above her head, turned it all the way up, and sat down on one of the benches by the door, closing my eyes and trying to relax. Lucy reached up and turned the steam back down.

"Well, Blue Bear, do you remember last Saturday when you were getting on my case for not having done anything?"

"Yes."

"I've had a busy day."

"Did you?"

"I did. Did you do anything today?"

"Just the usual. I slept in. Then I had my morning nap, and my afternoon nap. I puttered around a little, smelling things. Oh, and speaking of smelling things," I looked at her cigarette.

"Give me a break," she croaked back at me. "It's been a long week."

"Whatever."

"You didn't hear anything strange upstairs in the servants' quarters today, did you? Like, in Natasha's room?"

"Did something happen today?"

"Did something happen today? Oh, let me tell you."

She told me the whole story, all about the unexpected ride to school, the mail theft (now, if I'm not mistaken, the second time in her life she's committed a crime involving the mail), the visit to the Greg and Starbucks, Luca Speziale's new job, the plan hatched with Yvette, the conversation with Virginia, Natasha's room being searched, and her failed attempt to seduce Gambetti.

"And to be clear, I wasn't really seducing him. I was just acting like I was trying to seduce him." She put out another cigarette, picked up her loofah, and started scrubbing herself. "Oh, and by the way, what do you know about picking locks?"

"A bit."

"So you can teach me?"

"I don't know if that's a good skill for you to have." I didn't give her a chance to respond. "So do you think Natasha did it?"

"It's possible. I mean, for sure she's involved. But I don't get it. What does she have to do with inheritance money? She would've been in the building at the time of the murder. She'd have had access to my rain pants and the rain jacket. The cops think it's a woman about my size. But why? I hadn't even met her at that point, and she had already tried to impersonate me in a murder. What the hell? I mean, it just doesn't make sense for someone to want to set me up for this."

"Does it make much sense for someone to kill someone else at all, with or without someone else to blame it on?"

She stopped scrubbing herself and pondered the floral patterns on the ceiling.

"Yes," I went on, "there will be a motive — inheritance, or whatever — but who knows what else is going on. There's still too much we don't know."

"And that's the part that's not fair, Blue Bear."

"What?"

"There's so much we don't know. Today I know twice as much as I did yesterday, but now I'm twice as confused about what I still don't know."

"Yeah, that sucks."

"Oh, come on, don't you have some sort of ancient proverb or something? Maybe like, 'Well, you know, Lucy, the willow is a tree of wisdom, but the Oak has experience' ... or maybe, like, 'The owl roosts in the heart as winter in the snow of patience.' Y'know. Shit like that?"

"Did you just make those up, or are those real proverbs?"

"No, I just made 'em up. But you know what I'm saying? Don't you have something wise-sounding to say to a poor young soul who's feeling all lost and searching for meaning in her life?"

"Oh, I don't know. Let's see what I can come up with. Hmm." I thought out loud. "How about this. Embrace the mystery. Live the tension."

She took the last *Marlboro Gold* out of the pack and held it just above the rim of the tub with two fingers to avoid getting it wet. She watched the small bit of tobacco that was visible at the tip of of the cigarette as it packed down farther in towards the filter when she dropped the butt a few times against the rim of the tub. Placing it directly in the center of her mouth, between her lips, she leaned over to one of the candles, placed the tip into the flame, inhaled deeply, held the smoke in her lungs, and then mumbled back, the cigarette still between her lips, "Embrace the mystery. Live the tension. Great."

I closed my eyes and sat there in the sweat lodge for another hour in silence, and woke up whenever Norah Jones stopped singing. Lucy had turned the steam nob off completely. She was snoring with her mouth wide open and her head perched on the side of the tub. I reached down into the water by her feet and pulled out the plug. She snorted and woke up. I chuckled and went back upstairs to my storage room.

CHAPTER TWELVE

SIAMO DELL'AMBASCIATA SUDAFRICANA

Lucy, Brian, and I came up the steps of the Policlinico metro stop a week later. But unless you looked at us very closely, you wouldn't have recognized any of us. Luckily, the Policlinico metro stop is the kind of place people try to avoid looking closely at anyone else. Of course, you wouldn't recognize me because, most of the time, Lucy's the only one who can see me. Brian and Lucy, on the other hand, are almost always visible.

Brian was in a black suit, a white shirt, and blue tie. He was wearing wide glasses — the kind popular in the eighties with a bar across the top — and was sporting a thick head of red hair, combed in a large swooping motion from right to left. He carried a briefcase and had a look of purpose in his walk.

Lucy walked slightly behind, with less confidence, in a black business jacket, a matching skirt, nylons, and shiny dress shoes that clicked at irregular intervals every time her heel struck the sidewalk. Her real hair had been meticulously straightened and pulled back into a series of braids ending in a tight bun, then immobilized with gobs of hair product to keep any of it from slipping out from under a very real looking blond wig, with a straight conservative hairstyle, parted on one side to form a perfect dome around three quarters of her head, ending at the exact point where it met her shoulders. The rich ladies at Palazzo Mortimer could sure afford some expensive wigs. Her eyebrows had been tinted blond, and she had special contact lenses with no prescription that turned her eyes blue. Brian's glasses came with a weak prescription, but Lucy's heavy pair of glasses, with thick and pink round plastic frames, were strong. She could only walk by keeping Brian in her peripheral vision and following one step behind.

For Brian, formal business attire was simple. He took his suit out of his closet. He put it on.

For Lucy it was not. Ever since coming up with her plan the week before, she had been going through another moral crisis, spending long sessions deliberating with herself every afternoon, walking back and forth from one end of her rug to the other. She knew she would have to wear business clothes, but had to fight all week to bring herself to buy something with a clean conscience. On Wednesday, she entered a women's business attire store on Via del Corso. The smile from the saleswoman sent a chill straight up her spine, and she ran out immediately, gasping for air. On Thursday, she looked down at the ground and entered a similar store. Keeping her eyes square on her feet, she explained to the saleswoman what she needed and handed over a note with her measurements. When she returned on Friday, she immediately accepted the first proposal, and refused to try anything on. She walked straight to the cash register, proffered a pile of cash, stuffed everything into a paper bag, and got out of the store as quickly as possible, so she could breathe again out on the sidewalk.

Yvette had done a spectacular job on their fake I.D.s, dangling around their necks from identical *South Africa World Cup 2010* lanyards. They were now employees of the Embassy of the Republic of South Africa in Rome. Yvette had even changed their hair and eye colors in their I.D. photos.

"Alright, there, mate. You ready?" Lucy asked Brian.

"That's Australian, Lucy. You're spending too much time around Andrew."

"Crap."

"Try again."

"Hmm... I don't know... what does Natasha sound like when she talks?"

Brian put his nose in the air, "Just pretend to be English. It's close enough."

"Okay. Here we go. Let me give it a try." Lucy corrected her posture, elevated her nose just slightly, and used a very breathy tone. "Hello. My name is Ms. Alice Kloepfer. This is my colleague, Mr. Ronald Lindbeck. We're from the Embassy of the Republic of South Africa. Would it be alright if we came up and asked you a few questions?"

"That's good. That's good."

"Really?"

"Not really."

"Dangit!" She threw her elbow and most of her weight into Brian's side. "I really thought I had it there." Brian's weight was such that he wasn't moved.

"No, you wouldn't pass for English." He turned his palms up in the air. "But it's not like it matters. What are the chances this lady can tell the difference between different accents?"

"Pretty low. But still."

"We'll just do all the talking in Italian. There's no way she could identify us as Americans."

We all turned the corner heading down the block where Eugenio Galli's apartment was. Lucy stopped and turned to face Brian.

"Listen," her voice was low. "You don't have to do this if you don't want to."

"Ms. Kloepfer," Brian was now using his own terrible English accent, "please do make an effort to get into character."

"Okay, okay." She put her face into her hands and breathed deeply. "Watcha! What I mean to say, is that if you really don't fancy coming along, you mustn't feel that you need to do this for my sake. I'm quite ready to leg it alone, if need be."

"I say, Holmes! Are you off your trolley? What are friends for if not these sorts of grand adventures, eh?"

"Ah, indeed. Smashing."

"Hip, hip, cheerio. Bob's your uncle."

"Splendid. Shall we?"

"Let's."

They stood up straight, smoothed out the fronts of their jackets, and strolled down the block with as much of a posh English attitude as they could muster. Lucy peered over her lenses to read the names on the intercom.

"*Eccolo qua, Galli e Spiga.*" She pushed the button and we all waited. Nothing happened for a good thirty seconds — which actually feels like an incredible amount of time when you're working undercover.

A light on the intercom came on, and a crackly female voice asked, "*Chi è?*"

"*Ehm... io mi chiamo Alice Kloepfer, e sono qui col mio collega Ronald Lindbeck. Siamo dell'ambasciata sudafricana a Roma.*" Even in Italian Lucy kept her fake English accent.[128]

"*Sì? E che volete?*"[129]

"*Se non La disturbiamo, vorremmo salire un attimo e farLa qualche domanda sugli eventi dell'ultima settimana.*"[130]

"*Va bene ... l'ascensore è a destra, terzo piano, ultimo apartamento.*"[131]

The door buzzed and Mr. Lindbeck swung it open, holding it for his colleague, Ms. Kloepfer, to pass through.

"Thank you, kind sir."

"My pleasure."

The door to the apartment swung open as they walked down the third floor hallway. From far away, Irene Spiga looked about thirty, once you got close you would say she was actually around forty, but the look in her eyes made her look much older. She held the door open, looking defeated, but almost, deep down, I would say, perhaps even somewhat relieved. Her clothing itself was its own white flag of surrender — slippers, a t-shirt, and jeans — probably

---

[128] "Um... my name is Alice Kloepfer, and I'm here with my colleague Mr. Ronald Lindbeck. We're from the South African Embassy in Rome." *Even in Italian Lucy kept her fake English accent.*

[129] "Yeah? What do you want?"

[130] "If we're not a disturbance, we'd like to come up and ask a few questions about last week's events."

[131] "Fine... the elevator is on the right. Third floor. Last apartment."

the best that she could throw on in the time it took her unexpected visitors to come up three floors.

Upon seeing her — realizing that they were tricking a real person, not an imaginary one — both of the "South Africans" felt a panic in their guts, and I knew that Lucy and Brian regretted coming. It's one thing to tell tales to an arrogant police officer. It's another thing entirely to present yourself dishonestly to a woman who has just lost her husband.

"Please, come in." She spoke to them in English — strongly accented, but English nonetheless. "Can I offer to you a coffee?"

"That would be delightful, thank you." Brian compensated for his embarrassment by feigning professionality. "Ronald Lindbeck."

"And I'm Alice Kloepfer. It's a pleasure," said Lucy.

Very good, this way. Italian architecture is usually imaginative, but you would never say the same about their furniture. So the impressive aspect about the Galli apartment was not just its very un-Italian open floor plan, but its even more un-Italian array of furniture, which occupied every available square inch of the apartment. While mismatched, it somehow all worked together, from austere modernity to Victorian elegance, from Amish simplicity to contemporary shock. Natasha would have hated it. Lucy wanted to move in. She lowered her glasses and her eyes moved shamelessly from piece to piece, the same way Gambetti's eyes moved up and down her legs. Her initial panic went away and her jaw dropped in a moment of complete postmodern harmony and bliss. Every eclectic contrast was exactly how it should be and where it should be.

"You don't mind Italian espresso do you?" Irene was already filling the machine in the kitchen with two plastic espresso pods.

"That's wonderful," said Brian.

Lucy snapped out of her HGTV trance and tried to match Brian's professional pose, fighting off the weakness in her legs brought on by Galli's absolutely perfectly furnished apartment — the same weakness that was also sometimes caused by proximity to Scott. She pushed her glasses back up. "You speak English very well, Mrs. Spiga."

"Oh thank you. There is no need for false flattery. My English is far from where it was a time ago." She placed two espresso cups beneath the machine's spout. "I am an English teacher.

Or, at least I was… um… eh… a teacher before the children came. They are away with my parents right now."

Irene turned back to the machine and Brian looked over at Lucy with worry in his eyes. Lucy couldn't see any detail of Brian's face through her glasses, but she knew just what that look was about. She smirked back and shrugged her shoulders. What are you going to do? That's a rough break, but we'll do fine.

They sat at the dining room table — a long heavy rectangle made of repurposed antique wood and old plumbing pipes. Two blurry shapes arrived in front of them, which Lucy assumed must be the coffee.

"Sugar?"

"No, thank you," they responded in unison.

"Mrs. Spiga." Brian's accent turned into a 1970's trendy Anglican vicar. "We were saddened to hear of your recent loss."

"We'd prefer not to take up too much of your time," continued Lucy. "So perhaps we should just get right to it."

Irene sat across from them, and Brian set his briefcase on the table, removing a folder and a stack of papers.

"We understand your husband had significant business interests in South Africa," said Brian. He set a number of forms in front of her, all printed in color on what appeared to be official embassy letterhead. "As such, in concert with local authorities, we would like to ask you for some more information, so that we can file a police report in South Africa as well."

Irene looked back confused.

"Here, of course, is a document explaining all of your rights." Lucy passed over ten pages of absolutely incomprehensible — even for native speakers — English legal jargon, followed by ten more pages of Harry Potter in Zulu, formatted to look the same as the legal documents. If you can present people with letterhead, sections full of unchecked boxes, abbreviations, and areas of 'Do not write: for certified office use only,' then people will trust you with their lives. Irene remained, deep down, defeated, but she became trusting in front of official paperwork.

"Well, okay," she said. She took the pen that Brian offered her, and got to work filling out the forms.

I took the liberty of searching the apartment. There were three perfectly arranged bedrooms, one of them with two beds for two young boys. The walls of every room were full of art, but there were hardly any family photos. One corner of the master bedroom did have photos, but they were all clearly full of Irene's family, not Eugenio's. Based just on the photos, you would think Eugenio only started to exist beginning with their marriage. Everything smelled just like a typical Italian apartment — a little more wood polish than normal, but that's about it. No blood. No drugs. No hidden piles of cash. No guns or anything even slightly illegal anywhere. Even the desk with their tax returns smelled honest.

By the time I returned, Irene had finished filling out the forms and had passed them back to Brian. Lucy leaned over, and peered at them from the bottom of her glasses. It was all filled out neatly in block capital letters until... Lucy stopped and slyly pushed up her glasses to look at the form more clearly.

"There is no one written down in the parents category for Eugenio," she said to Irene.

"Yes," said Irene. "He never met them."

"Was he adopted, then?" Lucy asked. Brian's silence grew heavier. He degraded from professional to uncomfortable.

"No, he was growing up in an orphanage in Varese, staying there until he came to University in Rome."

"Did he ever know who his parents were, then?" Lucy pressed.

"No, we never knew."

"Hmm. Perhaps you could put the name of the orphanage on the form?"

"Sure. Why not." Italians are very familiar with bureaucratic nonsense. An administrative insistence that forms be complete was not foreign to Irene.

"Can you describe your husband's business interests in South Africa for us?" Lucy asked Irene. Brian grew even more uncomfortable.

"Yes. His job was to... how do you say?... import?"

"Yes, import."

"Okay, yes, he was importing luxury furniture to Italy from Africa. So he was there, maybe, for a few months every year to look at nice furniture, traveling around with business partners to various of the furniture workshops in Western Cape province to search for popular products to sell in Italian stores."

"Very good," said Brian. "Thank you very much, Mrs. Spiga."

Brian gathered up all the forms, closed his briefcase, and stood up to leave. Lucy wasn't going to give up that easy. She wasn't quite sure why they had come in the first place, but she wasn't going to leave empty handed. "Just one more thing."

"Sure."

"What do you know about anyone named Ginevra?"

"Ginevra?" Irene frowned and looked at the ceiling. She shook her head and raised her shoulders. "Nothing. I am sorry."

Brian was already on his way to the door, so Lucy stood up and followed him. Irene was the last to rise.

"Thank you, so much, Mrs. Spiga," said Brian, shaking her hand. "Again, we're so sorry to hear about your loss."

"Thank you so much for your time," said Lucy, distracted again by the furniture. She lowered her glasses and took one last unabashed look at the perfection of beauty in the most well furnished house she had ever encountered.

"Yes, it is… uh… no problem," Irene answered.

Lucy returned an unfeigned consoling look to Irene, shook her hand, and followed Brian out the door. They got on the elevator and I took the stairs. It was all over much quicker than any of us had imagined. By the time I got outside, Brian was already halfway down the block, still in silence, with Lucy trailing after him from behind. So I left them and headed off to Villa Ada, a large park that I hadn't smelled in a while.

Brian and Lucy went the other direction, back towards the metro stop, under a pall of silence for three blocks. Lucy fought to keep up with Brian, who suddenly felt the need to walk quickly, and to throw his weight around more than normal. When she was sure they were far enough away from the apartment, she took off her glasses and her embassy badge, and almost jogged to catch up to Brian. He came to a sudden halt in front of the metro stop and waited impatiently. When she was close, he held out his briefcase.

"Here."

She grabbed onto the bottom and held it as though she was only going to keep it for a second, but Brian was already backing away.

"I'm done," he said. "I'm never — ever — doing anything like that again."

His jacket fluttered as he turned around and the heels of his shoes clicked away. It was amazing how so much angry weight could move so swiftly while balanced on such small and shiny dress shoes. Lucy lowered the briefcase and held the handle in front of her with both hands, watching the back of his suit descend down the stairs into the metro station, wondering what emotion she was supposed to be feeling after such a bizarre half hour.

Before she could come up with an answer, her phone went off. After just one week of smartphone ownership, the only people who had called her were in her contacts, a long list of just two names, one of whom was Brian. It was clearly not Brian, meaning it must be the other contact. She dropped the briefcase and shot her hand into the exterior pocket of her jacket. But it was not a real pocket — friggen' business suits! — So she dug both of her hands into both pockets on the inside of the jacket and finally extracted her phone, almost losing the jacket off her shoulders in the process. Cell phone amateur.

"*Dai, porca troia, lavora!*" she swore at her phone when she had to remember how to work the screen lock. "Come on. Just work with me."

Despite her derogatory words, a subtle grin of anticipation had already spread itself over her lips, and the tension of the last twenty minutes was suddenly a distant memory. She finally got the screen unlocked and … no… *cazzo*… it wasn't Scott. Who the…

"*Pronto?*" she answered.

"Hi, this is Cristiano Ludovici from *La Repubblica*."

"Yeah?"

"Can we meet?"

"How do you have this number?"

"Can we meet?"

"Sure."

"Can you be at Piazza Navona in half an hour for an *apperitivo*?"

"Sure."

"Okay, sounds good. See you then."

"Alright, *ciao*," she said, but Cristiano had already hung up.

Lucy dropped her phone back into her jacket pocket, doing her best to make it look like a phone call was something normal for her. She turned around to get her bearings, picked up the briefcase and caught the sixty-four from termini. All the way down Corso Emmanuele, up to the stop in front of Sant'Andrea della Valle, she couldn't help but think of the Galli furniture, trying to remember as much detail as possible. Piazza Navona was just a short walk away, but she took her time navigating the paving stones, this time without Brian's assistance.

From what I understand of human feet, in moccasins it's easy to feel the pavement or cobblestones beneath you and get around without having to look at the ground too much. In dress shoes, though, you constantly risk a sprained ankle on Italian streets. Roman women, although they can't run to save their lives, still manage to break the laws of physics by the way they skate around the city sidewalks in high heels. And what's more, they do so while sending texts, and yelling at the person next to them, seemingly oblivious to the dangerous streets, and never missing a beat. Though she was dressed completely in Italian clothes, Lucy was immediately identifiable as a foreigner by the way she walked with clear attention to the objects beneath her.

And below the cobblestones, a few yards still further beneath her feet, Piazza Navona sat upon the ruins of the large oval shaped ancient Roman stadium, that still mimicked its stadium shape. Contrary to popular belief, in ancient times, the venue had never been used for horse races, but only foot races, so on Sunday mornings — when the light was best for viewing monuments, when nobody in the city was awake, and when Lucy scheduled her long runs in the empty city center — she would always make a point of taking a lap of Piazza Navona.

At midday, though, it was packed to the gills with vendors dressed as artists hawking paintings, obnoxious tour groups taking pictures and buying paintings, and migrants peddling selfie sticks, laser pointers and authentic designer purses. One side of the piazza across from Sant'Agnese was full of expensive outdoor restaurants where important or rich people would sit and watch the world go by, somehow under the impression that the world was interested in watching them. Lucy took a seat on a bench right in the middle, in front of Bernini's fontana delle quattro fiumi. A young german couple asked her to take a picture of them. She pretended not to speak English, so they made sign language at her, and she said, "No, go away."

The young couple then thrust their cell phone on a tall woman who was standing next to the bench with a large camera around her neck. That woman looked familiar. Very fashionable. Lucy stood up and surveyed the crowds. The other two weren't hard to spot, stationed on opposite ends of the piazza. They all occasionally glanced over at Ludovici, who was seated at an outdoor café across from the fountain, scanning the crowd for Lucy. She put her glasses back on, straightened her wig, and headed for the Piazza's exit, texting Ludovici:

I'll be at the Abbey Lounge down the street. Call off the sharpshooters.

She pushed the frames of her pink round goggles down to the tip of her nose. Cristiano picked up his phone, extinguished his cigarette, and pounded out another message on his phone. Even when texting, Italians still talk with their hands. In unison, all three models pulled out their own phones, met in the center, and wandered away.

Cristiano left a few euros on the table and strolled in Lucy's direction with his hands in his pockets. As he passed by, she took out her phone and pretended to be texting. He didn't recognize her, and progressed down the narrow lane that led to the Abbey Lounge.

CHAPTER THIRTEEN

ANCORA IL GIORNALISTA

Lucy followed Cristiano Ludovici as best she could, which was not very fast at all. By the time she rang the little bell attached to the pub's heavy wood and stained glass door, Cristiano was already seated at a corner table behind a pint of Guinness. The Abbey Lounge was an Irish pub tucked away in an alley in central Rome that's popular with local English speaking residents. The place was mostly empty, but there was already a steady trickle of people in and out — those leaving work early, or taking a very late lunch. Within an hour it would be packed, and would stay that way until the wee hours of the morning. It was a small thing, but Lucy preferred to meet Cristiano on her territory, not his.

She headed straight for the bathroom, where she removed the blond wig and glasses, and did her best to put some life back into the compressed helmet of braids and hairspray that her real hair had become. She tore off her suit jacket, took a long look at the trashcan, but, just in case it might come in handy later, she stuffed it into the briefcase. Rubbing water on her eyebrows did nothing to make them any less blond, so she shrugged her shoulders at her reflection and went out to meet Cristiano.

"*Ciao* Cristiano. Sorry, I hope you weren't waiting too long."

"Not a problem."

"Lucy Fox!" a round Irishman with a black Dropkick Murphy t-shirt and three day's worth of gray beard stubble approached their table with a big smile on his face. "It's been a long time! Why the hell did you just up and disappear on us? Some of us were worried stiff and we were all beginnin' to place bets on when your body would turn up somewhere."

"I'm alive."

"Well, let's see if we can't fix that. You'll have a pint then?"

"Yeah."

He shuffled off towards the bar humming along with the background music.

"I like this place," Cristiano glanced around at the wood panelling and the laid back atmosphere. "I must be the only Italian here."

"Shhh," she put her finger in front of her lips. "Don't let 'em know. They'll kick you out."

"Really?"

"No, not really. As long as you pay, they're happy to have you. But you're not going to be anybody's favorite here if you don't speak English."

"I worked at an Irish pub in New York for five years." Lucy felt like kicking herself in the back. So much for meeting on my own terf.

"An Irish pub with Italian staff?" she said. "That's very New York."

"Very New York indeed. This must be a place that you expats keep as a secret among yourselves."

"I mean... I don't know if it's a secret... I'd just never thought of inviting an Italian here until just now."

"There you are, love." The waiter returned with a coaster and a pint, and turned to Cristiano, "Now, listen, do you realize what you're getting yourself into with this girl here?"

"I have a vague idea, but I'm not sure," he answered.

"Did you ever read any Patrick Kavanaugh?"

"No."

"It often occurs to me that we love most what makes us miserable. In my opinion, the damned are damned because they enjoy being damned." He wandered back towards the bar, turned around, pointed at Cristiano and yelled across the room, "Now don't say I didn't warn you!"

"That's Pete."

"Seems like a nice guy."

"Jovial, yes. Nice isn't the first word I'd use."

"Anyways, that guy Kavanaugh's wrong. *La grandezza dell'uomo sta in questo,*" Cristiano muttered quietly at his beer, more to himself than to Lucy, *"che esso ha coscienza della propria miseria. La vera dignità dell'uomo sta nella sofferenza."*[132]

Cristiano remained silent, and Lucy wasn't sure what to do with that, so she said the first thing that came to mind, "I used to come here a lot," she held her glass aloft, clinked it next to Cristiano's, and took a sip. "Too much."

"There are worse ways to spend your time. Here, at least, there's a good spirit, friends, nobody gets killed."

"Oh, there's spirits alright."

"In vino veritas."

"We're still off the record, right?"

"Of course. You know, I didn't imagine you as the sort of person to be a regular at a bar."

"I'm not anymore. I was, but I'm not anymore. When I first got to Italy, the roommates at Palazzo Mortimer were all Italians, so I'd come here late at night when they broadcast American sports, to argue with other Americans about football and baseball and fight over the remote control."

"So you're into sports, too, then?" Even off the record, Cristiano was always a journalist.

"Well, I'd actually never really been big into sports before coming to Italy. To be honest, I was just interested in a place where I could speak English for a while and feel like a normal person. If

---

[132] *"Anyways, that guy Kavanaugh's wrong. The greatness of man is in this," Cristiano muttered quietly at his beer, more to himself than to Lucy,* "that he has awareness of his own misery. The true dignity of man is in his suffering."

you're going to argue about something, it's probably better to argue about something totally inconsequential, like the Broncos, right?"

"I know what you mean."

"Or at least most of the time inconsequential." Every once in a while, Lucy would open up about her personal life to someone she hardly knew, and say things she would never say to her best friends. Cristiano had one of those calm attentive demeanors. When he looked at you, you were convinced he was listening, and usually he'd wait a few seconds before responding, inviting you to say more. Cristiano remained silent and attentive, so Lucy kept talking. "Do you follow American football much? Remember Super Bowl XLVIII?"

"No and no."

"The Broncos lost to the Seahawks, forty-three to eight. That was a bad night. That was a *really bad* night. I was too embarrassed to show my face here for another month. And then this summer," she shook her head, "the Rockies had one of their worst seasons ever. And this is the *Rockies* we're talking about, so it was *bad*. Anyways, I haven't been back here since July. I know. It's weird, but it's like…" she put her hands out in front of her, to grasp hold of an invisible concept suspended in mid air.

Cristiano put his hand on his chin and stared right at the invisible object in her hands, like he could see it.

"It's like…" Lucy explained, "all of the sudden… you're alone, you're in a foreign country, you've got no one to talk to, and then the most important relationships in your life become these random casual acquaintances in a bar, who are sometimes there and sometimes not. And the only thing I ever had in common with any of these people was a language, and a vague appreciation of football and baseball. And then, it got to the point that, like, the Broncos' success became the measure of my own self worth in front of everybody else, y'know? Is this making any sense?"

"You're much more European than you realize."

Before she moved to Italy, she would have taken that as a compliment. Now she glared back at Cristiano, having received an insult.

"No, really. You've been talking to me about sports for how long? And you've only used one set of statistics: Broncos, eight, Seahawks, forty-three. Everything else you said was in emotional and existential terms. If that's not the textbook definition of a fanatical Italian soccer fan, I don't know what is."

Lucy took a drink and resolved to be more guarded around Cristiano. "I mean... the point is I got better. That was a weird time, yeah, but I grew out of it."

This was true. The change worked in her just after Brian's arrival at Palazzo Mortimer is a testament to how much normalcy he reintroduced — or introduced — into her life. Of course, *I* had always been there, but an invisible animal can only provide so much emotional support to a human being. They all want human interaction. For a while the only place she found it was the pub, but now every time she saw a Seattle Seahawks logo her fist began to curl.

"Lucy, I wanted to talk to you about the case." Cristiano moved out of his soothing listening mood and became a negotiator.

"You didn't just want to see me?"

"Have you been talking to any other reporters?"

"Nope. I've been very faithful to you, Cristiano. Anyways, it seems like nobody knows who I am yet. Or at least nobody's approached me, and I haven't seen anything published on me, yet. I think that's a good thing, right? You haven't published anything, either. It'd be nice to keep things that way, if we can."

"For now, we can."

"Yeah?"

"Well, the problem with you is that nobody knows what to do with you. You're obviously innocent. The documents that you gave me prove that. So, as far as anyone knows, you're not interesting."

"That's great."

"Well, kind of. It's great for you, but not for everyone."

"Who are we talking about? Who needs me to be interesting?"

"Nobody needs you in particular to be interesting, but we do need someone to be interesting. We need a suspect or someone involved. The police need a case, and I need — " Cristiano abruptly cut himself off and left the end of his sentence hanging in the air.

Lucy's eyes looked at the ceiling, then focused in on Cristiano. "You need a story," she finished his thought.

"Nobody's made any progress on anything after Speziale was fired. It felt great doing it, but it really threw off the investigation.

We really should have waited to do that. Nobody at the station knows why he was fired, so they're all spreading rumors about you, and, in the meantime, nobody has touched the Galli case since last week. It's now a file that gets passed around from desk to desk. Everybody's worried about what'll happen to their own jobs if they get involved, so they all pass the buck."

"What rumors are they spreading about me?"

"Everything. They say you've got high up connections with the U.S. Embassy, or that you were having an affair with Speziale and the chief found out, or that you found out some dirt on the chief and used it as blackmail, or even — and I'm not making this up — quite a few people at the station are even going around saying that you're someone who can read minds and who talks to an invisible friend. Anything you can imagine, they're saying it.

"So you've been looking into things?"

"As much as possible, yes. But I'm a journalist, not a detective. I can only look into things to a certain extent. I can't get warrants and subpoenas. I need to work with people. But I'm not the only independent looking into things."

"Who else is on this? That *Corriere* guy you were telling me about?"

"No, no. That guy moved onto other things a while ago. The only other person I know who's working on this case is sitting right here with me." He put his elbows on the table, folded his hands, and stared across at her eyes in silence.

Lucy sat back in her chair, played with her coaster, and looked up at the ceiling, avoiding a strong urge to squirm.

"Oh, come on," Cristiano gave an encouraging smile. "You don't have to look so defeated. You've certainly had some moments of brilliance, but let's be real. You're still an amateur."

She rubbed the back of her neck and tried to smile, "What do you know about what I've been up to?"

"Well, nothing really. But based on how you just reacted to my accusation, I now know for certain that you have indeed been up to *something*. God, you're really an amateur!"

She sighed, put her forehead square on the table and wrapped her arms around the top of her head.

Cristiano spoke loudly at the braids on top of her head. "Lucy Fox, are you in there? Is this Lucy? Is this the same Lucy Fox that I met last week? What happened to that girl in the interrogation room? Where's the girl who outsmarted Luca Speziale himself and who convinced a professional journalist to blackmail the police? God, you were brilliant last week. Come on. Pull yourself together."

There were a few deep breaths from Lucy's spot on the table, and then a muffled response, "Can we start over? Can we just go back to Piazza Navona and pretend this conversation never happened?"

Cristiano laughed.

Lucy sat back up with a huge frown and begging eyes, "What do you know about what I've been up to?"

"Not very much, really."

"Really?"

"Really. Not very much.

"What do you know, and how do you know it?"

"Okay, this is all I know. I've only met you twice, so it's not a ton, but it's something." He sat up straight and put his finger down at a different spot on the table every time he made a point. "One. The first time I saw you, you had just been let out of prison. My colleagues — the ones you didn't want to meet today — have very good zoom lenses and very high-resolution cameras. You were wearing just a white dry fit t-shirt and close fitting orange running shorts. You had nothing on your person except one square shaped object in the front pocket of your shorts — an object with the exact dimensions of a U.S. passport — and one set of keys zipped into the back pocket. Then you got picked up by a limo — a limo that you weren't expecting — and taken back to Palazzo Mortimer. That's strange."

"You were stalking me?"

"Not like that... but... well... yes. Whatever, it's my job to stalk people." He shrugged his shoulders. "Second, when you went to open the door to Palazzo Mortimer you had keys for a Fiat rental car in your hand, keys that you didn't have when you got into the limo. Third. You were also wearing a jacket when you got out of the limo. When we zoomed in on those pictures, we saw you had a ticket stub for a one-way flight from Zürich to Denver sticking out of your jacket pocket — a ticket made out in someone else's name. Fourth. By that point, you also had something shaped like a U.S. Passport in *both* the left and right front pockets of your running shorts. I'm going to venture a guess and say that it was somebody else who wanted you to get on that flight, because I don't think you could afford that kind of expensive ticket and fake passport. It was probably the same person who provided the limo services from prison and did all the legal work to bust you out. But I don't know. Maybe you're rich. Your family certainly is. At any rate, you live like you're not. It's strange, but we don't need to get into that. Anyways, fifth. The next day, you didn't take the rental car to Switzerland and you didn't get on that flight, which means you have a strong reason to stay. You're invested in something here. Maybe even this case. Am I right so far?"

"That's all you've got?"

"Today I called you to ask for a meeting. You agreed immediately, but when you saw the photographers in the piazza, you insisted that we come here instead. That was probably a good idea. When you arrived, though, you blew it. You walked in with blond hair and glasses, and you pretended not to notice me. You went to the bathroom, then sat down a few minutes later across from me with black hair, and... if I remember correctly... the last time we met, you didn't have blond eyebrows or blue eyes. This can mean three things. One, you're just a very weird girl. Two, you're in some kind of witness protection program. Or three, you're up to something fishy. Let's say it's number one... well... Okay, it's true. You are actually pretty weird for an American girl of your age, but you're not *that* weird. Let's say it's number two. If it is a witness protection program, it's a pretty bad one, which means it's probably number three — you're up to something, and I have a feeling it's related to the case. Am I right?"

"So, really, you don't know anything?"

"I know something's weird. And I pay close attention to details. Anyways, whatever you've been up to, I don't need to know about it. I'm just interested in the fact that you *are* up to something, and I care about your willingness to *continue* to be up to something."

"And we've come full circle. You," her pointer finger came off of her glass, "need a story."

"Exactly."

"Why should I help you?"

"Here's the thing." He lowered the volume of his voice. "Most people spend, maybe, one to three years covering homicides before moving on to something else. I've been doing it for five. It's not great, but it pays the bills. I need a few more good stories before I can get a promotion, and I feel like this could be one of them. The time between October and Christmas seems to be the slow season for murders in Rome, so it gives me the opportunity and free time to do some investigative journalism. Lucy, I know you're interested in this case, and probably for a good reason. I'm asking for your help."

"But I thought… I thought…" Lucy's eyes narrowed and she shook her head. The chic journalist and intellectual had suddenly become human and needy.

"You thought?"

"I don't know… I thought… remember last time we met?"

"Yeah."

"You told me you help people because that's your business. You *stalk* people 'cause that's your business. You're a journalist and you need to write. You're — I quote — 'not interested in charitable work.'"

"Correct."

"Okay, so then why should *I* be interested in charitable work?"

"I'm not asking you for a handout. It's true, I'm here for business. That's obvious. You're nice, and I'm very happy to be sitting across from you. But I wouldn't be having a beer with you just because you're nice. This is business. But, look, Lucy, business doesn't exclude a certain kind of friendship. In fact, it demands it. Just because the motives of an encounter are not specifically for friendship, this doesn't exclude the possibility of that value emerging anyways. Haven't you read any Aristotle?"

"Go on."

"Forget it. No, I mean, the point is, true friendship can exist on many plains — even a friendship of utility. It's not the same as marriage or a friendship of people who freely choose each other out of spontaneous affection, but it's not something to be ignored. Even business relationships are true relationships. I'm telling you — yes, as one businessman talking to one student — that I could use your help. I'm laying my situation out in front of you," he put his hands on the table palms up, "making myself vulnerable to you, so that I can ask for your help."

She leaned in and considered his palms. "How would *I* be able to help you?"

"Can I tell you what I think of the murderer?"

"Of course."

"I think he's someone who has access to the servants' quarters on top of the building. I think he probably lives there."

"Or she."

"Sure. He or she."

"What makes you say that?"

"Well, let me ask you, who has access to the roof?"

"The *principessa* is the only one who controls the keys. She told us it's just us residents who have keys, and nobody on staff... and I get the feeling the porter probably has keys... and well... now there's this other guy from down the block who uses the kitchen."

"And that's it?"

"Well, the *principessa* has keys too, but she's been out of Italy for a while now."

"Alright, so eight people."

"Right."

"Here's what I think. It only makes sense if the murderer is a resident in your quarters. You've seen the surveillance video, right?"

"How did you get access to that?"

"You've just got to pay that guy in the porter's office."

"Can I see it?"

"Swing by my office some time. But there's not much to see. Eugenio walks in at 14:40, and walks out at 15:10. At 15:30 you leave. Then at 15:50, somebody else rushes out of the front lobby covered in your rain pants and jacket with the hood up. At 16:05 Eugenio walks into the lobby, soaking wet, but is confronted by the rain gear person, running in after him. They exchange words, Eugenio gets killed, and the murderer escapes out the door, filling the lobby with exhaust from his vehicle, which was parked right outside the door. At 16:11 the porter finds the body, the cops are there by 16:16."

"Sounds about right."

"That day it was threatening to rain at 15:50, when the murderer first left the building, but it didn't start raining on the Janiculum until 16:03. So here's what I think. The murderer needs to go out and find Eugenio. But just before he leaves, he sees —"

"Or *she* sees," interrupted Lucy.

"This *person* sees that it's about to rain, so at the last minute, as he's running down to find Eugenio, he grabs... I mean, this *person* grabs your rain jacket and rain pants, which were hung up on a hook, just by the open room door. And this person also realizes it would be a good disguise, so he puts them on before leaving the building. Think about it. It must have been someone who lives there or has regular access. Why would someone who doesn't normally have access run upstairs and break in, just to grab your rain gear before leaving?"

"I don't know. That's weird."

"Exactly. Unless they were already at the Palazzo when they left to find Eugenio."

"We found the jacket."

"You did?"

"Yeah, it was in a dumpster on Via dei Corridori."

"Are you serious? Those are some of the worst smelling dumpsters in Rome." He scrunched his nose at her.

"Yeah."

"How on earth did you think to look there?"

"Don't worry about it." She closed her eyes and shook her head. Cristiano didn't press further.

"Okay, so the killer takes your jacket, drives out to look for Eugenio, comes back to the palazzo, finds Eugenio running into the Palazzo, confronts him in the lobby, kills him, runs away to Via dei Corridori, takes off your rain gear, and then comes back to the palazzo again like nothing ever happened. Does that match the description of anyone's movements that day? Anyone besides you and Brian?"

Lucy looked at the ceiling and went through the list of her roommates. "If that's all we know, then it could have been any of them."

"But you see why I think it was at least one of them?"

"Right. But you don't think that it was somebody trying to set me up?" asked Lucy.

"Stealing a random jacket as a disguise probably had the added benefit of framing somebody else, but I don't know if that was the primary intention or not. It was about to rain, and your jacket was on a hook by your door. I think it was an opportunity crime.

Anyways, the *intention* of stealing the rain jacket is not what's important. The important thing is the *fact* that it was stolen, and the fact that it was easily stolen. Am I right?"

Lucy stopped to think about Natasha and Eugenio's South African connections.

"Am I right?" Cristiano asked again.

"I suppose," she narrowed her eyes and rubbed her chin.

"Well, if you're interested, I'd like to do some investigative journalism and find out which one of the residents it was. Are you in?"

"I'm in."

"Very good." Cristiano smiled, stood up, left twenty euros on the table, and put his hand on Lucy's shoulder. "I have to go, but you've got my number. I'll be in touch soon. Call me if anything comes up."

Lucy stayed, finished her beer and the half of a beer that Cristiano had left in his glass, and then used the change to order french fries and watch the Monday morning NFL report broadcast from America.

She was sure to wander out of the pub before any of the old regulars would show up. She wound her way back up to the Palazzo, thinking of Eugenio's furniture, Cristiano's ideas, and his hands turned upwards in vulnerability. Her dress shoes, the pints, and the day's adventure made her walk in a much more lackadaisical and contemplative mood than normal. Coming down the dark hallway of the servants' quarters, the irregular click of her shoes reverberated down the corridor. The light coming out from the kitchenette faintly illuminated the old prince's hair and smile. She hurried to open her door before anyone could see her in dress clothes. Life had been much easier when she didn't have to lock everything. She finally managed to insert the key, but no matter how hard she pushed, it wouldn't turn to unlock. She tried turning it the other direction and felt the bolt slide into the wall. It had already been unlocked.

"Is that Lucy?" Andrew's voice yelled from out of the kitchen. "Lucy is that you?"

She turned the bolt back to the unlocked position and slipped into her room just as Natasha's head poked out into the hallway. "I think it was Lucy. Hey! Lucy, you've received a letter. Andrew's brought it up from the mail room for you and he's got it here in the kitchen."

"Alright, I'll be down in just a second," she yelled back, before shutting the door behind her.

She was used to her room being messy, but what she found before her as she turned around was a new low. She reached straight for the pepper spray in her suit coat pocket (which she had started to carry everywhere on her person) and checked in the wardrobe and under the bed. Nobody was there.

All of her belongings had been completely turned inside out. All of the books, all of her clothes, everything. Absolutely nothing was in the place where she had left it, including all of the furniture. Whoever had conducted the search had been incredibly thorough. She scrubbed the blonde out of her eyebrows, changed her clothes, and walked down to the kitchenette. The important thing was to pretend that nothing had happened.

"Keep it cool, girl," she whispered to herself as she walked down the hallway. "Friends close. Enemies closer. Sun Tzu... or the godfather... something like that."

"Guess who's got mail!" Andrew was sitting at the table facing the door, grinning and holding aloft a padded envelope for Lucy with both hands. Natasha was at the table too with an Italian grammar workbook, a verb conjugation chart, and a dictionary open before her. Lucy had a dislike for people who insisted on doing homework in public spaces.

"Oh, thanks." She took the envelope. "I thought you said you were going to be down in Calabria today."

"Yeah, I came back to Rome this afternoon."

"What's in the envelope?" Natasha asked.

"Just some things I ordered off Amazon." Lucy should have just left it at that, but given the contents of the envelope she felt the need to lie. "Y'know, some hair clips, and stuff like that."

"Oh neat!" Natasha dropped her pen and sat up. "Well let's open them up and have a look."

"Oh... I don't know... maybe later," she said, and then reached for the nearest subject change at hand. "So how's the Italian going?"

"It's alright, I guess. It's coming along. We're still learning sort of basic stuff. Andrew's trying to help, but he doesn't know anything about grammar."

"My parents were both born here," Andrew defended himself. "The only Italian I ever heard growing up was at home in Little Italy in Sydney. It was way different from what she's got written in these books. If either of you would ever like to know anything about real Italian, though, I'm always happy to explain it all. Or you should just come down south with me some time, where they speak the real thing."

"Like I said, don't listen to Andrew," said Lucy. "He only speaks Calabrian dialect, and a few words in Italian. It's enough for him to get by, but it's always embarrassing to go out with him anywhere. Everybody thinks he's some kind of back country redneck or something. Don't listen too much to him, you'll just pick up bad habits."

"Well, what can you tell me about the subjunctive mood?" asked Natasha.

"I don't go near the subjunctive and the subjunctive doesn't come near me." Lucy backed out of the room. "Just keep talking to the residents. After a year you'll be up to speed. You guys take it easy."

"*Ciao.*"

Back in her room with the door closed, she picked up the office chair from its side, and set it back on its wheels. She sat down, opened the envelope and arranged a new set of lock picks on her desk, which, for the first time in three years, had been completely cleared off. She got out her phone and called the person who, as the alphabet would have it, had recently been moved down from the second to the third person listed in her contacts, after Brian and Cristiano.

"Fox."

"Scott, what's up?"

"Just keeping it real at Wisconsin night."

"Sounds awesome."

"Don't you dare insult my state."

"Hey, so what are you up to Monday morning?"

"Um… why?"

"Is there any way you can get access to the tower for me and three Italian models?"

CHAPTER FOURTEEN

PIOMBATO

On the next Monday morning at 6:55, Lucy left the servants' quarters with two sheets of paper in her hands. She crumpled them both up, and left one of them in the doorway between the terrace and the roof access door, and the second in the door that led from the fifth floor hallway to the servants' staircase. The main entrance is one of those heavy doors that usually closes itself by the force of its own weight after you let it go. But if you guide it back as it closes, it's possible to catch it and leave it barely ajar, so that the door doesn't lock back on itself automatically.

By the established 7:00am meeting time, she was constantly looking down at her watch and tapping her foot on the sidewalk out on Via del Gianicolo, one hundred yards down the street from the main entrance to Palazzo Mortimer, right in front of the North American College — Scott's seminary residence. Three Italian models with arms full of camera equipment towered over her, making smalltalk in the air above her, and sometimes looking down to include Lucy in the conversation. Her business jacket had been spared the trash, and she was back in formal attire, this time with less fuss. For his part, Cristiano had to do a lot of convincing to get the models to dress in normal business attire. Sometimes, he insisted, investigative journalism involves not being noticed. But they had their real names and their real *La Repubblica* press credentials clipped onto their suit jackets.

Their point of access to the NAC didn't show up through the front gate until 7:15, fifteen minutes after the established meeting time.

"Hey, what's up?" He gave Lucy a side hug. "Sorry. We had some random bishop show up for mass this morning. Whenever it's 6:15 in the morning, they always seem to think we're interested in listening to a drawn out homily."

"Sounds like you guys have it rough over here, don't you?" She pointed at the plastic bag in his hand. "You probably had to make your own sack lunch this morning, didn't you? ... Oh wait, no... You've got someone to do that for you."

"Hey, it's not my fault if they don't let us into the kitchen. And come on, it's not like you guys have to cook for yourselves over at the Palazzo. Don't talk to me about privilege. What's this?" Scott took a step closer to her — using Italian standards of personal space — and took hold of the press credentials clipped onto the collar of her suit jacket. Her heart rate increased, and her breathing became slightly irregular. "Marianne Medlin," he read, "Catholic News Agency... and a picture of Lucy Fox... why does this not surprise me? What are you guys up to?"

"I'll tell you later. We're late, though. Let's get going."

She introduced Scott to the three photographers and they went into the North American College. The Italians followed Scott through the gate to the campus and Lucy turned around to look at Cristiano who was stationed at the bus stop across the street. She nodded at him. He nodded back and set off walking towards Palazzo Mortimer.

Unlike Gambetti, the NAC porter was very thorough. He wanted to know who they were and what they were doing there. Any building with "American" written on it in Rome has to be very careful to filter out thieves and operators. Scott had to vouch for them, and say they were his personal guests, conducting interviews on behalf of the Diocese of Oshkosh, Wisconsin.

Once inside the grounds, the first thing that strikes any visitor is the size of the NAC. Compared to the other buildings nearby, it's big – designed by a 1950's post fascist architect to look big. That's not to say it's ugly, like most other buildings of the era. It has its own strange sense of austere beauty. Cozy, no, but not ugly. It's not home, but it's much. Scott used his key card to let them into a heavy steel side door. The group descended a series of staircases to a basement level with lots of piping on the ceilings.

"Okay, so pay attention," said Scott. "You wanna get from here to the top of the tower. Right now we're in the negative two level. You're gonna walk about a hundred yards down this hallway, then take a right. Just before that hallway ends you'll see an elevator on your left. Don't take it. Keep going until you see a hallway with a flight of steps. Go up the steps to the negative one level, where you'll see two elevators. You want to take the elevator on the right, because the one on the left doesn't go to the seventh floor. So take the one on the right up to the top. Then take two rights once you're out of the elevator to another steel door to get onto the old roof terrace. Walk to the end, and take the steel staircase up to the terrace of the tower, and another spiral staircase to get up to the roof. You got it?"

"Got it."

"Alright, good luck. I got to get some eggs at the Palazzo before class. If anyone asks you what you're doing here, just say you're with CNA or the Diocese of Oshkosh or something like that."

Scott said his goodbyes and left them to navigate the basement, the staircases, the elevators, and terraces without his help. Whenever Lucy had been a guest at the NAC – Thanksgiving and other occasions – Scott or other people had always been there to show her around the main levels. The deep basement hallways full of machinery and storage, lined with tubes carrying in American air conditioning and pipes carrying out clerical waste water, and the terraced rooftops with dizzying views were a whole different story without any help from a resident guide. The group was immediately lost. It took them a good twenty minutes to reach the top of the tower.

Climbing up one of the last set of steps, walking slowly because of a difficult tripod, one of the models asked her, "*Allora,*

Lucy, ci spieghi che cos'è che facciamo qua sopra? Cristiano non ci ha detto niente."[133]

"*Eh ... sì ... guarda, il concetto è abbastanza semplice. Noi, da qui sopra, possiam vedere la terrazza di Palazzo Mortimer là sotto.*"[134]

"*Okay*"[135]

"*Abbiamo ragioni per credere che l'assassino è una che lì ci abita."*[136]

"*Ma non ci abiti lì anche tu?"*[137]

"*Sì."*[138]

"*Allora, che cosa facciamo qui?"*[139]

"*Cristiano è l'unico che sta in giro ad investigare l'omicidio, ed è stato l'unico che sta pubblicando qualche articolo su ciò che è successo a Eugenio tre settimane fa. Tendenzialmente, assumiamo che l'assassina seguirà gli articoli pubblicati da Cristiano. Allora, Cristiano si metterà a sedere sulla terrazza di Palazzo Mortimer. L'assassina saprà chi è Cristiano. E allora, noi possiamo essere sicuro che colui ... anzi colei ... che lo riconosce è l'assassina. Capito?"*[140]

"*Sì ... e noi, che fammo?"*[141]

---

[133] "Alright, Lucy, could you explain to us what we're doing up here? Cristiano wouldn't tell us anything."

[134] "Eh... yeah... Look, the concept is simple enough. From up here, we can look down on Palazzo Mortimer's terrace over there."

[135] "Okay."

[136] "We have reasons to believe that the murderer is someone who lives up there on the roof."

[137] "But don't you live there too?"

[138] "Yep."

[139] "So then what are we doing up here?"

[140] "Cristiano is the only one who's been investigating the murder, and he's the only one who's been publishing articles about Eugenio and everything that happened three weeks ago. Basically, we're assuming that the murderer is following Cristiano's articles. So Cristiano is going to sit up there on the terrace of Palazzo Mortimer. The murderer will know who he is. Therefore, we can be sure that the guy... or rather, the girl... who recognizes him is the murderer. Understood?"

[141] "Yeah... And what are we doing?"

"Noi ci mettiamo qua sopra a filmare l'incontro fra Cristiano e l'assassina. Vogliamo vedere le reazioni di ognuno degli studenti quando escono dalla caserma degli studenti alla terrazza e vedono Cristiano là seduto. Lui avrà con sé un registratore di audio, quindi, dopo, possiamo mettere insieme l'audio con le nostre riprese videografici. La persona che ha una reazione quando vede Cristiano è anche l'assassina. Capito?"[142]

"Eh ... sì ... ma non sarà pericoloso?"[143]

"Io ho detto la stessa cosa a Cristiano l'altro giorno quando abbiamo parlato del piano, ma lui ha insistito. E alla fine ... dai ... se l'assassina è colei che pensiamo ... non penso che ci sarà tanto pericolo per lui."[144]

All four of them were out of breath by the time they summited the tower, and were greeted by an unprecedentedly beautiful view of Rome from above – even better than Palazzo Mortimer's terrace. They say that the NAC has the second best view of Rome, after the viewing deck on top of the cupola of St. Peter's Basilica. However, there are then some who claim that the NAC has the best view, because you can't see St. Peter's basilica from the cupola of St. Peter's Basilica. Then of course, there are further still who say, therefore, that the NAC's view is inferior to St. Peter's, because from the NAC you can't see the NAC, but from St. Peter's you can.

"Bastardi seminaristi" Lucy whispered under her breath to herself, looking out over Rome. (Although, if you ask me, Lucy's dislike of the place had little to do with jealousy of the physical conditions and more to do with the fact that most of the guys who

---

[142] "We're going to be up here filming the meeting between Cristiano and the murderer. We want to see the reaction of each student as they come out of the door on their way to class, and they see Cristiano sitting there. He'll have an audio recorder on him, so later we can put together the video with the audio. Do you get it? The person who has a reaction to Cristiano being there is the murderer."
[143] "But won't it be dangerous?"
[144] "I said the same thing to Cristiano the other day when we came up with this plan, but he insisted. And at the end of the day... come on... if the murderer is the person we're thinking... I don't think he'll be in much danger."

lived there, at any given moment, seemed to be happier than her. But that's another story.)

It was a beautiful and crisp fall morning. She was chilly with just a skirt, suit jacket and a scarf, but stimulated nonetheless about the prospects of doing real investigative journalism with a professional. They all stopped and admired the view in fresh morning silence for a few minutes, and then quickly got to work, setting up the tripods, and camera equipment and zooming into the Palazzo's terrace.

"*E quand'è che ci dovrebb'essere Cristiano sulla terrazza?*" one of the models asked.[145]

"*Ci dovrebbe essere già lì,*" responded Lucy.[146]

"*Non ci vedo nessuno.*"[147]

Lucy looked into the camera, which was zoomed in and focused on the terrace of Palazzo Mortimer. She saw only me, standing at the railing, looking down at Andrew, who was hanging onto the side of the building at a fifth floor window sill. Below him, on the ground five floors further down, lay the body of Cristiano Ludovici.

I had been woken up in the storage room of the servants quarters a few minutes earlier by something that sounded like someone screaming outside. I rolled over and tried to ignore it, but eventually curiosity got the better of me. I came out into the hallways and heard just the normal morning banter of Brian, Scott, and Natasha coming from the kitchenette. Walking outside, there was no one there, but I heard the voices of people yelling from down below. So I walked to the railing of the terrace and looked down to see Andrew flailing to get himself into the open window, and Cristiano's body with a few bystanders and doctors from the hospital all gathered around. They were all yelling and gesturing at each other in Italian, arguing about what to do with the body and with Andrew's legs still hanging from the window.

---

[145] "What time is Cristiano supposed to be up there on the terrace?" *One of the models asked.*

[146] "He should already be up there," *responded Lucy.*

[147] "I don't see anybody."

The door to the servants' quarters opened behind me, and all of the other students – Natasha, Scott, Brian, and even Fr. Damien – came out onto the terrace. Gambetti or somebody must have called from downstairs to tell them what had happened. Natasha glanced over the railing, then backed away, covered her mouth, turned pale, and stood there shivering. Brian stood at the railing with his mouth open, shaking his head, and looking out over the horizon. Scott started swearing to himself and pacing back and forth with his spatula still in hand. Fr. Damien signed himself with the cross, and went downstairs to bless the body. Andrew's legs finally slipped into a fifth floor apartment.

I set out to sniff everything thoroughly. I should have done so before everyone else got there. The terrace had everyone's smells on it. One chair smelled strongly of Cristiano, which must have been where he had taken a seat. I examined all the railings, and saw that they were all normal, except for the ground in front of the spot where Cristiano must have gone over. There were a few fresh black scuff marks on the floor from the bottoms of somebody's shoes. There must have been some sort of confrontation before he went over the edge – or rather, before he was thrown over the edge.

Up on the tower it took them a little longer to piece together what had happened. From their angle through the cameras, they couldn't see the place where the body was. They only saw Andrew climbing into the window and all of the student residents filing out onto the terrace, looking frightened at the ground, and then sirens as police cars rushed to the scene. Lucy got out her phone, called Brian, and looked at him through the zoom viewfinder of the models' camera.

Brian had started to pace back and forth with Scott on the other side of the terrace. He took his phone out of his pocket, and answered, "Lucy, where are you?"

"Turn around."

He turned around. "Okay?"

"Now look up at the new tower, over at the NAC."

She waved.

"Are you that speck of a person way up there waving your arm?"

"Yep."

"What are you doing up there?"

"Um ... I don't know ... I guess you could call it investigative journalism."

"Lucy, what the hell is going on?" his voice was very severe.

"I don't know. That's why I'm calling you. What's going on?"

"Can you see the ground in front of the Palazzo from up there?"

"No."

"So you can't see the guy who just fell to his death from somewhere in the Palazzo?"

"Holy Shit ... no ..." She gasped and held the phone away from her face. She was now breathing heavily and felt her legs start to give out from under her. So she turned around, gripped the railing, and slowly sank down onto the floor."

The models all stared at her with wide eyes, and she could hear Brian's voice yelling from the phone, "Lucy! ... Lucy, are you there? Lucy?"

She put the phone back up to her ear, "Brian, say that again."

"Are you okay? Are you still up there? I don't see you anymore."

"I had to sit down for a sec. The thing you just said, the thing about somebody falling down, say that again."

"It looks like somebody just jumped to their death from somewhere in the Palazzo, or I don't know. Andrew fell off the roof too, but he caught onto a fifth floor window."

"Shit."

Brian quieted his voice, "Dear God, Lucy, please tell me you're not involved."

"Wait ... no ... it might not be him ... what if it's the murderer? Maybe the murderer fell off."

"What are you talking about?" Brian had now separated himself from the other residents and was standing by himself near the roof access door speaking quietly.

"Brian, the guy who just fell to his death, I need you to tell me what he was wearing."

Brian walked over to railing and looked down, "It looks like a black jacket, grey scarf, and black pants."

"Oh, shit, that's him. Oh shit. Oh shit, I'm an idiot!" she was shaking her head and sniffling, and could no longer see clearly through the tears in her eyes.

Though they didn't speak English, the models seemed to understand what was going on. They went to a table and chairs on the top of the tower, and sat down, staring at each other in silence.

"Lucy, what's going on?" Brian insisted. Lucy's arms had gone limp, and Brian's voice was only faintly heard coming out of her phone from somewhere near her hips, "Lucy, are you there? Lucy!"

Brian stayed on the line trying to talk for another minute, but Lucy was now far too distracted and disturbed to pay attention to anything. Her cheeks were drenched, her chin was shaking with every breath, and the hole in her stomach had opened itself up again – a hole that was not just a sense of loss, but a gaping sense of guilt and responsibility.

Finally, after a few minutes that seemed like hours, one of the models asked, "*È morto?*"[148]

Lucy could only nod her head.

The model looked frightened, "*E allora?*"[149]

That *allora* was the first thing to bring Lucy back to her senses. What to do? Lucy could only stammer back, "*Allora, niente! Allora siamo delle ragazze più sceme del mondo. È morto per colpa nostra ed è morto in vano. Non capisci? Non abbiamo ripreso niente!*"[150]

"*Lucy, l'ha voluto fare lui. Non è mica colpa nostra.*" The model wagged her finger at Lucy.[151]

"*Va be', pensate quel che volete,*" Lucy responded. "*Per adesso ... non so ... per adesso ... non so cosa fare.*"[152]

---

[148] "Is he dead?"
Lucy could only nod her head.

[149] *The model looked frightened,* "What now?"

[150] *That* what now *was the first thing to bring Lucy back to her senses. What to do? Lucy could only stammer back,* "Nothing! We're the stupidest girls in the world. He's dead and it's our fault, and he died in vain. Don't you get it? We didn't film anything!"

[151] "Lucy, he wanted to do this. It isn't at all our fault." *The model wagged her finger at Lucy.*

For now Lucy and the models agreed it was best for them to take down the camera equipment and leave the NAC property. Nobody else at *La Repubblica*, the models said, knew anything about Cristiano's project. Whenever the cops asked, the models would say they went into the office like normal at 9:00, and Lucy would say she had been at class all morning. Hopefully nobody would ask around at the NAC for information or security footage. The models went down first, and Lucy followed ten minutes later. She removed her fake press credentials, and didn't look at the porter when she exited the property. Out on Via del Gianicolo, she just barely glanced to her right, one hundred yards down the street. There was the same sort of crime scene that we had found three weeks earlier. This time, though, she didn't go near it, but took a left, walked a hundred yards, and then got onto the number 877 which was miraculously passing by. She took another two busses to Sapienza, and spent the rest of the morning sitting in the back of her lectures, trying not to cry – and failing – and drawing cartoons in her notebooks to distract herself.

Before getting on the bus back home, she had to find a sharp rock and put it into her hand, so she could spend the next half an hour squeezing it while listening to rap music. Walking up the Janiculum hill, she inserted a few small pebbles into her already uncomfortable business shoes. By the time she walked up to the crime scene, she was perfectly in character and perfectly in control of herself. I was at the front door waiting for her. By that point, there were just a few bits of yellow tape and a small group of police standing around chatting.

Lucy stood by the crime scene tape and stared down the cops. They all got nervous and spoke very quickly to each other in hushed voices, shooting furtive glances back at her. But nobody dared look straight at her, and nobody moved to speak with her. Lucy could just barely hear the word *"strega"*,[153] repeated a few times between the cops. They fought with each other for a while until one of them finally pulled rank. A shy young officer had been chosen for the

[152] "Fine. Think what you want," *Lucy responded.* "For now… I don't know… for now… I don't know what to do."
[153] "witch"

unlucky job. He broke off from the group, took out a note pad, and approached Lucy, mostly looking at the ground. Lucy decided to play along. She stared right back at him, and convinced herself that she was the terrifying creature the poor young man believed her to be.

"*Scusi signorina ... eh ... Lei ... eh...*" the poor officer mumbled, "*Lei per caso abita qui?*"[154]

"*Sì.*" Lucy snapped back at him, and the officer almost whimpered.[155]

"*Come si chiama?*"[156]

"Lucy Fox."[157]

"*Va bene, signorina Fox, La devo fare un paio di domande.*"[158]

"*Avanti.*"[159]

The interview was incredibly brief. Lucy proffered her alibi – school – which he was more than happy to believe. She said she did not know anyone named Cristiano, and then firmly insisted that she would like to go upstairs. He immediately accommodated her demand and let her go, breathing a sigh of relief when she was a few steps away. The other officers folded their arms, stood up straight and looked at her through the corner of their eyes as she passed through the door. Lucy remained in character – confident and smug – until she closed the small elevator gate behind her and the box started to rise. She put her back against the wall and slid down to the floor, ripping her shoes off once she was seated, and leaving the pebbles on the ground. She threw the sharp rock that she had held in her hand onto the opposite wall. She pulled out her phone and edited her contacts. They were now back down to two.

---

[154] "Excuse me, miss… um… Do you… um…" *the poor officer mumbled.* "Do you by chance live here?"

[155] "Yes," *Lucy snapped back at him, and the officer almost whimpered.*

[156] "What's your name?"

[157] "*Lucy Fox.*"

[158] "Okay, Ms. Fox, I need to ask you a few questions."

[159] "Go ahead."

CHAPTER FIFTEEN

IL PIANO

She spent a while sitting alone on the elevator floor — quite a long while — waiting patiently for her cheeks to dry. By the time she arrived up on the terrace, her gaze was blank. She thought she had gotten it all out of her, but the sight of Brian and Andrew seated at the table in front of a bottle of whiskey was enough to make her break down again. Cristiano was dead, Andrew had almost lost his life, and it was her fault.

Before she could object, Andrew had already gotten up, and pulled her into his arms.

"No, Andrew, you don't understand."

"Lucy you're safe now with us. Nothing can happen. I'm okay too. We're all alive and safe. It's okay now."

"It's just that… it's just that…"

"It's okay now. Nothing can happen to you now."

"It's just that —"

"You're safe, Lucy," he interrupted. "You don't need to worry."

She saw no way to explain the real situation to him. How do you tell someone you were almost responsible for his death? Are you even obliged to tell him? She would need a lot more time on the rug before she could come close to figuring that one out. At least Andrew had survived and she could hold onto that. She wrapped her arms around him, leaned her ear onto his, and squeezed hard, holding him tight against her, glad to feel something human, something she had not messed up entirely. The longer she held on, the easier it became to ignore that pit of guilt in her stomach.

Andrew, Brian, and Lucy spent the rest of the afternoon drinking straight from the bottle and going over the day's events. That morning, Andrew had walked out onto the terrace, saw Cristiano sitting there, and started chatting. At a certain point in the conversation, Andrew stood by the railing — the edge of which came up just above his knees — and pointed out the Castelli region in the distance. He heard a door slam, and feet approach from behind, which he thought must have been Cristiano. Before he knew it, he was shoved over the railing, and hit the window sill one floor below with his feet. He slipped off the sill, but just barely managed to grab onto the curtains with his hands through the open window. For about a minute, he said, he heard a struggle and hurried conversation above him before Cristiano came flying down too. But instead of hitting the sill, he fell all five floors to the ground. After a brief struggle with the curtains, Andrew was finally able to pull himself up, and get his gut onto the sill and slide into the apartment.

"So then who pushed you over?" said Brian. "That's what I don't get."

"Well, they're saying that Gambetti is already selling the surveillance recordings," said Andrew.

"Yeah?" said Lucy. "Is he telling anybody what's in them or just selling them?"

"Well," said Andrew. "I chatted with someone in the laundry department who talked to someone in the kitchen who says she talked to Gambetti."

"Sounds reliable," said Brian.

"Well what did they say?"

"It's pretty weird," said Andrew. "All they know is that this guy, Cristiano, just waltzes on in, and then half an hour later these two massive guys wearing ski masks park their Subaru Impreza in front of the door, and then run through the lobby to the staff elevator."

"Bizarre," said Lucy. She started buttoning and unbuttoning her suit jacket.

"I can't believe they haven't improved security since the first murder," said Brian.

"Three minutes after they arrive," continued Andrew, "the big guys from the Subaru run back through the lobby, get in the car and take off before anyone even notices Cristiano's body is there."

"Did they get the plates?" asked Brian.

"Three minutes," said Lucy. "Damn that's quick."

"They taped over their license plates," said Andrew. "They're professionals, these guys."

The three of them went over the story again and again. Brian kept eyeing Lucy, seeing if she would tell her side of the story, but she couldn't bring herself to explain to Andrew why he had almost died. At one point, Natasha came walking across the terrace. They all fell silent, and Lucy had to hold onto the armrests of her chair to keep herself from getting up and pummeling her. Natasha looked hurried, and did not stop to chat as normal, but went straight to her room.

"What are you all dressed up for?" Andrew asked Lucy when Natasha left. "I don't remember having ever seen you in fancy clothes like that."

"Oh... I... I... we had this famous author come make an official visit to the literature faculty," she lied, pulling on the end of her skirt. "And a group of us were responsible for showing him around. He didn't speak Italian, so you can guess who got volunteered to be the tour guide around campus."

"You'd make a great tour guide, I'm sure," said Brian. "But don't you have to go to class every once in a while to know the campus well enough to give tours?"

"Lucy goes to class," said Andrew. "I've even taken her myself. Anyways, you look fantastic."

For just a half a second, Lucy felt at ease in her business attire.

"Did this famous guy tip his tour guide well?" asked Brian.

"No. Not at all."

"The bastard. You deserve it," Andrew passed her the bottle. "Maybe this'll make up for it."

"This'll do." She took a final swig, and retreated to the servants' quarters.

The next morning, Tuesday, Lucy stayed in her room — skipping class — until she heard everyone else depart for school. Then the two of us got straight to work.

"Alright, Lucy, so you've got the lever in. There you go. Okay, yeah. That's right. Now twist it just slightly and keep some tension on the pins."

"Okay."

"Now insert the pick."

"Alright."

"Do you feel the first pin?"

"Wait a sec ... no ... okay ... wait ... yeah, there it is."

"Alright, now count how many pins there are."

"Okay, there's one ... um ... wait ... No, that's the spot in between ... so then ... yeah, there's two ... three ... four ... and that's it. There's just four."

"Okay, go back to pin number one."

"Got it."

"Do you still have tension on the lever?"

"Yep."

"Now see if you can get number one to click."

"Alright ... let me see ... um ... nope. It keeps dropping."

"Okay, try pin number two."

Lucy squinted hard at the door, and struggled until her face lit up with a smile. "It clicked."

"Great! Now go back to one. Keep the tension on the lever."

"Yes! There's click number two!"

"Now try the third pin."

"Got it!"

"And four ... nice and easy. Nice and easy ... this one's the hardest ... just like we practiced."

"Holy shit, we're in!"

Lucy turned the lock and opened the door to Natasha's room, wearing the rubber medical gloves she'd taken from Natasha the day she had helped her clean her room. I followed her in and Lucy closed the door behind us.

"I can't believe how easy that was!" she was beaming. "Why have I never done that before?"

"Okay, we've probably got a lot of time ... but let's hurry just to be safe."

I set about sniffing everything. Nothing exceptional. A standard twenty-five year old human female. Lucy took pictures of everything and went through the desk drawers, the wardrobe, and the small number of books on the shelf. She found nothing of interest.

"Blue Bear, there's a lock on the nightstand drawer."

"Let me have a look."

"What do you think?"

"It's tiny, but I think you can do it. Try the number four pick."

She rummaged through her bag and pulled out a smaller lever and lock pick. This lock was much more poorly made than the door lock, and much tinier. It was easy to get the pins to click once you could find them, but there was not much room to maneuver the pick in such a small lock. On her third attempt, though, she finally made it. The drawer slid open, and there were only three items inside. A black leather journal. A box of ammunition. A small handgun.

"How the hell did the cops not find this?" she asked.

"I don't know." I sniffed all the contents of the drawer. "The only person I recognize who has touched all these things is Natasha. Or at least ..." I sniffed again. "Yeah, this gun is very new, and nobody else has touched it recently besides Natasha. It's also been very well cleaned — inside and outside — quite recently. Let's have a look at the journal."

"Is there anything in this room that hasn't been well cleaned?" Lucy asked.

I sniffed in the air. "No."

Lucy picked up the book and flipped through the pages. The first half was covered in Natasha's handwriting, and the rest of the pages were left blank.

"What language is this?" Lucy couldn't read anything.

"Looks like Afrikaans. Just take some pictures. We'll translate later."

Joseph M. Grady

Lucy laid the book flat on the nightstand, and took out her camera. Before she could take any pictures, a number of photos fell out of the back cover and onto the ground.

"Well, look what we've got here. Old fashioned film and development. Cute." Lucy reached down to pick them up, and saw that the only two people featured in all of the photos were Natasha and Eugenio. "Well, aren't they an adorable couple?" Lucy shook her head at the incredibly cheesy photographs.

"I don't know," I said. "She's mid twenties and it looks like he's pushing fifty."

She shot me a dirty look. I'd forgotten about a certain episode of her past that I was not allowed to mention. One of those unwritten rules.

She turned back to the pictures. "Oh, here they are are at a vineyard. Here's them at a restaurant. Here's them making out on top of a mountain. Here's them on the beach. Wow. it sure looks like Eugenio managed to get a lot of work done on those business trips, doesn't it? Look at this one. This is great. Even on the beach in South Africa she's wearing long sleeves and pants, when everyone else is in swim suits."

"That's fine. Let's just move on."

"Hold on a second." Lucy put the photos back in the journal, and the journal back into the desk drawer. She picked up the gun, opened the clip, removed all the bullets, and then took all the bullets from the box of ammunition and poured them into her bag. She filled the ammo box with a bag of marbles that she'd found in Natasha's wardrobe.

A door closed in the hallway. Lucy's face turned white and her heart rate doubled. She shoved everything back into the nightstand and softly shut it. She went to the desk, picked up the lamp and stood behind the door. Footsteps came down the hallway. They passed by Natasha's door and went to the end of the hall by the kitchenette.

"Lucy, we've got to get out of here. Whenever Natasha gets groceries, she puts them straight into the fridge before going to her room."

She put the lamp back on the desk, opened the door, jumped out into the hallway. As soon as she turned around a figure came out of the kitchen, and Lucy almost screamed. Fr. Damien shuffled by with a Mountain Dew and a plastic container of fried rice.

"*Buon giorno, Lucy.*"

"*Buon giorno, Padre,*"

Fr. Damien returned to his room, Lucy's shoulders collapsed, and she disappeared into her own room.

That afternoon I was sniffing around the spot where Cristiano had landed, not far from the main entrance, when Lucy came outside with her running clothes on.

"Do you have your pepper spray?" I asked her.

She glared back at me, the same way she used to glare at her parents when she'd be forced to put on a suit.

"I'm just saying."

She looked around to see if anyone was nearby, then held up her right hand and showed me the pepper spray. "I've been thinking about getting bear spray instead." She put it in her pocket, and started stretching.

"That's not funny. Bear spray is not something to joke about. And don't leave it in your pocket! A warrior should have his weapon ready at all times when in a place of danger."

"*His* weapon?"

"Whatever. You may have disabled the gun for a while, but that doesn't change the fact that two grown men broke into the Palazzo and threw two grown men off the roof. It's not safe for you here anymore. You can't just go walking around like you normally would under different circumstances."

"It had to be Natasha." Lucy thought out loud.

"What do you mean?"

"Think about the timing. Andrew said there was over a minute between both people being thrown off, and that the bad guys were only here for three minutes. It would be impossible for them to go up, wait a minute, and then come down. The two big guys threw over Cristiano and bolted straight back down. But somebody else must have surprised Andrew. Andrew said he heard *a* person approach from behind, thinking it was just Cristiano — singular. One person. It had to be Natasha. Who else would have advised her thug friends in the Subaru? Those guys had to have been tipped off by someone on the inside. You don't just randomly show up somewhere in ski masks to kill somebody unexpectedly unless there's someone to tell you what to do."

"But why would Cristiano just sit there for a minute waiting for the thugs to arrive after Natasha pushed over Andrew?" I asked. "He would have yelled or something in the meantime.

"She had the gun!" said Lucy. "She must have used the gun. She pushes Andrew over with the sheer force of surprise, and then keeps Cristiano at bay with the gun until the Subaru guys arrive. We already know she used the gun once on Eugenio. Obviously these two random strong guys who keep showing up in odd places weren't the ones who killed Eugenio. Those guys are nowhere near my size. That one was definitely Natasha. She used the gun to kill Eugenio and she'd be stupid not to have the gun pulled on Cristiano."

"This sounds very complex," I said.

"Life is complex," she came back.

"Remember Ockham's razor?"

"Oh screw Ockham!" she yelled.

"You're right, I'm not a huge Ockham fan either," I said. "Ockham can go —"

"I'm definitely right," she interrupted. "And maybe we could use it to our advantage." Lucy stopped stretching, and saw a plan forming in the air in front of her. "Do you think Natasha's the type to double check the ammunition before rushing off to kill someone?"

"Would you?"

"Probably not, I mean, at least if I were in a hurry, probably not. Natasha kept it loaded right by her bed. Sure, it was locked in the drawer, but it was still loaded. If we could get her to rush in, grab the gun, and come to confront one of us, all the while thinking that she's carrying a loaded gun ..."

"I think I see where you're going with this."

"We'd have to do it, like, within the next day or two, though, before she notices the ammo box is full of marbles."

"True," I said, "but don't you think that would be rushing things?"

"Well, you're the one who's uncomfortable about my safety all of the sudden. Why not rush things?"

"I mean, how sure are we about Natasha?"

"Who else could it have been? It has to be her."

"Let's go back to basics, Lucy. What do we know about motive? She was Eugenio's lover at one point, but then all of the sudden she shows up in Rome and decides to kill him, why?"

"Oh, I don't know," Lucy put on her sarcastic voice, "maybe because he was *married*! He was keeping her as a girlfriend on the side, down in South Africa. Then one day, she reads that stupid fairy tale — what's it called again? — *Under the Tuscan Sun* and decides to surprise him by moving to Italy without his knowing about it. She shows up, finds out he's married, and that's the end of that."

"But that has nothing to do with what we knew before this morning. You still have to explain the threat letter about inheritance, and the keys. What's that all about?"

"I don't know. I don't have to know. Maybe that's all just a red herring. Something Natasha planted so she could throw us off."

"But the keys? You're saying she planted the keys too? That's extremely unlikely."

"Look, Blue Bear, I don't know!" she yelled gesturing at me with her hands. Two people who were walking by on the sidewalk gave Lucy a strange look. She turned her head, and put one hand up to her ear as though she were talking into a cell phone. "You're the one who was telling me to live the tension, embrace the mystery. Maybe I don't have it all spelled out, but at this point, we definitely know enough to act on what we've got. We've got a gun. We've got an opportunity. We've got a motive. What else do you want?"

I shrugged my shoulders. Lucy started her phone's GPS timer on her left armband and hesitated, looking up and down the street. She picked a direction and ran up Via del Gianicolo, at a much quicker pace than her normal starting speed, maybe eight minutes per mile.

Lucy tended to do most of her thinking while running. She didn't like listening to music or the radio while exercising, so there's really not much else to do except think. She can be a somewhat difficult read. Sometimes she's an open book. Sometimes she's not. But over the years, I've learned that observing her gait is one of the only surefire ways to know exactly what kind of mood she is in. If there's a slight bounce in her step, I can expect a jovial Lucy. If she's dragging her feet, she'll be tired, cranky, and won't want to talk.

That afternoon, judging by her starting pace, and her lack of direction, I could tell something about the content of her mood and thought. She was clearly angry with me, not the sort of mild anger she gets when I annoy her, but the more gnawing anger that she gets when she knows I'm right, but doesn't want to admit it. She was probably going to spend the next hour convincing herself that I was wrong, and she was right. I've heard her say the most bizarre and irrational things at the end of her runs, but with deep conviction and certainty. It's amazing how people are capable of self-deception.

While she tends to run *faster* when she's angry, she'll run *longer distances* when she has something on her mind that she needs to ponder, or when she feels a great responsibility to get something done. Americans are weird. When something is wrong, they'll get to work on anything and everything, regardless of its relationship to the problem at hand. Any kind of work, even exercise, for some strange reason, is cathartic to them. Lucy is a great example of this. Whenever final exams come along, she'll go on long slow runs, not because she feels the need for exercise, but because running clears her conscience of the need to study. I do the best I can to appeal to the one eighth Cree in her. It's down deep in there, and comes out just faintly every once in a while, but it takes some effort on my part.

As she took off up the hill, I saw in her gait a mixture of all of those three things at once: anger, something on her mind, and a deep feeling of responsibility to get something done. A perfect storm. I went upstairs to take a nap in my storage room, not expecting to see her come back for a couple of hours.

And she didn't. She set a personal record from the front door of Palazzo Mortimer to the gate of the Doria Pamphili park, and then went all seven miles around the circumference of the old estate. Leaving the open space, she didn't return home, but flew down the Janiculum, a mile and a half towards Porta Portese, and got onto the bike path that runs alongside the Tiber river, which she took four miles upstream until Piazza del Popolo. Under normal circumstances, she's perfectly capable of going thirteen miles without feeling very tired, but given her lack of sleep, the previous afternoon's whiskey, two weeks of heavy tobacco use, and her exceptionally quick pace beforehand, once she hit the switchbacks leading up the hill to Villa Borghese – another spacious park in

Rome, slightly more frou-frou European than Doria Phamphili – her legs finally protested. Her pace slowed considerably and her breathing became labored. When she finally summited the hill and entered the park, she kept a sloppy form and a slow pace for a mile and a half. She looked like a local.

The footsteps of a quick group of runners approached her from behind. Middle aged Roman men love running in groups. The first to pass her, surprisingly, was a characteristically young American – with bright red hair and terrible form. Then two more Americans, and then, a pair of shoes approached rapidly from behind, very close to her. She tensed up and adopted a defensive position, clamping her fist firmly around her pepper spray. Someone's right hand shoved her left shoulder. Immediately, she came to a halt, and swung as much of her weight as possible into her left elbow making contact with somebody's firm abs.

"Good God, woman!" Scott was doubled over clutching his stomach with one hand, and shielding his face from Lucy's right hand, which was threatening him with the unused bottle of pepper spray.

"Oh ..." Lucy was breathing hard, "hey ..."

Another seminarian and something blonde ran by. Scott and Lucy stood there breathing, hunched over, looking and sweating at each other, until Scott said, "Well ... y'wanna... go... uh... catch up with the group?"

"Sure."

The group was moving fast, so they had to keep a steady pace to catch up to the other seminarians. When they got near, Lucy thought she recognized the blonde thing that had gone by.

"Scott ..." she breathed, "Is that ..."

"Natasha..." He quickened the pace. "Yeah."

It was a cool and crisp October afternoon, but for working out, everyone was comfortable in shorts and a t-shirt. Natasha, however, was wearing leggings, a heavy windbreaker and a headband. The group ran past a Roman family on the side of the path. The middle-aged father was standing there expressionless with his arms crossed. The mother, however, was making strange faces with her lips and doing a bizarre stretch. Their teenage daughter looked embarrassed. Her face turned to an expression of horror when the group of seminarians started to laugh at her mother. Scott turned to Lucy with a big grin on his face, but she only felt embarrassed for the poor young girl. She wanted to say something to Scott, but couldn't find enough air for a full sentence, so instead she just glared.

Natasha caught sight of Lucy out of the corner of her eye. She had been cruising along with a bounce in her step and chatting away with one of Scott's friends. She turned around, started running backwards and yelled "Oh, Lucy, I thought that was you!" Natasha's face became very encouraging, and she said one of the most insulting things that Lucy had heard in a long time. "Keep it up, you're doing great!"

If Lucy wasn't already angry, now she was livid. But she smiled back and waved at Natasha. (Like I said, Americans are weird.) So Lucy decided she'd have to keep pace. And she did for another four miles around Villa Borghese. On mile five, however, her legs, her lungs, and the previous day's whiskey refused to cooperate. She fell back about twenty yards behind the rest of the group. That is, until she saw that Scott and Natasha were talking to each other at the back of the group. They both laughed at something, and smiled at each other, and Lucy all of the sudden found a new source of energy in her legs. She started to bridge the gap, but before she knew what had happened or why it had happened, her left foot was caught in a pothole and her whole sweaty body was aching and sprawled out on the dirty ground next to the path. She instinctively pushed herself up, and tried to keep running, but her shaking legs refused to go any faster than a walking pace. Her lower lip trembled and her eyes felt damp. Scott and Natasha had stopped thirty yards away, and were looking back at Lucy and breathing hard with their hands on their wastes.

"Are you alright?"

"Just go!" Lucy yelled at them, "I'm done!" she yelled. She looked down and kept quietly repeating to herself while digging her fingernails into her hands, "Don't cry in front of Scott. Don't cry in front of Scott. Don't cry in front of Scott."

"Are you sure?" Natasha asked.

"Just go!"

Scott and Natasha turned around and took off. Lucy walked in small circles around a tree for a minute. She wiped off a couple of tears from her cheeks that she hadn't managed to suppress, and then collapsed onto a park bench to send a WhatsApp message.

> Brian, what are you doing? I really need your help to plan some things tonight.

> Hey Lucy. Sorry. Cant make it 2nite. i have 2 work. i have really good news tho.

"Whatever," Lucy said to herself standing back up. "This ends tomorrow."

She took public transportation back home. The metro and the bus were crowded. Normally Italian men are all too happy to have an excuse to stand or sit right next to Lucy. That afternoon, however, she found that she had more than enough personal space. There's at least one advantage to being covered in dirt and sweat.

Walking up the Janiculum hill, she spotted a large familiar figure coming down the hill towards her. He was not dressed for clowning though, but was wearing dress shoes, a white collared shirt, and khaki pants.

"What the hell happened to you?" Brian stopped to ask her.

"Don't worry about it. I had an intense run."

"Looks like it." He took off his backpack and held it in front of him. "Guess who got a job!"

She didn't answer.

"Oh come on, guess."

"Andrew?"

"No! Me!"

"You've already got a job."

"No, but a real job."

"Well, that's cool I guess."

"That's not just cool, that's great." He pulled a green apron out of his backpack and smiled.

Lucy just looked back at him.

"What do you think?"

"I don't know. I like green."

"No, look closer."

In the middle of the apron there was a small circular logo: white block letters surrounding a siren. Lucy's eyes turned to pity, "Oh, God, no."

"What?"

"You can't work at that place. This is terrible. You've got a great job already."

"What are you talking about? I loved working at Starbucks in America. Best job I ever had. Plus now I'll have regular hours."

"Just because something is enjoyable doesn't make it right." And then she remembered another reason he shouldn't work there, "But Brian, no, you *can't* work there! What about Speziale?"

"I thought of that too. Now we'll have someone to keep an eye on him."

"No, Brian," she was begging now. "Whose team are you on? I told you that I need your help tonight."

Brian got serious too, "I told you what I think of helping you with ... you know ... helping you with – "

"Brian, I promise, you don't need to lie or anything. I just *need* your help. I can't do this alone. And this is it, Brian. This is gonna be the last thing."

Brian looked away, "Lucy, just promise me you're not gonna do anything to put yourself in danger."

"I won't if you're there."

"Lucy."

"Okay, I won't."

"Do you promise?"

"Do you promise to skip class and be around tomorrow morning?"

"Sure."

"Alright, then I promise."

"You know they've got a lot of new security measures at the Palazzo, right? Don't try anything stupid, okay?"

"Don't worry. I've met all the new, like, security guys or whatever they are."

"Still."

"And there's, like, a whole bunch of cameras and two security guards on duty twenty-four seven. Stop worrying. The Palazzo is safe now, Brian. And the murderer ... well ... if she can surprise us, she's dangerous. But she's not going to surprise us. We're going to surprise her, and cut her off from her strong friends."

Brian sighed, "The Palazzo is safer than it used to be, maybe. But you have to be smart too. Just be safe, Lucy." He looked her square in the eyes, and Lucy looked away, "Look, Lucy, I just don't want you to get hurt or anything. Or worse."

"Don't worry," she was already walking past him up the Janiculum. "Have fun at work. Say 'hello' to Speziale for me."

"Lucy!" Brian yelled after her, but she kept walking.

"Don't worry!" she yelled back.

He stood on the hill wondering whether or not he should go to work. He looked at the siren on the apron, at Lucy's back disappearing up the hill, and back at the apron. He shoved the apron in his backpack and headed down the hill.

CHAPTER SIXTEEN

IL BAGNO TURCHESE E LA PISTOLA

Lucy herself got to work that evening too. It took her several hours to cut out letters of the newspaper and glue them onto a threat letter. She snuck down to the basement servants' quarters and prepared a trap in one of the old bedrooms, complete with a place to hide her cell phone to film the whole scene, and handcuffs to detain the murderer once they'd gotten her to confess. It was all set to be used the following morning. She wrote and rewrote her whole plan on a bunch of different pages of paper, connected with a huge system of arrows representing contingencies and back up plans. Brian would receive a copy too, so that they could review it the following morning. It was foolproof.

I raised all of my objections that night over an hour of tense conversation in the Turkish bath. She wouldn't hear any of it, though, so I left and went to sleep in my storage room. Lucy stayed in the bath, knowing she wasn't going to sleep. Once I left, she turned on the steam, opened the drain, let the hot water run for a while, added more bubble bath solution, returned the plug to the drain, and turned off the water. She started the whale song CD, and laid her head back on the rim of the tub, closing her eyes and stretching her sore legs to the end of the basin.

The door opened and closed again, and Lucy thought she heard me enter the room. Without even opening her eyes, she immediately launched into me, completely sure that there was nothing that could go wrong. "Blue Bear. Look. We've gone over it how many times by now? I do not want to talk about it again, alright? What the hell could go wrong? She's one stupid and impulsive blonde girl with an empty gun against two strong Americans. End of story. I know how that one ends. Just leave me alone and let me relax tonight."

"Who the hell do you think you're talking to?" a young female voice with a South African accent asked her.

Lucy's heart went from nothing to pounding in no time. Her eyes flew open, and she found herself completely frozen and motionless while staring down the barrel of a gun.

"No really," Natasha asked. "Who the hell were you talking to?"

Lucy tried to respond, but she was only able to open her mouth and make a squeek, not unlike the whales on the CD.

"Put these on. Attach one end to the water knob, and another to your wrist." Natasha threw something into the water and a couple small pieces of metal fell on Lucy's legs.

Lucy didn't move.

"I said put them on!" Natasha yelled, wagging the gun at her.

Lucy fumbled around with the metal object, and finally understood that they were the handcuffs that she had prepared for the next morning in the trap room across the hallway. She grappled around in the water for a while, unable to work quickly under so much stress and confusion.

"Hurry!"

Lucy whimpered and started breathing very quickly. She finally managed to attach her right wrist to the cuffs, and then, after much shaking, to wrap the other end of the handcuffs around the hot water knob next to the spigot. She pushed the cuff closed, locking herself to the tub, and another thought crossed her mind. *The bullets. The gun's empty. I'm an idiot.* She squinted and looked straight at the gun. Natasha seemed to understand why.

"Don't think this isn't loaded. I know you broke into my room today and tried to unload all the bullets."

Her heart accelerated again.

"I want to know," Natasha stepped back and sat down facing Lucy on the tile bench that surrounded the edge of the room where I normally sit. She set the gun down on the bench, but kept her hand right next to it. "I want to know two things. I want to know why you killed Eugenio and I want to know why I shouldn't kill you."

Lucy was confused by the first question, so she decided to focus on the second one. "There's no way you can kill me and not get caught. The security guards will hear the gunfire. The new cameras already show you coming down here. Do you really want to kill me, try to outrun the two guards and the police, and become a fugitive right now?"

"Nobody ever comes down here. This gun isn't that loud. If I felt I needed to, I could be in Africa for a week before anyone discovers your body. But anyways," she held up her hands, which had rubber gloves on them, "I reckon that I needn't leave Italy at all. There's no indication they would be capable of tracing your death to me. You somehow managed to off two people and the Italian police are none the wiser. I imagine I could do significantly better."

"The cameras, though."

"They've installed twelve new cameras. None of which covers the path from the roof, and down the servants' staircase to here. Nobody knows you're here, nobody knows I'm here, and nobody will see me leave."

Lucy started grasping at straws, "The stench, though. Someone will smell the body."

"There are hundreds of liters of bleach in the laundry room, and your body is already conveniently placed in a bathtub. I promise, your carcass will be quite nicely preserved, and ready for repatriation whenever they find you. But you failed to respond to my first question, the question your life depends on. Why did you kill Eugenio?"

Lucy just shook her head with her mouth open.

"Why?" Natasha yelled, picking the gun back up.

"I didn't" Lucy croaked. "*You* did. You're the only one who could have killed him."

"I know it was you, you bastard. I know you were arrested for it, but your lawyers got you off the hook. And I know you weren't inside the servants' quarters when Andrew and that poor reporter got thrown from the roof. You don't have to play stupid with me. I don't need a reason to kill you, I need a reason *not* to kill you, and you're not giving it to me."

"Go up in my room. There's a whole package of information with a foolproof alibi. I promise."

"I'm not going to fall for that sort of trick. I've seen the security footage myself. I saw you kill him. And why should I trust any documents you have, Lucy? Or should I call you..." Natasha reached into her pocket, took out Lucy's fake U.S. passport, read the name, and threw it on the floor, "Emily Green?"

"I can explain that."

"Or is it..." Natasha took out Lucy's fake press credentials, read the name and threw it next to the fake passport, "Marianne Medlin?"

"That one ... that one can also be explained."

"Or is it ..." she pulled out the lanyard with the South African Embassy I.D., and dangled it in the air, "Alice Kloepfer?"

"Okay, so I can see why those are a little confusing, but they can all be explained."

"It's also interesting. My phone stopped working this evening, and then I found the battery in your desk drawer. I wonder how that got there."

"Well, I wasn't going to let you call your Subaru friends."

"My what? Never mind, Lucy – or whoever the hell you are – it's quite clear to anyone that you're full of shit. So just cut it out and explain to me why you killed Eugenio. I saw the security footage. Just tell me why!"

"You saw someone wearing my raincoat killing Eugenio." And then Lucy decided she didn't want to play this game anymore. "What the hell am I talking about? If you saw the security footage, then you saw *yourself* killing Eugenio. I don't know if you're crazy and don't remember, or what, but that's what happened. Look, I get it. You've got a gun pointed at me. I understand you've had a couple of crazy weeks. But you don't have to play innocent with me. At this point, it really doesn't look like you're in danger of getting caught – especially not by me. If you're, like, really looking for information from me, use the truth as your starting point, and stop asking me bullshit questions with premises that you yourself know aren't true."

Natasha set the gun down and stared at the wall above Lucy. "Alright, let's talk truth. Were you sleeping with him?"

"With who?"

"With *whom*?" Natasha corrected her.

Lucy looked from side to side, not seeing the value in a grammar lesson at such a time. Natasha continued. "With Eugenio. You got jealous when you found out about me, and decided to kill him, didn't you? Was he sleeping with you too?"

"I wasn't sleeping with him! I never knew who he was. And what do you mean *you too*?" Lucy looked up and stared straight at Natasha, "So you admit it, then? *You* were having an affair with him. Or at least, come on, that's obvious from all those cute photos you've got in your journal."

"Lucy, don't you understand? I'm the one with the firearm. You need to answer my questions, or you're going to die."

"And you didn't tell the cops about your relationship, did you? Sounds like you've got something to hide."

"Lucy, do try to understand. I'm threatening to *murder* you! I should think it's only in your best interest to respond to my questioning."

"I am answering your questions. I told you I wasn't sleeping with him. But don't you get it? It looks like I'm about to be a murder victim, and you're about to become a murderer ... again. What've I got to lose by speaking my mind? Doesn't the victim have a right to ask a few questions? And shouldn't a potential murderer take some time to figure out what's going on?"

"You're no victim." And Natasha added in a very unconvincing tone of voice, "If I kill you, it'll be revenge."

"Look, here's what's gonna happen. You can do one of two things. You can choose not to kill me, and then go look at my alibi, and realize that not killing me was a good idea. Or you can kill me, and then let curiosity get the better of you, look at my alibi, and come to the painful realization that you killed an innocent person. Not that you'd care, though."

Natasha folded her arms and stared at Lucy for a minute. Lucy stared back. The whale song CD continued. Lucy kept her shoulders as still as possible, while searching around under the waterline and bubbles with her free hand and her feet for anything she could use to help her. There was a rubber ducky, a rubber plug in the drain, a bar of soap, and a loofah. Nothing. Completely and totally trapped. Her only hope was to stare back and convince Natasha not to kill her.

"Alright, let's try to make a fresh start," proposed Natasha. "From the top."

"Let's."

"But I must insist on one thing. Do please keep in mind that I am the one wielding the gun."

"As long as you can keep in mind that I'm the one whose life is at stake."

"That's quite fair." Natasha extracted some papers out of the pocket of her coat. "There are a number of items which I've found on your desk that require an explanation."

"So you're the one who searched my room?"

"This evening, yes."

"And last week?"

"Last week?" Natasha looked in the air. "Not at all. But you have little reason to act so offended. I have photographs of you breaking into my room this morning."

"Really?"

"Yes, after your first break-in two weeks ago, I purchased a game camera."

"A what?"

"Aren't you a hunter? Remember, slaughtering bison for your moccasins?"

"No, that was just ... nevermind."

"I know. I can understand sarcasm. Apparently you can't. Anyways, a game camera is a device used by hunters with a motion sensor that takes a picture of animals every time one walks by. It works well to track animals, so I'm not surprised it managed to work on you as well."

"Oh," Lucy's eyes lit up. "That's what that thing was on the bookshelf. I was wondering. But seriously, though, that first break-in wasn't me."

"Indeed." Natasha unfolded the papers. "Well then how on earth am I to understand these?" She showed Lucy the threat letter made from the letters cut out from the newspaper that Lucy had prepared that evening, "And these," she had also stolen Lucy's elaborate plans to lure Natasha down to the basement the following morning and into a trap in the old bedroom across from the Turkish bath.

"That letter's not real. Or, I mean, yeah, it's a real anonymous letter, but I'm not the one who sent that first letter. I thought you were the one who sent that first anonymous letter from 'the true heirs'. This one's just designed to lure you down to the basement tomorrow morning."

"Well, it appears your plan worked fantastically. Here I am. And why am I to be lured into the basement? You claim you didn't murder anyone, but you are, nonetheless, beginning to sound awfully creepy."

"I wasn't going to kill you. Just handcuff you and turn you over to... I don't know, maybe the police. I just wanted to confront you with those pictures of you and Eugenio and get you to confess the murder."

"Well aren't you a good one. But I don't get it, Lucy. Why should you care? It doesn't have anything to do with you."

"You killed my friend and — " Lucy stopped herself because she was a little surprised to have heard herself use that word to describe a relationship with a man she'd hardly known, but then she remembered what Cristiano had told her about friendship at the Irish bar.

"Your friend?" Natasha asked. "So now you say Eugenio was your friend?"

"No. You killed my friend, Cristiano, the reporter. Yesterday. Don't murder my friends and then tell me it doesn't have to do with me. And you threatened to kill my friends in the servants' quarters of Palazzo Mortimer. I can't have that. I *won't* have that. And you'll have to kill me first before you ever get close to them." Lucy was shocked at herself for having said something that sounded so cheesy and heroic at the same time.

Natasha remained silent, so Lucy stopped to listen to the whales and wonder whether or not it was true. Why was she trying to catch the murderer? Curiosity? Morbid obsession? Self defense after having been accused? No. None of those explanations were sufficient to explain her behavior. In all the last weeks of investigating, she'd never really stopped to ask herself why she had gotten herself so involved, and all of the sudden she'd explained it to herself using words that were far more noble and idealistic than what she'd have formulated when not under duress. But now that she'd said it, she couldn't help but see that, to a certain extent, heroic or not, cheesy or not, it was true. Why else was she behaving so rashly in front of a girl threatening to kill her?

Natasha, however, was not convinced. "You're telling me you want to give your life for an oddball group of foreign roommates at a retirement home?"

Lucy didn't need to reflect to come up with a response, "You're right. Fine. I'll admit it. I am kind of pathetic. I'm a foreigner whose only meaningful relationships in life are these weird roommates at a retirement home. You're right. I mean, what am I, if not an oddball roommate?" and she added something even more cheesy sounding, "If I can't give my life for them, then for *whom* can I give my life? But you wouldn't know what it's like to be an oddball, would you? It's not like there's anyone on our hallway who's so weird as to be a germaphobe or anything like that."

"This discussion is becoming a little abstract," Natasha immediately changed the subject. "Let's get back to the details."

"Let's."

"So let's say for a second that you're not the murderer. Explain to me who is. I just don't see who else it could have been."

"That's funny. I said the same thing about you just this afternoon."

"Well... who was it?"

"Well, you, obviously!"

"Lucy, don't waste my time."

"I'm not wasting your time. And come on, you're trying to decide whether or not to commit murder. It's midnight on a Tuesday. Don't tell me you don't have time. In fact, you'd better take your time, and make sure you're one hundred percent certain."

"Alright, tell me why I'm a murderer."

Lucy swallowed, and looked at the gun. She didn't have time to come up with a good lie, so she gambled on the truth. She started from the top, from the time she went running in the park and ran into a weird guy in a red tracksuit with keys. She was extremely thorough, including even details that I've left out. She went from the very first moments all the way through the arrest, the interrogation, the release, her first conversations with Cristiano, the jacket, the Galli mailbox, their visit to Galli's wife, the plan with Cristiano to find the murderer, her search of Natasha's room that morning, and her plan to confront Natasha the next day. The story took over an hour. As time went on, Natasha kept making more and more connections, nodding her head as Lucy pointed out details that Natasha herself had verified over the past weeks. When it was over, Natasha picked up the bubble solution and squirted some into the water, which was getting dangerously clear.

"Thanks."

"There's some parts of that story that are difficult to believe."

"I'd say the same thing, but it's the truth. If you want to ask Brian tomorrow, he'll tell you the same story."

"I guess it sounds like you're not the killer. And things all of the sudden look pretty damning for me."

"Well, I'm sure if you just explained – "

"Oh God, no, not tonight."

"I mean, at this point, in good conscience, you can't leave me handcuffed in the tub all night. And I don't think you're going to kill me ... so ... I'd like to think I've earned an explanation."

"I'll be brief."

Natasha dug through her pockets. A small splash of water in front of her face struck Lucy and a tiny metal object landed on her thigh. She unlocked herself, and stretched out her hand, feeling the blood return to her fingers.

Lucy stayed seated in the tub, as Natasha began, "Well, whatever... he was an Italian businessman who used to stay at the rental house next door to Mum and I for a few months every year. What's not to like? Two years ago we started to ... well ... y'know. Anyways. I more or less knew that he was married and all, but ... Have you ever been to South Africa?"

"No."

"Well, I'm sure it's fun for tourism and whatnot, but to live there all the time is so dreadfully boring. To be honest, well ... I don't know ... we were in love I guess, but, I don't know... Well, not like, you know, all *in love in love*, but sure, love, I guess. I mean, I was bored with everything else, and he was definitely the only interesting part of life. My whole life became sitting around waiting for the weeks when Eugenio would come down for business. So I convinced him I could come to Italy and not cause him any problems with his family, and eventually he agreed. He found digs for me at the Palazzo. He said he had connections here, but I still have never understood how. My flight changed and I showed up to Rome a couple of days earlier than expected. When I finally got ahold of him on that mobile he freaked out, and told me to stay at the Palazzo. He sounded really worried and said he was coming to get ..." Natasha paused for a second, swallowed, and continued. She was much better at controlling her emotions than Lucy, "He said he was coming to get me. Anyways, that's the last I heard from him. I tried to call back. Then you and that police officer showed up and told me someone had been murdered. And that was that I guess."

"But the gun? Why do you have a gun?"

"Oh, I bought this last week, after Eugenio was murdered."

"After the murder, I just bought a thing of pepper spray," said Lucy. "Maybe I should have gotten a gun."

"But you've stolen all my bullets, you said? Good on you." Natasha removed the clip out of the handle. It was empty. She reinserted the clip and started to fidget with the gun, polishing it with the sleeve of her jacket.

"So I was right. It was unloaded all along." Lucy smiled.

"And it's not like Eugenio or Cristiano were killed with a gun like this anyways."

"How do you know?"

"Oh that's right, you haven't seen the video. It was a nail gun."

"The thing that killed Eugenio was a nail gun?"

"Yeah ... quite gruesome to watch, really. Got him seven or eight times in the forehead."

"How did you get the video?"

"Easy. You've just got to pay Gambetti to have a look. It was positively expensive, though, and probably not worth it."

"Well that explains why my fingerprints were on the murder weapon. You know we spent two weeks building that awning over the terrace before you showed up. Brian and Andrew were always too scared to use the nail gun. Mine must've been the only fingerprints on it."

Natasha twirled the gun on her finger.

"Natasha?"

"Yeah."

"Brian knows everything. But yesterday... I don't know... I couldn't bring myself to tell Andrew that I was the reason he almost got killed."

"What do you mean? That wasn't your fault."

"I know. I mean... I don't know... I'm going to tell him at some point. I want him to know. I just don't know how he'll react. I just couldn't tell him yesterday. What I'm trying to say is that I would really appreciate it if you didn't tell Andrew about my whole investigative project. He doesn't know yet. He will know when things cool down. Andrew and I have been on egg shells before, and I want things to be right with him for a while."

"Mum's the word. But why do you want things to be right with him?" Natasha arched an eyebrow.

"You know I'm not into him. I'd just like things to be right between us. I guess I've kind of been an ass to him lately, and he's been surprisingly patient with me."

"Oh, I know you're not into him. I can see the way you look at that seminarian."

"Is it really that obvious?"

"Overwhelmingly obvious to everyone but him."

"Now be honest," Lucy turned red and changed the subject. "Were you really going to kill me?"

Natasha sighed and played with the gun. "I don't think so. In theory I thought it was possible, but it's really quite a weird experience pointing a gun at someone. I don't know. If I was really convinced it was you, I might've shot off a toe or something. But I guess there wasn't any ammo anyways."

A loud bang set off. Natasha screamed and dropped the gun. A candle right next to Lucy's head exploded. After a long second of silence Lucy started to laugh, while Natasha sat frozen with her hands covering her mouth.

"So I guess I stole all the bullets out of the clip," Lucy dipped her head underwater, came back up and started picking bits of wax off her neck, shoulders, face, and hair, "but there was one already in the chamber. What kind of person leaves a caulked gun in her nightstand?"

"Oh my God, I'm so sorry."

"Don't worry, now we're even."

"What do you mean, we're even?"

"I was the one who replaced all your cleaning supplies with sugar water last week."

Natasha's jaw dropped. She stood up, moved to the side of the tub and asked very seriously, "Lucy, I know I've been kind of a ... well, let's say, I've acted kind of cold towards you, and I can see now why you have been rather mean towards me. But are we going to be friends, now that we no longer suspect one another of murdering each other's friends?"

"Wait, so today in the park, when you said 'Keep it up, Lucy. You're doing great,' you were being cold?"

"Absolutely. It felt wonderful."

"I've never been so pissed off at anyone in my life."

"I'm glad," Natasha smiled, "Well, what do you say? Are we going to be friends?"

"I think so," Lucy looked up and smiled back.

"Good." Natasha picked up some of Lucy's things, and walked over to the door of the Turkish bath. Before leaving, she turned, still smiling, and said, "*Now* we're even," taking Lucy's towel and bathrobe with her.

CHAPTER SEVENTEEN

DE FRATRIBUS

Before going to bed Lucy slipped a piece of paper under Brian's door:

> *The plan is off. A whole lot of new shit has gone down. Let's talk.*

But Brian was busy with school, two jobs, and his required hours of talking with the residents at the Palazzo. In the meantime, however, Natasha and Lucy had become inseparable. They'd even managed to allow the mean girls to let both of them sit at their table. They started spending every afternoon – after Lucy came back from her run – at the kitchen table studying together, Lucy analyzing long passages of Dante and Buzzati, Natasha conjugating verbs and reading Italian children's books.

The following Friday night, Lucy and Natasha sat deeply in the patio furniture behind small glasses out on the terrace after dinner with Andrew, taking in the view and sipping *digestivi*, the traditional assortment of Italian liqueurs that are often put out on the table at the end of large meals to aid with digestion, or something like that. The conversation had been pleasantly wandering from thing to thing and was about nothing in particular, until, out of the blue, as can happen under the influence of *digestivi*, Andrew took it in a serious direction.

"Now what if it was Fr. Damien?" Andrew suggested.

Natasha and Lucy looked at each other. No response.

"Well, just think about it," Andrew's eyebrows came up. His eyes flickered between Lucy and Natasha.

Still no response.

"Oh come on," he insisted. "You can't tell me you haven't been thinking about this."

"The first murder was in the afternoon," said Lucy. "Which means he was at the Greg library. There's probably footage of him leaving the palazzo and footage of him entering the library. You can go check if you want, but I seriously doubt it was him."

"No, no, no," said Andrew. "I'm not talking about the murderer. I'm talking about the person who received the mysterious bank account, or whatever the threat letter was talking about. Remember? Does anyone still have that letter anyways?"

Lucy and Natasha remained silent and looked at each other across their *digestivi*.

"I think it's still somewhere in the kitchen," said Natasha.

"Well, think of this," continued Andrew. "The murderer is trying to find out which one of us has the bank account access. What if Eugenio told Fr. Damien in confession? Think about it. He now knows, but he's not allowed to tell anybody that he knows. Isn't that how all that works?"

Lucy rubbed the back of her neck, feeling a sharp pang of annoyance as she remembered Brian's insulting comment about sin and confession from a few weeks ago. She sipped her sambuca and didn't respond. Natasha sighed and shrugged her shoulders. Andrew let it go.

"Well, whatever. You two seem to have become awfully chummy as of late," Andrew raised his glass of amaro at them.

"Do you know what Machiavelli once said?" Natasha asked Andrew, pouring herself another glass of limoncello. "Keep your friends close; keep your enemies closer."

"Or have you ever had to multiply with negative numbers? Do they teach you that in Architecture?" asked Lucy, watching the two whole coffee beans that she'd put in her sambuca float around as she swirled her glass, "The mean girls taught me a trick the other day to help with multiplication: *l'amico di mio amico è mio amico, il nemico di mio amico è mio nemico, e il nemico di mio nemico è mio amico.*"[160]

Andrew gulped the rest of his amaro and stood up, "And which one of those describes you two?"

"I don't know," said Lucy, "I s'pose we'll just have to do the math and find out."

"You're not going to bed already, are you?" asked Natasha, "It's still early. Stay with us."

"No, I'm going out. My cousins from Calabria are in town. You guys should meet them sometime ... or actually ... maybe you shouldn't."

"Sounds great."

"We'll see you later."

"*Ciao ciao.*"

The roof access door swung open before Andrew touched the knob, and a large tired looking Starbucks employee walked out onto the terrace. Andrew went down the stairs and Brian took a seat in the patio chair where Andrew had been seated. He threw down his backpack, unbuttoned his coat, tore off his hat, and placed an empty McDonald's bag on the table. Over the last couple days even Brian had noticed Lucy and Natasha's new attitude towards one another, but he was convinced that acting nice to Natasha was Lucy's latest scheme. Natasha poured a large glass or limoncello, and pushed it in front of Brian.

Before Brian could say anything, Lucy looked around to make sure it was just the three of them and said, "Brian, Natasha and I have something we need to tell you."

Brian sat back and put on an understanding face, "It's alright. You don't have to tell me. I already know. You two are... well... y'know."

---

[160] The friend of my friend is my friend, the enemy of my friend is my enemy, and the enemy of my enemy is my friend.

"No, Brian," Lucy struggled not to laugh, and quieted her voice. "This is serious."

"I know it's serious. I see the way you two look at each other. I mean it's okay if you are. In fact, good for you! Good for you for not being ashamed. We're all friends here. There's no need to hide it."

"Brian, come on."

"Alright, alright, tell me."

"Natasha," said Lucy, "is not the murderer."

Brian sat up and looked around the terrace, and then at Natasha, "Well... um... I don't know what to say... um... congratulations... I'm glad to hear you're not a killer."

"Thanks. I'm also glad I'm not a killer." Natasha nodded her head in agreement. "And I think you already knew, but I should also let you know that Lucy is not the killer, either."

"Well this is great," said Brian. "Yeah, this is really great. Nobody here's a killer."

"Unless you're talking about Lucy's killer good looks," Natasha made a face at Lucy, like the models in Italian perfume ads.

"Are you sure you guys aren't ... you know ... because it's okay if you are," said Brian.

"No!" shouted Lucy.

"So, is there a reason, though ... for ... for you know ... all of this sudden good will?" asked Brian. "I'm not a murderer, she's not a murderer, you're not a murderer, we're all not murderers."

"I can explain," said Lucy. "But you have to promise me you'll never tell anyone about the room I'm about to tell you about, and that you'll never go there yourself."

"Okay."

"Alright," Lucy began. "So in the basement behind the laundry room, through the door with all the electrical warnings – "

"Oh yeah, you mean the Turkish bath?"

"What? You know about the Turkish bath?"

"Oh sure. Kind of creepy down there. But you're the one who always sneaks off there in a bathrobe late at night, when you think nobody's looking."

"Does everybody know about the Turkish bath?"

"Everybody knows."

"*Cazzo*! Really?"

"Yeah."

"Anyways, so I was there in the Turkish bath the other night..."

Lucy and Natasha took turns telling the story, which also required them to go back over just about every detail of the case thus far. On previous occasions, Lucy had only ever seen Brian have, at most, two beers. A few hours went by, and as the story got more and more surprising, the bottles of limoncello, amaro, and sambuca grew more and more empty.

"But, so then," asked Brian once they'd reached the conclusion of the story, "how did you get back upstairs?"

"I'll leave that to your imagination."

The door opened, and Fr. Damien came out onto the patio and stood by the ashtray along the railing. They all glanced down at their watches. Over the course of the evening he had come outside, right on schedule, every forty-two minutes for a cigarette. Whenever this happened, the three of them got quiet, and made small talk, until Fr. Damien would put out his cigarette five minutes later and return to his room. This time, however, towards the end of his cigarette, something incredibly unprecedented happened. Fr. Damien came up to the table and took a seat.

"Brian," he asked, "how come you not have girlfriend?"

"What?" Brian responded.

"Girlfriend, why you not have girlfriend? *Fidanzata*? You are strong and big. You are single young man. Why you not have girlfriend?"

"Um ... uh ... I don't know ... I just ... I just don't. Why do you ask?"

"You have always around you two beautiful young girl who have not husband, and you have no wife. I see it in these girls' eyes. They want husband. Maybe they not think of you first, because you are too fat. But still, they want husband. I think if you insist one of them might be happy with you."

Fr. Damien's face became a statue. He leaned forward and stared at Brian. His intense gaze demanded an answer. Brian was more exposed and vulnerable than Lucy had ever seen him. He mustered all of his energy to try and think up a response. But he couldn't come up with anything and Fr. Damien was still staring. At a certain point, it seemed like he gave in and responded like a man who finally breaks under interrogation, saying as quickly as possible what had to be said, "I'm just not attracted to white girls, okay?"

Lucy, unfortunately, happened to be taking a generous sip of Sambuca at that same moment. On hearing Brian's admission, for just a second, she forgot how to swallow, and spent the next minute trying to breathe while laughing, crying, and coughing sambuca out of her lungs. In the meantime, Fr. Damien had heard Brian's response, considered it for a second, and then seemed to agree that it was reasonable. He put out his cigarette and returned to his room. Natasha was laughing at Lucy, but seemed to be completely fine with Brian's statement. Brian slouched in his chair, defeated and horrified.

Natasha emptied the bottle of limoncello, filling everyone's glasses. She pushed Brian's glass toward him. With a calm voice and curious eyes she said, "Tell us about white girls, Brian."

"I don't want to talk about it."

"Vell zen," Lucy pretended to be holding a notepad and paper, and put on a German accent, "Tell me about yohr relayshunnship viss yohr muzzer."

"I said I don't want to talk about it."

"Brian," Lucy came back to her American self, "you can't *not* be attracted to an entire *race*. There's beautiful and ugly people in every race."

"Oh, I suppose it's possible," Natasha piped in. "I'm sorry. I know what you're thinking. Here's the stereotypical Afrikaner speaking up. I promise you, I'm not like my grandparents. I mean, it's not really something I experience personally, so maybe I shouldn't talk. But it's not something I haven't heard people say before."

"But didn't you have white girlfriends in college?" Lucy asked Brian.

"I had *a* white girlfriend in college."

"And she was attractive?"

"Yes ... very ... I mean ... no ... circumstances can change. Things can happen that can make you no longer attracted to certain races."

"Such as?" asked Lucy.

Brian finished his limoncello in one gulp. "I need both of you to swear you'll never bring this up again."

The hybrid slowed and made a right turn off the desert highway onto a small dirt side road and Lisa, fidgeting with her hair, told Brian, "Okay, let's go over the rules one more time again."

Brian smirked about the strange rules, but, noticing the stern look on Lisa's face, he solemnly began: "Rule number one: no questions until after the weekend is over. Rule number two: do as you're told without questions. Rule number three: if you don't do as you're told, we're going back and you don't get to meet my parents."

Over the past hour, Lisa had grown more and more agitated and nervous. She had started muttering things like, "Oh God, why are we doing this?" and, "It's not too late to go back. Isn't this a little early? There's the turn for Moab. Why don't we just go camping and call it a weekend?"

Brian tried to console her with things like, "Well last weekend went relatively okay, didn't it?" or, "Oh, come on, there's no reason to be nervous, I'm sure your parents will love me, once they get to know me."

"Yeah, but your mom is a little more mainstream than my parents."

"Actually, Lisa, you might be surprised. My mom had her wild years too."

They had spent the previous weekend at the townhouse of Brian's mom. Overall it went off without a hitch, except for long dinners permeated with forced conversation, and the time Lisa vehemently objected when Brian's mom wanted to give him a haircut.

"Really, Lisa, just tell me. What are you so worried about? I'm sure it'll be just like last weekend. I mean, at least you know both your parents. I don't even know who my dad is. There can't be as many awkward silences as last weekend if we have two parents to deal with, right?"

Rather than answer, Lisa brought the car to an abrupt halt. "Okay, get out and put on your running shoes."

"My running shoes?"

"Do you remember rule number two?"

Brian's mouth hung open in defiance. Lisa was already outside, opening the trunk and pulling out her own running shoes. He protested, sitting in the passenger seat for a few minutes, before curiosity won over. They spent the next half hour running through the spring desert –

"Wait, wait, wait," Lucy interrupted. "*You* were running?"

"Lucy, please don't interrupt me," said Brian. "And yes, I used to be trimmer than you, before that weekend. Afterwards I stopped running and put on a little weight."

Lucy looked back at him with skepticism.

"Okay, a lot of weight."

"We need to talk about this when you're finished."

"There will be no discussion when I finish. Can I keep going?"

"Please."

"As I was saying..."

They spent the next half hour running through the spring desert. Lisa kept quickening the pace and Brian had a growing awareness of the increasing amount of perspiration seeping through his shirt, in relation to the decreasing amount of time between his impending encounter with Lisa's parents. Yet this was not enough to prevent his pride from keeping up every time the pace quickened, even to the point that, when the green Prius became visible, the two broke out into a dead sprint. Lisa fell back, giving Brian the lead, so that when he passed the car and raised his arms in triumph, he did not expect to be shoved straight into a pile of dirt.

"Hey! Damnit, Lisa!" yelled Brian, crawling up and dusting himself off. "Really, what's the deal? I'm meeting your parents, in like, a couple hours! Really, this is not okay!"

Lisa was already on her way to the car's trunk where she pretended to hear nothing, producing a shovel and a piece of paper. She paced off a few distances between a number of cacti, muttered numbers to herself, and eventually settled on an empty patch of dirt. Brian was again left speechless, torn between laughter and utter confusion, hoping that this was all some sort of joke, though not seeing the humor in it.

His thoughts were interrupted by a dull thud announcing that the shovel had found its intended target. Successive thuds, dings, and scrapes revealed a large wooden chest buried a few inches beneath the surface.

"What's all this?" Brian asked.

Lisa continued as though she had heard nothing, and Brian remembered *oh yeah, no questions.* The chest showed itself to contain heaps of unorganized dirty clothing. Lisa immediately began to select a variety of items and set them outside of the trunk. She stood up, and for the first time since they had gotten out of the car, acknowledged Brian's presence.

She took a deep breath, looked him in the eye, and, as seriously as could be mustered, said, "Okay, I need you to put these on."

"No way. What on earth are those?"

"It's some clothes I need you to wear."

Brian approached the garments and examined them more closely. "I guess you could call them clothes."

They were a pair of worn-out man-pris, a t-shirt with an Om symbol on it, a bandana, some hemp bracelets, a pair of Birkenstocks, and a bright wool sweater. The color drained from Brian's face as everything became clear: the protest at the haircut, the disappearance of his electric shaver that morning, the run, the sweat, the dirt, and finally the clothing.

"You're trying to dress me as a hippie."

"Please just do this for me. Listen, I told you my parents weren't the most mainstream people there ever were. Just trust me on this."

"No way, I am not wearing this crap."

Lisa fought to control her expressions as her face became redder with anger, and let out a stream of not so intelligible words. Lisa (unlike Lucy) had always been one of the most chill and laid back girls Brian had ever known. His eventual compliance was not so much a result of the force of her anger, but rather, Brian's fascination at this previously unknown side of her personality, which had in it something mysterious, and, although he wouldn't admit it to himself later on, very attractive. The only complaint offered when he took the clothes was a snotty, "What are you, my sister?"

All the clothing that they had brought from college for the weekend was hidden in the wooden chest and a few odds and ends were placed back in the hybrid.

"Wait, Lisa, what about our church clothes? I thought you said your parents were Mormon."

"Well, they sort of are – you won't need to worry about church clothes – definitely best if you don't bring a tie, unless you're gonna use it as a bandana or something like that."

Before leaving the place with the underground chest, Lisa had put on similar crunchy-people attire, messed up her dirty blonde hair, hung all sorts of beads and dangly things in the car's interior, poured mud all over the exterior, and covered the seats in those uncomfortable wooden bead seat covers. The whole makeover was crowned by a smattering of bumper stickers placed unceremoniously at various angles on the back.

The next hour of the journey was spent in silence. They continued deeper and deeper along the dirt road into what seemed to be a more and more desolate flat expanse of desert, followed by increasing rockiness until the car immersed itself in a wide canyon of rich colors that played against the rays of a sun growing closer to the horizon. Since they left the wooden chest under the ground, nothing discernibly human was encountered until they drove under a large stone arch with the words *I sorta am where I am these days* inscribed upon it.

At a high point in the canyon floor, Lisa stopped the car and motioned for Brian to get out with her. Two goats stood nearby chewing junk from a box of trash, observing the couple with casual detachment.

"Well, here it is," said Lisa, opening her arms out to the canyon.

"Here is what?" Brian saw only red rocks in the sunset.

"Here's where I grew up."

"Out here in the middle of nowhere? What, were you raised by wolves?"

"Well, sort of. They're a little hidden, but look at all the houses."

At first Brian thought about laughing, thinking she was joking, but upon looking closer, scattered around in all directions, there were small bumps of junk and adobe.

"Those are houses?"

"Sort of, they're actually called 'earth-ships'. Try not to call them houses."

"But you told me you grew up in a small town outside of Moab."

"This is a small town outside of Moab."

In the fading light, it was nearly impossible to tell that there was a town around them at all. The buildings were all slightly underground, built into the sides of the canyon, sheltered from view and the weather by poplars and pines. Once you knew what to look for, it was easy to see houses, windows, and more geometric shapes in the canyons. However, at many times, it was a tough call to know whether something was an interesting rock formation, or something man-made, or where a house began and the earth stopped. Behind the two, a lantern approached and a strong baritone voice called out in joy, "Earth be with you!"

To which Lisa rolled her eyes, took a deep breath and called back, "And with your spirit!" then in a softer voice, explained to Brian, "That's how we greet each other here."

The voice with the lantern called out, "Arbie!"

Lisa leaned to Brian and said, "Oh, that's what my parents call me, it's short for tree."

Brian braced himself for a weekend that he was now expecting to be filled with Lisa constantly leaning in to whisper explanations. Lisa turned to the lantern, smiled, and called back, "Papa!" before skipping off to the shape now emerging out of the shadows.

Lisa jumped into the imposing figure and was twirled around in the air a few times. The surroundings reverberated with a deep laugh and the faces of nearby goats shifted from casual detachment to annoyance. Brian approached with caution. Lisa's father was a large man with long gray hair past his neck and a short grey beard. He wore small, completely round glasses, a flowing blue shirt revealing a significant amount of chest hair, Birkenstocks, and, of course, lots of crunchy dangly things. Beaming with a large smile he approached and called out, "You must be Brian!"

Brian extended his right arm for a handshake but was intercepted by a great back popping bear hug. Lisa's father released Brian and held his shoulders at arm's length. Looking straight into Brian's eyes, he slowly intoned, "It's wonderful to meet you, son. Call me papa."

For the first of many times, something that Lisa's father said puzzled Brian. He knew Lisa's father's name was Fred, but why would he ask Brian to call him 'Papa'? Did Papa just have some eccentricity of calling relationships more than what they were, or had Lisa miscommunicated the seriousness of their relationship? Or rather, even though they were still rather young, they were actually talking about marriage, but they had decided not to tell anybody about it. Had Lisa told him?

"Welcome to our town. This is your first time here, right?"

"It is."

"Well it is good that you have come. I have found that there are few places on earth where the Chi is as deeply right as this place." Papa closed his eyes, spread his arms to gesture towards the valley floor – with a sparse number of lights now illuminating the valley – and filled his whole chest and gut with air, releasing very slowly, "There, do you feel that?"

Lisa nodded her head at Brian and mouthed the words *yes, you do*.

"Oh yeah, um, yeah that's great," said Brian, taking in a corresponding deep breath and wondering what Chi was.

"Alright, well, let's get down to the ship. Beth couldn't come up to greet you. She's busy relocating a fly. Come on, this way."

They collected the small number of things that Lisa had allowed them to bring from the car and walked around a path down to the other side of the high point on which they had been standing. A good portion of the high point turned out to be the house. The whole south-facing side was covered in angled windows with a garden out in the front. Brian later discovered that the parts of the house that weren't already part of nature were made entirely out of old tires, dirt and adobe – which was why most of the walls were three feet thick. Passing through the sheet metal door, they came upon a woman in a long dress and shawl with a small green box in hand, who was slowly prowling towards a large planter. She was intensely focused on a small fly near the planter until, without warning, the woman's hands flew swiftly together, sharply closing the box.

She delighted in her catch and was startled at Lisa's greeting, "Earth be with you, Beth."

Beth very slowly came towards Lisa giving a firm maternal embrace, "Oh, and with your spirit, my dear Lisa."

"Brian, this is my mom, Beth."

Beth – who, although she was Lisa's mother, insisted she be called 'Beth' – slowly pulled Brian into a rigid hug and then ceremonially kissed both of his cheeks. She tilted her head and considered Brian for an uncomfortable amount of time, finally saying, "Hmmm ... I am, indeed, always fascinated by people whose names begin with the letter B. I feel our energies shall correspond nicely."

Emily Post would have been shocked if she had taken part in that particular dinner. Although the quality and amount of the foods and the courses may have called for three plates, three forks, two knives, a spoon, and two glasses, they were all absent. The family preferred to use as few dishes as possible, so food was set out directly onto the table and eaten with hands. (More dishes require more wastewater.) If the explicit rules of dining were all violated, the unwritten rules of dinner conversation were even more severely violated. While other people, at all costs, avoid talking about religion, sex and politics, Lisa's parents acted as though they were the first items on the agenda. Coached again by Lisa, Brian deeply sympathized with Papa when he expressed his sentiments of betrayal at how terribly conservative the Obama administration had been.

Trying to avoid the subject, Brian piped in, "Certainly true. However, I must admit, I am mostly apolitical in my thinking." This was at least somewhat true.

Papa could only respond with a nodding of the head and, "Hey man, that's cool. No pressure at all to you, man."

When Brian mentioned his mother's first name, Papa chuckled and wondered aloud to himself, "Was it '87 or '88 when I slept with a woman of that name?"

"I would say it was '88," responded Beth.

Lisa stifled a groan and sank lower into her chair. Brian was so taken aback by this that he only returned to the conversation minutes later because of Papa's exhortation on the merits of not circumcising as infants – apparently he preferred the ancient Egyptian coming of age ritual at thirteen. When papa turned away, Lisa rolled her eyes at Brian and mouthed *thank God I wasn't a boy*. Eventually a rather personal question was addressed to Brian and Lisa, which both of them met with silence.

As the silence grew, so did the concern on Beth's face, "but you mean you're not – "

"Really, Arbie?" interrupted Papa with shocked surprise. "You're not feeling repressed at that Mormon school, are you?"

"No, Papa," said Lisa sinking deeper into her chair quietly adding, "we just haven't yet. Don't worry, I'm sure we will soon enough."

Papa and Beth then both turned at Brian with looks demanding an explanation, which was met only by Brian's deer-on-the-railroad-tracks face. At this, Lisa felt forced to sit up in his defense, "No, no, no! It's not him at all. I mean, no, that's not it. We just haven't, okay." And she tried to offer a token of good will to her parents, "We watched a movie the other day and made out. It's not like we're ... I don't know... just ... let it be, okay."

Beth skeptically accepted this, but added, "We're just concerned about your liberty is all. We want you to be well rounded, self-actualized people. If you need any help, don't hesitate to ask. You know we've got more than enough to help in our storage closet if you feel in the mood this weekend."

"You're not very religious, are you?" Papa asked Brian, still seeking an answer.

"Not really. My Mom grew up Mormon, but sort of rebelled after college and left the Church. Having me out of wedlock sort of sealed the deal. So I grew up somewhat nominally Mormon, occasionally going to Church with the grandparents. But for the most part, I guess I just avoid the issue altogether."

"Oh, we didn't know you had a Mormon background," replied the father, now with a new interest, having forgotten the initial reason for the question. "Fascinating. Although, please do us a favor and don't tell us too much about Mormon beliefs."

"Oh, don't worry, I'm not too familiar with them myself, so I'm really not one to be preaching to you anyways," lied Brian.

"Oh no, Brian, normally we would be absolutely delighted to discover other spiritualities," added Beth apologetically. "However, we happen to be *anonymously* Mormon ourselves, so we would prefer to know as little as possible. I do hope you understand."

"Um, not really, what do you mean anonymously?"

"Well, haven't you read any Karl Rahner?"

"Karl who?"

"Rahner, Karl Rahner," said Beth. "Papa and I first encountered him while living in a quaint commune near Innsbruck.

He was a professor at the local university scene that we had a habit of frequenting. He's a theologian of the highest caliber, although certainly we disagree with so much of what he has to say. He proposed the idea of *anonymous* Christianity. That is to say, people who have never had the opportunity to reject the Christian message could still be Christians, although in an anonymous non-explicit way. So Papa and I, for a while, considered anonymous Christianity as a good way for us to embrace the faith of our dear ancestors. We were obviously quite disappointed to discover that we could not become anonymous Christians due to the fact that we had already been baptized in our infancy. So in an arbitrary fashion, we chose a religion that we knew very little of, and decided to take up the title of anonymous Mormons. So of course, you must understand why we take such great care to learn nothing whatsoever of the Mormon religion, otherwise we could no longer maintain our status as anonymous believers. I do hope you understand."

"Oh certainly," replied Brian nodding his head in feigned comprehension.

"However, the truly funny thing is, that since Papa and I converted to anonymous Mormonism, we no longer felt the need to continue so much with the New Age practices in which we had previously participated. Something about them became rather banal, and we now spend most of our religious efforts in avoiding Mormons so as to remain blissfully ignorant – otherwise, you see, we would have to explicitly reject those beliefs. We used to be passively apathetic and knew very little about it, but now that we are intentionally apathetic, you would be surprised at how much more difficult it is to know so little."

Based on the bottle of wine on the table, the coffee maker in the kitchen, Lisa's status as an only child, and the general feel of the town they lived in, Brian guessed they were doing a pretty good job.

"But anyways, enough about us, what about you guys?" said papa. "How did you two end up in our dining room?"

Brian waited for Lisa to begin and Lisa waited for Brian to begin. They both wagered different lengths of an empty hanging pause for the privilege of not having to tell the story, until Lisa finally folded and began, "Well... um, so I guess Brian and I are the only two BYU Classics majors who aren't Mormon, which gives us nothing to do on Sunday mornings. So we made a habit of spending the morning reading the only copy of the New York Times in Provo at the only Starbucks in Provo, the only thing open in Provo on Sunday mornings. And then Monday nights are family night for most Mormons, (At hearing this, both of Lisa's parents coughed and fidgeted pretending not to hear what she had said) so Brian and I started to hang out then. It's kind of funny because they don't allow co-ed housing, so we've had to lie and say we're siblings to get access to one another's apartments. So it's actually been fun having to hide our relationship from our roommates – sort of like a forbidden love type story. And then, eventually, I guess we stopped making excuses for reasons to hang out with one another and started to call our relationship what it was."

Before bed, Brian brushed his teeth with a small dribble of water from the bathroom faucet. He was about to wash his face, but then remembered Lisa's strict instructions not to wash anything. Feeling there was more yet to be done, but unsure of what it was, he just stared at the mirror for a while. Brian returned to Lisa's room and found her sitting on the floor up against the wall with a similar look of shock on her face.

"I was going to tell you about them, I really was. I just kept putting it off until, well, until it was too late and here we are." Brian opened his mouth to say something but was cut off with, "Remember, no questions."

So instead he just sat next to her and two hours passed in silent contemplation of the opposite wall. Lisa woke Brian up and brought him out the window. They stopped by the car and got a bag that Lisa had hidden under the back seats. She led him towards the center of the valley to a statue where she met some old friends and delivered a load of contraband - candy bars, paper plates, inorganic fruit, a couple of books, cold McDonalds fries with a melted milkshake, and a framed picture of Ronald Reagan.

The previous weekend, Brian's mom had insisted that the two sleep on opposite ends of the townhouse in separate bedrooms, and use separate bathrooms. Lisa's parents, on the other hand, insisted there was only space for them in Lisa's bedroom, so Brian and Lisa pretended to be much more casual about the arrangements than they actually were: one small twin bed. But given the tension, they both spent the night in passionate disinterest of one another.

Cell service was rather sporadic in the canyon, so when Brian woke up, he found several texts from his mother all saying, *You didn't call to let me know you arrived safely. Call me when you get this.* Brian put on a thick wool cardigan that he found near the door and walked into the middle of the valley where Lisa had told him he could get some service as the first rays of the sun began to creep over the canyon walls. He sat on a large sandstone slab, faced the east, and opened his flip phone.

"Hey, Mom ...

"Yeah, we got here just fine ...

"Sort of an odd place ....

"Oh, I mean it's just kind of a hippie environment. Lisa never really mentioned how crunchy her parents were. I'm sure it would've been just your thing a few years ago...

"Yeah, I mean they're really nice people, Beth Kochivar and, get this, Lisa's Dad has a different last name than her. They decided it was too patriarchal to give Lisa the father's last name – Fred Russo ...

"I said Russo ...

"Russo ...

"Hello ...

"Are you there?"

Brian looked at his phone to check and make sure he still had service. Lisa approached, still half asleep, carrying two cups of coffee and still in her pajamas. She placed one cup in his hand and kissed his cheek. She sat next to him and leaned her head on his shoulder.

She whispered to Brian, "I put in a little something-something to make it a little stronger. It's gonna be another long day with the parents."

Brian smirked, kissed the top of her head, and then continued into the phone, "Yeah, I'm still here...

"I think one of us might've just lost service for a second there ...

"Is everything okay? You sound a little shaken up ...

"Yeah, actually that's exactly what he looks like. Round glasses and everything ...

"Yeah, I haven't had a chance to see the art studio yet, but yeah, they make, what did you call them? Oh yeah, raku pots. How did you know they were artists?

"Well, yeah, judging by the quality of their house and cars, I'd say they're pretty good at it too ...

"Yeah, he has a lot of Karl Rahner books. Wait, but how do you know all this? Were you talking with Lisa about this last week?"

Lisa's head came off Brian's shoulder. She looked more awake and puzzled at the conversation. She shook her head and mouthed *no, I didn't tell her any of that.* Brian passed the phone to Lisa.

"Hello ...

"Hi, yeah, this is Lisa ...

"Oh sure, odd questions are fine ....

"um ...

"yes ...

"Yeah, definitely. He's gotta be my biological father. We have the exact same eyes and nose ...

She passed the phone back to Brian, who was scrunching his nose in disbelief that his normally straight-laced mother would ask such a question.

"Mom, is everything really okay? You really don't sound okay ...

"Um, Okay ...

"Can't we talk about this later ...?

"Wait, he's my what ...?

"How on earth did you know him ...?

"No way ..."

Of all the looks of stunned confusion that Brian had worn on his face during the entire visit, the one that appeared next took the cake. Without saying a word, he shut the phone. Lisa took hold of his hand and demanded an explanation. Brian just looked at Lisa's hand in fascination, as though he had never seen it before.

After a minute, Brian faltered for words and avoided Lisa's gaze, "Well, um, Lisa. There was a time when my Mom wasn't really as uptight as she now is. I guess, I guess I ... I didn't really know how much, but, but ...

He tried a few times to mouth the next words, but couldn't quite get them out. He took a few sharp breaths and continued, "Well, I mean, Lisa, you, you ... I mean, you know how I never really knew who my father was ... well it turns out ... well, it turns out that, that, your dad, Papa, or Fred, or whatever, is also my dad."

At first Lisa's expression was joyful with the surprise of the coincidence. This was followed by a look of horror as she did the math. She shook his hand out of hers and wiped it on her pajamas. Lisa's eyes filled with tears as she turned and ran into the canyon away from the house. Brian contemplated the sunlight on a nearby cactus for the next hour sipping his coffee, thankful that his sister had given it a little extra strength.

CHAPTER EIGHTEEN

SBRONZA E POSTUMI

At the end of his story, Brian stood up and stumbled straight to bed. All three bottles of *digestivi* stood empty, or close to empty, in front of Lucy and Natasha, who contemplated them in silence, having trouble digesting what they were just told.

Natasha finally spoke. "Did that just happen?"
"Shh," I just thought of something.
"What?"
"We need to be very *very* quiet when we go inside."
"Okay. Why?"
"I can't let Blue Bear know about me being ... you know."
"Who?"
"Nobody," said Lucy. "Okay, so let's pretend for a second, that I'm not totally, but at least somewhat ... y'know. Okay, so I know Blue Bear would be disappointed, but he doesn't have to know, does he? Well, whatever, so yes, so just, so just pull yourself ... pull yourself together, Lucy, okay?"

"You didn't have that much. Not so much. Not so much at all. Alright, maybe, like, a bit of sambuca ... or maybe, like, what? Two limoncellos, right?"

"That's right!" Lucy yelled, slamming her fist on the table. Then she grew quiet again, "Who the hell thinks that this is fun, anyways? It just totally impairs your ability to interact with reality. Alright, so maybe the first hour was fun ... and the second and the third ... but after that, come on. It's already, like, it's already three hours since the last time I had a drink ... kay, maybe like two hours ... or even one hour ... at this point I don't know ... anyways, it's been a while, and I haven't touched anything, and now, all of the sudden, why is it my fault that I'm all dizzy? It's not my fault. And if I remember correctly, Brian just told a bizarre story. That's not my fault either."

"Y'know that's life sometimes."

"Right. Sometimes you get dru .... sometimes very tipsy, not drunk ... and sometimes you make out with your sister. Not me. Brian. Not me."

"That's life."

Lucy stood up, unsteady on her feet. "Wow, okay, so that's not the dynamics of the physical world that I remember to be in order the last time I sat down, I mean, the last time... I stood up. Okay, so something must have happened." She tried to balance, putting one arm in the air, but still wobbled. "I just put my hand above my hand ... above my *head*, but nonetheless, there was absolutely no effect towards balance. What the hell is ... I mean ... what the hell is ... is the worth of putting your hand above your head, or putting your arm out, if it has not any effect in achieving balance? It's not like it was my fault to not have balance."

"Maybe you should go to bed. Here, let me help." Natasha took Lucy by the arm and both of them stumbled towards the door.

"All of the sudden there was, like, sambuca, Natasha, and who knows how many you consume without the consensus of your conscience? Remember, we have to be quiet. There's all kinds of bears sleeping inside here."

"Whatever you say."

Before opening the door Lucy stopped, and held her new friend at arms length. "Remember, Natasha, there's sleeping bears here, so be quiet," she pulled Natasha in towards her, and wrapped her arms around Natasha as tight as she could. "Bear hugs, I mean. Bear hugs. Let's not do this again. It's no fun. Okay. It was fun. Kind of. Once or twice a year, maybe, but not often. *Una vez al año no hace daño.* But because I'll be too embarrassed to say it tomorrow when I'm not slightly ... mostly ... inebriated, you should know that I hope we're going to be great friends, Natasha. Great friends. We're great friends already, right?"

"We are."

"Great."

The next day – or rather, later the same day – at an hour that felt far earlier than it actually was, Lucy woke up and noticed three things at once. Brian was snoring louder than normal in the next room over. Her head hurt. And there was a knocking on her door. Living at the Palazzo was getting so creepy lately that someone knocking on your door was something that could not be easily ignored. As quietly as possible she crept out of bed, grabbed a nine iron and pepper spray, and shimmied up to the door.

"Lucy, it's me," Natasha's voice could be heard through the door.

She removed the newly installed door chain, unlocked the door, and cracked it open just slightly, allowing Natasha to shimmy in, before closing it and redoing the chain.

"We've got another one," Natasha brandished a folded up piece of paper. She headed straight for the curtains, and pulled one of them open. Lucy fell into her chair, shielded her eyes with one arm, and almost hissed like a cat at the light, which only exacerbated the throbbing in her head.

"Lucy, we've got another letter from *the true heirs!*"

"Water," was the first word Lucy managed to croak that morning, while putting on her sunglasses, to screen her headache from the light. "I need water. And I have to pee. Really bad. But I don't want to move again. Moving hurts."

"What? Did you want me to bring you a bedpan?"

"I wouldn't object if you did."

"I was given to understand that our work involved conversing with the residents, not providing direct physical care to other students."

"Just get me some water."

Lucy closed her eyes, and Natasha looked around the room. "Am I really doing this?" she asked herself out loud. Using the sleeve of her jacket she grabbed Lucy's water bottle, and used the other sleeve to turn the knob on the sink. Lucy squinted her eyes and reached out with both hands to receive the bottle, and gently nursed on it, trying to move as little as possible.

"Well, you did drink quite a bit —"

"I don't have a hangover ... I just got a little dehydrated, I think. There's too much sugar in sambuca."

"Oh, right. I'm sure it was just the sugar, Lucy. But if you ask me, the alcohol probably didn't help, either. I'm feeling a bit hungover too, but I'm fairly certain it wasn't the sugar that caused it. Just a good old fashioned alcohol hangover for me, thank you very much."

"So maybe I've got a little bit of a headache or something, and a sensitivity to light and sound. I'm getting old, Natasha. I didn't drink that much. Or… well maybe I did. I'm just out of practice. Do you have an Advil or a Tylenol, or something like that?"

"But the letter, don't you want to see the letter?"

"I don't want to see anything right now."

"Okay?"

"You read."

"Alright. Dear Student Residents..."

"Gently, Natasha," Lucy whispered. "Gently. No sharp sounds."

"You do know we're leaving for the park in half an hour?"

"*Porca troia...* why did I sign up for that?"

"Do you want me to tell them you're sick?"

"I'm not sick. I've just got a hang — well, you know. And, no, I've been skipping too much lately. I gotta show up to something every once in a while. No, it's not that bad. It's not that bad. I just need an Ibuprofen and some coffee or something. Read on."

"Dear Student Residents. It has come to our attention that you're not taking our threat seriously. Listen. We know quite suredly that one of you, for certain, has the desired information. We're not joking. Once we can tell that one of you in particular is *not* the person who holds said information, that person will become superfluous to us, and will be offed, as a warning to the person who does. I repeat. We are not joking. Give us the information we need, and you can save your own life, as well as that of those around you. For example. It was quite clear that poor Cristiano was not the resident in possession of the bank account numbers, and it was also clear that he was sticking his nose where it didn't belong. On the spur of the moment we had to arrange for him to have an accident on the rooftop. Poor Cristiano. And yet his death could have been avoided if one of you would have just coughed up what does not belong to you, and rendered it to those who are the rightful owners. That is all. You have little time. Signed. The true heirs."

"Do you have an Ibuprofen?"

"How about a Nurofen?"

"Whatever it is, I'll try it."

"I'll go get one for you."

"Two!"

Natasha returned with a cup of coffee and two pills. Lucy took them both at once, and burnt the back of her throat gulping down the pills with the hot coffee.

"We've got to find out who's sending these letters," said Natasha.

"Where did you find it?" Lucy was still cringing from the burning in the back of her throat.

"It was tucked under the door to the terrace. It wasn't there when I went into the shower this morning, but it was sticking out when I came out of the bathroom."

"Is that where we found the first one?"

"I don't remember."

"But you don't think anyone besides us two has seen this one?"

"I don't know. I don't think so. If somebody else had already seen it, I doubt they would've folded it up and tucked it back under the door."

Half an hour later, the Palazzo's nine-seater white '96 Fiat Ducato rattled up to the loading area in front of the main entrance, where seven residents were already milling around in puffy jackets and scarves, ready for an arctic expedition. The sky was completely blue, but the temperature had already maxed out at a frigid high of 52° Fahrenheit. Life can be difficult in the Mediterranean too. Lucy, who believed herself incapable of driving in her present condition, urged

Natasha – who, as a South African, was ill prepared for driving on the right side of the road, shifting with her right hand, and dealing with the sensitive old Fiat clutch – to climb behind the wheel. Any progress that Lucy had made against her headache with coffee, water, and South African drugs was lost when Natasha insisted, it seemed, on hitting every Roman pothole in the mile and a half that separated the Palazzo from the park's pond. When the van finally lurched to a stop, the residents filed out, and Natasha distributed stale pieces of bread so that they could feed the ducks. Lucy stayed put in the middle front seat, with her feet on the dashboard, her elbows on her knees, and her head in her hands.

"Wouldn't you like to come along and feed the ducks, *Signora*?" Lucy heard Natasha's voice from just outside the open window.

Before Lucy could answer, someone in the front seat next to her responded, "No, Lucy is still in the car, I will... how do you say *fare compagnia?*"

"Keep her company."

"Yes, I will keep her company."

Lucy peered out from behind her right hand. The woman still seated next to her was the "mean girl," Virginia.

Natasha wandered off, and Lucy turned to Virginia. "Since when do you speak English?"

Virginia shrugged her shoulders, "Since when have you ever spoken to me in English?"

Lucy shrugged her shoulders.

"The other two – how do you call us? – *mean girls*," Virginia smirked and arched one eyebrow, "hate it when I speak English, so we speak only Italian. Besides, you need to learn Italian."

"But you speak English with Natasha?"

"What can I say?" Virginia turned and looked out the window at Natasha, who was tearing off pieces of bread for an old man whose hands were too shaky to do it himself. "I like Natasha. I see too much of me in her. Who knows? I am rich old mean woman. I can do as I please."

"Well alright, then. You've always been a mysterious one."

"And you are too!" Virginia thumped Lucy's shoulder with her pointer finger. "I observe a lot of things. I do not have much else to do. I observe that Natasha, all of the sudden, has trust in you. She trusts you very much!"

Speaking of trust and observation, Lucy got an idea. "Virginia, what do you know of anyone named Ginevra? Was there ever a Ginevra who lived at the Palazzo?"

"A long time ago," Virginia looked back out the window.

"How long?"

"I don't know. Perhaps a decade. Maybe two. I have not heard of her in a long time."

"What do you remember about her?"

"Little. She was also a mysterious woman."

"Oh, come on. Do you remember if she had any family?"

"Listen, that is all I know. Enough questions for now, let's go feed the ducks."

"But wait, no, tell me more about Ginevra. What did she look like?"

"She hated people who asked too many questions. Come on. No more being a bludger all day. Let's get to work and feed the ducks. Stop faking. Your hangover is not so bad." Virginia dug around in her purse, and handed a bottle to Lucy. "Here. You take one Panadol and you feel better. If not, later, we go and steal more powerful drugs from Martina."

Lucy didn't want to press her luck. She'd have time with Virginia later on. She let the topic of Ginevra go, took the pain killer, and got out of the car.

The ducks all flocked to Natasha, even after she ran out of bread. Lucy still had plenty, but the ducks hesitated to approach.

"Look, you bastards! I've got bread. Hers is all gone!" she hucked a chunk of her loaf towards Natasha's feet, and the ducks scattered away quacking.

"You've got to be more gentle. They can tell your intentions."

"I'm feeding the ducks with old ladies in the park. I want to give 'em bread! That's my intention! What else do they need?"

"Yeah, but you must be giving off nervous energy or something. They can tell when you're malicious and they can tell if you're calm and friendly." Natasha picked up the bread, and handed it back to Lucy. "Here, close your eyes and breathe deep. Pretend the ducks are your good friends."

Lucy closed her eyes, breathed deep, and tried to imagine that her friends were ducks.

"Alright, now try and feed that brown one. Show him you've got a token of friendship."

Lucy crouched down and crept towards the duck. The duck waddled away. She stood back up, "But this isn't how I treat my friends. If that duck were you or Brian, I'd have just flung the loaf right at him."

"Well, I don't know. Perhaps you can't succeed at everything. Are you feeling better, at least?"

"I'm feeling kind of drowsy, but really loose. Virginia just forced some kind of pill down my throat in the van. I guess it's working."

"Have you thought about the letter?"

"Yeah. It's interesting. The night you searched my room, you found the fake letter that I wrote from the same," Lucy used her hands to make quotation marks, "'True heirs,' right?"

"Right."

"So how are we to know that this morning's letter was from the *true* 'true heirs'? What's to say it's not another fake letter from the true heirs?"

"It looks creepy enough to me," said Natasha. "I don't know if we have the luxury of not taking it seriously."

"Well, let me throw this out there. One of us – me – has still got the keys, but the true heirs still have no idea which one of us it is. So we've got that over them. They still need us all alive, otherwise they don't get what they need, for whatever reason they need it. They say they wouldn't, like, risk killing one of us, until they could figure out, for sure, that their intended target doesn't have the keys ... or the bank account numbers, because if they kill that person they'll never get what they want. I guess they don't even realize it's not even a bank account they're looking for, do they?"

"What about Andrew? They tried to kill him, didn't they?"

"Somehow he must have made it too clear too soon that he doesn't know what's going on. I guess you're right, they could eliminate him, and they tried unsuccessfully. Us on the hand... they need us."

"So you're saying we've got an advantage?"

"They're the ones who've told us that." Lucy pointed out across the pond. "They've told us they need us."

"What are you getting at?" Natasha's gaze followed Lucy's finger.

"We've got wiggle room. Let's screw with them."

"Don't we need to know who they are in order to... ehm... *screw* with them?"

"That's exactly the point!" said Lucy. "They're anonymous, right?"

"Right."

"Well, then that's the only thing we can screw with. We'll screw with their anonymity itself."

"Okay? I don't know if I've ever screwed someone's anonymity." Natasha leaned her head back and looked down her nose at Lucy, suspicious of such a proposal. "You'll have to explain what that entails."

"No, I mean, gosh, come on, try and keep up with me for, like, just a minute more, okay?"

"I'm trying, Lucy, I'm really trying."

"What if we didn't show this morning's letter to anyone else and wrote our own anonymous letter from the 'true heirs,' and delivered it to the servants' quarters residents. It would say the exact opposite of the letter that you found this morning. 'Don't worry guys. We don't need the bank account numbers anymore. We found them ourselves. You're all off the hook. Carry on as normal. It's all good. Have a nice day.' They've obviously got some sort of inside guy. They'll find out about the fake letter soon enough, and we'll see how they react."

"And what would that achieve?"

"We could draw them out. If they don't have *anonymity* to fall back on, they'd have to identify themselves somehow. Prove their credentials."

"Haven't they done as much killing Eugenio and Cristiano?" said Natasha.

"Sure, but those were individual acts in the past, probably attributed to one person. But that's the problem with being a killer who wants to remain hidden, while at the same time identifying himself. In order to get what he wants, he has to communicate. But he needs a *name* if he wants to communicate through time, with any continuity between his person and his acts, but he can't use a real name. So if we rob him of his fake name, we rob him of his anonymity, and his power to communicate with words. We rob him of his anonymity, and he'll be forced to use his real name to communicate."

"How long do I have to live in this country before I start sounding so weird and abstract?"

"Three years."

"I think I see what you're saying. If it works as well as your plan to trap me in the basement, it sounds like a great idea."

"It's worth a shot."

"I reckon it couldn't hurt to try. I've got another idea, though," Natasha suggested. "You might not like it, though. It's awfully practical."

"What's that?"

"We go to the orphanage where Eugenio grew up, snoop around, and try to find out who his parents are. Eugenio was the illegitimate kid. So if we find out who Eugenio's parents are, we can then find out who the legitimate kids are – the true heirs, that is, the killers."

"Good God, you're a genius!" Lucy's mouth opened and she put her hands up on her head.

"You really haven't thought of that yet?"

"No."

"Anyways, it's really great you and Brian managed to get Eugenio's wife, Irene, to tell us where the orphanage is when you pretended to be South African embassy officials. Eugenio would never talk about it with me. I've e-mailed the *principessa* and asked for the use of the van next weekend. I've told her we want to take a weekend to do 'team building exercises' as a group. You, Brian, and I can head up to Varese and poke around a bit. I've already checked into the property. It's not an orphanage anymore. It's just a retreat center. But who knows, maybe we'll find something."

Lucy looked across the lake. It had been over a year since the last time she'd left the city limits of Rome. A weekend in Varese sounded like a trip to the other side of the world. She'd have to do a lot to convince herself over the next week, "Alright." She took a deep breath, "Let's go."

The next Friday morning Lucy kept a death grip on the van's steering wheel, hurtling down the *Grande Raccordo Anulare* (literally, the "Grand Ring Road"), the circular beltway that goes around Rome's suburbs. The road was smooth and well maintained, but always packed with massive semi trucks moving slowly, and miniature European cars zipping from lane to lane at high speeds. On the beltway, a nine-passenger van can't throw its weight around like a semi, nor can it speed around like a car, so it requires a lot of extra stress to drive one in heavy traffic.

Scott was in the front middle seat, fiddling with the radio, jumping from station to station, changing every time he got bored in the middle of a song. Natasha scowled out the window from the front right seat. I was alone on the middle bench, and Andrew was on the back bench by himself, already fighting with sleep. The decisive moment didn't come until they reached the northern tip of the *Grande Raccordo Anulare*, where the road flies up to an overpass. Every driver is confronted with a decision: you can either set out into the unknown, following the road sign to *Milano*, or return to the comfort and familiarity of *Roma Centro*.

For a long time the beltway had represented the absolute outer limits of Lucy's sphere of activity. They passed a sign giving them one more kilometer before decision time. Now was the moment. The city of Rome — *O Roma felix!* — would be left behind for an entire weekend. Her pulse quickened, and she tried to ignore the road signs, but couldn't ignore the very thin layer of perspiration forming on her neck and arms, which, given Scott's vicinity, made her even more uncomfortable. She reached across to turn the heat off. It was already off.

"Isn't there AC?" she asked.

"No," said Scott, "But you can roll down the window."

"Oh God no," Natasha turned towards them. "We're going far too fast. Open the windows and I'll be sick."

"I've never heard of that before," said Scott. "I might be ready to believe the whole front seat thing, but you're definitely making up the window thing."

"Just leave 'em shut for now. I promise you, it's not worth finding out if I'm lying or not."

Lucy swallowed, stared ahead, and intensified her gaze. The Milan exit was now less than half a kilometer away. She took off her aviators, and put them up on her forehead. They merged into a line of cars headed up towards the overpass. The van rose. Lucy shifted down to fourth, held her arm against Scott, and then shifted to third.

The three were seated together, right next to each other, on the front bench of the tiny European van, leaving all of the middle seats and two of the back seats empty – except for me and Andrew, of course. When they first boarded the vehicle in front of Palazzo Mortimer, Lucy had refused to let anyone else drive. Natasha claimed that she had to have the front seat, otherwise she would get sick. Andrew staked out the back seat for himself, because he planned on sleeping. Scott said it was a terrible idea to let only Lucy and Natasha sit up front and navigate, so he squeezed himself into the middle front seat, a feature of most European vans. Natasha put up a fight, saying there wasn't enough room, and that Scott would cause her to get sick. Lucy gave a very half-hearted objection, but in reality, was actually more than happy to brush up against Scott's left arm every time she needed to shift, and feel her thigh against his every time she needed to move on or off the accelerator. She pretended the cruise control was broken and spent most of the time with her foot on the accelerator. Once Andrew finally fell asleep sideways in the backseat, it looked like three grown adults in a van had all chosen to sit up front, with six open seats behind. This would be a strange sight in America, but is actually not all that uncommon in Italy. Little by little, inculturation happens.

Once the exit ramp lifted above the normal street level, Lucy caught sight of the split ahead in the road and the two arrows – one pointed towards Milan, the other back to Rome. The traffic in front of them took off at high speeds, and Lucy should have accelerated and shifted up to fourth. But she lost heart and went to second instead.

I leaned forward from the middle row, "Come on, you can do this."

The van decelerated even more.

"Lucy!" I yelled, "Come on!"

She turned back at me, "Well I guess I'll just have to dive in. Live the tension, right?"

Scott and Natasha looked at Lucy with puzzled expressions. Lucy narrowed her eyebrows, tightened her grip on the wheel with both hands, and punched in the accelerator. She cringed and stared at the sign, willing herself so strongly to take the left to Milan that she forgot to shift. The RPM readout on the tachometer went way into the redline, and the van lurched back and forth. In shock, Lucy let her foot off the gas, too wired to remember the clutch. The van stalled. She kept her foot on the brake, right in front of the fork in the road. She was now full on sweating and breathing hard, the van at a full stop right in front of the fork. Every Roman driver behind them set off honking and yelling. Lucy heard nothing. Her mouth hung open and her eyes were fixed on the sign with the arrow and the word *Milano*. Scott reached behind himself, and put his seatbelt on, then leaned away from Lucy towards Natasha, not sure whether to make fun of her, ignore her, or if he'd have to say something out of character and encouraging. I put my paw on her shoulder, and she rubbed her cheek up against it.

"We got this," Lucy told herself. "We got this. Sorry, guys, I think it just stalled or something. This thing's old."

She put her sunglasses back down on her eyes, turned the engine back on, glared at the word *Milano*, grabbed the stick, put her right leg back up against Scott's, gently tapped on the accelerator, gradually eased off the clutch, and took the left fork for Northern Italy. In no time at all the van was back in fifth gear. Rome became a shrinking mass of apartment blocks in the rearview mirror, and the van plunged deep into open countryside.

The old Fiat hadn't gone so fast in years. Lucy rolled down her window – Natasha didn't dare object – and filled her lungs with non-Roman air. She'd forgotten the sweetness of breathing clean air. Leaning back, she left one hand on the wheel and let her hair whip around her head, while Scott and Natasha fought for control of the radio.

"Alright, everybody smile," said Natasha, approaching the Umbrian border. She propped her phone up on the dashboard.

Natasha leaned into Scott and smiled. Scott stared down the camera without smiling. Lucy gripped the wheel and kept her eyes on the road.

"Shall we try another?" Natasha looked at the results. "I want to send a photo to tease Brian and show him what he's missing out on."

"Don't mention that name again," said Lucy. "Brian's dead to us."

In the days following the infamous story night on the terrace, whenever Brian saw anyone, he would turn red and find an excuse to leave the room. He had become so busy that it was hard to find him anyways. At a certain point, though, Natasha and Lucy finally cornered him, and explained their plan to go visit the orphanage. He hemmed and hawed, talking about work and school, but eventually agreed to come.

Unfortunately, when she finally did give her consent for the students to borrow the van for a team-building weekend, the *principessa* sent an enthusiastic e-mail to all of the residents, not just Natasha, wishing them a good time. Fr. Damien, of course, refused to come, but Andrew was immediately on board, and thankfully Scott, who was in the kitchen at the time they got the e-mail, insisted on coming along.

That morning, already twenty minutes after the agreed upon departure time, Lucy came tearing through the lobby, running with her carry-on pack. Brian was sitting on a couch.

"Okay, okay," she said. "I'm here. Sorry. We can get going."

She stopped by the door. Brian wasn't getting up.

"I said we can go now. I'm here. Sorry."

"I can't."

"What?"

"I can't go. Work called. They can't give me the weekend off."

"What?"

"Work, Lucy. I can't."

"I don't understand what you're saying."

Scott, seated in the front seat of the van, saw Lucy through the glass doors and started honking.

"I'm sorry. I can't," he said. "Anyways, I already told you. I'm fine going to some retreat house, but I'm done with any of this..." he looked around the lobby, "investigation crap. It's not safe."

"Brian," Lucy walked over to the couch. "I don't think you understand. You said *yes*."

"I said 'yes... *if* I can get work off.'"

"I don't give a shit about your word games right now. We need you. Like... we *need* you. Get in the van. Call work. Tell them it's too late to cancel. This is not a discussion that I'm going to have with you right now."

"Right. Discussion over." Brian got up and moved towards the elevator.

"Brian, do you know how much you'll regret it if something happens to us?"

Brian opened the elevator grate and got in. "You're responsible adults. What you're doing is risky as hell, but I have to trust you not to do something stupid. You're a grown up, and you can make your own stupid decisions without me."

"If you're too fricking embarrassed to hang out with us, just because you made out with your sister and accidentally told us about – "

"What the hell is wrong with you, Lucy?" croaked Brian. His mouth hung open and he looked hurt.

"I'm just... this is very... I'm just... I'm sorry about... no! What the hell am I saying? Screw you, Brian!" She reached into the elevator, pressed the buttons for every floor, and stormed through the lobby to the van.

The ride from Rome to the Umbrian border was as smooth as possible, given the circumstances. The large toll highways between provinces in Italy are extremely well maintained – even better than American interstates, not that Lucy would admit it, though – whereas all other non-toll roads are built with potholes already pre-installed. Lucy had always thought the van shook so much because of the Roman cobblestones. This was certainly a factor. But now, on smooth open pavement, the van could no longer blame its behavior on the roads. It was rickety and sporadic the whole trip. Crossing into Umbria, there was a loud bang from somewhere underneath the car, and the whole carriage shimmied.

Andrew woke up in the back seat, "What the bloody hell was that?"

"You were just dreaming," yelled Natasha. "Go back to sleep."

"Alright," he lay back down.

Ten minutes later, though, it happened again.

This time Andrew didn't sit up, but just yelled, "Bloody hell!"

All the way through Umbria the bang and shimmy would happen every ten minutes. Andrew stopped yelling and learned to sleep through it, but Natasha looked worried and Scott would scratch his chin and ask questions. Once they crossed into Tuscany, the frequency had increased to once every five minutes, and on the stretch between Florence and Bologna, Natasha spotted a sign for an *Autogrill*, an Italian rest stop.

"Lucy, we're pulling over here, now now," said Natasha. "Look, it even says there's a service station. We absolutely must have this van looked at."

"It's fine. I promise. I think I know what the problem is," said Lucy.

"I gotta piss like a race horse," said Scott. "We gotta pull over."

"We can stop for the bathroom. That's fine," said Lucy. "But the van is okay, I promise."

She took the right lane, and decelerated onto the highway exit. Italian rest stops are closer to what most Americans would know as truck stops, just a little smaller and slightly more civilized. There's always a coffee bar, a gas station, bathrooms, people milling around, truckers taking their afternoon naps in their cabs, and a restaurant called *Autogrill*, that somehow has a monopoly on all Italian rest stops. Before Lucy could park, Scott climbed over Natasha, jumped out of the van and made a beeline for the bathroom. Lucy and Natasha wandered into the restaurant, and Andrew volunteered to guard the car.

"Are you sure, Andrew?" said Lucy. "This place looks pretty safe to me."

"Better safe than sorry."

"You can take the man out of Calabria, but you can't take Calabria out of the man." Lucy handed him the keys.

I started sniffing around the van, trying to find the problem. It wasn't hard to figure out. As I've said a number of times already, one of the biggest disadvantages of being human is the crippling lack of a sense of smell. It makes auto repairs so much easier if you can just sniff your way straight to a problem, rather than having to look at things. After just one minute I went into the building to tell Lucy what was wrong with the van.

It was Friday on the Milano-Roma stretch of highway, which meant the line for the women's room was out the door. I explained the problem to Lucy while she was in line, and also explained how to fix it. After the bathroom, and some time at the coffee bar, Lucy went over to the mini mart section and Scott and Natasha headed out to the parking lot. The van was not where they had left it. One hundred yards away, Andrew was having an animated discussion with a mechanic in front of the garage. The hood was open and the mechanic kept frowning and gesturing inside the engine. Scott and Natasha got closer, and Andrew put his hands on his hips.

"Hey guys. So Lucy was all like 'It's no problem'... my ass it's no problem."

"What's up?" said Natasha.

"Yep, it's definitely buggered. This guy says we might need a whole new transmission. Whatever it is, it's serious."

"Sounds bad," said Natasha. "Where are we? Are we going to make it to Milan?"

"Not today, it doesn't sound like. It'll take quite a while to get this all sorted out."

Lucy sauntered up with a new hammer, duct tape, and an open bag of chips. The other three turned and gave her accusatory looks.

"What's going on, guys?" she asked. "Why are we talking to a mechanic?"

"It turns out the van's in much worse condition that you thought," said Andrew.

"Oh yeah?" Lucy was still skeptical.

"Yeah, we probably need a whole new transmission or something."

"How long did you talk with this guy?"

"Five, ten minutes," said Andrew. "And he can already tell it's that bad."

"Exactly," said Lucy. "Did he tell you that he looked at the transmission?"

"Yeah."

"In five minutes?" Lucy walked in front of the engine, put her back to the mechanic, and turned to Andrew. "If I were to ask you where the transmission is, would you be able to identify it?"

"Yeah," Andrew walked up next to her. "It's one of those things in there. Maybe that one there."

"I guess they don't teach you auto-mechanics in the architecture faculty," Lucy put her forehead on Andrew's shoulder and giggled at him. She forced the hammer and duct tape into his hands. "Come on, let's go. Give me the keys. I'm gonna move the car."

She gave a knowing smile to the mechanic, trying to say, *you almost ripped off a group of foreigners. Well done. But not good enough.* The mechanic shrugged his shoulders back at her with a guilty smirk that said, *You win some, you lose some.* She got behind the wheel, and drove the van to an empty spot. Natasha, Scott and I sensed that we weren't going to be leaving for a while, so we escaped back to the *Autogrill*. Lucy got on her back on the pavement behind the van and shimmied her way behind the back tire.

"Andrew, give me the hammer," her hand appeared from underneath the van.

His left eye was healed, but he was still slightly hesitant to hand her a hammer. Given her position on the ground, Andrew judged that she didn't pose an immediate threat to him, and gave it to her. She banged away at something metal on the underside of the car, striking repeatedly on a hollow spot, and then asked for the duct tape. While Andrew was staring across the highway, someone tried to park in the spot next to the van, and Lucy almost had to fight the car off with just her legs – the only thing visible from underneath the van. Just in time, Andrew came back to his senses, and wagged his finger at the driver with one hand, and gestured at Lucy's legs with another.

"Okay, now help me up," said Lucy, shimmying out from underneath the car.

"What did you do down there?" Andrew put his toes on top of hers, grabbed both her hands, and brought her up to his level.

"I fixed the problem." Their noses were level and just an inch apart.

"What was the problem?"

"The muffler. Didn't you hear it keep backfiring?"

"Yeah... so you mean that's what that sound is?"

"That's what that sound *was*. It'll stop now."

"You mean that sort of sound... on the van or on any other sort of vehicle is always the muffler?"

"Yeah." Lucy let go of his hands and took a step back. "Haven't you ever heard an engine backfire? In fact, I should have a look at your scooter some time."

"That guy told me it was the transmission."

"No." Lucy was amazed. "How much money were you about to pay this guy to fix a transmission that he didn't even look at?"

"What was wrong with the muffler?"

"The pipe going into it was slightly bent, and the back part was rubbing up against the back bumper. It kept overheating."

"So what did you do?"

"I bent the pipe back and shoved a few balls of duct tape between the bumper and the muffler. It should stop overheating for now. Problem solved. Fifteen euros." She ran her fingers through her wavy black hair, stopping here and there to remove small pebbles. "And the parking lot of an Italian rest stop in my hair."

"Wow. But you never looked underneath the car after you parked. How could you tell that was the problem?"

"I've got good ears. Come on, let's go. I'll pull up to the front. Go get Scott and Natasha. Oh, and here." She handed him the hammer and duct tape and winked. "You can even keep these."

CHAPTER NINETEEN

COSA VUOI?

Lucy didn't wake up until nine in the morning. *Where the hell am I?* It was always jarring to wake up outside of the Palazzo, which, aside from prison a few weeks earlier, had been a very rare occurrence since her arrival in Rome. Her eyes jumped around the assortment of objects in the poorly illuminated room, and she let the memory of the journey slowly return: a tiny desk, a rigid chair, a rickety iron bed with only one pillow, a Brady Bunch style crucifix, high corniced ceilings, and – the room's one saving highlight – a connected bathroom, which must have been added whenever the orphanage had been turned into a retreat center.

Oh the glory of spending an entire weekend in a place where you don't have to shuffle all the way down a public hallway in a bathrobe and sandals just to get to the shower! It's amazing how modern humans – especially Lucy – can experience such a change in mood with a slight adjustment in bathing habits. She stretched in bed, slouched over to the curtains, and peaked outside. It was foggy out. Fair enough. In the bathroom she cranked the knob marked *caldo* in the shower and stayed there long enough that the inside turned foggy as well.

Well over an hour after waking up, she finally moseyed down to the massive dining hall, where there was only one place set remaining at the breakfast table. An eager Filipino sister poured her coffee and hot milk, set a tray of biscotti, juice, and fruit in front of her, and stood by the kitchen door, twenty yards away, watching Lucy eat. She nibbled on a few cookies as quickly as possible and escaped the dining room to explore the retreat center grounds. It was a large complex of many residential wings all connected to each other around a number of courtyards. At the center there was a big church and dining room. Outside it was chilly and still foggy. You could barely see one building from the next one over, which gave the impression that the campus was much larger than it really was. She found Natasha, bundled up like the Michelin tire man, in one of the courtyards, seated next to an ancient nun in a grey habit and a wheel chair. They were clucking away at each other in a language Lucy didn't understand.

"Lucy, this is Sister Madelon."

"It's very nice to meet you, sister." Lucy shook the old nun's hand and sat down on the bench next to Natasha.

The nun looked back at Natasha with a blank expression.

"Lucy, she doesn't speak English," said Natasha. "Try and use some of the Afrikaans that I taught you."

"Okay, let me see if I can remember anything," Lucy looked into the air in concentration, then turned to the nun and said, "*Sama sama.*"

Natasha and the nun sat in silence for a second before turning to each other and laughing.

"I'm sure that was very funny," said Lucy.

"Oh, it was."

"Did you ever teach me Afrikaans or just ways to make a fool of myself?"

"Yes and yes."

"But what are the chances there'd be a South African nun in the middle of northern Italy?"

"She's not South African. She's Dutch. More than half the old sisters here in the retirement home are Dutch. I guess their order, or whatever you call it, was from the Netherlands."

"Have you been able to find out anything about this place?"

"Yeah, I was just talking to her about it. It's a little slow going, though."

"Well then, keep going. I shouldn't interrupt."

"No it's fine. She's only *mostly* there," Natasha tapped on the side of her forehead that wasn't facing the old nun. "I've been sitting here for an hour and I've already had to introduce myself five of six times. Long term memory still seems to be mostly intact, though."

"Wow. That's perfect. Well, no, I mean, that's not perfect, but for us, it's like, perfect."

"I suppose so."

"So this place is a retirement home too?" said Lucy.

"This wing here is."

"Sure feels great to get out of the Palazzo Mortimer retirement home for the weekend, doesn't it?"

"It's partially a retirement home. It's also a novitiate and a retreat center. Oh, you missed it, Lucy. It was absolutely stunning. For an hour and a half this morning, there were perhaps forty or fifty novices – girls from all over the world, but in identical grey habits – and they all got out buckets with heaps of bleach and other things. They swept and they mopped and they scrubbed every inch of this entire facility. I asked sister Madelon and she told me they do that every morning. It was incredible, absolutely incredible. You must wake up earlier tomorrow to see it."

"Sounds like someone might have a vocation."

"After all that spectacle, I'm beginning to wonder."

"Have you asked her about Ginevra or Eugenio?"

"I don't know if we need to be that direct yet."

"What has she told you so far?"

"Yeah. Like I was saying, I've just been asking her about this campus. It was entirely an orphanage when it was built in the 1920's. Then in the '40's it became the Italian novitiate too. Around the '60's no more Dutch sisters were entering, so it became the only novitiate. Then around the '70's they stopped accepting children at the orphanage, and started all sorts of foster programs through the eighties. In the '90's they started making it into a retirement home and retreat center. And here we are today. I mean, there was quite a bit more to it, but that's the essentials."

"So Eugenio must've been one of the last generations to grow up here," said Lucy.

"I suppose so."

"And that explains why he spoke Afrikaans."

"He didn't, really. He spoke Dutch. But they're just about the same."

"Have you found out who's in charge, or who'd have access to records?"

"Madelon told me that Mother Superior is the grumpy one we met last night at the gate."

"No," moaned Lucy. "Not her. I saw her glaring at me from reception this morning too."

"That's the one."

"Well, whatever. It's alright, we'll figure something out."

The day before, traffic on the stretch of highway between Rome to Milan hadn't been that bad, but once in Milan itself, the highway became a parking lot. What made things worse was Natasha's insistence that they stop in Milan's city center and have a look around. Parking, at first, was a nightmare, until Scott remembered the name of the Italian patron saint of parking – *San Pancrazio, facci spazio* – and they found a free spot immediately. Lucy was surprised that she liked Milan. She liked it a lot. But she wasn't sure how to feel about that attraction. Over the years she had absorbed too much of the central Italian inferiority/superiority complex to go in with objective eyes. It was organized. Calm. Everyone was beautiful and they were dressed exactly as they should be dressed. People walked with purpose on sidewalks that were much cleaner than those in Rome.

While Rome has a unique and undeniable heart-piercing beauty that makes you long with existential nostalgia for the infinite, Milan's beauty is more intuited, perceived through its thick skin and its classy locals. For example, people say New York is beautiful, but if you actually take a look around, not many of the particular things in New York are really all that beautiful. It's a confluence of factors that makes it beautiful. Milan is the same. Even more. Some people say Milan is ugly. These people have no personality. There's a certain character that pervades the city and that tells you that life is life. Milan is Milan. You're in Milan. This is how it's done. Sure, we're Italy. But we're Milan.

They all hoofed the two hundred and fifty steps up to the roof of the Duomo, the second largest gothic cathedral in Europe, and spent an hour just above the city skyline with the Madonnina, amid a forest of gothic spires, watching the sun light up the horizon through the evening smog of industrial no-nonsense northern Italy. After finding dinner and before heading back to the car, Lucy bought a lighter with the words written on it: *Milano è la città più europea del mondo. È ancora più europea di New York.*

Varese is only forty miles north of Milan, squeezed between a giant lake and the foothills of the Alps, right up against the border with Switzerland. Like I said, Lucy doesn't get out of Rome much. What's a bear to do? That weekend was not exactly my finest hour as a spirit animal. The Alps! I mean, come on, the *Alps*! And you want me to spend the weekend closed up in a retreat center looking for old records? Nature called, and I was drawn to the mountains, to the fresh air, to the smell of other animals in the forest. I wasn't completely absent from Lucy's life, but I'd be lying if I said I was completely present.

After the sun set, it took them an hour to find the place where they parked the van in Milan, and with traffic and poor navigation skills it took them two hours to get to Varese, and another hour of being lost in Varese before finding the retreat center. The old Italian nun who had to wake up to let the car through the gate was not happy. She showed the group their rooms, gave them their keys, and Lucy collapsed into her bed. I headed for the hills. Alpine Italy. Switzerland. It was too good to be true.

"So what do you think we should do?" asked Natasha. "We've only got today and tomorrow."

"I don't know. For the time being, see if you can get any more information out of sister Madelon here. We're on retreat, right? I'm gonna go see if Mother Superior's available for spiritual direction."

Lucy went to another courtyard, and sat in a park bench by herself. She placed her head in her hands and worked herself up into a spiritual crisis that would require the immediate attention of an Italian nun. If police detectives could crumble at her feet, any old crotchety nun wouldn't offer much resistance, right?

After just ten minutes of concentrated reflection, she had turned herself into a spiritual and moral wreck, and because she was on "retreat", she went straight to the authority. Mother Superior was still at the reception desk in the large lobby, leaning back in a captain's chair and reading a collection of Leopardi's poems. Lucy's moccasins made little noise on the stone floor, and by the time she was standing in front of the desk looking down at the nun, Mother Superior was still looking at her book.

"Good morning," Lucy began in English. The night before, the nun had spoken to them only in English, but with a bizarre accent that pronounced every word very clearly and slowly, and gave an exaggerated weight to the vowels. Lucy figured that in English she'd have an advantage over the nun.

"Good morning," the nun looked up from her book.

"Ehm ... well ... I'm not really sure how to say this ... um ... would it be alright if we talked for a moment?"

"Sure." The nun didn't move and continued to look back at Lucy, holding the book open in front of her.

"Um ... I mean, do you have some time to talk to me about some things? Some issues? I feel like I could really be helped by talking to a sister."

"Why not? Come over here."

They went into an office with a glass wall behind the reception desk. Lucy sat down in a modern armchair, with her back to the glass. The nun took an identical chair, diagonal to Lucy.

"What's your name?"

"Lucy."

"Lucy, I'm sister Gabriela. And what would you like to talk about?"

"Well ... so I came here on retreat with my friends – "

"You must speak slowly," interrupted the nun. "The American accent is a little difficult for me. All those R's deep down in the throat. What are they doing down there? Why don't you bring them forward a bit?"

"I'll try to speak slowly, okay?"

"Very good."

"So we're on this retreat. And, well, just like, a lot of stuff has come up, just being at the retreat center and all ..."

The nun leaned in and furrowed her eyebrows, trying to keep up with Lucy's foreign speech patterns. Lucy leaned back and looked at the abstract painting on the opposite wall, a bunch of black and white curves that might be angel wings or might be the hoods of a group of monks. In high school she had learned that police interrogations and court mandated counseling sessions were always two different ball games. The first game, interrogations, involved crafting an alibi, sticking to it, and getting the police to commit a procedural error. The second game, counseling, was trickier, because it involved understanding what sort of image the psychologist has of himself. What sort of problem does the psychologist delight in solving?

After that first time she got arrested, during her first round of court ordered counseling, Lucy somehow got her hands on the DSM-IV. Throughout the end of middle school and on through high school, she would get passed along from shrinks to counselors, from gurus to pastors. She would spend weeks studying a certain mental disorder, and whenever she would get sent to a new psychologist, she would do her best to manifest certain symptoms. But whenever the psychologist could finally identify the symptoms and send her to a specialist, she would completely change the set of problems, and throw off the new guy by coming up negative on all the tests, and positive for a completely unrelated disorder. Her file became a convoluted mass of misdiagnoses and she especially enjoyed pitting different specialists against each other. It took her six different private schools to make it through four years of high school. She even managed to leave with a diploma that sent her to college – not without the intervention of the CFO of Initech, of course.

The nun was very attentive, scratching her chin and leaning forward to catch every word. Every once in a while she would stop Lucy and ask her why certain points were relevant. Lucy had learned that whenever she had to sit across a large desk from an upset private school teacher or mustached Jesuit principal, or whenever her parents sent her to some new hotshot evangelical youth pastor, who was finally going to figure her out, it was always enough to speak of her problems in terms of Immanuel Kant's duty ethics, mixed in with psycho-babble about a father wound. All of this, of course, she disguised in Christian terminology, but at the end of the day, Kantian ethics and pop psychology were the only things most of them were really interested in talking about.

So Lucy launched into a long tale of woe, the details of which were mostly true, but which her experience had taught her to embellish here and there. Sr. Gabriela was patient enough at first, struggling to pay attention, then grew more and more interested. A nun who works as a receptionist, thought Lucy, she'd probably prefer to be saving poor souls like me. She's gotta be loving this.

"Wait. Lucy. Okay, I think this is enough for right now."

"Okay..."

"What were you thinking of doing on this retreat? Will you have time for silence?"

"I guess."

"Do you know anything about Ignatian prayer?"

"Yeah," said Lucy. "You've got to be the change you want to see in the world. *Magis*. Be the more. Y'know, making a difference and all that."

"Hmm ... okay, that's definitely a component later on, but for today the first thing you'll need to do is find a comfortable place where you can spend a few hours in silence – "

"A few hours? Sister, I don't know if I have a few hours."

"Well, take twenty minute chunks if you're a beginner. Now I'm going to write down some meditations on scripture passages. You have a bible with you, right? You can use this one if you understand Italian."

"Don't you want to talk about my problems?"

"You've certainly got problems. I don't know the answers. Here. Write this down."

Sr. Gabriela flipped through a bible. Lucy, however, was completely lost. Hearing the words *I don't know* coming from an authority figure was something completely new for her. And so in a moment of panic, knowing she didn't have time for a few days of retreat, she jettisoned her original plan. She departed completely from reality and came up with a completely artificial sob story, trying to get straight to the point. I should have been there to tell her not to. She was out of her league. "Well, sister, I think there's still more to the story I was telling you."

"I'm sure there is. For now, though, do these meditations, and tomorrow we'll talk. You can't attack everything at once.

You've got to choose the hills you want to die on. You're here 'til Monday morning, correct?"

"I think this next part's important, though."

"Alright, alright," Sister Gabriela smiled and chuckled for the first time, shaking her head. "Tell me. Tell me."

"Okay, so where were we?"

"You were just out of college and trying to understand what your Christian duty is in life with respect to your latent need for a parental figure ... something like that ... can I ask, who taught you to speak like this? Is this a normal American way of speaking? You poor people."

"Well let me just skip ahead a few years. So before I came to Italy, I found out that I was adopted."

The nun got serious again, and looked Lucy deep in the eyes.

Lucy looked away from her, at the painting across from her and continued, "Yeah, so I found out I was adopted. In Colorado they just passed this new freedom of information law, so adopted children can find out who their biological parents are. Anyways, my real mom's a deadbeat in San Francisco now ... but I found out that my dad's Italian. In '89 he was very young and on vacation in America. He spent a few nights with my mom, and nine months later I was born. He was back in Italy, and I was given up for adoption before he ever knew anything about me ... but ... but ... I don't know ... I'm not sure he ever knew I even existed."

"And so this explains what you're doing in Italy."

"Right, well, I came here to figure out, you know, who I am, where I come from."

"And here we are."

"But not just, like, Italy in general," said Lucy. "I'm here this weekend because I finally found out where my dad grew up. Here. The orphanage."

"So you haven't managed to find him, yet?"

"No ... but he ... um... he died last month."

"I see," said Sister Gabriela.

"So I'm here to see what I can see."

"You're not on retreat."

"Well, it's a kind of retreat."

"Sure."

"So you can help me?"

"Maybe. What was your father's name?"

"Eugenio Galli."

"Okay, I remember him."

"You do?"

"Very little, but yes. For some reason the Dutch sisters really loved him. I was only here for two years as a novice, and we did not have much interaction with the children. But I still remember a lot of them. And I remember Eugenio."

"And ..."

"Oh, he was boisterous. Active. Loud. Always trying to get his way. A good kid, though. I'm sorry, though, that's really all I remember. I was just here for two years as a novice, and didn't interact much with the children. I'm sorry to hear he's died already."

"Do you remember anything about *his* parents?"

"So American. So practical. Now I see why you're really here."

"So you can help?"

"This is Italy. We have laws. I can't just hand over confidential records."

"Well, can you tell me something about them?"

"Probably not. Well ... whatever, this isn't confidential, I don't think. It's just rumors from older sisters. Anyways, Eugenio was a great kid, but he never got adopted. They say this was because he was the illegitimate child of a powerful family. Who's to say, though? I was not here at the time, but the older sisters told me that his mother — your grandmother I suppose — lived for nine months on the grounds here during her pregnancy. A nice lady. At the time she was neither particularly young nor old, they said. She told the rest of her family she was abroad or something. And then, when Eugenio was born, I think she finally did go abroad."

"So there is some kind of record?"

"Sure ... but I doubt she used her real name, anyways. I don't think it would help you. They said she sounded very southern, said she was from Basilicata, but demonstrated no knowledge of the geography of Basilicata."

"Maybe there're pictures somewhere?"

"To be honest, if you ask me, you're better off staying away from that family."

"But they're *my* family."

"Lucy. Look. I came back to Italy two years ago for medical reasons. But I spent the previous forty in Nairobi, running one of the largest pharmacies in the country. After treatment I got better, but they wouldn't let me go back to Africa. Now I'm mother superior of the retired nuns. Do you know what that means?"

"What?"

"It means I used to be very powerful. People needed me. Now half the people I'm in charge of are senile. I'm a receptionist, but you know what, I am happy. But, what am I saying? That's not my point. The point is, I spent the previous forty years around people who really needed something, and were willing to lie to get what they needed."

Lucy sank back in her chair and looked down at her lap.

"Oftentimes, though," continued Sr. Gabriela, "I would give people what they needed, even knowing that they were lying. I hope that I'm wrong, but everything about the way you are behaving is telling me that ... at some point along the road ... you are completely full of garbage. You are telling me all kinds of stories. Why don't you just tell me the truth?"

"I don't know what to tell you, then. That's ... that's the truth."

The nun stared her down. Lucy looked back at her lap and suddenly felt like crying, but didn't.

"Here's the thing," the nun said. "Despite your lies, I think, somehow, your heart's in the right place. And if I could, I might even help you. But life – both now and in general – would be so much easier if you would just say what you want. Why not do that? Just say what you want."

"Say what I want?"

"Yes."

"I want information on Eugenio's birth family."

"Good. That's obvious. Now tell me why."

"I ... I already told you."

"Well then you're not going to get it. Come find me when you're ready to tell me something that at least resembles the truth." Sister Gabriela stood up, and left the room. The click of her heels echoed all the way across the lobby and down the hall towards the retirement wing.

What was left of the morning, Lucy spent pacing back and forth in her room. She was torn. Thinking of Sr. Gabriela's obstinacy, she felt like breaking something, but knew that wouldn't help the cause. At the same time, remembering the nun's penetrating eyes, she felt like balling herself up in bed and crying. So in the end, she neither broke anything, nor cried, but settled for pacing back and forth in her room.

The security cameras at the facility were too comprehensive. Breaking into the records was off the table. The only way forward was through the nuns – some of whom were mostly senile, and at least one of whom, Sr. Gabriela, was incredibly far from senile. Everything, perhaps, was riding on Natasha, on whether or not she could find a way forward through the old Dutch sisters.

"Any progress?" Lucy pulled Natasha aside and asked her before lunch in the dining room.

"Not really."

"Did you ask about Eugenio or Ginevra?"

"I didn't know if we wanted to be that forward already."

"I think we have to be. Go for it. Also ... this is a long shot ... but if you can find out a way to blackmail the nun in reception, Sister Gabriela, that could help us a lot."

"I'll see what I can do."

At lunch they were the only four guests at a cramped table. Four overeager, petite, young nuns, who plied them with more food than they wanted, and made sure their water and wine glasses were never empty, served the four-course meal – *primo, secondo, insalata, frutta.*

When she had been pacing around her room, Lucy had also spent a great amount of time reflecting on Sr. Gabriela's words: *say what you want.* Forgetting the case for a second, Lucy knew what she wanted. Now was the time to act, to say what she wanted. After lunch she let the others leave, then went up to the sisters and told them that only two of them would be at dinner.

The fog lifted in the afternoon so the four students borrowed bicycles from the nuns and rode the fifteen-mile loop path around Varese's majestic lake in front of the Alps. Afterwards, Lucy spent more time than she had intended showering and getting ready for the evening, and just barely intercepted Scott on the way to the cafeteria for dinner.

"Scott. Hey. Natasha and Andrew told me they were bored and went to Milan for dinner."

"What? I could've sworn I just heard – "

"Come on. Are we gonna stay here or go some place fun?"

"What do you mean?"

"I saw some cool places in town here in Varese. Come on. Let's go out tonight."

"I thought we had plans to have dinner here?"

"I already signed us out. It's too late to stay here. Come on. Let's go."

"Well, okay."

Walking out the gate of the sisters' property, and turning towards the city center, Lucy took her right hand and placed it inside Scott's left arm. He tried to shake her off, but she held firm.

"Lucy, what are you doing?"

"You guys are so formal over there at the NAC. Don't they teach you the proper etiquette for walking a lady to dinner?"

"We don't have ladies over there."

"Well then I'll have to teach you tonight."

"Oh, and you're a *lady*?"

"And how."

"Do you have any idea how much trouble I'd be in, if someone from the NAC were to see me going out to dinner on a Saturday night with a girl like you leeching onto my arm?"

Lucy leaned closer to him, linked her right elbow with his and grabbed his arm with her left hand. "Well, here let me just grab on tighter, then. Like a leech. It just makes dinner all the more fun doesn't it? Plus, come on, nobody from the NAC would come to Varese for a travel weekend, would they?"

"Well, I guess we'll find out."

They smiled at each other and walked into town. That's as much as Lucy would ever tell me about that evening. She was often an open book on all kinds of things, but every time I plied her for more information on that evening in particular, she either teared up and stormed off, or got a dreamy look on her face and refused to speak.

Late that night, just after she and Scott had parted ways, Lucy knew she wouldn't be able to sleep, so she went for a walk around the retreat center grounds. I emerged from the forest and found her in her coat slowly putting one foot in front of the other, and vaguely smiling at the dark trees along the path circling the grounds.

"Well, well, well," she finally caught sight of me. "Look who decided to turn up this weekend."

"Lucy, we're right next to the mountains. I'm sorry if I can't help myself. You do understand I'm a bear, don't you?"

"It's fine. Everything is fine."

"How's it been going?"

"Great ... really *really* great. Perfect. Life is great."

"Oh good, so you haven't missed me then. What have you found out?"

"Well ... no ... the case is terrible. We haven't found out anything."

"So then what's great? And what is that scent that I smell on you?"

I sniffed her neck. She was giving off all kinds of pheromones that I hadn't smelt on her in quite a while. Her hair and clothes were all still in order, so it didn't look like anything had happened, and the scent suggested that she was still feeling the need to ... well, anyways, she understood that I had figured out what was going on.

"Your nose is really not fair," she said.

"I know. If humans just had a halfway decent sense of smell it would seriously reduce over ninety percent of all the ambiguity in your relationships. Whatever. I don't need to know about it. But the case? What do we know about the case?"

"Oh nothing. That's been terrible. Thanks for all your help, by the way."

"What have you tried?"

She told me all about her long session in spiritual direction, and Natasha's endless chats with senile Dutch nuns, but nothing about her evening out. "Whatever, though. This place is nice ... and it is ... nice to get out of Rome, I guess."

"There you go. Not all is lost."

CHAPTER TWENTY

'NA GAMBA SPEZZATA

Sunday morning they hiked up the mountain that was just behind the
retreat center: *Sacro Monte*. The path was steep and long, but it was
wide and cobble stoned, with fifteen small renaissance chapels along
the way. They walked slowly. It was Sunday, so the locals were out
strolling up and down the mountain too. Each chapel was dedicated
to a mystery of the rosary, designed to hold at bay the advance of
Swiss Protestants into the Italian peninsula. It worked, I guess. Like
all good hikes in Italy, after spending hours working your legs
through an isolated wilderness area, you arrive at the top of the
mountain to find a parking lot next to a church, a gift shop, and a
terrace where you can sit and buy expensive cocktails. Two sides of
the terrace bar on Sacro Monte were on the side of a cliff, and the
third side was along the path, so you could sit and look at the view
on two sides, and on the other side, watch people as they came up
and down the path.

"Allora, eccoci qua, ancora un'altro spritz per tutti. E ancora un paio di cose da mangiare."[161] The waiter set four large drinks with straws on the table, and a couple of baskets of potato chips, and cleared away four empty glasses with straws and a couple of empty baskets of potato chips.

Scott raised his glass, "Here's to the Madonnina."

"To the Madonnina," they all replied, and clinked glasses.

"What's the Madonnina?" asked Andrew.

"Who's the Madonnina? She's that speck of gold you see right there." Scott pointed out over the cliff towards Milan. On the top of the Duomo, miles away, there was a giant golden statue of Mary. On a very windy Sunday, from the top of the mountains in Varese, when the factories are closed and the cars aren't driving to work, you could see her reflecting the sun off herself from the center of the city.

Natasha came out of left field and asked the group. "So what did you all think of that letter from the 'true heirs?'"

Lucy sent her a sideways look and nudged Natasha's foot under the table, while clearing her throat.

"Oh, you mean that letter you guys got that day that Lucy punched Andrew in the face?" said Scott. "I'm sure Andrew wants to talk about that, doesn't he?"

"Whatever, it's all fine," said Andrew. "Yeah, we got another one from those same people a few days ago. Sounds like they're all chummy with us all of the sudden."

"Really?" said Scott. "What did they say?"

"Not much really," said Andrew. "They just left a letter saying that they weren't worried about the inheritance money anymore, and they're sorry for having made us worry about bank accounts and all that rubbish. It's a bit strange, if you ask me. I mean, why would they just say sorry and tell us to go about our normal business after all that drama?"

"Maybe they found out I was around," said Scott. He was a little louder than normal, after one and a half spritz on an empty stomach. "The true heirs got scared and went away. I understand. I would too if I were them. Man, this country. I tell you what."

---

[161] "Okay, here we've got another spritz for everybody. And a few things to nibble on."

"Guys, is this really the best place to be having this conversation?" said Lucy. The terrace was full of tables with people drinking Sunday afternoon cocktails. Their table was up against the railing that looked over the cliff ledge on one side, but packed in on the other three sides by tables full of Italians.

"Well, we're up here in Varese, hundreds of kilometers from Rome," said Andrew. "I doubt anyone knows what we're talking about."

"I don't know, though," said Scott. "I get the feeling whatever we're doing here isn't unrelated. Let's be real, girls, I know something's gotta be going down. You've both been spending the entire weekend creeping around an old convent talking to nuns on the sly. Call me crazy, but I'm almost certain that that would not be your first choice for a weekend get-away."

Lucy looked at Natasha, with eyes that said, *I told you so. You should not have brought this up in conversation.*

"Come on," Scott slammed his fist on the table and the people at the surrounding tables all shot exaggerated Italian glares at them. "Be honest. Just tell me. What are we doing here?"

"Scott!" shouted Lucy, "what did we tell you about not ... y'know ... not drawing attention, especially not when we're talking about ... Just try to speak quietly and on the D.L."

"Whatever. I'm going to the bathroom," answered Scott. "But when I get back, I want some answers, okay?"

"I have to use the toilet too," said Natasha.

"I'm gonna go buy a selfie stick. We've gotta get some group pictures," said Andrew, pointing at the parking lot area where he saw some vendors who had been selling them earlier.

And Lucy found herself alone at the table, guarding the drinks, and munching on potato chips. She was leaning across the table, drinking from the straw in Scott's spritz when she heard the yell. It was loud, deep, desperate, and short. It was followed by a thud with the unmistakable crack of breaking bones, and a very explicit series of English swear words, interspersed with the word, "Help!"

Everyone who was seated on the terrace got up, rushed over to the railing opposite the path, and looked down over the cliff's edge. Some of them already had their cell phones out, and were calling for emergency help. A waiter came running through with a rope, and Lucy had to shove and dig her elbows into people to make her way to the railing. Scott was thirty feet below the bar, hanging onto a very small lonely tree that had grown out of an extremely narrow ledge on the side of the cliff and yelling in pain. His feet were dangling right above a two hundred yard drop.

The door to the single bathroom was in the bar building, next to the place where Scott must have gone over the railing. Someone flushed inside, the door opened, and Natasha pushed her way through the crowd to where Lucy was looking over the edge. Andrew showed up too, wielding a selfie stick. There was little that anyone could do.

"Scott!" yelled Lucy.

He looked up, but couldn't identify any of the faces. He was clearly in a lot of pain. "Lucy!" he yelled back, followed by a long list of expletives explaining exactly how he felt.

"Scott! Hold on!"

"Hold on, Scott!" yelled Natasha. "Hold on tight! Help's coming!"

Help, though, in the form of professional paramedics, took over half an hour to arrive. Andrew stayed by the edge, yelling encouraging words and laughing, as Scott's profanity got even more sarcastic and colorful. Lucy and Natasha paced back and forth on the terrace, sometimes crying and hugging, sometimes yelling encouragements down to Scott, always looking like they were on the verge of a breakdown.

The waiters managed to put together a very impromptu harness using rope they'd found in the basement. They dropped it down to Scott, and he even tied it around his waste, but he refused to let go of the tree, not trusting his life to the knot tying skills of waiters. It took a paramedic with a harness to repel down the side of the mountain and clip him in with professional ropes to finally convince him to let go of the tree. His right leg was very swollen, and once up on the terrace, they immediately immobilized him in a full body brace. Lucy, Natasha, and Andrew were kept away. He was hauled off to an ambulance and sped along the road that led down the backside of the mountain.

Lucy sprinted down the path that they had walked up, leaving Andrew and Natasha behind. At the retreat center, she fired up the

van, drove to the gate, looked left, then right, and only then realized
that she had no idea where Scott would be. She parked the van, and
ran to her room in the retreat center, opened google, and called every
number for every hospital emergency room anywhere near Varese. It
took an hour to find anyone who knew anything, and by the time she
did find out where Scott had been, they told her that he'd already
been sent to a specialist in Milan.

"*Milano. Ma dove a Milano?*"[162]

"*Il Grande Ospedale Metropolitano Niguarda.*"[163]

"*Vado subito.*"[164]

"*Guardi, le ore delle visite sono già finite. Può andare
domani alle dieci.*"[165]

"*Va bene.*"[166]

She hung up. Natasha was standing at the door, leaning up
against the doorpost.

"Lucy, he'll be fine. He's safe now. There's nothing we can
do." She sat on the bed next to Lucy and put her arms around her.

"I know ... it's just ... knowing that's not enough. Why don't
we go to Milan? Are we safe here?"

"We're only safe because they think we might have the bank
account numbers."

"What do you mean?"

"Scott started talking too loud," said Natasha. "Somebody
sitting around us must've understood what he was saying. He
basically admitted to everyone that he had no idea what was going
on. They did exactly what they said they'd do. They told us that as
soon as they could establish for sure that one of us doesn't have the
bank numbers, they'd off that person – as a warning to the one who
does have the numbers. Perhaps they didn't understand that he's not
a resident. Either way, it's clear. They're not messing around. It
won't be long before they come after one of us and use more direct
methods. We don't have much time."

"Right, so I'd feel a lot better if we got out of here."

---

[162] "Milan? Where in Milan?"
[163] "The Metropolitan Niguarda Hospital."
[164] "I'll be there right away."
[165] "Listen, visiting hours are over. You can go tomorrow at ten."
[166] "Fine."

"You're right. Let's get out of here."

Lucy, Andrew, and Natasha checked out of the retreat center and spent the night in a cheap hotel near the hospital – three tiny beds in the room, and one bathroom down the hall. Breakfast not included. Lucy was the first to charge into the hospital at the start of visiting hours. After a brief search, she spotted Scott at the other end of a long hallway in a wheel chair with one foot propped up in a thick plaster cast. She immediately started walking and then running towards him. Scott's eyes grew wide, and he made a very subtle stop gesture with his right hand, followed by two fingers at his neck imitating a knife. Lucy halted and looked back scared. Two old men in black suits and clerical shirts came out of a hospital room, and carted Scott off. Turning the corner, Scott finally got an angle to look at Lucy. He smiled and winked. She followed at a distance and watched from the windows of the waiting room as they loaded him up into a white van with the North American College logo pasted on the side, and drove away.

Turning around, she spotted the last person she would have wanted to see at that moment, lurking at the other end of the waiting room in a grey habit. The nun gave a nasty grin to Lucy. Alright, thought Lucy, with a clear mission consciousness. Game on. Let's give it one more shot.

"Sister, can we talk one more time?"

"About the truth?"

"Let's just talk, okay."

"Okay."

They took seats at right angles from each other — Lucy with her feet tucked under her chair so that her knees wouldn't touch the nun — in perpendicular rows of plastic seats, and chatted in hushed voices below the whir of a Coke machine.

"I'd just like to give you one more opportunity to help us," said Lucy.

"That's very generous of you," the nun smiled back.

"I know why you're back in Italy and not Nairobi. It's not medical. You were illegally selling prescription drugs there."

"What are you getting at?"

"Nothing. Since we're on the topic of truth, I'm just saying I know the truth about you. And if you want, I also know how to remain quiet about that truth."

"Would you stop and think for a second."

"I've already thought about it quite a bit. We came here on a mission. One of us almost died in carrying out that mission. I'm not at all interested in leaving here empty handed."

"I mean, really. Think. Your blonde friend got that story from an old Dutch nun with no memory. If a senile nun can remember a story like that, do you really think it's a secret from the rest of the community? I am in Italy for medical reasons. And your cute blackmail story, clearly, everybody already knows all about it. You can tell whomever you like."

Lucy leaned forward like she was going to stand up. "Well it was worth a shot."

"Stay seated!" yelled the sister.

Lucy sat back down and crossed her arms.

"I have been blackmailed with various false accusations at least twice, annually, for the last forty years. Welcome to the third world. Say what you want about me, but much worse has already been said. You're an amateur. Now are you going to tell me the truth about what you were doing in Varese?"

"At this point, why should I?"

"Who knows? Maybe I'd help."

Lucy sighed, looked at the ceiling, and then fixed her eyes on the Coke machine. "Maybe we're investigating a murder."

"There. Now was that so hard?"

"Yes."

"You're right. You are here on a mission. Your friend Scott seems to know nothing about it."

"You talked to Scott?"

"Of course."

"And Scott talked to you?"

"We chatted. An interesting fellow, that one."

"Chatted about what?"

"Life. You realize he almost died? That can be a rude awakening for someone so young. He has a lot to discern in the next few weeks. You know he has a different life than yours. Maybe he hasn't realized that yet, and maybe a brush with death might wake him up."

"Wait... no... you need to stay out of this."

"I will. I will. Though, I must say that I did consider contacting his superiors, given his ambiguous behavior. But I thought better of it."

"I'm not having this conversation."

"Nonetheless, he convinced me about you."

"About me?"

"Alright, well I have been doing my own research on the Eugenio case. It is indeed strange. There's not much material except for a few articles by a certain Ludovici, who then turned up dead a few weeks later on the scene of the crime – the crime scene where you also happen to live. It's weird, and if you ask me, you're better off staying out of it. But I don't know, like I said, Scott convinced me that your heart is in the right place. Whatever you are doing, you are doing it for a good purpose. I hope. But I must ask you, please, be careful. In fact, you are much better off staying out of it."

"It's too late for me to get out."

"Well. In Eugenio's files, there's nothing written about his mother. And this is not a surprise. It was clear that she was from some sort of mafia family, hiding because she had been found pregnant at the wrong moment or from the wrong man. The older nuns called her 'Ginevra' but that was clearly not her real name. The family must have been very influential because, even last night, years later, the older sisters all got shifty eyes when I asked them about it at dinner. If you look inside that envelope of yours on the chair over there" — a large brown envelope sat unaccompanied three chairs down from the sister — "you would notice that somehow you've procured a copy of Eugenio's files and a picture of baby Eugenio with his mother. It's truly surprising that you managed to get your hands on those. You must be very crafty."

Lucy looked back through the glass wall at the traffic outside, then at the envelope and back at the whirring Coke machine. "You mean you ... you mean ..."

"It's quite unusual that those copies got in your hands. You must be very crafty indeed."

"Did you – "

"It's better if you don't ask questions. But you might notice those documents, nonetheless, in that envelope of yours."

"But that's not —"

"In that envelope of yours!" the sister cut her off.

"Oh my God, I'm such an ass."

"Yes you are. But that's not the point. If you got to know me better you'd say the same thing about me."

"But why are you helping me?"

"To be clear, I don't want to acknowledge helping you with anything in particular. But in the abstract, looking back at my time in the pharmacy, I've learned to judge who needs help and who doesn't. You're lucky you have good friends like Scott. In the future, just try to remember. You don't have to manipulate to get what you want. Sometimes the truth is enough."

"I'm so sorry."

"Don't be."

"No really. I'm sorry. You don't know how bad I feel."

"I can imagine. You don't have time to feel bad about yourself, though. Go on. Get out of here and worry instead about your friend who had the accident. Between you, me, and the wall, I think he actually does have a vocation. It's going to be quite difficult for both of you when he finds out, but you can help him to make his decision more clear, by staying away from him. Anyways. Go. Get out of here."

Lucy stayed there and looked back at Sr. Gabriela with sympathetic eyes.

"I said go!" she shouted.

Lucy got up, but didn't move until the nun shoed her out of the room with her hands. She picked up the envelope, left the hospital, and went back to the cheap hotel to find Andrew and Natasha.

Feeling unable to drive back to Rome, Lucy took the front middle seat, Natasha the passenger seat, and Andrew the wheel. She texted him:

Where are you? When do I see you?

Over the next three hours along the highway she sent twelve similar texts, each with more dramatic expressions of her need to see him, but he didn't respond until they entered Tuscany.

> Tough to say. Once we get back to Rome, me and my foot will be immobilized in my room upstairs for at least a few days. There's no sheilas allowed on the seminary corridors. Sometime soon I'll be headed to Wisconsin for surgery on my ankle. Call me.

"No," she sighed, turned off her phone, and slammed it into her bag.

"What's up?" asked Andrew.

Lucy looked to her right at Natasha, who was asleep with her head bobbing up and down, and then turned back to Andrew, "Nothing's up."

"Was that Scott?"

"I don't know what to do, Andrew."

"Lucy, this is all weird." Andrew lowered his voice.

Lucy had to lean in to talk over the motor. "What's weird?"

"The whole Scott thing. I think he's a great guy and all, and I'll do what I can for him. But it's just weird. I'd keep my distance if I were you."

"What do you mean?"

"Can I be frank?"

"You already are being frank."

"There's a lot of people who care about you. Maybe I'm one of them, alright? I just don't want to see you getting mixed up with this whole murder thing anymore. I've almost been killed, Scott's clearly a target. Maybe you were right a while ago. We'd be better to just keep our heads down and not get involved. I want you to be safe. I care, you know?"

"What does that have to do with Scott?"

"Nothing. I'm sure it's nothing. All I'm saying is that what happened to him is weird, and maybe that's something to stay clear of."

"I just need to talk to him before he leaves."

"He's leaving?"

"Within a couple days. You said you'd help me with whatever?"

"I'll do anything to help you, Lucy." He nudged her with his elbow. "Even if I don't know what's going on, I'll help. But you know I don't like it."

"That means a lot. Thanks."

"Remember, just stay safe and stay out of it. We care about you."

She laid her head on Andrew's shoulder, stretched her calves out on top of Natasha's legs — Natasha grunted, but allowed Lucy to stay — and pretended to fall asleep. She was in the middle of nowhere Italy, and for at least the next couple hours, far from Rome and Milan, she knew she would be safe with those two by her side. And somewhere in Umbria, she actually did fall asleep.

CHAPTER TWENTY-ONE

LA CHIAVE DELLA CHIAVE

Within an hour of her return to her room at the Palazzo, she heard an envelope slide under her door. Inside, there was a note and a key card.

> Like I said, I'm here to help, and I've got connections in this country. Scott's in room 503. Don't go until after midnight when everybody's asleep or you'll probably be seen on the hallways. Promise me you'll be safe. - Andrew.

She opened the door, and looked up and down the hallway. Andrew was nowhere to be seen.

By 11:30pm she was walking back and forth along the street between the NAC and the Palazzo, and by 11:58 she tried the key card on the NAC's gate. The light beeped and turned green, and the heavy door ceded to her frantic shove. Alone in the elevator, she pressed a number forbidden to her except twice a year whenever she gate crashed the open houses they held for benefactors — and certainly forbidden to any beautiful young woman any time after midnight, when nothing but sin happens for those who are not pious enough to be sound asleep.

Room 503 was near the end of a long corridor of thirty bedrooms. She didn't knock but quietly cracked the door open, slipped in and shut it behind her. Turning around, her eyes flew open and her jaw dropped in embarrassment. She did not find a dark room with Scott deep in pious slumber, but four guys sitting around gripping Manhattans and staring at a presence totally foreign to them in such get togethers.

"Scott," one of them finally said, "I didn't know this was going to be that kind of a party."

"Can I get you a drink?" offered a second.

"I knew it!" said a third with a fake grin and exaggerated hand gestures. "I just knew it. There's something electric in the air. Just electric. Don't you feel it? I've felt it too, Scott. Isn't it invigorating? The Spirit's just moving! They're finally gonna get ride of that celibacy rule."

It took Lucy a while to figure out he was joking. She didn't laugh along with the others.

"Scott," she said with solemnity. "I just... I just... I needed to see you."

"This is probably not the best time."

"We need to talk."

"Guys, could you give us a minute?" Scott poked at the pillow behind his back, and grimaced as he adjusted his right foot and the massive plaster cast surrounding it.

His three friends gave each other looks.

"Oh come on! You know me."

The three got up, clearly reluctant to leave, wanting to see how things would play out.

They exited the room and she brought a chair up next to his bed, and took his hand. "When are you leaving?"

"It's not fair. I am on way too many pain killers and too much gin to have this kind of discussion with you right now."

"*In vino veritas.*"

"*In morphino absurditas.*"

"Look. I think you know what I want to say. I wish we didn't have to, like, talk right now, this early in our ... in our ... well, whatever it is. But here we are. You're leaving."

"No. Look, Lucy, I had to do this all day yesterday. I mean, don't worry, I know, it's normal and all. All the nurses at the hospital were clearly attracted to me, and they kept coming in and telling me, '*Oh che bello, che bello*,' and I'm like, 'Come on, babe, just, like, put the cast on, and get about your business. I get it. I do. But get about your business.' And they did. They did. Italians. Whatever."

"You can't just diffuse the situation with humor."

"Oh, wow. This is going to happen. Yeah, this is happening. Okay. Serious Lucy. I'm speaking with serious Lucy. No, you're right. Let's be serious. Okay. Do you know how bad I feel about the other night? I gotta apologize. It wasn't right."

"Scott, stop letting yourself talk that way. You've never been ideological before, and you're not going to start now. I won't let you. You say the truth. You know what happened. You know what you felt. Now's the time," she grabbed harder onto his hand and leaned over the bed. "You know we could make this work."

"No, I get it. I get it. We could have a beautiful life together, 'cause I'm beautiful. You're beautiful. We'd make beautiful babies and I would, just, you know, become a very successful entrepreneur or an attorney or something. And we'd go on and it'd all just be great. We'd move back to Wisconsin and just live the best life ever. Is that what you want?"

"Yes! Sure, maybe's it's a little early to say that, and when you phrase it like that it sounds crazy, but yes. There you have it. I've said what I want. Now you just – just take a risk – you have to say what you want."

"Lucy, there's something else. And you gotta believe that I betrayed that something else the other night when I behaved like that with you. And the fact that I did is a comment on the smallness of my soul and the greatness of who you are. You just gotta trust me. There's something else already at play in my life. I know you're not interested in moralistic platitudes, and to be honest, I'm not interested either. Just trust. There's something else, alright? I'm sorry."

"Is it money?"

"No."

"There's a lot of people at the Diocese of Oshkosh paying way too much for your pathetic education over here. I get it. You'd feel like you betrayed them if you ran off with me. Whatever, Scott, money's not an issue."

"I know money's not an issue."

"No, *literally*, money's not the issue. Some people kill to get their inheritance ... some people run away from theirs. I'm telling you, though, any debt you've got to the diocese can be solved with a phone call. Don't let that be an issue."

"I know your daddy's loaded. Brian told me. Money's not an issue. I know."

"So there's nothing holding you back then. The other night you made it clear what you want, and right here, just now, you've told me as much implicitly. Why don't you just put on your big boy pants, take a risk, and say it now again, in no uncertain terms. I'm putting my heart on the line. You think this is easy?"

"You think it's easy for me to say no? You think I'm not making a huge risk by saying no?"

"I don't want to fight. This isn't going anywhere."

"Good, then let's not fight."

Lucy stood up, sat on the side of the bed, grabbed both his shoulders, leaned in and forced her lips onto his. He didn't resist. She heard snickering from Scott's friends watching through the cracked door.

She sat back up, looked him in the eyes, and walked out the room into the hallway. All three of Scott's friends jumped up and tried to act casual with her presence.

"Lucy," Scott yelled at her from his room.

She brushed a tear off her cheek and continued down the hallway.

"Lucy!" he yelled louder. "Your keys! You just dropped your keys on me."

She stopped, and checked all her pockets. She pulled herself back together and came into the room. Scott was smiling and dangling Eugenio's two keys in his hand.

"Sorry... I didn't mean to ruin your dramatic exit or anything."

She didn't say anything, but took the keys and turned around to leave.

"But can I ask why you have a public storage locker?"

"What?"

"Public storage. Why do you have one of those storage garages?"

"How do you know that's what this is?" she asked, with her back still to him.

"There's the logo right there on the key. We've got one for the lounge at the NAC too. We're remodeling, so we put all the furniture in storage. How much stuff could you possibly have that you'd need a storage garage?"

She didn't know how to respond, so instead she just left the room.

When she got down the street and back upstairs to the Palazzo, the light was still on in Brian's room.

"Lucy, I'm sorry." Brian sat up. He had been laying on his bed reading Karl Rahner's *Fundamental Theology.*

Lucy sat down at his desk chair. She'd been getting ready with responses to an I-told-you-so approach from Brian, but was deflated by an apology.

"Brian, it was... it was..."

"I can't image. Natasha's been texting me."

"I should probably also say I'm sorry for... for y'know... the things I said when –"

"Don't bring it up again."

Lucy threw the keys over to Brian.

"What's this?"

"Those are the keys."

"*The* keys?"

"Yep."

"I thought we agreed it's better if I don't know where they are or what they look like."

"Do you understand what those symbols are?"

"No," he looked at them more closely.

"There's the initials M.P. written on the one key."

"Member of parliament?"

"It means *Magazzini Pubblici* – public storage. It's a key to a storage facility unit. The company Magazzini Pubblici has three locations in Rome. We need to go check all of them tomorrow."

"But how does this work? We just walk around with the key and try to open every locker?"

"Brian, are you gonna help me or not?"

He sighed, looked down, and rubbed his forehead.

"I'm really sorry about what happened to Scott."

"I didn't ask you about Scott. Are you, Brian, going to help me, Lucy, right now?"

"I've been at work all day."

"I've been driving all day."

"I've got a seminar presentation tomorrow."

"You disappoint me, Brian."

"Listen. If you're really in danger, just tell me what's going on and I can help you. But if not..."

Lucy had already walked out of his door.

The next evening after class, Lucy and Natasha tried the location closest to them first, a short bus ride, just a few miles from Palazzo Mortimer, right next to Villa Doria-Pamphili. From the outside it didn't look that big. The gate was open, so they came right into the maze of garages without having to think up a way to get through the entrance. There had to be up to five hundred units. It was late on a Monday evening, but there were a few people moving things in and out of cars and trucks. They walked all the way down one aisle, and across the back row. In the middle of another row, they saw a group of people all gathered around a storage unit.

"Do you know what they do with public storage lockers when people stop paying their rent?" said Natasha.

"Take your stuff?"

"No. They open them up and auction off the contents of the locker. Didn't you ever watch television in America?"

"I don't remember that happening on any of the shows I watched."

"Let's go," Natasha went down the row towards the group of people. "I've always wanted to see one of these."

Fifteen very serious people crowded around an open storage locker in a semicircle, frowning at the contents inside: a treadmill, a mannequin, a bunch of boxes, and a weed wacker. A grey haired man, who was belting out Italian words at an impossibly fast pace, seemed to be the guy in charge. He kept yelling numbers and numbers and numbers, and pointing at people whenever they flinched. The price was raised over eight hundred euros, and the fight narrowed down to two people, flinching back and forth at each other. Eight hundred fifty. Nine hundred. Finally, one of them stopped flinching, but the auctioneer kept yelling nine hundred fifty at him, to try to provoke the non-flincher to flinch again. He frowned and wagged his finger 'no', so the auctioneer turned to the other flincher and yelled, "*venduto!*"

Everybody clapped, the two flinchers shook each other's hands, and the winner counted out a large pile of cash for a lady next to the auctioneer.

"Eugenio died over a month ago," said Natasha. "What if he didn't pay the October rent? What could that mean for November?"

"It could mean we showed up just in time, if they're gonna do any more of these today, or it could mean we just lost the inheritance to this guy. I don't have any cash, do you?" she dug around in her bag and could find only four euros in change. "It's too bad, that's a nice looking treadmill. I can see why the true heirs wanted to kill for it."

Natasha checked her own resources, "I've got a twenty. Do you think we could convince this man to give us a look for twenty four?"

But the group set off again down the row, so Lucy and Natasha followed them to another large locker.

"*Allora, l'ultimo magazzino per oggi!*"[167] the auctioneer yelled, and opened up the garage door.

Everyone crowded around the unit, and two employers spread their arms to prevent anyone from going in. Unlike the last garage, which had been packed to the gills with stuff, this one had just one item: a large red Nike duffel bag lying on the floor. People started shaking their heads, and about half the group even headed for the exit. Lucy and Natasha both gave each other knowing looks.

The auctioneer began at twenty Euros, and Lucy raised her hand immediately.

---

[167] "Okay, the last storage locker for today!"

Thirty? There was a challenger standing at the other side of the semicircle.

Forty? Another challenger raised his hand.

Fifty? Lucy raised her hand.

Sixty? The first challenger was back.

Eighty? Lucy fired again.

"How on earth are we going to get money?" Natasha whispered in Lucy's ear. "These kinds of things are always cash only. Wouldn't it be better to just let this guy win and then rob him on his way out?"

"I've got a hunch about this one. If I'm right we'll have a lot of money in just a second."

Ninety?

The challenger scratched his chin, and looked over at Lucy. Newcomers, it seemed, were not appreciated at the storage locker auctions. "*Due cento!*" he yelled and glared at Lucy.

The auctioneer looked at Lucy and offered her two hundred and fifty. She agreed.

The other guy upped it to three hundred.

Lucy accepted three fifty, crossed her arms and glared back at the challenger.

"Lucy, three fifty for Eugenio's duffel bag? I'm sure we can buy it off the guy after he's had a look."

"Not if I'm right. And hey, if I'm wrong, this wouldn't be the dumbest thing I've ever done. Just pretend like we don't speak Italian. Did the auctioneer just say three hundred or did he say thirty-five? It's tough to say. Are they on the euro in Italy? I thought Italy was still on the lira."

The challenger, at that point, started scratching his chin, and looking anxious.

Four hundred? He accepted.

Lucy immediately accepted four hundred and fifty without hesitating. The challenger finally wagged his finger at the auctioneer, ducking out of the race. Some of the crowd clapped, others chuckled at Lucy, having made the worst gamble of the day. Lucy ran straight into the locker and opened up a corner of the bag.

The auctioneer yelled at her, telling her she had to pay first, in cash, before she would be allowed into the locker. "*Non si tocca niente! Non si tocca niente finché non si paga! Vai fuori! Prima si paga!"*

She turned around and apologized to the auctioneer, placing five crisp hundred-euro bills in his hands. He immediately forgot his anger and smiled at Lucy. They shook hands. She took a fifty in change, and accepted a set of keys for a new *Magazzini Pubblici* lock on the unit. They made her sign a contract on the unit that would terminate within a month unless rent was paid on time. Some of the others in the crowd stuck around, curious to see whether or not Lucy's gamble had paid off. Natasha placed herself between the group and the bag with her arms crossed.

The auctioneer walked away. Lucy turned on her phone's flashlight app and closed the garage door. There would be no audience when they opened the bag. She and Natasha stood on opposite sides, looking down.

"Well, it's your bag now," said Natasha. "Let's have a look."

"Here, hold the flashlight."

Lucy knelt down, and unzipped the duffel. It was absolutely packed full of bundles and bundles of one hundred, two hundred, and five hundred euro bills. Natasha immediately took a seat on the floor, and had trouble holding the phone steady. Lucy took out a bundle and flipped through the bills. Neither of them could speak. Here it was. The true heirs weren't lying. They were really after a lot of money.

Lucy kept digging around in the bag to see if there was anything else. Just piles and piles of cash. Nothing more.

"Shall we count it?" Natasha finally asked.

"Well ... it's gotta be millions at least. I don't know. Three, maybe four million? These bundles of five hundreds have... who knows... fifty bills in each bundle. This is ridiculous. Who has this much cash? Maybe it's better if we don't know an exact number right now."

"What are we ever going do with this?"

"I'm kind of hungry."

"No, I mean ... long term ... we can't just keep three million euros. Wouldn't somebody notice if one of us deposited such an extraordinary amount of cash into an account?"

"I don't know. We can figure that out later. But I would like dinner. And hey, we did win this unit fair and square, didn't we? Can you go to Google on my phone and type in 'Rome, very expensive restaurant'?"

Lucy put a bundle of five hundred euro bills in her bag. Natasha refused to touch anything. They left the rest in the storage unit, and headed out for a very expensive meal.

CHAPTER TWENTY-TWO

IL BAGNO TURCHESE E LA CATENA

After the sixth course and *digestivi*, very satisfied, they had the restaurant's concierge call them a cab. They both slouched in the back, without seat belts, cradling their stomachs, and soaking in the experience of newfound privilege.

"It feels very different this time," said Lucy.

"What's that?"

"Having money. It feels different this time."

"How do you mean?"

"This time it's mine ... well ... kind of mine, I guess."

"As opposed to?"

"Y'know, before. Back then, there were always all kinds of strings attached. Do this. Don't do that. Be responsible. Forget it. Now I can be reckless and it's just me being reckless. It's more fun but it's also, like, less fun." Lucy sank down farther in her seat and closed her eyes. "I think I like it, though."

"Would you say you're in a particular mood, lately? You know, with everything that's been going on? It's not just a matter of having money all of the sudden."

"Well there's that too. I can see what you're saying," said Lucy. "But I like to think that every bite of expensive food is just enough to make a corresponding amount of anxiety disappear."

"How large was the bill?"

"€580.00."

"Food is one thing, but how much did we pay for the wine pairing?"

"Something like a hundred each."

"For *that* wine?"

"For that wine."

"Well, if it takes away your stress, that's fine," said Natasha. "The wine was quite good. Not exceptional, but quite good. Of course, far too overpriced. Except for maybe the Chardonnay. That Chardonnay was exceptional. I would drink that all night. But don't they know how risky that Pinot Noir pairing was? How stupid was that? In Italy of all places. Really. An Italian Pinot Noir. Were they joking? If you're serious about stress relief, the first thing we're doing with that bag of money is hiring a car, going to Tuscany, and finding out if there's any decent wine in this country."

"Absolutely."

"Why did I leave South Africa, again?"

"Um…"

"Wait, no… Don't answer that. We will not be talking about that."

"Good. Tonight we've spent way too much on food and wine to talk about anything stressful."

"Indeed. Did we pay enough to make your stress go away?"

Lucy leaned over onto Natasha, "I think so."

The car pulled up to the Palazzo. Lucy reached into her bag for her wallet, but was distracted by bright flashes of light from both sides of the car. There were at least ten people crowded around outside the cab, surrounding it with cameras and flashing bulbs. Lucy made the mistake of lowering the window to ask what was going on. As soon as there was enough room, two cameras with hands attached were immediately inserted into the crack in the window and began firing at will inside the car.

"Ms. Fox! Ms. Fox!"

"Lucy! Lucy!"

"Just one question!"

"Ms. Fox, look over here!"

"One question, over here!"

"Ms. Fox, how are you connected to the murders of Eugenio Galli and Cristiano Ludovici?"

"Ms. Fox, look here!"

"Lucy! Lucy! Lucy! Lucy! Lucy!"

She rolled the window back up, first closing down on the paparazzi's wrists, which held on fiercely to the cameras, unable to remove them from the car. Natasha reached across Lucy, rolled the window down a smidge, pushed the cameras out, and rolled the window back up.

"What do we do?" asked Lucy.

"I don't know. Pay the cab and fight our way inside?"

Lucy gave the driver his money, but didn't move out of the car. The door opened, Lucy's fist curled and she turned to see who it was. Andrew was there. He was yelling and pushing off the reporters. He turned around and grabbed Lucy by the wrist, yanking her out of the car, while warding off reporters and photographers with his other arm. Natasha pulled off her scarf and covered most of Lucy's face. For Lucy, everything between the car and the building was one giant flash of light and sound. She let herself be pulled along by the wrist, unable to navigate herself with all the flashing and yelling. She was soon inside the building, seated on the floor in the hallway behind the porter's office breathing hard. Some of the reporters continued to call out her name from outside.

Within a half an hour, a simple search of her name rendered more than fifty results on different tabloid news sites. If you don't count the photos taken by Cristiano's harem a month before, more photographs of Lucy had been taken in the minute in front of the Palazzo than in the previous three years combined. All of them were confused snapshots of Lucy from bizarre angles, either curled up in the car or being led from the car to the Palazzo door with Natasha's scarf on her head.

After Scott had almost been killed, both Natasha and Lucy were reluctant to sleep in their own rooms, now that they were back at the Palazzo. So they pulled their mattresses to the floor in Andrew's room. Andrew fell asleep early, but Natasha and Lucy stayed awake, staring at the ceiling until two in the morning. Lucy finally managed to close her eyes, but she kept turning from one side to the other, with no results. Five hundred and eighty euros of food, wine, and stress relief were not enough to make her sleep. Once Natasha's breathing grew deep and consistent, Lucy slipped out of bed, went to her room, changed into her bathrobe, grabbed a towel and headed downstairs to the negative one level. If anyone had been planning on breaking in and committing murder, they would have done so already, right? I followed her down. She soaked, and I sat in the steam.

"Did you have a look at the picture we got from the orphanage?" she asked me after half an hour of silence.

"I did."

"What do you think?"

"I think it's pretty clear," I said.

"I just can't believe we were so stupid. Ginevra wasn't even a fake name, just short for the name of a mean girl we already know well."

She lit a cigarette. I turned up the knob on the steam. For once she didn't seem to mind. We both breathed deep.

"I guess it's time for us to leave the Palazzo, isn't it?" she said. "How much longer can we stay here before somebody else gets killed? They weren't kidding. It's real money. A lot of it. They know who we are and they know where we are. We still know nothing other than who the rich grandma is. And even if we knew who the kids were ... I don't know ... what is there for us to do? We find out who they are and then what? I can't do anything. The police won't do anything. Maybe it's just best to take the bag of cash and get out of here. Have you ever been to South Africa?"

"Yes."

"And?"

"What's wrong with Colorado?"

Lucy never had the chance to answer that question. The door slammed open and was swiftly closed behind two very large figures that entered the room. They were wearing black leather jackets and black ski masks. Before Lucy had time to think or react, they had grabbed her shoulders and pulled her back against the side of the tub. One of them had his hand on her mouth, preventing her from screaming, and another held a heavy metal chain around her neck. But scream she did. Muffled, yes, but still an intense life-threatening scream coming out from the bottom of her lungs.

They were professionals. They were able to do an amazing amount of things in a short amount of time with just four hands. They shoved her face down into the bubbles. They pulled her arms behind her back and tied her hands together, then placed a wooden dowel through her elbows and behind her back. As soon as she came out of the water, her mouth was suddenly full of a bandana, and her scream turned more into a gagging and choking sound. I could do nothing but pace back and forth. Once she could breathe again, through her nose, she made another attempt at screaming, but not just arbitrary noise like before. Through the gag I could just barely tell that she was screaming my name. But there was nothing I could do. So I walked back and forth even more quickly, and uselessly growled at the men. I think my noise didn't help the situation. Lucy certainly wasn't thinking clearly. I wasn't either.

"*Non sbagghio termini cu tia,*" one of them told her. "*Assittati e lavora, e puoi vivere. Per sfortuna non abbiamo molto tempo per gioccare stasera. Au primo segnu che non ti assitti e lavori, ti uccidiamo subito. U capisti?*"[168]

Lucy just whimpered.[169]

"*U capisti?*" he yelled, slapping her face from behind. A red mark appeared.[170]

Lucy nodded yes. The man's tone of voice was enough to tell her that they meant business. They were quick and professional. She was no longer dealing with Natasha, stumbling in and innocently waving a gun around.

---

[168] "I'm going to talk straight with you," *One of them told her.* "You can cooperate and if you're lucky, maybe even survive. Unfortunately we don't have time for games tonight. At the first sign of your not cooperating, we will kill you immediately. Understood?"

[169] *Lucy just whimpered.*

[170] "Understood?" *he yelled, slapping her face from behind. A red mark appeared.*

"Dunque. M'hai a dire i numeri del conto del banco." He took the bandana out of her mouth.[171]

"There is no bank account."[172]

"C'hai un'opportunità in più pi dicci a verità, oppure ti uccidiamo."[173]

"No really, there's no account ... there – "

Before she could finish answering the question, though, the thick metal chain was back around her neck. This time, however, it was tightened. Hard. Very hard. It was clear they had no intention of leaving her alive. Her eyes widened, and even using all her strength, she was able to make only weak gagging sounds. She kicked the other side of the tub and thrashed her shoulders around, but it did nothing other than splash water over the rim and spread bubbles around. The man tightened the grip and Lucy's face turned from white to blue. Her chin moved up and down, gaping for air, but not able to take anything in. After a minute – an excruciatingly long minute – her eyes stopped focusing on anything in particular. The movement in her chin became mechanical. The tremble and tension in her shoulders was released. Her whole body grew limp. Her shoulders sank deeper into the water, and her neck rose higher as the man pulled up on the chain. The water surface calmed down.

By now, I was roaring, and banging on the wall with my paws. It had been hundreds and hundreds of years, since the last time I can remember ever roaring that loudly, completely losing control of myself. It's hard to explain. I had forgotten my voice could get that loud and deep, and that my mouth could open that wide.

Every once in a while, it's true, we can become somewhat visible, even to other groups of people. It's rare, but it happens. And that night, for the first time in a long time, someone other than Lucy recognized me. When Lucy went limp, something deep down inside me snapped. Something I didn't even know was there. Certainly, I've seen hundreds of people die before, oftentimes even unjustly. On so many of those occasions I was saddened, but able to accept it all. Human nature is human nature, right? But this was different.

---

[171] "Alright. Good. What are the bank account numbers?" *He took the bandana out of her mouth.*

[172] *"There is no bank account."*

[173] "You have one more chance to tell us the truth before we kill you."

What exactly was different, I still can't say, but something deep within me snapped. Lucy went limp and I breathed in deep, with the intention of ruining my vocal chords. I let loose with every bit of strength in my whole four hundred pound body.

Both of the large men turned and looked straight at me. The one man let go of Lucy's neck. Her head flopped back onto the edge of the tub. Only a few feet from their faces, the two men were now staring down a humongous blue bear, who had completely lost his mind, roaring at the top of his lungs and spraying them with slobber. I can even remember it as though it were in slow motion. Their faces were blank at first – total and utter confusion. Then they breathed in together. Their jaws dropped simultaneously, and they started yelling. And for the amount of time it takes to empty your lungs after a deep breath, there were just the three of us large animals in that small room, all yelling uncontrollably at each other, while Lucy lay unconscious right below.

I picked up my right arm, let out my claws, and took a swipe at one of them. He moved back, but my claws made a clean swipe through the leather jacket, cleaving four deep diagonal cuts right in his chest. I stumbled backwards and stared at my paw. They both ran for the door and fumbled with the knob. Once out in the hallways, their legs pumped in seemingly random directions, stumbling down the corridor of the old female servants' quarters. Having already given myself over to anger and instinct, I chased them out — not quick enough to catch them, but just to scare them off — across the laundry room, up the stairs, through the lobby, into a black Subaru Impreza and away from the Palazzo. They didn't look back to see if I was following. As soon as I got to the street I snapped out of my fit of rage. I remembered Lucy and ran as fast as I could back to the Turkish bath.

The back of her head was still perched on the side of the tub, but she was now gasping for air, coughing, gagging, dry heaving, and in general, looking miserable. A little color had returned to her face, but not much. Her eyes were clenched shut and tears were streaming down the sides of her face into her hair. She sat up in the tub, still coughing and gasping. She removed the stick from behind her back by pressing it up against the sides of the tub, pushed her arms underneath her legs so that the rope was in front, and held the rope right in the flame of a candle. The knot was very well tied, but somehow they'd managed to leave almost an inch of rope between her hands. The rope dried out and I sat there staring at my right paw, which still had blood on it. Lucy sat there staring at the flame, slowly getting control of her breath, and every once in a while looking back anxiously at the door.

"I don't think they'll be coming back soon," I said.

She tried to say something back to me, but just started coughing again. Once the rope was on fire, she used the tub's faucet to snap it apart. She put on her bathrobe without drying off and hurried out into the hallway, but stopped. Where to go?

"I don't think they'll be upstairs," I said.

"Who?" she croaked, and rubbed her throat.

"The ... uh ... the bad guys with the masks. They probably won't be upstairs. I mean, it's probably safe."

"No," she whispered. "No. I'm not going anywhere where Kelly or my shrink will expect me to be. Where would I not be expected to be?"

She looked up and down the hallway. She was very jumpy, even jittery, understandably so, of course.

"I can't stay here. Blue Bear, I can't stay here. We gotta get out of here." She turned around a few times.

"It's almost four in the morning. Where are we gonna go? Like I said, I don't think they'll be back. You might as well just hide out somewhere in the Palazzo."

"We gotta go. Where's my bike."

"You haven't owned a bike in three years..."

"Where's my... no... Juanita, I'm sick. *¿No entiendes? ¡Ya dije que estoy enferma! Juanita, pórque no vas a decirlo a Kelly que estoy enferma? Hoy no puedo.* I can't go to school today. I gotta get out of here..."

She walked up the hall and then back down. It wasn't entirely clear to me whether or not she even knew where she was. She stopped and grabbed at the door to the old bedroom right across from the Turkish bath. The light worked. It was full to the brim of random furniture, all labeled and appraised by notes with Gambetti's handwriting. She climbed around the room, opening cabinets, drawers, and chests. One dresser contained a huge pair of thick red curtains. She threw one of them onto the oldest couch she'd ever sat on, used it as a pillow, and wrapped herself up in the other curtain.

A few hours later, she woke up, with all of her faculties of reason once more functioning perfectly. Or, well, they'd never really ever been functioning perfectly, but I think it's clear what I mean. The fluorescent ceiling light was still on, and I was sleeping in front of the door.

"Blue Bear."

I snorted.

"Blue Bear!"

I groaned and turned over.

"Blue Bear, wake up! What happened last night?"

"What do you remember?" I asked, yawning.

"I don't know. Just images. I was in the bath. There were two men, I think. Hands tied behind my back. A metal chain on my neck. Some weird dialect. Lots of pain and noise and squirming. Choking. Waking up in the tub. Breathing, and wanting to hack up a lung. A candle with a flame on my wrists. And now I just woke up in a pile of curtains and a bathrobe."

She rubbed her throat. Her voice sounded normal. Her neck still had a red mark, but her facial skin tone was back to how it was before. Her wrists still had the ropes on them. She sat up.

"Two men broke into the bath last night and tried to kill you," I said.

"Right. I remember that part."

"They didn't succeed."

"That's the part that's a little hazy."

"Something happened."

"Obviously something happened. *What* happened?"

"Something happened that I can't explain."

"What? Did they decide not to kill me?"

"No they were set to kill you for sure. No, I don't mean that something happened that I can't explain *to you*. I mean something happened that I can't explain at all."

"Yeah?"

I sat up and showed her my right paw, with blood still crusted on it.

"What the... is that blood?"

"It is."

"Gross."

"Lucy, do you know what this means?"

"It means... I don't know... you hit one of them with your paw and he ran away?"

"Right."

"Wow... you... Blue Bear, you saved my – "

"Sure, but do you realize what this means?"

"That I really owe you now."

"*Metaphysically*, Lucy, do you know what this means?"

"I'm not allowed to ask you questions about metaphysics. It's too complicated."

"It is too complicated *for you*. But what do you know thus far? What have I told you about all your questions about how things work?"

"I know I'm not allowed to ask you about metaphysics. You always said it's a waste of my time and yours, that I'm much better off studying literature. Narrative is where you really touch the substance of reality, not science or abstract ontology."

"Well," I looked down at my paw again, still in disbelief, "Something new happened. The logic of the drama has changed. What have you been able to observe about my interactions with the physical world?"

"That it makes no sense."

"To you it makes no sense. But what is it that makes sense to you?"

"Right, which is why I'm better off paying attention to the narrative value of your actions and not worrying about the spatial or physical realities. If I focus on the physical or non-physical aspects, everything stops making sense, but if I think of it as within a narrative, it does. It's narrative law that's important – aesthetics and journey and all that – not categories of being."

"But what's the one law that you've observed, even if I won't let you talk about it or call it a law?"

"You can't touch people other than me. But wait... that means... "

"That's right."

"You touched someone."

"This has never happened before, to anyone," I said. "Ever. Not to anyone that I know of."

"That's crazy."

"No... not just 'that's crazy' like I-just-won-a-free-t-shirt 'that's crazy'... Lucy... this is a complete and total unheard of singularity. All the laws of the narrative – not as you know them, but as I know them – just bowed down in your favor."

"I don't know what to say."

"That's the point. I don't either!"

She stood up. "What time is it? Where's Brian? Where's Natasha and Andrew and Fr. Damien? Is everyone okay?"

"I chased off the two guys last night."

Lucy climbed over all the things in the room to get to the door, opened it, and ran all the way upstairs to the rooftop servants' quarters in bare feet and a bathrobe. By the time I got up to the terrace, she was coming out of the servants' quarters in an orange running zip, black leggings, aviators, Brooks, french braids, and a smartphone armband.

"What's going on?" I asked.

"Nobody's here. Brian texted. He's at work. Natasha's A.W.O.L. Fr. Damien's here, but asleep like normal. Andrew's gone too. I'm worried about him. He doesn't go to class early."

"Okay," I said. "What are we gonna do?"

"Wait, I've got another question for you," said Lucy.

"Yeah."

"The two strong guys who tried to kill me last night, did one of them — the one that didn't speak Italian, and didn't actually speak at all — did he have a limp in his right leg?"

"I... I don't know... I can't say I remember. I was pretty angry. I guess both of them might have hobbled a bit, but that's normal when a bear's chasing you."

"Was it a hobble or a limp?"

"I just don't remember. Take your pick."

She took off towards the roof access door.

"Where are you going?"

"I'm getting out of here."

"Okay?"

"I need to think, and I need to get out of here. Running's the only way I can think lately."

"Well, Brian's the only one whose location we know for sure. You need to go and stay close to him and then find Andrew and Natasha. Figure out where they are."

"Brian doesn't want me or my problems."

"Did you explain the situation to him?"

"No. But I already know how he'd react. His friends are in danger of death and he only cares about school and work."

"If you tried to explain, I'm sure – "

"I've tried to explain. I don't need him. I'm a grown woman."

"Lucy!" I raised my voice at her, something I rarely do. "You owe me! You just said you owe me. Promise me you'll go find Brian and stay close to him. I am so not in the mood to discuss whatever ideology right now. I'd tell Brian the same thing about you if he were in your shoes right now. Alright?"

"Alright. But I don't – "

"I don't care about your excuses right now!" I interrupted. She looked down at her shoes. "Promise me you'll go get Brian and Natasha to help you, whatever it is you plan on doing next. Try to find Andrew too."

"It's just that – "

"The laws of all the entire universe just bended in your favor. Does that mean nothing to you? It's not gonna happen again. You're still free," I said.

She kept her eyes on her shoes, shifting weight from one leg to the other, itching to get going.

And I then added something I had never felt about or said to any of my assignments, "And I'm not telling you to do this because it's some duty of mine as guide, I'm telling you that you have to go and find help because I... because I love you."

She glanced back up at me and then quickly back down at her shoes.

"Listen. I mean... whatever... don't take that the wrong way... but yeah... I mean it. The laws of the universe – the laws of the drama – just bent in your favor and maybe there's a reason. Maybe that's the reason. Maybe there are laws that are deeper. A law of... I don't know, love or something. Not all sentimental and all that crap. Something else. I don't know. Whatever. Just don't go it alone. That's what I know for certain."

"Okay."

"You promise you won't go it alone?"

"I promise," she said.

"Whatever. Get out of here."

"But what do I do about his job? He won't take time off work."

"Just explain to him what's going on."

"Or maybe... Don't worry. I think I have a plan."

CHAPTER TWENTY-THREE

LUX ET ANTHROPOS

Given how well that phase had worked in the past, I was not able to stop worrying. I took a seat on the terrace patio furniture and Lucy ran downstairs.

"*Ciao bella.*" Gambetti was opening up the porter's office.[174]

"*Ciao Gambetti.*"[175]

"*Oh, Lucy, spetta. C'è un tipo qua fuori che vuole parlare con te. Dice che non è giornalista, ma l'avvocato di tuo babbo.*"[176]

Lucy stopped. "*Cazzo. È ceco?*"[177]

"*No. Mi sembra che veda bene.*"[178]

"*No, cazzo, Gambetti. È della Repubblica Ceca?*"[179]

---

[174] "Hey there, beautiful," *Gambetti was opening the porter's office.*

[175] "Hi Gambetti."

[176] "Oh, Lucy, wait a second. There's some guy outside here who wants to talk to you. He says he's not a journalist, but your Dad's lawyer."

[177] *Lucy stopped.* "Shit. Is he Czech?"

[178] "No, it seems he can see just fine."

[179] "No shit, Gambetti. Is he from the Czech Republic?"

"Diciamo che c'ha un accento particolare, sì. Ed è biondo, quindi, non so. Direi di sì comunque... In ogni caso..."[180]

Lucy was no longer listening. Outside Mârek Mikulaštik stood in front of a black limo, parked just in front of the Palazzo. Lucy took a few steps forwards and then backwards and looked from side to side. There was no other exit from the Palazzo Mortimer property than through that front gate. There was only one way forwards.

When Lucy came out the front door, Mikulaštik opened up the back door of the limo and stood to one side. She stopped and folded her arms.

"Good morning, Ms. Fox."

"What do you want?"

"If I might kindly ask for you to board vehicle."

"What do you want?"

A hand reached out from inside the limo and passed a pile of magazines to Mârek. She approached with caution. From Mârek's hands, Lucy's own confused and frightened face stared back at her, printed right on the covers of six Italian tabloids – all pictures snapped of her last night or stolen off her Facebook profile.

"Ms. Fox, perhaps you have noticed that this morning there are no paparazzi outside your residence. At great costs, your father's foundation has purchased, for temporary period of one-day, armistice with tabloids. You are to leave the Italy immediately. No discussion." He stepped to the side and gestured at the limo.

The back of that car did look comfortable. Heated seats. Leather. There was an Italian lawyer waiting with a pastry and a cappuccino. Further inside, there was another lawyer with a folder, which would, for sure, be full of fake travel documents, and another lawyer holding a piece of luggage, probably already packed with business casual clothing in her size. She looked down at the tabloids and back at the limo.

"Please, Ms. Fox. We have little time."

She threw the tabloids on the ground and raced down the Janiculum hill. Mikulaštik sighed and got into the backseat.

---

[180] "Let's say he has a somewhat particular accent, yeah. And he is blond, so, I don't know. I'd say yes... anyways..."

It's only a mile and a half From the Janiculum hill to the Trevi fountain, so within eleven minutes, Lucy was already tearing around the corner to Brian's Starbucks. Looking up at the siren, she decided she needed a moment to figure out what to say. Around the block she found a small alley where the various restaurants all had dumpsters behind their back doors. A short balding and bearded Starbucks employee stood next to a dumpster, lighting up a cigarette.

"Luca."

He looked up and glared. "Oh, look who it is. Here to gloat more?"

"No, I, no... listen... I feel really bad about what happened. It was a mistake."

"Wow. Things must be really difficult for you, having to live with such a conscience. I can't imagine. Poor you."

"If you found out who murdered Eugenio Galli would they give you your job back?"

He didn't respond.

"The only people who know why you were fired are me, your boss, and Ludovici. Ludovici's dead. I'm right here. I haven't told anybody anything. Here we are. Whatever Ludovici threatened you with is now in the grave with him. Your boss, I imagine, would be willing to reconcile. I'm the only other one who knows about the rest."

Luca took a heavy drag on his cigarette.

"You weren't a smoker when I first met you," said Lucy.

"I smoked that night. I imagine you remember that cigarette?"

"Right. You smoked like an amateur. Now you look like a pro."

"What do you know about the Galli case?"

"I met the killers last night. They'll be back. We've just got to wait around Palazzo Mortimer and open the door for them when they come."

"And how do you know they're the killers?"

"I know."

"Why do you want my help?"

"Three reasons. First. It couldn't hurt to have a hand from a former cop, someone who knows what he's doing. Second. Well. I can't say I feel great about what happened to you. Sure, it felt great to win, but afterwards, I'm sorry about... you know. Third. I need Brian's help. I need Brian around the palazzo. I need all hands on deck. You know he's not right for this store. You need to get him a few days off or something."

"It's too late to get him just a few days off. He'll be fired this morning."

"What?"

"Actually, right now, I think he's having a nice chat with the manager."

"He's getting fired right now?"

"Yes."

"Why?"

"Listen. I'm willing to help you, if you really know what you're talking about. I'm sorry it had to happen this way. But if you are up for it, sure, I am interested in helping. Brian... well... listen... you can imagine that I have been looking for pithy ways to get revenge at you. For a while I wanted to do something great, but the opportunity has not presented itself, so I thought the only way to seek for revenge at you was to procure Brian's getting fired. Let's say, he has been caught sneaking cash from the register."

"Really?"

"No, not really, but I've set him up. Come on."

"Oh... okay, like 'caught' stealing from the register."

"Correct."

"That's great. That's perfect. I mean, that sucks for Brian, and all. I feel bad for the guy, but it works."

"So you see how ridiculous my revenge plot is," Luca laughed at himself. "I do something mean to Brian to get revenge at you and I find out that I only – how do you say? – beat you to the punch." He flicked his cigarette butt on the ground and stepped on it. "You sure sound like a great friend to Brian."

"It's not like that. You understand why I'm doing this."

"Sure. I understand your calculations. They're cruel, but I get it. Anyways, let me know how I can help with the investigation."

Luca went back into the store and Brian came out looking very distraught. He dropped his backpack on the ground, pulled out a green apron, and threw it in the dumpster. He picked his backpack up and only then realized that someone was standing there watching him.

"Oh... hey Lucy... what the hell are you doing back here? You're not going to believe what just happened to me. Wait... what's going on? Why are you back here?"

"Brian, I need your help."

"Wait a second. Did you... oh my God... Fricking Judas Iscariot herself."

"Are you kidding me?" At Brian's words, Lucy put her hand up to her heart, feeling an intense and sudden anger seethe through it. She gave up any intention of seeking Brian's help. "Is that what you think of me?"

"Did you just get me fired from my job?"

"Do you think I did?"

"I don't get it, Lucy, it's a very simple question. Did you just get me fired from my job?"

"Oh, your job. Your job! Great, you've got a job! Well, what about your *life*. Huh? *Life itself* is in danger at the Palazzo, and you don't give a shit."

"Lucy," Brian tried to be calm and clear, "did you just stab me in the back and get me fired?"

"Is that what you think of me? Judas Iscariot. Is that all I am to you?"

"What the hell is wrong with you? I just don't get it."

"Don't try to take the moral high ground," she raised her voice. "You just called me something, and I want to know if that's what you really think about me. Judas Iscariot. Just my sinner friend. That's all I am to you."

"I'm not going to let you get all philosophical on a very simple argument. This is not about ideas, this is about you being an ass to me, Lucy."

"Oh, give me a break." Lucy put her hands on her hips and walked back and forth. "Whether I did or didn't doesn't matter. The point is that those words sounded pretty damn easy coming out of your lips. How long had they been sitting there? You think I'm a sinner. Fine. But if I'm Judas, then what does that make you? You think you're some kind of Christ figure. Don't you? You've got the whole Year of Mercy on your team. You get to walk around with your nose in the air, carrying around your Rahner books, dispensing mercy to poor sinners like me. Isn't that what you think? Isn't that all I am to you? You use me to be better than everyone else."

"What does this have to do with you getting me fired? Be real for a second. If anyone has a right to be pissed it's me."

"You're using me. If you've got a Christ complex, then that means you've got to keep a Mary Magdalene around, doesn't it? But y'know what? At least Jesus drove out her demons. He didn't just keep her around so that he could feel better about himself around his Pharisee friends. Isn't that it? You go to the Greg and look down on the other Americans and their scholastic manuals, because you're full of mercy, and they're not. Y'know what. I know what your mercy looks like. And if that's all the mercy you have to offer, then you're the biggest Pharisee of 'em all."

"Mercy and pharisees aside for a second, you still haven't answered the question. Did you steal from my register and get me fired?"

"Yeah, I did. And I'm glad I did."

"I can't believe you," Brian was barely able to whisper. His mouth was open and it looked like he was on the verge of tears. "You scheming and manipulating little bitch."

"I can't believe *you*," Lucy whispered back, hurt. She finally said something close to the real reason why she was angry. "Last night I was this close to death, and you don't give a shit. Don't you get it? They tried to kill me, I narrowly escaped, and you could care less."

"Wait, what?" said Brian.

"Don't act like you care all of the sudden."

"Lucy, what happened?"

She was already running away down the alley.

"Lucy!"

She ran as fast as her legs would take her, taking random turns at every street corner, not even really sure where she was after five minutes. She's incredible at distances, but she's not much of a sprinter. At a certain point she doubled over next to a dumpster to catch her breath. She saw a can and kicked it, launching it down the street. It smacked straight into a car's bumper in an explosion of expired apricot jelly. She ducked into an empty alley to get away from other people's stares and the car alarm. The anger left quickly enough, but was replaced by a deep emptiness. She had not really gotten him fired, but it felt like she may as well have. She did her best to distract herself and tell herself she was right. She had said all the correct words.

"Brian was wrong, and I am right. I have nothing to be ashamed of!" she yelled at an empty crate. "This is not my fault. None of it."

The box remained silent and stared back.

The pit of guilt in her stomach did not go away. She looked at the box and felt the temptation to sit down and cry, but yelled even more loudly at the box, "No. Now is not the time for that. I have nothing to feel bad about."

She called and texted Andrew and Natasha again. No responses. She stretched her legs and set off jogging. Summiting the Spanish steps, she went around the corner to the Quirinale, the residence of the Italian president. In the piazza in front of the Quirinale she slowed to a walk. Natasha still wouldn't answer her phone. Lucy paced a little in the square, and caught the eyes of the military *bersaglieri* next to a big green Iveco who were scanning her nervously and fiddling with their M-16s.

It was seven o'clock. An hour and a half before Natasha would be expected in school. For the first time ever, Lucy was in downtown Rome, unable to go home, and without any particular plans or place to go.

"This is why so many tourists look miserable."

Thus began five of the most anxious hours in Lucy's life. She went to Piazza dell'Orologio, and sat on a park bench waiting for Natasha to go to class. She didn't come. She didn't come for the second hour of class either. After the second break Lucy went up to the group of foreigners smoking outside the Italian Language School.

"*Scusate ragazzi. Qualcuno di voi per caso conosce* Natasha Abramova?"

They all gave her blank stares.

"Does anyone know Natasha Abramova?" repeated Lucy.

"Oh yeah, she's in our class."

"Have you seen her today?"

"No, she's not here."

"If she comes, can you tell her to call Lucy Fox immediately?"

"Sure."
"What's my name again?"
"Lucy Fox."
"And what are you going to tell Natasha to do?"
"Tell Natasha to call Lucy Fox."
"*Bravo.*"

So Lucy wandered. She walked down to one end of the old city, Piazza San Pietro, and then turned around and walked to the other end, over to the Coliseum. If you walk slow enough on the off season, the guys dressed up like Roman soldiers will pester you and try to get you to pay for a picture with them. Strolling through the ancient sights, Lucy grew sick of seeing young lovers holding hands and forcing themselves to look happy because of how much they paid to see piles of old Roman rocks. How many poor souls have been willingly duped by the garbage they read in *Eat, Pray, Love*? So she slowed down, and was glad to have the opportunity to sneer at the soldiers and other vendors when they pestered her. She'd never been inside the coliseum before. It was a chilly day in November, but the sky was as blue as can be. She told the guards at the exit that she'd forgotten her umbrella inside. They asked if she had a ticket or receipt. No. Alright, go look for your umbrella. The coliseum was nice. Very old. Her phone buzzed, and she grabbed at her shoulder to see who it was. A text from Brian.

Hey Lucy, what's up?

"What the hell?" she said to herself. Why would Brian send a text like that? She didn't respond, but returned to her solitary slow march around the ancient stadium. Another text:

How's it going? What are you up to today? My classes got cancelled today so I'll just be hanging around home. Are you gonna be around?

Something was wrong. That made no sense at all. Either he was a very weird passive aggressive jerk, or something was very wrong. The Gregorian was about a half mile from the Coliseum. She ran through the forum and across Piazza Venezia to the flagship Jesuit university. It was the last break of the day before the fourth and final hour of morning lectures. The third year theology auditorium was surprisingly full. She stopped the first American seminarian she could find.

"Hey, have you seen Brian today?"

"Um... I don't remember. He might be here. He usually sits right up there." The seminarian pointed at Brian's seat.

Lucy walked up the stairs and into a long tight row of foldable chairs and desks bolted to the ground. The students meanwhile, were all making their way back up into the tight stadium seating. In the middle of the row, a very tall American stood reading his Kindle, next to Brian's empty spot.

"Hey, you're Brian's friend, right?" the seminarian asked Lucy, looking up from his reading. He spoke very slowly and deliberately.

"Yeah, have you seen him today?" she replied.

"He normally sits right where you're standing, but I haven't seen him today."

"He hasn't been to class at all?"

"Nope."

"Have you seen Scott Valentino?"

"You heard about his foot, right? He's on a plane for America right now."

"Seriously?"

"Yep. They carted him off this morning."

"So your classes weren't cancelled?"

"Um... no..."

"That bastard. Something weird's going on."

"No kidding. We just got to a really weird point in Anthropology. The professor's pretty good though. Nice guy." The seminarian pointed at an almost middle aged skinny professor in a black suit and a grey clerical shirt. "He speaks perfect American English, but they say he's actually French and Hungarian. Nobody can figure it out."

The bell rang and the seminarian curled himself into the flip down chair and kept on reading his kindle. Lucy, in the middle of the row, turned around, and found herself facing a row full of six large German seminarians, taking notes as the professor had already begun speaking into the microphone, in a very clear and precise Italian, but with a thick French accent. Lucy turned around again to see if she could get out the other side of the row. Four other Americans were sitting there and did not appear easily moveable. She sat down in Brian's spot. What better way to kill another hour while thinking up what to do next?

The professor got going, and everyone furiously scribbled notes on pads of paper or typed away on laptops. Only a few sat back, folded their arms, and just listened. Lucy thought about the case and Brian's text. She fumed about Brian's non-cooperation and worried about Natasha's whereabouts.

The seminarian next to her, who was reading a Jane Austen novel, placed a piece of paper and a pen in front of Lucy, "Hey, you know Italian, right? How 'bout you take some notes for us?"

"You don't understand Italian?"

"I get by."

"And you're in your third year of theology?"

"Could you please stop talking in class? I'm trying to pay attention."

He returned to Jane Austen and Lucy wrote her name on the top of the page. She considered the blank space below her name, and thought about drawing a picture of the professor. The professor mentioned something in Latin, so at the top of the page she wrote her name again, but in Latin, *Lucia.* Then next to that, she wrote the etymology of her name: *lux,* and the English definition: the light. Then she wrote, in the middle of the page, the true heirs: *heredes veraces* and a question mark. Between *lux* and the *heredes* she wrote *Ginevra,* then scratched it out, using Ginevra's full name: *Virginia,* from the Latin *Virgo,* meaning Virgin. Another question mark. From Virginia there was another arrow to the word *Mater* and an arrow from *Mater* to the word *Eugenio,* from the Greek Εὐγένιος, which means the noble offspring. And behind Eugenio, she wrote Ludovici, from the latin *ludum vici,* meaning 'I won the game'. Ironic. Along one side of the paper, she wrote down the names of everyone else at Palazzo Mortimer and their Latin or Greek etymologies. One of those names would have to belong to the "true heirs." Brian. The clown. *Pagliaccio.* Andrew. Ὁ ἀνήρ. Τοῦ ἀνδρος. Ὁ ἀνθρωπος. The man. Natasha. Natálya. *Dies Natalis.* Christmas Day. Fr. Damien.

Δαμαζω. The tamer. Scott Valentino. *Valentia*. Strength. Gambetti. Little legs or shrimp cocktail.

But who were the true heirs? And what was their connection to anyone else in the Palazzo? It couldn't just be two random giant thugs in leather jackets. The guy who killed Eugenio was not at all their size. Otherwise the police wouldn't have thought it was Lucy. They'd even measured Lucy next to the height of the person on the security recordings. Next to the true heirs she wrote the word anonymous, from the Greek α-ὄνομα, without a name.

An American seminarian at the end of Lucy's row raised his hand.

"*Sì*," said the professor, pointing at him.

"*Um... scusa... ma io non capisco... cioè,*" his Italian was horrendous. "*Questa cosa... um... questa cosa di Gaudium et Spes...*"

"You can just say it in English," the professor told him. Just like Scott, the professor had a Wisconsin accent.

"Alright, so here's the thing. We're talking about the document *Gaudium et Spes*, paragraph twenty two, and it's relationship to Rahner's anonymous Christianity. He's trying to be anthropological, but the most anthropological thing in Vatican II clearly contradicts him, right? If we say that by creation, man already has redemption, what's the point of *Gaudium et Spes*'s affirmation that *only in the mystery of the incarnate Word does the mystery of man take on light?*"

Lucy's head picked up when she heard the word *anonymous*. Meanwhile most of the class had set down their pens and were stretching their hands. Once the professor went into English, they all checked out, and the Americans, for the first time during the whole lecture, looked like they were paying attention.

"But it also goes on to talk about the first Adam being only the figure of the future Adam, not vice versa," the professor responded. "Rahner's not talking about creation in our terms, which have a bifurcation of natural and supernatural. Remember the implicit athematic knowledge of the Logos that we were talking about earlier? We can affirm the same about created man. Even in creation, he's still talking about the incarnate Word. And here's another thing. Rahner's not talking about man being a mystery, meaning, like, something that we don't know, that we've still got to find out, like an Agatha Christie novel, or what's for lunch today. I don't know right now, but I'll find out in an hour. Probably pasta. He's saying a mystery that is, in itself, impenetrable, but that is also, at the same time, the horizon upon which I can understand everything else. That's something to consider. "

Bill leaned over to Lucy and whispered, "But what if pasta is the horizon upon which I understand everything else?"

Lucy ignored him and wrote the word "mystery" on her paper next to the true heirs, and put an unequal sign between the two.

The seminarian at the end of the row raised his hand again, "But professor – "

"Listen I'm on your side," he interrupted. "Rahner's certainly problematic, but perhaps not so much for the reasons you point out."

"So what's problematic?"

"Well, it's right there in *Gaudium et Spes* twenty two. Man is not the measure for the incarnation. Despite how much he claims to be doing *a posteriori* theology, Rahner risks making the incarnation necessary and therefore not free, given what he's said about man. Against Rahner, *Gaudium et Spes* affirms that the light comes in freedom, not necessity. The light is the measure of man, not man the measure of the light."

"Right, so anonymity is impossible," said the seminarian.

"Well what's anonymity? It's the *lack* of a name. And what's a name?" The professor then pointed at the people along the row of Americans. "You're Jack, you're Kevin, you're Michael, you're Bill, you're... I've never seen you here before."

He was pointing at Lucy.

"I'm Lucy."

"Well, it's five weeks into the semester and you've finally decided to bless us with your presence at lectures today. Does Brian know you're in his spot?"

"I'm an *ospite*."

"*Va bene*. Anyways, you're Lucy. The point is that you have a name, and that means that someone else calls on you by name. Like Balthasar said, name, mission, and identity are all the same thing. You don't have an identity without a name that expresses your mission. Without a relationship, a name has no sense. It's not about your own consistency. The name is yours, yes, but it's not yours. It's for the other. Something else is the measure. Someone else calls you by name. Perhaps that's where the difficulty lies. Anonymity, perhaps, works in theory. But in reality, anonymity is horrendous. It's hell. It's to be without relationship."

Before the American had a chance to ask another question, the professor went on with his lecture notes, switching back to Italian, and Lucy wrote down on her paper *the light is the measure of man, not man the measure of the light*. And in one blinding second everything made sense. She rewrote it, but in Latin and Greek: *lux is the measure of* ανθρωπος, *not* ανθρωπος *the measure of lux*. She rewrote it a third time, this time all of it back in English, substituting the Latin and Greek with the modern names of the people from the Palazzo. Her jaw dropped, and she put her hands on her head.

"The light is the measure of man," she said out loud. "Lucy is light. *Lucy* is the measure… the police told me that… Lucy is the measure."

"What was that?" The professor looked up.

"The light is the measure of man!" this time Lucy blurted out, sitting up straight and yelling at the professor.

"Correct," he narrowed his eyebrows and looked back.

"The light is the measure of man, but what if the light is also man? Or woman, I guess, in my case. What if the light is a human person?"

"That's exactly the proposal."

"Then that means that *lux* and ανθρωπος are the same height! What if man is the same height as *lux*? Then we're the same! We *can* measure!"

"Yes and no. Man and the light are exactly the same but still very different, aren't they?"

"Very!"

"That's the mystery."

Lucy stood up. "Thank you! Thank you! Thank you! You're brilliant!"

All hundred and fifty students in the lecture hall had turned to stare at her. She climbed over Bill, Michael, Kevin and Jack. They each tried to get up and move out of her way, but the Greg's rows of desks were too tiny and she was moving too fast to give them time to get up. Once in the aisle, she sprinted down the stairs, across the front of the lecture hall, and out the door.

CHAPTER TWENTY-FOUR

LA CHENOSI

Coming down the front steps of the Greg her phone buzzed. Another text from Brian.

> Listen. We've got your friends Andrew, Brian, and Natasha tied up on the terrace. If you'd ever like to see them alive again you need to come home within half an hour. The True Heirs.

She texted back.

> I can be there in an hour.

They weren't having it:

> You've got half an hour or they're dead.

At Brian's pace, the Greg is a forty-minute walk from the Palazzo. She sprinted across Piazza della Pilotta, and was about to turn the corner when she heard a clicking sound. An American seminarian on a black bicycle was moving along very slowly through the piazza, carefully avoiding pot holes. Every time the petal went around one rotation, the bike made a terrible clicking sound. He was thin, was wearing a helmet and clerics, and a fleece jacket with the word Denver written on it.

"Hey, hey, hey!" she flagged him down. "I need your bike."

He stopped and put one leg on the ground. "Um... you need my bike? Do we know each other?"

"It's an emergency, I don't have time to explain. You're at the NAC, right? I'll give it right back, I promise. It's an emergency"

"Well... um... I guess I wanna believe you... but..."

"Just give me the bike! It's life or death! I promise. I live right down the street from you," she walked up right next to the bike and put her face right next to his.

He leaned back, and put his leg out farther, now very unsteadily leaning to one side of the bike. "No, I'm sure it sounds like you have a great reason to need the bike more than me right now, it's just that I... I don't know... it's a little weird don't you – "

He was interrupted by Lucy, who had firmly planted her lips right on his, in an attempt to end the discussion. She kept pressing forward with her lips, and grabbed onto the handlebars, maintaining her lips on his face, until he let go of the handlebars and fell backwards off the bike. He lay on the ground with a stupid smile on his face, and Lucy helped herself to his bike.

"I'm sorry, I just really need a bike right now."

She got on, and started to petal away.

"Hey!" the seminarian yelled back, now laughing. "If you'd like to come convince me to lend you the helmet too, I've still got it. Oh, and don't worry, I won't tell Scott about anything. We can keep this little moment between us two."

Lucy didn't have time to worry about what the Scott comment was all about, because she was already in the highest gear, halfway down the block, yelling *permesso* at all the tourists on the narrow lanes between her and Starbucks, where she hit the brakes, dismounted, and left the bike on the ground outside the store. Within three minutes, she was back on the bike, headed towards Piazza Flaminio, where she made another brief stop at the biggest modeling agency in Rome. The clicking noise that the petal made every time it went around was louder and faster than ever. From Flaminio she cut around the Vatican, Via della Conciliazione, then past San Pietro's and straight into a tunnel that led into one of the ugliest places in Rome: the underground bus station beneath the Janiculum hill. Lucy only ever used that bus station short-cut in times of extreme need. The crowds were not very thick, so she cruised through the fluorescent-lighted tunnels, with a strong odor of urine, riding directly on the moving walkways, to get to the tour-bus parking garage, and emerge at the top of the Janiculum, ten minutes ahead of Brian and Natasha's threatened execution time.

She skidded to a stop, dismounted and left the bike unlocked on the ground outside the entrance to Palazzo Mortimer. I was sitting there in the lobby waiting for her. Gambetti and the security guards were sound asleep, snoring and slobbering on the porter's desk, gripping Gatorade bottles that had clearly been laced with some strong sleep aids. I explained the situation to her.

"You could just call the cops," I said.

"That ship's sailed a long time ago."

"Well, what are you thinking?"

"Walk with me."

She took me to the basement, and into one of the old servants' rooms, full of antique furniture. In the corner there was a large safe with a broken lock. It was packed with antique guns.

"You've never seen any ammo down here, have you?" she asked me.

"No."

"Well, what can you tell me about one of these?"

She handed me a wooden bow, and picked up five arrows from the floor of the safe. I helped her string the bow, and taught her the basics. She'd always refused to learn before. Now she regretted it. We also found an orange feather in the room, which she tucked into her hair behind her right ear.

We crept up the narrow servants' staircase, all the way to the roof access point, making as little noise as possible. On the top step outside the door, she took her phone out of her armband. One minute to go. She took a seat on the step and breathed in deep, extending her right hand out in front of her face. It was trembling. She closed her eyes and sat up straight, breathing softly through her nose until her hand became steady as a rock. She hit the play button on her phone's recorder and set it on the top step. She knocked one of the arrows onto the bowstring, got to her feet, and put some tension on the bow, holding the arrow downwards. Using her foot, she slowly pushed the door ajar. And it creaked. No! She had no choice but to kick the door wide open immediately.

Both of the large leather jacketed thugs were standing on the terrace, this time with no ski masks. Natasha, Brian, and Andrew sat behind them, gagged and duct taped onto the patio furniture. The thugs stared at Lucy, just fifteen feet away from them, with confusion on their faces.

Before either of the men had a chance to react, one of them almost fell backwards, and looked down, still confused, at an arrow which had just lodged itself into his gut. Her aim was great, but unfortunately, Lucy did not have a great reload time. When the second arrow went flying, the other thug had already become a moving target. It pierced the shoulder of his jacket, but missed any flesh. Arrow number three did find its way onto the bowstring, but not before the thug's fist found its way onto Lucy's face.

When she came to, she was also duct taped to a chair next to the others. Her mouth was taped shut. Her head was throbbing, and her right cheek would soon have a good bruise. The guy with the arrow in his stomach was lying down on a deck chair across from her. His accomplice had already cut away the jacket and t-shirt, revealing a round gut with an arrow sticking straight in the air. His upper chest was also covered in long strips of gauze, which corresponded to a few long bear claw wounds. They were trying to put gauze and rubbing alcohol around the base of the arrow wound. It hadn't gone deep, and his belly was large enough that the arrow posed little serious threat to his long term well being.

Lucy looked at the others seated next to her. Natasha, to her right, was exhausted and frightened. She tried to give Natasha an encouraging look. Andrew was anxious and fidgety. Lucy scowled and shook her head at him. Brian looked both upset and somehow also guilty. Lucy raised her shoulders and eyebrows at him.

"*Avaja, t'arrusbigghiasti?*" the uninjured man asked Lucy, leaving his accomplice to treat his own wounds. "*Sei pronta a parlare?*"[181]

Lucy nodded her head.[182]

The man took out a gun – Natasha's gun – and placed it on Brian's forehead. He planted his feet right in front of Lucy and towered over her. "*Non t'hai a gridare o nuddu. Se c'hai a farlo, spariamo a chistu inciu a capa. U capisti?*"[183]

Lucy nodded. He ripped the tape from her mouth.[184]

"*Dunque. M'hai a dire i numeri del conto del banco,*" he said again.[185]

"And I was trying to tell you last night that there is no bank account," said Lucy. "There's just a bag full of money."

The man looked over his shoulder at his shirtless accomplice, and again at Lucy.

"Oh come on," she said. "Don't act like you don't speak English. You sure as hell can't speak Italian. You must've grown up in Australia. Your mom, Virginia, certainly uses all kinds of Australian expressions when she speaks English. Last week she used the word *bludgers*. I mean, really, who says bludgers?"

Andrew's eyes pealed open. The three of them — the two big thugs and Andrew — all spent a while giving each other knowing looks.

"You were about to say something about a bag of money," the large man continued his questioning with a thick Australian accent.

"Shouldn't Andrew be asking the questions? He's the only one who's committed murder for it, and it's not even his inheritance.

---

[181] "*So you're awake now?*" *the uninjured man asked Lucy, leaving his accomplice to treat his own wounds.* "Are you ready to talk?"

[182] *Lucy nodded her head.*

[183] *The man took out a gun — Natasha's gun — and placed it on Brian's forehead. He planted his feet right in front of Lucy and towered over her.* "You must not scream or do anything like that. If you do, we'll shoot this guy in the head. Understood?"

[184] *Lucy nodded. He ripped the tape from her mouth.*

[185] "Alright, you need to tell me the number for the bank account," *he said again.*

You two, on the other hand, could walk away right now without any charges. Think about it."

"Andrew's got nothing to do with it," he answered. "I never met him 'til today."

"If he's got nothing to do with it, then don't you think it's kind of strange that he killed Eugenio?"

The thug looked over at Andrew. "I told you, Andrew. I told you you're a pathetic idiot. I told you you'd get caught. There's a difference between roughing someone up and killing 'em."

He ripped the tape off Andrew's mouth.

"She can't prove anything."

"You're the same height as me," said Lucy. "The police measured me against the person on the security cameras wearing my rain jacket. I'm the same height, the same measure as the murderer. You're the only resident who's the same height as me."

"Like I said, she can't prove anything."

"That afternoon," Lucy turned to talk to all three Australians, "you were all at the Palazzo waiting for Eugenio to come. You knew he was going to come see his mom on the sly, and you somehow knew she was going to give him money. Money that you two," she nodded at the large ones, "thought would belong to your inheritance. So you emptied the Palazzo of the student residents — me running, fake jobs for Brian, Fr. Damien at the library, etc — to make sure we wouldn't get in the way."

"She still hasn't proven anything," said Andrew. "It's just a stupid girl coming up with crazy ideas."

"But your half brother, Eugenio, came to the Palazzo earlier than you expected, and by the time you three arrived, he had already made off with the money. He stashed it in a storage locker, and almost got away until you two thugs caught up with him in the park, but Eugenio had already crossed paths with me in the park. He must have seen me when he first visited Virginia, and recognized me. He ditched the keys with me, knowing that if you guys caught him, you would take them. You could never catch him on foot in the park, though, so you called your cousin Andrew back at the Palazzo, and told him to help find Eugenio using the scooter. When Andrew got the call he was still up at the Palazzo, but he didn't want to go out immediately to track somebody down in the rain. So he grabbed the first rain jacket he could find, and the first weapon he could think of, the nail gun in the storage room."

"What a waste of time," said Andrew. "This story is so far fetched."

"If Eugenio had stayed in the park, he probably could have lost you three for good. In the meantime, though, Natasha showed up at the Palazzo. He received a call from her when he was talking to me, and told her he was coming to the Palazzo to get her to safety. He managed to run back to the the building, but Andrew caught up to him in the lobby — still wearing my rain gear. They chatted, trying to come to an agreement. Andrew demanded the bank account numbers, and Eugenio said he'd already given them to a student resident. But before Andrew could get any more information, he lost control of himself and shot Eugenio in the head with the nail gun."

"Right," said Andrew. "And if you don't shut your mouth, maybe I'll lose control again. You may have everything right, but you'll never prove any of that to the police."

"Your fingerprints were never identified on the gun because you're already a citizen. You didn't get scanned when you entered the country. You've never had your fingerprints taken here. I'm sure if they run your prints they'll come up all over that nail gun."

"Prints aren't enough. You've demonstrated that."

"You parked the motorino by the door, so when you got away, you filled the lobby with smoke. You really should have let me look at that muffler. A little duct tape and a hammer could fix that."

"Still not enough," said Andrew.

"You threw away the rain gear on Via dei Corridori and hurried back to the Palazzo in shorts and a t-shirt without putting your helmet on. You always wear your helmet... but that day you were too distracted with the hood on my rain gear to remember to put it on. I remember when you pulled up in the scooter at the Palazzo next to me and Brian. You still didn't have your helmet on."

"Who cares. The cops'll never agree with any of this. You may be one hundred percent right, but it doesn't matter. I forgot my helmet. Big deal."

"And it seems that these two Australians, who tried to kill me last night, agree with me that you killed Eugenio —"

Joseph M. Grady

"To be clear," the wounded man with the arrow interrupted. "We weren't going to kill you straight away. You'd be surprised at how long it takes to really strangle someone. You're sure lucky that animal showed up."

"These guys killed Cristiano, though," said Andrew. "We know that."

"No we didn't" they responded in unison.

"Yeah, that's another thing," Lucy said to Andrew. "Just look at that footage. Your cousins never could have made it upstairs in time. They heard the screams as you threw Cristiano over the railing. Cristiano hung on to you, and you almost shared his fate, but you grabbed onto the curtain. These two guys only made it up the elevator and headed straight back down when they got scared hearing you yell."

"Now, to get back to the point," the large non-wounded Australian said. "My cousin's stupidity and recklessness aside, you were about to tell us about a big bag of money."

He bent over Andrew with a knife and freed him from the duct tape.

"Cousin?" said Lucy. "Andrew's your cousin? This is all making a little more sense."

"Whatever," the thug said. "I didn't ask you about my family. I asked you about a big bag of money!"

"A big bag of cash from Virginia's mafia family that belonged to Eugenio, not you," said Lucy. "And it definitely never belonged to Andrew. Does your mother, Virginia, know that you two are here? We could solve a whole lot if we just went downstairs and had a civilized chat about your recent behavior. But you probably wouldn't want to do that... you might lose all the inheritance if she were to hear how you treated Eugenio and Cristiano."

"Don't act like you understand what's going on in my family!" yelled Andrew. "There's far too much blackmail that we could use on Auntie Virginia for that to ever happen. I warned you to stay out of this!"

Andrew walked over to Lucy, looked down at her and slapped her on the face, knocking her head to the side. Hard. Brian yelled as much as he could through the tape on his mouth and rocked his chair back and forth. Lucy slowly moved her head back. It was throbbing even harder now, and she felt a salty taste in her mouth.

Blood. The large non-wounded cousin took Andrew by the shoulders and moved him a few feet from Lucy.

"If you ever want to see Brian and Natasha alive again," said the larger Australian. "You better get us that big bag of money right now. That's mob cash that never belonged to that halfbreed Eugenio, and it sure as hell doesn't belong to you."

Lucy sighed. "Like I said, it's in a storage unit a mile from here."

"Give us the keys and the locker number."

"The keys are in the golf bag in the storage room. I don't remember what number unit it's in."

"Give me the gun," Andrew told his cousin.

"You got us into this mess," said the cousin. "Don't make it worse."

"I can make this alright in the end," said Andrew. "Lucy knows how to keep quiet, right?"

Lucy nodded.

"Good. Lucy and I are going to get the money. If we're not back here in half an hour, go ahead and off one of her friends, alright? Preferably Brian first. Or, whatever. Flip a coin or something."

Andrew held onto the gun in his jacket pocket, and walked Lucy downstairs, out the building. They stood next to his motorino.

"Don't try anything stupid," said Andrew. "I will shoot you without a second thought."

"I would have already done something stupid if other people's lives weren't on the line."

"Just get on the bike."

She swung her leg over the back seat.

"No, how is this going to work?" Andrew thought out loud. "I can't have you in the back seat. Scoot forward. It'd be too easy for you to get away."

Lucy was given the keys and told she'd be driving. He quickly explained the braking and acceleration. She put on his helmet, turned on the motorino, and lurched out into traffic. She shuddered feeling Andrew's left hand gripping hard onto her belly button, and the barrel of the pistol digging into her back.

They picked up the bag of money, put it into the motorino and headed back to the Palazzo.

"When we get to the Palazzo," yelled Andrew into her ear, Lucy's stray hair whipping in his face, "I want you to keep going and drive up to the NAC, and park inside there."

The gate to the NAC property was just opening as they pulled up, because a bicyclist was exiting. They parked, and the porter came charging out of his office, walking across the parking lot and glaring at them, asking who they were, "*Ma chi siete?*"

At that same time, a Volkswagen full of three elderly Cardinals pulled up and parked directly between the porter and the motorino. By the time the porter figured out what to do with the Cardinals and turned around to find Lucy and Andrew, they were already inside the building.

"Am I allowed to ask what we're doing here?" said Lucy in the elevator, the gun still fixed on her.

"I need to find out why you kept looking at the top of the NAC. It looked like there was somebody standing up there, and you kept looking up there at that new tower with hopeful eyes. There will be no witnesses."

Lucy swallowed. They exited the elevator and then the building, walking out onto the rooftop and then up to the tower, first a steel grated staircase to reach the tower's highest level, and another steel spiral staircase to the viewing area. A 360° degree panoramic of central Rome surrounded them at their feet, nine stories down.

"I see people and movement, but can one of you explains what's going on down there?" Luca Speziale was standing by the railing – which came up just above his knees – holding a camera pointed down towards the terrace of Palazzo Mortimer.

"Give me that camera," Andrew told him.

"Who are you?"

"Give me the camera," Andrew took the gun out of his pocket and pointed it at Luca. "Set it there on the table and walk away."

Andrew collected the camera from the table, still keeping the gun trained on Speziale. He told Lucy to go stand by Luca, then picked up Luca's camera, held it high in the air and sent it hurtling to the ground as fast as possible. The lens shattered. He kicked it to the side.

Andrew threw a roll of duct tape to Luca, "Now tape her to the chair."

"Again?" said Lucy. "Is this necessary? We destroyed the evidence. Let's go."

"Shut up."

After a bit of work, Lucy and Luca were both duct taped to chairs. Again.

"Andrew, we need to get back to the Palazzo in five minutes so they don't kill Brian and Natasha," said Lucy. "Or at least call them or something and tell them we're on our way."

Lucy received yet another blow on the face. She and Luca both got tape on their mouths. Again.

"You really think we're going to risk leaving you and your friends alive? My cousins might be dumb enough for that. But I'm not."

Andrew got out his phone and called his cousin. "Bad news .... yeah, she got away. She's got the money too. We seriously can't risk leaving anyone alive. Just kill Brian and Natasha right now. I'm serious. Like right now. Good. Then straight away, come up to the top of the tower at the building across and down the street. Yeah, that's me waving at you. Good. See you in ten minutes."

Andrew pulled up a chair and sat in front of Lucy. She had remained uncharacteristically calm from the moment she shot the first arrow up until that point. Now she was no longer calm. To say the least. Her chest heaved up and down, continually filling up with air, and never fully exhaling. Her face was soon drenched with tears, mixed with the blood that had been trickling from her nose after the latest blow to the face.

"You've got less than ten minutes to make peace with your maker," Andrew told her. He removed the feather from her ear, and brushed her hair out of her eyes. He caressed her ears and then massaged her neck. She shivered and her shoulders just grew more tense, the more he massaged. "It's really too bad about you having to get mixed up in all of this. We could have been friends. Who knows. You're pretty. We could have been even more. I know we had a rough patch that one day when you got violent with me, but I tried as hard as I could to be nice to you after that. You probably think now that I was faking. I wasn't. Damnit Lucy, we could have been something. We were so close to being something. Holding my hand in the rest stop. Leaving your head snuggled up to mine the whole way back to Rome. But you're just too stupid to understand how things work. Too stupid to understand what's good for you. I told you to stay out of it. I really tried to keep you safe, because I cared about you. It's a shame. It's really a shame."

He took his hand off her neck, and got up to stand by the railing of the terrace, squinting down towards the palazzo.

"It looks like there's a good bit of movement on the terrace down there. Looks like they're dragging the bodies somewhere. My cousins are quite dumb sometimes, but they can sure be quick when they need to be."

Lucy closed her eyes, and put her head back. That's it. She'd failed. Brian and Natasha were dead. Whatever happened next didn't matter. Andrew stayed by the railing for a few more minutes, squinting and shielding his eyes, trying to understand what was going on below.

"And there he is," he said finally. "A big man with a black coat and jeans just walked through the porter's office... and there he goes into the building. Now I reckon that from the building entrance to the elevator is, what? One minute? And from the elevator up to here could be another minute or two? Which means that I've got to get both of you over the railing before he gets to the top, but not before it would be reasonable for him to have feasibly arrived up here in time to do it himself. Otherwise who am I going to blame for your deaths? In any case, I hope to be halfway to Sicily before the cops ever get here. Better safe than sorry, right? Who's first? Ladies first."

Andrew squatted down next to Lucy. He picked up the chair she was sitting in, cradling her with one arm beneath the seat, and another on the backrest.

"You're much lighter than Ludovici or Valentino. Ludovici put up quite a fight, but he went over in the end. Scott would've been impossible, but luckily I caught him by surprise. But this, I'm going to enjoy. And, if I may, perhaps I can offer you a final thought for your life, my dear Lucy. Your friends just died – disappeared into nothingness. And the last thing they got to think about, just before leaving the world forever, was the fact that you abandoned them. You let them die, so that you could run off with a bag of money. You've always been such a great friend, Lucy."

The sky that day was extraordinarily blue, and the sun didn't allow her to see anything else than its blinding rays and the surrounding blueness. Andrew's words registered, but they didn't ring true. They became completely meaningless background noise. Lucy focused instead on the last thing she would see. The sky. It was so immense and so peaceful. So incredibly different than the place where she was right now. But it was always there. Always had been there. Why hadn't she spent more time looking at the sky? Well, at least in this last moment, she was still free to do so.

Andrew, of course, wanted to make things dramatic. He stepped up onto the small tile lip on which the railing was connected to the floor, lifting both himself and Lucy another six inches above the ground, and bringing the top edge of the railing to just below his knees. He held Lucy over the railing, above the ground. A nine-story abyss yawned open beneath her. He leaned back slightly to get his arms underneath Lucy, and then grunted, pushing her up even higher, so he could really hurl her.

And Lucy, paradoxically, rising up higher, felt every muscle in her body relax. Pure abandonment. Whatever had just happened to Brian and Natasha was now going to happen to her too, and that was good enough for her. Everything that could be done, right or wrong, had been done. The only thing left to do, was take one last look at the sky. She hardly even perceived the voice of the Italian model who had just reached the top of the tower, so intense was Lucy's gaze upon the sky. And then she heard her name.

"Oh, ciao, Lucy. Scusa il ritardo, eh. C'è stato un po' di traffico. Allora, che famo?... eh... Dio mio! Ma che cavolo state a fà?"[186]

There was a slight jerk, and the support of Andrew's hands that had been beneath her gave way. She tumbled downwards into the emptiness beneath her. This was it. The descent into the abyss. The final plunge. It was over much sooner than she thought it would be. She felt a violent slam on the right side of her body, and then... wait... no... a tile floor, and, was that Andrew's foot she saw disappear over the edge?

---

[186] "Oh hi, Lucy. Sorry I'm late. There was a bit of traffic. Okay, what are we up to?... um... Oh my God! What the hell is going on here?"

In any case, the wind had been knocked out of her. It took her a few empty breaths before her lungs would finally cooperate and allow her to take in fresh air. Her already aching head ached all the more, and the whole right side of her body was just beginning to feel the reverberation of falling straight down onto the hard tile floor, while strapped to a chair, and landing hard on her side. The ringing in her ears barely allowed her to hear the scream of the Italian model who was looking over the railing, eyes fixed on Andrew's body, nine stories below.

Right in front of Lucy's face, on the floor of the tower's terrace, in front of the railing, at the spot where Andrew must have stepped backwards off the lip, distracted by the arrival of the model, there was a roll of duct tape. It was still rocking back and forth, and part of it still had the imprint of the bottom of what must have been Andrew's shoe.

CHAPTER TWENTY-FIVE

L'ESCATON E IL TEMPIO MORMONE

The entire tower became a crime scene, and the parking lot filled up with vehicles. Over the next hours, there were all kinds of very official looking people who took Lucy from one place to the next, asking her questions, stinging her with rubbing alcohol, shining lights in her eyes, twisting her limbs to check for sprains and broken bones, demanding documents and explanations, dealing with a team of Czech and Italian lawyers who had also descended on the crime scene. She gave blank stares to investigators who wanted to know where to track down a long list of names of people who they thought might be involved. She gave blanks stares to a third group of police who explained that everything had not actually happened in Italy, but an extraterritorial Vatican property, thus complicating the whole process even further.

For Lucy, though, it all happened at arms' length. She had given herself over to being taken from one place to the next, demanded one thing, and then another, poked and prodded. But what did it matter? That is, until, looking over the shoulder of the person in a suit talking at her, on the other side of the parking lot, she saw the police questioning a blonde girl dressed up in way too much winter clothing, an overweight American in Starbucks dress code, and a giant blue bear standing behind them. They were all there, safe and sound.

Her cheeks grew wet again, she stood up, and – knowing she wasn't allowed to move around the crime scene, but needing to express herself to someone – grabbed onto the U.S. embassy official who had been explaining her rights to her, and squeezed him into a tight bear hug. "They're alive! They're alive!"

When Lucy had left with Andrew to pick up the bag of money from the storage locker, I couldn't fit on the scooter, so I had to stay at the Palazzo. We spent a very strange time in silence. The guy with the arrow moaned about the pain in his gut. The other thug sat on the patio furniture playing a game on his phone. Brian and Natasha breathed through their noses and shot scared looks at each other. When the cousin got the phone call from Andrew with the orders to kill, he stood up, took out his knife, and without saying a word, walked up to Natasha. He removed her scarf and put the knife up to her throat. She was breathing heavily. But then he returned the knife to his pocket and stood there looking puzzled, scratching his chin. He grabbed her head and pushed it to one side like a barber, and began feeling around the side of her neck.

"Hey," he said to his brother. "If you were looking for someone's jugular vein, how would you find it?"

"Just find the pulse."

"Oh right." He felt all the way up and down Natasha's neck, until, after much searching, he found the pulse. "Got it!"

He took his knife back out of his pocket, but in doing so, had also lost the location of the pulse.

"Well this is just downright tricky, isn't it? None of you by chance has a marker or something like that, do you?"

Brian and Natasha both shook their heads.

"And bloody hell, look at the size of your neck," he said to Brian. "It's hard enough trying to figure out how to slit this girl's throat, but how on earth am I supposed to get through all of that? Well, I'm sorry if this is gonna be a bit messy, but I promise I'll do my best."

He put the knife back up to Natasha's throat, and grimaced, like he was about to do something he didn't want to. The door to the servants' quarters creaked open, and everyone turned. Fr. Damien walked out. He had a red nose, baggy eyes, and was wearing pajamas. He took a new pack of cigarettes out of his pocket and removed the plastic wrapper.

He lit up and asked, "What is happening?"

"Excuse, me, but who are you? You must be that Asian priest Andrew was telling me about."

"Yes."

"But you're not supposed to be here. You're supposed to be at school right now. You've got a very strict schedule, Andrew told us all about it."

"I am sick."

"Clearly. Crikey, this makes things much more complicated. I'm really sorry, but I am going to have to tape you to a chair. Do you mind coming over here?" He gestured at an empty patio chair with his knife. "Now, where did we put that duct tape?"

Fr. Damien took a drag of his cigarette, and walked up to the man. "I cannot comply with your request, and I must ask for release of these two."

The man tried to take a swipe at Fr. Damien with his knife, but somehow his wrist was already in Fr. Damien's hand. Fr. Damien twisted the man's wrist in just the right direction and he let out a scream of pain, dropping the knife. With his free arm, the Australian took a swing at Fr. Damien, who had ducked at just the right time, and already had both of his arms around the thug's midsection. In an amazing display of physics and martial arts, the large man's feet went flying in the air, and he was, in no time, slammed hard on his back, on the floor, staring up with a blank expression. Fr. Damien put one knee on the man's gut, removed the string from his own pajamas, and tied his hands together. He stood up, breathed in, and removed the cigarette from his mouth. The shirtless brother, still lying down on the deck chair with the arrow in his gut, stayed lying down, and put his hands in the air.

"What's this?" Brian set down his coffee on the kitchenette table and picked up a piece of paper that Lucy had just slammed on the table in front of him.

"Read."

"United Airlines, December 13th, Rome to Chicago, Chicago to Denver, ticket in the name of Lucy Fox. Is this real?"

"Oh lovely," said Natasha, "You're going home for Christmas."

"It's real. And I don't know if 'lovely' is the first word I'd use to describe it, but yes. I'm going home."

"Well that's great," said Brian. "It's too bad you won't be here, though. I just heard from Papa and Beth. They'll be out here in Rome for Christmas."

"You win some, you lose some," said Lucy.

"Oh, speaking of Vacations," Natasha said. "I got a call from my Dad. He doesn't want me to come to Moscow this summer, but he'll be renting a Villa for a couple of weeks in some place called Rimini this August. I guess it's by the beach and is popular with Russians. Any takers?"

"You mean, do we want to come?" asked Brian.

"Yeah, would you like to come?"

"I'm in," he said. "Lucy?"

"Why not?" said Lucy. "You said there'll be Russians for two weeks in a Villa? Maybe we can solve a crime there too."

"Great. When do you come back from Christmas break?" Natasha asked Lucy.

"Not 'til January 7th."

"Orthodox Christmas," said Natasha. "My name day."

"And you're really going to spend all that time with your family?" said Brian.

"I have a hunch she's got ulterior motives," said Natasha. "You don't have a ticket for Wisconsin too, do you?"

"And what if I do?" Lucy got up and poured herself a cup of coffee. Brian smirked, and Lucy changed the subject, "I was just walking downstairs to the printer, and I went past Virginia's room."

"Yeah?"

"The door was open, and the whole apartment was, like, totally empty. Martina and Elena were just standing there with their arms folded, looking sad. I asked them where Virginia was and they told me she'd just up and disappeared. Gone."

"That's the end of an era," said Natasha. "No more mean girls. How are we going to break in the new students arriving in January?"

"Are you allowed out of the Palazzo today?" Brian asked Lucy.

"The lawyers said no."

"So are you going out today?"

"I don't know. We'll see."

"Do you need anything from the store," Natasha asked.

"We're running low on coffee," said Lucy.

"Speaking of coffee," said Brian. "The budget's looking pretty bad for the rest of the year."

"Oh, we should talk about that," said Lucy. She bent down below the sink and took out five kilo-sized bags of store brand coffee beans.

"Oh, that's awesome," said Brian. "Where'd that come from?"

She threw them on the table in front of him. The bags made a thud that didn't sound at all like coffee beans.

"The police did search the servants' quarters, but I guess not very thoroughly."

Brian opened one up and removed a wad of cash.

"You didn't think I was gonna leave all that cash in the storage unit, did you?" asked Lucy.

"Are you kidding me?" Brian leaned back and laughed.

"Good night, Lucy! How much is that?" asked Natasha.

"Only two million Euros. But that'll keep us good on coffee for at least the rest of the year."

"So the police said they found two million in the bag," said Brian. "How much was in there to begin with?"

"The police were right. There were two million in the bag when they found it in Andrew's motorino," said Lucy. "If three million happened to wind up at Irene Spiga's house, and two million somehow slipped its way into that coffee bag... I couldn't tell you how it got there."

That afternoon, after three transfers, and an hour and a half of bus time, Alice Kloepfer and Ronald Lindbeck — with blond and red hair and formal business attire — got off the thirty nine near the *Grande Raccordo Annulare.*

"Where are we? Are you sure it's here?" asked Lucy.

"Yep," said Brian.

"Inside the mall? Are you kidding me?"

"Right on the other side."

They had to trek another half an hour around Rome's largest and ugliest shopping mall and then another twenty minutes under and around a highway overpass full of weeds and abandoned construction material before arriving at their destination: another construction site.

"And here we are," said Brian, standing in the weeds on top of an abandoned metal tube, looking over the fence, and trying to imagine what the building behind the scaffolding looked like. "I guess it does kind of look like a temple, doesn't it?"

"Do you feel at home?"

"A little bit. More so for the shopping mall than the Mormon temple... or well, to be honest, the two don't look all that different from one another. Unbridled Americanism on both sides of the highway."

The pair took a lap around the construction site to the visitor's center, which had already opened.

"How long have they been building this thing?" asked Lucy.

"Seven years," said Brian.

"Seven years? They built the NAC tower in one. That thing does not look fancy enough to take seven years."

"Mormons are efficient, but they can't work with Italians. They don't allow smoking on the job site... it's holy ground, I guess. When was the last time you saw an Italian construction worker who doesn't smoke?"

"Seriously? No smoking? How have they managed to build anything at all?"

Entering the grounds for the visitor center, they left Italy behind, and entered what could have easily been mistaken for any other building in Utah. Two smiling young ladies in shapeless ankle length skirts and name tags stood as sentinels in the reception area to greet them.

"*Buon giorno.*" They said in perky unison, with hopelessly thick American accents.

"Hi," said Brian, extending a reciprocal fake smile and a hand shake to both of them, "Ronald Lindbeck, and this is my colleague Alice Kloepfer."

"Great to meet you! I'm Sister Smith."

"And I'm Sister Young."

"Nice to meet you," said Lucy, wondering why they were called sisters. Do mormons have nuns now too? Have they come full circle from beginning in polygamy and ending in celibacy?

"What brings you out to the temple construction site?" one of them asked.

"Oh," said Brian. "We both work for Initech, and we've been out in Rome on a business conference for the last couple of days."

"Wow! Welcome to the city."

"I'm LDS," lied Brian, "but Lucy... I mean... Alice grew up unaffiliated with any Church, and we've just had some great conversations the last couple days working together in Rome."

"How exciting."

"Two things," said Brian. "We were wondering if we could get a copy of the Book of Mormon for Alice. She's really interested in reading it. And second, Alice and I have been talking a lot about the importance of family history, and making sure that all of our deceased family members have the same opportunities for Church membership like all of us."

"Wow!"

"Yeah, so I've been trying to help Alice get logged onto Ancestry.com to find out more about her ancestors, but my own log-in doesn't seem to work here in Italy."

"Oh, shucks. That's too bad. I'm sure we could definitely help you out here. I've got an admin Log-in that we could use together."

In no time at all, Lucy was cradling a free copy of the Book of Mormon, and both of them were rushing down a hallway towards a computer. They spent the next half hour on the Mormon run ancestry website looking up the family history of some poor girl named Alice Kloepfer with one of the missionaries smiling over their shoulder and a healthy dose of giddy excitement. A telephone finally called the missionary away, and Lucy and Brian were left to navigate themselves.

"Alright, here, type in Giovanni Fasani," said Lucy.

The old prince was not hard to find. He had just one wife, one heir — the current *principessa* — and an incredibly noble pedigree.

"Okay, so let's bookmark this," said Brian.

"Now to find Virginia Pironi."

Being part of a mafia family, it was a little trickier, but they eventually tracked her down. They also found Irene Spiga and Eugenio Galli. They were already marked as married. Irene's entry had a good deal of ancestry history, but Eugenio's lineage was blank. Using the administrator log-in, Brian changed Eugenio's status to deceased and entered the date of death.

"Alright," said Brian, "are you sure about this?"

"One hundred percent." Lucy pulled out the small framed photo of the prince — the one that had always hung from above her sink — and removed the back cover. Inside was a sappy love letter written from "Ginevra" to *"Mio Principe."*

Brian linked the prince's profile with Virginia's by a dotted line to indicate an extra-marital affair between the high class aristocrat and mafia princess. He then connected both of the parents' profiles to the illegitimate fruit of their encounter: Eugenio.

"And there we are," said Brian.

"That simple?"

"That simple."

"That was easy," said Lucy.

"Now what?"

"Now we mail this love letter to the tabloids, and see if anyone cares."

The Mormon missionary came back into the room, Lucy and Brian hurriedly closed the browser, shook hands with their helper, and ran out of the visitor center.

Lucy stopped in the lobby, "Wait, I'm going to slip into the bathroom."

"What? No. Let's go. We can stop at the mall. I don't want to have to talk to these people again."

Lucy was already gone. She emerged five minutes later in her running outfit and handed off her briefcase to Brian.

"What did you change for?" he asked her, walking out of the visitors' center.

"I'm going to run home."

"From here?"

"Yeah."

"It took us an hour and a half to get here on the bus."

"Yeah, It's only seven miles from home, though."

"Are you kidding me?"

"Welcome to Europe," said Lucy. "Why didn't we just take a cab? Aren't we rich now? When I go home for Christmas, if I hear any young American talking about how great public transportation is in Europe, I swear, I'm going to punch them in the face."

"An hour and a half and we only got seven miles. You can run and get home faster."

"Exactly," said Lucy. "*I* can run and get home faster. I'll race you."

She took off running and Brian shuffled back towards the mall and the bus stop.

I was along the bank of the Tiber River, sitting on a step and admiring the water, smelling people as they travelled up and down the bike path. Upstream I saw a runner in Lucy's clothes, with Lucy's gait, but with blonde hair and sunglasses. She slowed down to a walk when she came around the path to where I was sitting. She took a seat right next to me, pulled her new phone out of her armband – her old phone now belonged to the Republic of Italy – and placed it next to her ear.

"Hello?"

"What's up?" I said. "Were there any paparazzi outside the building?"

"Just one, but he was on a smoke break. I probably could have left even without a disguise. This wig is gonna be gross if I have to keep using it for running. It's so dumb. Nobody's published anything on me for two days. I'm not interesting. I should be allowed to leave."

"That doesn't seem to be stopping you."

After the previous week's events, things had gone extremely well. Between the combined corroborated testimony of Luca, the model, Natasha, Brian, and Lucy, as well as the audio recordings from Lucy's phone and the memory chip from Luca's camera, it was pretty obvious to everyone what had happened. The two Australian-Italian thugs were in custody, Virginia had disappeared, and Lucy's lawyers had her on lockdown at the Palazzo. Luca Speziale was back to work at the station, and the police finally had some resolution regarding the Galli and Ludovici cases.

"Well Blue Bear, I survived." She scooted up next to me and leaned in.

I wrapped my paw around her, "I'm glad."

"Not just survived though... thrived. Wouldn't you say?"

"Sure."